Tom offered his lips as their faces met and they were drawn into one another. They fell to the floor and rolled over and over as lips opened and tongues tasted. They twisted around and around on the floor, drinking in the scent of each other, kissing, moaning. Then they began a battle, each trying desperately to know every inch of the other's body, to take every morsel of flesh into their mouths and taste it, lick and kiss and bite it, chew it off and have it forever. Tongues dragged over eyelashes, lips swallowed skin, hands fought for territory. They took a crash course in each other, and graduated with honors.

I love you. I love you. I love *you,* Tom thought.

Tom moved closer to Mitch and locked his head in the pillow of his shoulder as a protective arm came around and held him tight.

TOMCAT: A searing—and poignantly sensitive—novel of a man and his experiences with love.

TOMCAT

THOM RACINA

ace books

A Division of Charter Communications Inc.
A GROSSET & DUNLAP COMPANY
51 Madison Avenue
New York, New York 10010

TOMCAT

Copyright © 1981 by Thom Racina

All characters in this book are fictitious. Any resemblance to actual persons, living or dead, is purely coincidental.

An ACE Original

Excerpt from *The Tiger in the House,* by Carl Van Vechten. Copyright 1920, 1936 by Carl Van Vechten. Reprinted by permission of Alfred A. Knopf, Inc.

First Ace Printing: November 1981

Published simultaneously in Canada

2 4 6 8 0 9 7 5 3 1
Manufactured in the United States of America

DEDICATION:

For Saxon, my very own tomcat, the best damn cat in the world. . .

For Paul, who believed in it from the start, and helped so very much. . .

And for Susanne, who finally gave the stray a warm home. . .

With love.

THE EXEMPLARY CAT

There is no single quality of the cat that man could not emulate to his advantage. He is clean, the cleanest, indeed, of all animals, absolutely without odor or soil when it is within his power to be so. He is silent, walking on padded paws with claws withdrawn, making no sound unless he wishes to say something definite and then he can express himself freely. . . .

He is entirely self-reliant. . . . If he is suddenly thrown on his own resources in the country he can support himself on the highway; he can even support himself in town under conditions that would terrify . . . the dog. . . .

He is beautiful and he is graceful. He makes his appearance and his life as exquisite as circumstances will permit. He is modest, he is urbane, he is dignified. Indeed, a well-bred cat never argues. He goes about doing what he likes in a well-bred superior manner. If he is interrupted he will look at you in mild surprise or silent reproach but he will return to his desire. If he is prevented, he will wait for a more favorable occasion. But like all well-bred individualists . . . the cat seldom interferes with other people's rights. His intelligence keeps him from doing many of the fool things that complicate life. Cats never write operas and they never attend them. They never sign papers, or pay taxes, or vote for president. An injunction will have no power whatever over a cat. A cat, of course, would not only refuse to obey any amendment whatever to any constitution, he would refuse to obey the constitution itself.

Carl Van Vechten,
The Tiger in the House

ONE

Chloe gave him the name when they lived together for that short and bittersweet time in Chicago. That period of life when they were reckless, when they pretended to be Bonnie and Clyde and robbed supermarkets instead of banks. The winter when they made the giant snowman in Lincoln Park, a work of dubious distinction that many took to be the spitting image of Hizzoner Mayor Daley. Yes, he was alive then. It was the time when Chloe was still sane and Lord & Taylor hadn't yet moved into town and life was more or less uncomplicated.

They liked mornings best, got up at seven or eight, made love as much to take the chill out of the bedroom air as to show affection for each other, and then sat for long periods of time over steaming muddy coffee. Chloe never could cook. Tom let her make the coffee, sometimes the tea, but nothing beyond that. They'd once ripped off two thick filets from the market in Sandberg Village—Chloe waddling out of the store with them stuffed between her thighs, moaning about freezing her genitalia to death—and found there was nothing in the apartment to fix to go with them. Nothing but jello. A box of strawberry jello. So Tom did the steaks, Chloe the jello. Her accomplishment was something like a layer of thick red rubber covered with a sea of floating pink. And it tasted like it.

So they sat this morning drinking the coffee, munching the peanut butter cookies Tom had baked a few days earlier. Chloe had marveled at the sight of that, this tall Texan bent over an open oven with an apron around his bare waist, protecting his cherished pair of Faded Glory jeans. And what was even more amazing, he was mighty good at it. Better even than Chloe's mother, who was the best cook in the world until she choked to death on a martini olive while flying somewhere over the Everglades. But Mama Chloe was still very much alive and cooking this day Tom and her daughter were eating his cookies as the snow fell outside the iced window panes.

Suddenly, the little kitten they'd adopted jumped up to the table top and sat and stared at them, tail curled around itself. Tom had found him in the garbage can behind the apartment house. He'd dumped the trash and heard a faint squeak. He stopped and listened and looked around. Nothing. He began to put the beat-up steel cover back on the can when he heard it again. He lifted the bag he'd dropped in and under it was a little ball of reddish-brown and white fur. His heart fluttered for a moment and then he was filled with rage. He could kill the bastard who'd put a kitten in a garbage can in the middle of winter. He pulled off his gloves and lifted the shivering little creature from the egg shells and coffee grounds, tucked him under his shirt, and took him inside to Chloe.

That night the kitten slept with them. Chloe got up at three to give it a bottle, a toy baby bottle with a nipple that really worked (which she had run out and lifted from Woolworths on Clark and Dearborn just before they closed that afternoon). She felt for the first—and what would turn out to be the last—time in her life like a mother. But she was also an artist and a scribe, so she spent the hour immediately following the feeding sitting on the floor with her legal pad, the yellow pages filling with scribbled poems to a yet unnamed but already much-loved cat. She wrote and wrote and dreamed of one day doing a monologue on stage, a Chekhov heroine rescuing a cat in the snow. It was all very dramatic and moving there in the frosty room with the candlelight doing a dance on the ceiling and the kitty full and asleep on Tom's chest. She felt the beauty of the situation zinging her consciousness all over creation. And the speed she'd taken helped some too.

After a Valium finally calmed her pencil, she crawled into the bed once again, snuggling up to her lover as though she were another lost and defenseless animal. Tom opened his eyes, and without disturbing the sleeping kitten, put his arm around Chloe's shoulder. "What will we name him?" he whispered, looking at the little white whiskers just inches from his nose.

"Tomcat," Chloe said.

Three weeks later, when Tom came in from shoveling the sidewalk, Chloe had an announcement to make. "We've got a problem."

"What?"

"It's Tomcat."

Tom's eyes narrowed.

"No, nothing's wrong with him," she said. "It's just that he isn't."

"Isn't what?"

"Isn't a tomcat."

It took a full minute for what she was saying to sink in. "You mean. . .?"

Chloe nodded.

"You sure?"

She nodded again. "I looked."

"But we tried to figure it out last week." He recalled their spreading the little kitten's legs, looking closely down there, laughing as they did it. Tom insisted the cat a macho fighter.

"I got a book," Chloe said. "He's a girl."

"Surrounded by women." He pulled off his jacket and sank onto the mattress. He crossed his arms and muttered, "Shit."

"Can we call her Ophelia?"

He looked at the kitten now curled up at his side. "Sorry, kid, destroying your masculinity like this in one fast move. But the lady of the house says you're Ophelia now. There'll be another Tomcat someday, sometime."

Chloe sat down and petted Ophelia. The cat purred, which they both acknowledged as *her* acceptance of her new name, recognition finally of her gender.

A few minutes later—delayed reaction, one of her most singular traits—Chloe said, "Someday? Sometime?"

"Huh?"

"There won't be another Tomcat *some*day."

He looked at her blankly. Sometimes he didn't know what the hell she was talking about, probably because often *she* didn't know what she was talking about. But this time she certainly did. "There won't be another Tomcat someday because there's one right now."

He just waited.

She smiled and pointed to him. "You."

He just sat there a long while and then grinned. "You know, I think I like that."

And so his name was Tomcat, but no one ever called him that. No one but Chloe. And then, two years later, Rachel. And finally Mitchell, a year after that, but he only did it to tease Tom because by that time Chloe's condition had become hopeless and Tom dreaded picking up the phone and hearing her drone, "Tommmmm-cat?"

Chloe.

Rachel.

Mitchell.

The three forces in his life, the three people who

would mean so much to him in such different ways at the same time, the three energies. Guiding his life, or at least the first part of his life, the past. The past, dissonant yet harmonic, his whole existence right up until the time this story ends a kind of song, like many of the songs he'd written, a tune containing both happy words and sad thoughts, minor chords and major ones. Music had a lot to do with his life. Just the way cats did. And chocolate. And Christmas trees.

In fact, he would become a cat for Rachel many times over the years he knew her, purring and playing with her breasts as if they were balls of yarn, biting her nose as Ophelia had bit his in the Chicago days whenever she was hungry early in the morning, letting Rachel stroke his fur with her exquisite fingers. . . .

TWO

Tom's involvement with Rachel was different from any other. Maybe that's why he thought it was the best, the most valuable of all. With Chloe they'd gotten to know each other on a beam of some kind of wild potent energy which was spouting from both of them at that time of their lives, linking them together by candles and poems and shoplifting and music and pills and a cat.

With Madame Zena, who had walked into his life even before he met Rachel, it was a business arrangement before anything; but on another level Tom always looked on her with amusement, as a truly outrageous character in history to whom he felt just a little bit dear, in a strange and curious way right up until the horrible end.

With Kevin it was friendship, pals, an element he'd lacked in his life to that point. And with Mitch, it was at first an encounter void of any curiosity, something unique to his experience, something hungrily attractive.

But with Rachel it was frantic, as though they had three hours left in which to live and they were going to damn well pack some three or thirty years of living into that time. He met her at Rockefeller Center the day the Christmas tree was put up. They went ice skating togeth-

7

er. He bought her a hot chocolate and she told him if he
came home with her she'd turn him on to chocolate de-
lights, the likes of which he never dreamed. Fry cocoa
from Jamaica. Mexican hot chocolate. Krön bananas.
Mocha rum cake. . .

Tempt him with chocolate and he'd go home with
Godzilla.

Or even Florence Hendersen.

So they went to her apartment, a high-ceilinged place
on West End Avenue in the Eighties from which you
could see the river if you stuck your head out through
the bars crossing the living room window. The elevator
was very slow, the super always out, two gay priests
lived above her and someone downstairs, she was sure,
practiced voodoo because she'd seen the dead chickens
out in the garbage on Thursdays, but all in all it was *the*
place to live. She'd lived there almost twenty years, and
fashion had caught up with her at last; the Upper West
Side was finally "in".

The living room, dining room, closets, even the
bedroom was filled with records, shelves of them, crates
of them, piles of them. The cavernous living room was a
collection of wonderful dreck and truly beautiful items.
Oriental rugs. A Donald Duck lamp. Overstuffed furniture. Henry Moore and Pla Domenech lithographs on
the walls. Framed child's drawings. Giant old Hardman
piano in the corner. Books, plants, antique dolls and a
Robert Kennedy campaign poster.

The dining room was filled with glittering Baccarat
crystal and Wedgwood china, piled right next to plastic
New York World's Fair souvenir cups and saucers.
Multi-colored Woolworth's forks and spoons. Scottish
sweetbreads and Kieller's marmalade in the kitchen.
Kidney pie in the refrigerator and something called
borscht.

A bathroom filled with scents and lotions and potions
and the first cushioned toilet seat he'd ever put his ass

on. And a bedroom which seemed to be all bed—a California king—and a stack of mismatched pillows and a Sony Trinitron and Betamax, and an air conditioner and an electric blanket and tons of jewelry heaped on the dresser like the treasures of Tutankhamun's tomb; and a truly beautiful art deco lamp, exquisitely placed on the marble nightstand next to the bed. "This is . . . wonderful," he said. He never felt so comfortable anywhere in his life, not even in his own apartment.

A few months later he would move into his own little house in Los Angeles, made possible by the "graciousness" of the Countess, and then he would feel very much at home. But there was something special about Rachel's. There would always be. Something *special*.

Because she was.

They sat on the floor of the living room, pillows propped all around them like a little fortress. She put a Pink Floyd album on the turntable, but it proved too heavy for the mood; she changed to James Taylor, then Ella Fitzgerald. She fed him with her fingers, something no one had ever done before that he could remember. A William Greenberg brownie. The richest, chewiest, gooiest, best he'd ever eaten. That did it; he was hers forever.

He asked what she did in life besides lure men home with chocolate. She told him she worked for a record company, one of the biggest and best, and thus the collection piled everywhere but in the dishwasher. "I write jacket notes mainly. Liners. Last year I collaborated with two others on a book on rock, a photo book which the label pushed. But save me from collaboration. It was a horror working as a threesome. I write promo stuff too. I love music and I love the people who make it. And I can whip off some good lines about any record you hand me."

"That's terrific. I always wondered who did that kind of stuff."

"And you?"

"I just ice skate around the country."

She laughed. "God help my rubber ankles. Oh, pain. What do you mean, around the country? You fell flat on your ass twice out there. You're no Sonja Henie, baby."

"Yeah, I guess you're right." He shrugged. "I don't do anything much. I work for a clothes designer in L.A. and I travel around for her. That's about it."

"Any hobbies?"

"I tinker around on the piano. You?"

She pushed some brownie into her own mouth. "I get fat."

He studied her. Well, she wasn't slim. She was . . . big. Not fat. Plump. Ripe. And very very sexy. The sexiest older woman he'd ever— He suddenly realized he was trying to guess her age, but he couldn't. So he asked, "How old are you?"

She laughed. "Let's just say you're in your twenties and I'm in my forties and leave it at that."

He nodded. (But curiosity got hold of him a month later, and he dug through her desk drawer until he found that she was forty-three.) Yes. She was the sexiest woman he'd ever know. It was in her incredible eyes. They pierced and penetrated. They shone with maturity and experience and knowledge. He had the strange feeling she could read him perfectly, without even asking him any questions.

Tom looked up at the many photographs of a child on top of the upright. "Are you married?"

"I have a son, if that's what you're asking. No, not married anymore. I was. Horror of horrors. To a librarian. We would sit around at night with five cats and listen to Mahler before Mahler was listened to and read Plato and Saint Augustine to each other—aloud yet! I'm not kidding you. Then one day I heard Mick Jagger, read Fanny Hill, bought a diaphragm and got a divorce."

"Is he still a librarian?"

"You kidding? He finally discovered acid and lives in a tree in Central Park."

"Where's your son now?"

"Away at school. In Vermont. He's twelve and it was his idea, his big dream, going away to school, very fashionable with his peers or something. I think I have to be nuts. I miss him desperately. But he likes it, and I see him most weekends. His father has a say in the matter as well. It's the military school *he* never got to go to. So I look up in the tree and say all right. We'll let him go. We'll let him have what he wants, let him be happy. I'll visit and bring chicken soup." She leaned back and crossed her arms. "How about you? You have a family? You're barely old enough to be out after ten."

"A family. No. Well, sorta. It's a long and unpleasant story."

She lit a joint and held it to his lips. "I suspect you don't want to tell it."

"Not now."

"That's fair." She inhaled and put her head back. "Let's just sit quietly for a few minutes," she whispered. She took his hand. Their eyes met. Then she saw him put his head back as well, as his fingers clasped hers, and they relaxed as they smoked the grass and held hands like schoolkids. They felt something already reaching one another's hearts, and when the joint was gone and they began to feel the effect, they talked about her life and his life and how they both wondered what in hell was happening because it was the first time she'd found herself on her living room floor with someone young enough to be her son, because he was discovering a new excitement he'd never known, something he was sure no one would understand.

She kissed him and opened his shirt and placed her bare hand on his nipple. It hardened. He did the same to her, sliding his fingers inside the warmth of her bra.

"We're much alike," she said softly into his ear.

"But yours are so much bigger." He cupped her large breasts in his hands and then he opened her blouse and unfastened her brassiere. He looked at her breasts for a moment, and then he took one of his lips and gently suckled. His eyes flashed up to hers and he whispered, "Ummm, they're *definitely* bigger."

She did the same to him. She put her lips to his left nipple and bit a little, felt its form with her tongue, licking at it. Then she did the same to the other, and she giggled and said, "Yours are hairier. About four hairs, exactly." He laughed. No one had ever done that to him before, no one had ever seemed remotely interested in his chest. Sometimes when he masturbated, he pinched his nipples a little. It added something. It was as if Rachel knew that.

They cooed. They giggled. They were turned on. She told him she only liked games when they both agreed to play them and they didn't hurt anyone. So they played games. They played doctor. They played spin the tea cup. They played war, a game in which, Tom explained, Rachel would always be wounded in the area of the breast or crotch, and he being the staff physician and the only doctor on the battlefield, would examine her for the extent of her injuries. As she smoked another joint and he gave her a thorough check-up, she asked, "Okay, Hawkeye, don't I sometimes get to play the nurse and see what hit you?"

"That's not the way we played it when I was a kid." The truth was it was a fantasy; he'd never played such games as a child.

"*When* you were a kid?" She tossed a pillow into the air.

He shrugged. "Well, then, how about giving this hungry little tyke another brownie."

"Addict." She got up. "I'll fetch one if you change the record." She started toward the kitchen, but he stopped her, reaching out to touch her leg. Then he stood and kissed her. She brought her hands up and held his head, framing his cheeks, feeling the thick blond hair behind his ears entwined in her fingers, looking into the blue eyes. "You're the prettiest cat anyone ever dropped on my doorstep," she said, and then went forth to gather up more fudgy treats.

He put the Pink Floyd back on and turned up the volume. The furniture vibrated. He wondered if the gay priests' bed was shaking. He flopped back down on the pillows and felt his penis standing hard across his thigh in his open jeans. He could still feel the warmth of her breast in his mouth. And the scent of her, cinnamon and sparkling. He'd never foreplayed like this before—touching, teasing—without moving right along to a manly climax.

She came back and handed him another brownie. He gobbled it up, all smiles. "You're purring!" she said.

"You called me a cat." He said it as if it was some kind of revelation. "You called me a cat and. . ."

She nuzzled her face into his chest hair. "I love your fur, Tommy cat." She was calling his hair fur. The bright eyes blazed in amazement. He loved it. Then she moved her head down to the other hairy patch on his body and she said it again, "I love your fur."

And he purred some more.

Then he made love to her with more tenderness than he thought he possessed.

They slept, Tom curled in Rachel's arms. The last person he'd slept with—actually had fallen asleep with—was Chloe, and that had been over two years ago, when she asked him to stay in Chicago that one last day, to see her parents. The day before he set out for California and the dream of striking gold turned to rusty reality and hard times and cheap tricks and TV dinners in a crummy Hollywood apartment. That time not so long ago—but didn't it seem it?—when he tried to make it on his own, before Chloe had given up the life of an actress in New York and decided to pursue the career of a filmmaker in L.A. and moved in with him again, bag, baggage, feathers and yellow pads full of feminist poetry.

But he'd saved himself finally, pulled away from her, gotten rid of her. He had another dingy apartment, working his ass off for the Countess, but she was taking good care of him and maybe soon he'd even be able to save enough money for the down payment on a piano. He missed having one.

He woke up in the middle of the night, still curled in Rachel's arms. The air conditioner was on high and so was the electric blanket. Outside, the dead of winter, and he was sure hers was the only air conditioner running east of the Colorado River. The room was pitch black, not a hint of light, no shadows, nothing. A cave in the woods some place, and he was lying in protection from the wolves by the motherly warmth of the woman next to him.

He had the urge—just for the moment, because he felt so good, because there was a celebration going on inside him—to get up and play a song. He'd been dying to do that since he laid eyes on the piano. But it could wait for morning. For now—forever?—he wanted to stay in bed with her and be her kitten. Now he knew why Ophelia had purred like a motorboat all those nights.

The best thing was that he wasn't playing a role; he didn't have to act the stud or the strong one or the central casting cowboy with her. Maybe, just maybe, with Rachel he could be himself. It frightened him. He'd never been himself, even when he was alone. Maybe he'd give it a try. Because he felt she would understand him and accept no matter what.

He stretched a little and thought of her on the silly ice skates that afternoon and snickered. Then he moved his hand and rested it in the warmth between her legs. He wanted to fall asleep like that, touching her. He'd never done that before either, not even with Chloe.

They woke up in that position around eleven. It still seemed the middle of the night. Rachel turned on a light, and Tom saw his breath. She punched the button on the air conditioner and the blast of air ceased. Then she gave him a hug, and told him to sit tight, read the papers, and she'd be in with breakfast.

She served him on a white wicker tray, complete with steaming silver teapot and a fresh rose—where in hell did she get a goddamn rose?—and crisp bacon, onion muffins, mounds of jams and butters, and a tomato omelette, sprinkled with fresh dill.

After they ate, they made love, and in the midst of their passion Rachel screamed.

"What is it?" Tom asked, startled, pulling away.

She reached under her body and pulled out a hunk of cold greasy bacon. "Not by any means a Kosher fuck, Thomas," she deadpanned.

He cracked up and fell backwards on the bed and laughed until his cock went limp.

"It wasn't all *that* funny. . ."

They spent the day like that. Playing, laughing, talking, eating. In bed, all the time. Oh, she made a few necessary trips to the kitchen—she discovered he ate like a horse *all* the time—and he made a pilgrimage to the piano to prove to her he had something more going for him than good looks and eight inches. They showered together and went back to bed to watch TV. And they got wrecked again.

Late in the day, as they grew sleepy and exhausted from the satisfying experience of discovering each other, she lifted her reading glasses up to her dark hair, and closed the book she'd been engrossed in. "I just had a *zetz*."

"Pardon me?"

"I just had a *zetz*."

"Huh?"

"A *zetz* is Yiddish for 'stabbing feeling'."

"Should I call the doctor or the rabbi?"

She smiled. "Silly. The stabbing feeling is just that—*feeling*. I feel something that's very nice. Very strong. Very good." She ran her hand through his hair again. "Come, furry cat, let me hold you."

He fell into her arms. "Chloe—I'll tell you all about her sometime—once named me Tomcat."

"You are. Most certainly." She kissed him on the nose. "And you play a hell of a good piano."

"I wanted to ask you, think maybe you could get me an audition somewhere? I've got a lot of songs on tape."

"Sure. And when they record your album, we'll call it *Tomcat*." She was kidding.

He wasn't.

THREE

Rachel once asked him, "What's your life all about?"
Tom replied, "Cats."

And there was more in that answer than anyone knew, beyond its facetiousness. His mother, Annie, who was called Tugboat, identified with Maggie the Cat. She saw a performance of *Cat On A Hot Tin Roof* at a community theatre in Dallas and longed to be as beautiful and clawing and sure and mysteriously exciting as Brick's strong wife.

Her mind craved a communion with Maggie and Brick. She sat in Twisters, the local hangout on the outskirts of Dallas, propped atop a bar stool, holding court. The place had previously been called Dire Straits—which was what the patrons were in—when it had been strictly a shitkicker's saloon. Now it was a trendy omnisexual disco, Annie's haven from working the streets of the Big D, and night after night she bored truckers and drag queens, prosties and cattlemen for hours on end with her stories of how she and her Bronco—her Brick—were just like the characters in that there play.

But the men sitting around her, all of them blessed with large frame and pea-sized brains, listened politely as long as there was some shred of a chance of getting into her pants when the lecture was over. Annie was

17

known as a little kooky, a little off, and a mighty good
lay. Let her drone on about Elizabeth Taylor in the movie version, she had every right to lecture on Liz; she was
a star in her own right. She'd dropped a kid and gone
through seven or eight abortions and screwed maybe
half the men in all of Texas before she'd even turned
twenty-one, and still she was renowned for possessing
the tightest pussy north of the Gulf Coast.

And there was some truth in her tales of
Annie/Maggie and Bronco/Brick. She married to make
Tom legal, and in doing so became wife to a man who'd
made a name for himself in rodeos throughout the West
—Colorado, Nevada, Arizona—and had finally settled
down to take over his daddy's big ranch. No "Big Daddy" here, just a big spread; Bronco's father was a small
sniveling old crow, detested by all who knew him. But he
was money, land money, cattle money, oil money. Bronco believed it would all be his someday, so home came
the prodigal son, home to the hope daddy would kick
off soon. Home to the fortune.

Bronco had already made daddy proud. The old fart
had always written in his scrawled hand how "danged
pleased you done so fine on that steer, son" after yet
another victory. Now Bronco would work the ranch
while the old man settled down to die, making him
prouder still in his old age, managing the ranch as it had
never been managed before.

Tennessee Williams could not have penned a better
ending:

Bronco drags home his bride, Annie, a smiling woman, pleasantly, pregnantly plump. She knows in her
heart if not elsewhere that this child she's carrying is
Bronco's, and it will be a son. But Old Man Brassen
takes one look at his daughter-in-law and spits in her
face. Walks away muttering. Annie tells her husband his
father's behavior is peculiar. Bronco runs off to find
daddy sitting in one of the barns, which he always does

when he is pissed. Bronco demands an explanation from
the crusty gent. "You got no right, daddy, no right doin'
something' so mean as that to a lady who's now my
belov'd wife."

"Belov'd wife, horsepoo!" The old man spits again. "I
screwed that whore myself, ten times in a flophouse on
Post Office Street in Houston four summers ago. She's
mighty good for what's keepin' your pecker up, but she
ain't no lady. And you gone an' married her and brung
shame on the family, you asshole."

Bronco is sure the old man is mistaken in his senility.
"Daddy, you gotta be giffurin' the wrong little lady
here."

"Quit callin' her a lady. She ain't no lady. I'd remember those tits in my grave, which is right where
you're puttin' your pappy, you miserable bum."

The old man finally accepts what is and the three of
them live rather happily in the giant wood frame house
which fittingly looks like the manse in *Giant*. Except for
the old man constantly referring to Annie as a tramp
(Where's that whore-wife a yours?" and "Hey, whore-
lady, you gonna watch the television with us tonight?"),
things do go along quite pleasantly. Until little Tom is
born. Then the friction begins between Annie and Bronco.

She is depressed and eats chocolates from Neiman-
Marcus by the shovelful, which she charges in the old
man's name. She's not wasting her time waiting for him
to drop dead; she's going to have as much as she can get
right now. The old man can't stand Bronco and her yelling at each other all the time. He orders a pow-wow.
Shades of Brick and Maggie here. Bronco has a secret,
it comes out, a shadow of the past eating at him. He's
drinking heavily, the truth serum in his blood taking
hold of his brain. Annie the Cat tries hard not to listen
to the two of them because she's bored with this crap
already. Bronco tells daddy in nebulous terms some-

thing about not being "a man" in the past, in one of them rodeo shows. "I done somethin' against nature, daddy!" Tears run down his thick skin, his handsome face. Annie has started to play solitaire, ears slightly perked.

The old man asks something about Bronco having maybe taken a try at sheep.

Annie chimes in, without looking up from her cards, "More like the sheep*herder*, the way I heard it." Brick and Scooter out on the athletic field.

Bronco and Tom—that was the guy's name, the same name Annie picked for their baby, which was the cause of Bronco's sudden impotence after birth, which was the cause for Annie's melancholy, which was the cause for all the yelling and the whole basis for this sorry scene— out on the coliseum floor. Love amongst the manure, as Annie once put it.

So Bronco confessed, guilt-riddled and shaken, and shortly thereafter daddy has his long-awaited stroke, but when he did kick the proverbial bucket, it turned out to be filled with steer shit. The will divided the ranch and the rest of the man's holdings into many small pieces, each of them going to various relatives, charities, even churches, which was curious because the deceased had pledged himself a "born heathen" all his life. Not a penny to his son who'd done so much to make him proud.

Lest we think the old man was all cruelty and heart-lessness, a quote from the will is in order: "And the two acres up there past Rig Number 4436, I bequeath to my son, Bronco, the prevert, and his wife, the whore." The two acres named were the lousiest, most arid land under the Brassen banner, complete with a shack which had a Nehi Cola sign for a roof, and which the old man had sometimes referred to as "the Guest House for Wet-backs." Bronco went into a severe depression.

Annie went to New Mexico. She took a family car and everything she could pack into it, driving frantically, not only to get as far from the Brassen Ranch as possible, but also to get what she hadn't been getting all through the period of mourning—a good lay. When Bronco stopped sleeping with her after Tom's birth, she was reduced to sneaking in on the ranch hands every once in a while, when she thought she could pull it off, but they were clumsy and scared because she was the Lady of the House and they feared Bronco would shoot on sight if caught with their pants down. Little did they know, he probably would have shot *her* first and continued where she'd left off.

So Annie drove to Albuquerque and fell in love with a Mexican magician (he made bottles of beer disappear faster than anyone she'd ever known) and after seven months of semi-bliss, he cracked her skull with an empty Coors bottle and as soon as she got out of the hospital, she bashed in all the windows of his pick-up truck with a decorative cement pink flamingo she pulled from the yard next door, and left him and the Land of Enchantment forever.

She returned to Texas, the Yellow Rose come back to her roots, living first in Houston where she knew the trade better than any girl in town, and settled in. The years went by quickly. Tom thought he had a pretty decent childhood. His mother worked nights, but so did a lot of other mothers. Annie provided food, clothing, even gave him an allowance. No matter what her line of work, she took care of her boy.

And he took care of himself. He got lost in daydreams. He read *Photoplay* and other movie star rags and pretended he was one of them, Lana Turner's lover, Clark Gable's best friend, living on a street paved with gold. Little Tom had seen the mansions in the River Oaks section of Houston and he imagined those in Hollywood to be even more magnificent. But the streets in Houston were like streets everywhere. Hollywood would be different. He'd live there one day.

But that would be the future. For now, life with Annie

was okay. He liked her. He wasn't sure he loved her, but he knew he liked her. She was more a pal than a mother. She'd been saying "shit" around him long before he was old enough to hear such poetry, which was something none of the other boys' mothers did. It made her unique. She let him take a beer every once in a while. Sometimes she brought tricks home and he heard the springs creaking through the paper-thin walls. One day she even played father and told him what his penis was really for. Although he was pretty sure himself by that time, it was reassuring to hear it from one who knew.

It wasn't all wonderful; there were difficulties. Going to the police station to fetch her. The cops would call and tell "Tommy" they had his mom there again, would he like to come walk her home? The cops were nice guys, and they treated Annie and her boy well; one of them even became a regular customer for a year or so. Waiting for her to return home one Christmas Eve turned out to be like waiting for Godot. After decorating the tree he'd bought with his own money as a surprise for her, he found himself watching the Christmas morning sun come up with no more tears left in his body. And yet, the unaccountable joy when she showed up three days later.

Some of the binges lasted longer than that, and he learned to survive on peanut butter and Tang, two easy things to steal from the Safeway. For recreation he had television and masturbation. Annie fell in love often and hard. A few times the guy moved in with them, but Tom never liked any of them. She sensed it and kept her affairs out of the apartment as much as possible. If tricks didn't play father to Tom, he didn't mind them as much. But when her lovers left her, she became a little girl, crying, moping, depressed, and he would cheer her, comfort her, cook for her and pamper her by telling her she was beautiful, very beautiful, and another Prince Charming would come along on his great horse and sweep her off her feet very soon. He never believed it, but he wished it would happen. For her sake.

Tom respected Annie because she never pretended to be anything other than what she was. She was Annie Brassen, the plump whore with a mouth full of nails and lots of strength in the hammer of her fist; she could punch a guy out with the best of them, or tell a raunchy joke over a foamy beer and yet still be able to break down and cry when some jerk was kind enough to send her a tall rose on her birthday. She could drink any cowboy under the table, even go down under there with him for a spell, and still come up to appreciate the drawings her kid had made for her that day.

She was a stereotype in most folks' eyes, the whore with the heart of gold, and it seemed God could not have fashioned a better replica. But that was on the surface, the level on which everyone knew Annie. Few were allowed to penetrate the vulnerability under the skin, for it was too precious, too distinctly out-of-the-mold of her environment. She'd been open and sensitive and warm-hearted as a child, only to find herself eaten up with the pain and anguish of her parents' marital problems. She grew a protective coat of armour as she began to realize neither her father nor her mother had any interest in being a parent, that she was really not loved.

And now she was a parent herself, and one of the privileged few to penetrate the person under the tough exterior was her son, for he *was* loved, loved deeply; perhaps, as it came to pass, too much. Annie was outrageous. It drew attention. It drew business. It created another reality from the dull one in which she existed. Much of it was an act at first, playing Annie Oakley at the bar with tassles on her tits and a holster slung over her bulging hips, but the guise grew into a second skin, and soon she couldn't *help* being outrageous. It was fun. And Tom thought it was fun. Together they experienced warm, tender moments, private moments which strengthened the affection of the relationship. Annie desperately wanted to be a good mother, and in her own crazy way she was. In Tom's eyes she wasn't Maggie the Cat so much as she was Auntie Mame. And as her Patrick, he was always there, always waiting for her, accepting, smiling. He was so constant, she began to take his attention for granted. Then high school came along. And something began to happen.

Tom changed. Life changed for him. He began to do things he'd never done before: go to plays and concerts, read *books* instead of picture magazines, play the piano with gusto. Annie was losing him. She didn't come to visit the teachers anymore, dressed like a schoolmarm herself, the way she'd done in the old days, not now when he was a young man; she knew he didn't want anyone to know who his mother was. He bought himself a big bolt lock to put on his door because she'd walked in one day while he was masturbating, and he thought he should be entitled to his private moments with his private parts, the way she was to hers. (In a drunken stupor a few nights after that incident, she made reference to his having a bigger cock "than your daddy had on his six-foot-three bucking bronco hulk," and he hated hearing that because it was the only time ever that she talked about his dad and he never wanted to hear about him. Years later he would be curious, but not then.)

He got a job in a warehouse after school and on weekends, and Annie saw less and less of him. The job was solitary. He was aloof, a loner. Girls longed for him. They made open passes and teased—he was sexy compared to most of the wimpy boys in the class—but no one ever broke through to him. The athletes invited him into their chosen clique, even thought he wasn't an athlete, which was an honor; he rejected them. The studybugs had no use for him because he wasn't a good student ("Never working to your potential!" the teachers drilled into him), but sometimes they would seek him out for a party or a dance; he never went.

Tom felt, those first and second years of high school, that he was having a rough time getting to know himself, much less work on a few others along the way. He had friends, plenty of them. They existed for him in books—in Fitzgerald's and Hemingway's Paris, where a light drizzle fell and the smell of fresh-baked bread was ever in the air. Who needed parties when Gertrude Stein was inviting him to her salon? Tom spent his time in parks, sitting under trees which had been there before Texas had been there, closing his eyes to dream, reaching for a land far away.

He read classics, adventure stories, history books and fables about knights in armor, fantasies about lands so splendid, he wished upon every star he could be there. He would have given his life to ride with Mr. Toad in *Wind In The Willows*. To touch Lancelot's sword. To mutiny right there alongside Mr. Christian.

But then, all at once, his taste in reading changed. *Willows* sat collecting dust while *Peyton Place* and *Lady Chatterly's Lover* took turns occupying the spot of honor under his bed. He seemed to keep having to buy Kleenex whenever he went to the store. Becoming a teenager was a discovery.

He did cultivate one friendship at school, that of a certain punk named Bobby. Bobby was the ranking cocksman of the sophomore class, a nasty little kid whose head was buried in the gutter and seemed to have more fun than anyone else Tom knew. Bobby had been called a "hit man" in grade school; for two bucks, he'd do anything: set fire to a house, toss a brick through a department store window, annoy with gusto the people you hated. He kicked a teacher in the ass in front of the class and shot a moon at the mayor of Cleveland when he once toured Houston's school district and visited a rally at Bobby's school. Everyone was afraid of Bobby. Tom had the guts to get up close.

Closer than he bargained for.

Bobby gave Tom some dirty comic books. Four black and white pictures of a Southern belle getting screwed by a burly black slave (the *"Gone With the Wind* Collection," as Bobby put it). And a few well-worn paperbacks with titles like *Lust Swamp* and *Sin Time At Girl's Camp*. And what did Tom give in return? His body.

Or, at least, part of it. Bobby gave him blow jobs. He just told Tom he wanted to do it to him. It was easy, Tom found out. And it felt good. They didn't talk about it. They just did it. No problem.

But on one occasion, curiosity reared its head and Tom asked. It was one of the few times they got into a discussion of some depth beyond disguised masturbation fantasies. Tom asked him if he really enjoyed doing it to him without him ever doing anything back. Bobby said he'd been balling girls for as long as he knew what to do with his dick, and since he was three years older than Tom (he'd flunked more years of school than he'd passed), that meant a lot of conquests. He said he got bored with it. He always liked looking at pictures of guys with girls going down on them, so he thought he'd try it himself, to see what the girls were all smiling about. He *knew* what the guys were smiling about; his Aunt Sophie went down on him in her parlor on Elm Street, right there under the kerosene lamp and big picture of The Last Supper, when he was only eleven.

"Why me?" Tom asked. "Am I the only one?"

"Yeah. I guess 'cause I heard some guy in your gym class say you had the biggest dick at Jefferson."

Tom blushed. "Funny. That's what my mom said."

"Huh?" Bobby's eyes widened.

"Never mind."

And that was the end of it. Until another occasion, after Bobby had done what he liked to do, after Tom had zipped up and they'd come out from the bushes, Bobby asked him why he'd been so curious the last time they talked. "I don't know," Tom asked. "I like to know why people do things, I guess."

"You maybe interested in doing it yourself?"

Tom shook his head. "Nope." It was true. He didn't have the slightest desire to do the same to Bobby or anybody. Hell, he hadn't even had a girl yet.

"Well, all I know is I like it. For myself. But I ain't gonna press anybody else into it. Maybe someday you'll dig it too. Anyhow, gotta go. See ya tomorrow."

"See ya."

BJ's (blow jobs, as Bobby labeled them) were so much a part of his life that it seemed damn fitting that they would be the spark to fire the cannon which would shoot him out of Houston and into his much-longed-for adventuresome future. He got up early one Saturday morning, and on his way to the warehouse, he stopped off at Bobby's to pick up some dirty pictures he'd ordered through the mail, and Tom dropped his jeans to his knees for five minutes. Then at work, on his break, he beat off in the toilet dreaming of having a girl go down on him, the girl in the photographs he was looking at, a blonde with very red lipstick. When he went home and flopped on his bed, the humidity and heat overpowered him, and he felt excited again. He pulled out his penis and started working it up and down, holding in the other hand his favorite fuckbook, reading the description that always. . . .

Annie came home and he forgot the whole thing. They ate cold fried chicken together, but she was drunk already, and he wanted out. He went for a walk, lying to her that he was going to the movies with his "pals," and went to the nearby dirty book store where the proprietor knew him and let him page through the under-the-counter books at leisure. He could feel himself on the verge of orgasm for almost an hour. It had been the horniest day of his life. He was going crazy. When he finally left, he mustered up the courage to swing over to Marjorie's house. Marjorie was a baton twirler who had holes in her underpants. When she twirled, the skirt flew up. When the skirt flew up, all the guys got turned on. Bobby had made it with her. So had every boy with the guts to ask. Tonight Tom had the guts.

But when Marjorie's mother opened the door and informed him, in her whiskey breath, that her daughter wasn't there, he was surprised to see her blouse open down to her navel. Her breasts were clearly visible. His mouth opened. He felt the guts leaving him. She murmured, "Wouldn't a big 'n strong young man like you wanna get outta this here heat and set a spell, have an orange Nehi with Marjorie's mama?" Her right breast completely emerged from the gaping blouse. Tom could see she rouged her nipples. He looked up. The same rouge graced her cheeks, but now seemed to be steaming off her face. He felt his legs shaking and his head pounding. He suddenly turned and hightailed it into the night, wondering as he ran if every Houston kid's mother was "Dirty Legs," as they called hookers. Where were *normal people?*

He found himself in his park, under his tree, if not with normal people, at least in normal surroundings, and he tried to shake the sexual frustration, but he just got hornier. He shut his eyes and rubbed his knees fitfully, nervously. Then his hand slid up to the inseam of his jeans where it was warm, and he saw the pictures flashing in his head and there was Marjorie and her torn panties and the feeling he always got when Bobby did it to him. . .

His pants filled with semen and soaked through the denim. It was messy and it would be embarrassing if anyone saw him on the way home, but the release had been exquisite and well worth it. At least now he could go home and get some sleep.

He walked into the apartment and froze.

What greeted him in the small living room late that hot night was the scene Marjorie would have walked in on at her house had he gone in to "set a spell" with mama. There was Annie, drunk, on her knees in front of the old mohair sofa. Sitting on it, bare naked but for his high cowboy boots, was a man, no, a kid, a damned kid who looked more *his* age. Maybe it wouldn't have been so bad had Annie not been giving the kid a BJ at the time.

The kid got very upset. Afraid, suddenly losing his erection, he bolted and ran around the room, holding a pillow in front of his genitals, screaming bloody murder. "Don't kill me! Don't hurt me, please. I didn't do anything—she did it! Don't hurt me!"

Annie pushed her hair back, put her head to the cushion of the sofa and closed her eyes. She moaned, disgusted, "Oh, Tom, can't you learn to knock first?"

Tom was more disgusted than she, however, and he turned away and took a deep breath. Here was a skinny kid running around their living room bare-assed and his mother sitting in a heap on the floor in her bra and panties with a bottle of bourbon next to her. He walked into his room and turned on his record player, full blast. Johnny Mathis. Blaring so loud it was distorted. He sat on his bed, trying to stay calm, and felt the dampness in his pants. It startled him. He had completely forgotten.

He stood up and slipped them off, tossed them in a ball into the closet, and slid on a pair of Jockey shorts. He sat down again and pulled his socks off and told himself he couldn't blame her, she was drunk and horny. *He* had been that way all day. *He'd* been desperate. Couldn't he understand that in her? And he hadn't knocked, after all. He just stared at the wall for about ten minutes while "Chances Are" tested his eardrums. Then he figured he'd better see if she was all right, to help her into bed if she needed it. The kid was sure to be halfway across the Panhandle by now.

Tom opened his door and fixed his eyes on the two of
them again. Annie knelt on the living room floor, her
face pressed against the boy's pelvis, her hands holding
tight to the balled-up jeans around his ankles. Tom
shouted, "Christ!" but this time Annie did not flinch.

Then it happened quickly, though it seemed eternal,
as though the scene had been caught in slow motion on
a movie screen. Tom grabbed Annie by the hair and
pulled her away, then grabbed the boy by the neck and
slammed his head against the wall. "Get the fuck outta
here," he shouted, and then, in sheer anger, he brought
his knee up to give the kid a great deal of pain where
Annie had just been giving him pleasure. The boy
doubled up and moaned.

Tom turned to Annie and tried to get her up from the
floor. "I need it, I need it . . . scared of the dark. . ." She
babbled, making no sense. Tom pulled her toward the
bed. "Bronco never let me do it to him, never let me do
that! Always thought it would bring back the memories
he didn't want to. . ." The door slammed. The kid was
gone. Tom lifted Annie to her bed and dropped her on
the mattress. Then he picked up a towel from her dressing table and wiped semen from her chin. It was the
most difficult thing he'd ever had to do in his life. He
didn't even know he was crying.

He walked to the window and looked out at the lone
tree in the sandy yard. There was something better out
there. Hollywood? Were his teeth straight enough for
the movies? Paris? Couldn't he hear Ingrid Bergman
calling him to Casablanca. . .?

No, it was Annie. She was whispering his name. He
walked to the other side of the bed and stood there, and
listened.

It was Rachel who got it out of him. He had never
told anyone. Not anyone. "There's something about

Annie you're not telling me," she said softly as she stroked his fur. "And you need to tell me. You want to. But you don't know how."

He nodded and turned away.

"I'm going to make you some cocoa." She got up from the bed and wrapped herself in her blue terrycloth robe. "Tommy, if you ever find the words, and you will, they'll come the way the right chords come to your fingers when you're writing a song. And I'm always around to listen."

He said nothing.

She went into the kitchen, and returned fifteen minutes later with a big mug of steaming chocolate and a plate of butter cookies. He sat cross-legged on the bed and savored the midnight feast. She crawled back in bed and watched him eat; it was one of her greatest pleasures, to see *him* gain pleasure from her cooking, even if it was only cocoa and cookies. He finally put his back against the wall and stretched his feet out in front of him and folded his arms. "I want to tell you now."

"Okay."

He cleared his throat. This would not be easy. But she had been right. She had felt his need to tell it. It would explain so much about him that had been left unsaid. . .

"She was calling me to come over to the bed, in a soft voice, kinda sexed-up, but I didn't realize it then, you know? Well, she says—she looks up at me and I'm her kid, remember—and she says, 'Tom, you're a man now, I saw you once and I know you're a man.' " He stopped and closed his eyes. The memory was intense even after so long. He could hear "Chances Are" pounding in the other room. "I told you how she caught me beating off that one time."

Rachel nodded, but he didn't see her.

"That's the . . . that's what she meant when she said, 'I know you're a man.' I just kinda shrugged and said,

'Ma, get some sleep,' or something like that. I guess I
said, 'Annie, get some sleep,' because I didn't call her
'ma' much.''

Rachel saw the difficult time he was having. She held
back from touching him; it would not help.

"Then she says to me, 'Baby, you're more a man than
that twenty-buck paperboy I had out there,' and I tried
to walk away but she grabbed my wrist.'' He stopped for
a moment and laughed. "Hey, I wonder if he really
was?''

"Was what?''

"Our paperboy.''

Rachel smiled, glad he could joke about it.

". . .she just grabbed my wrist and I was only dressed
in my shorts and she said something about us not having
any secrets from each other and how she'd seen the
books under my bed and she knew what passages were
underlined and she'd seen the pictures and could tell by
the frayed edges which ones were my favorites and she'd
read my diary and she knew all about what I liked having done to me. . .'' He put his head back so fast, in such
a jerking motion, he hit it hard against the wall, but the
shot of pain seemed to dull the ache of rememberance.

"Then she . . . she reached up with the other hand and
yanked my shorts down in front, ripped them.'' His
voice seemed to go hoarse and Rachel had to strain to
hear him. His eyes were wide and dry as the sandstorms
he remembered as a little boy. No tears, not even now.
He hadn't cried since that night. "I was paralyzed. She
started lifting her head, looking right above my shorts
and she said something about mama being good to me,
mama could give me what I needed.'' He doubled up,
knees to his chest, as if he had a stomachache.

"You don't have to go on,'' Rachel said softly.

He didn't hear her. "Then I yelled something. I don't
know what, but I yelled. And I hit her. Slapped her,
stunned her. I moved away, in a daze, out into the living

room. She started taunting me. She said my dad was a sickie and I was a sickie just like him. She knew about Bobby. My dad and I both liked 'sticking it in the wrong end.' She actually used those words. I had never heard anything like that about him. I didn't realize what she meant. I never really figured it out till later."

"What happened to your father?" Rachel asked.

"He died in a skidrow flophouse just about a year ago. I never met him." He took a deep breath. Rachel took off her glasses and rubbed her eyes as she listened. "You know, I wanted to kill her when she said those things, and yet I felt sorry for her. She was like a wounded pigeon, a frail little bird, and I felt that I was responsible for her."

"But even a frail bird must be released sometime." She knew what he was getting at. "You must let it fly away. That in itself is part of the responsibility."

He nodded. "I went to the fridge and got a bottle of beer and went into my room and then I threw the god-damn thing through the window and it shattered the glass into a million pieces. That shut her up. I knew at that moment there was no stopping me. I was leaving. It was heart-wrenching, because she was all I'd ever had, you know? We'd had a life together, not a terrific one, but a life, and, shit, we'd had lots of good times. But I had to get out.

"I dressed in my *Midnight Cowboy* stuff, the jacket with the fringe on it, heavy buckskin on the hottest night of the summer. I don't know why. Maybe I already knew it was going to get me money, that image. I got the money I'd saved in a box under the bed. She hadn't touched that. I guess she was only interested in the porn.

"In the living room I saw the twenty the paperboy had given her and I thought to myself, hell, dirty money can help buy me a clean beginning, so I stuffed it into my pants. She was sitting right there. All puffy-eyed and tears streaming down. I just said, 'Bye, Annie.' And she

said, 'My baby. . .' And I slammed the door. But I
didn't move in the hall. I leaned against the door and I
sobbed. I . . . I didn't want to leave her that way . . . I
didn't want it to end like that. . ."

Rachel could tell that was all. She reached back and
turned out the light in the bedroom. Then, in the
darkness, she pressed the button on the air conditioner
in the window right next to the bed, and in a few minutes
the sound of the fan droned them to sleep.

Bottles breaking through windows seemed to chase
him through life. Chloe vented her anger that way. After
he realized he could no longer afford new windowpanes,
he taught her to pitch them down the hall so they'd
break on the bathroom door. But that was after the time
an inch of snow fell in the bedroom before he could find
anything to cover the hole with. Once she came home
from work in the middle of the afternoon and screamed
that she got fired from Ma Bell. "The old bitch fired
me!" She slammed her purse down on the bed.

"What happened?" Tom asked, nervously eyeing all
the glass in the room. He had been sitting at the piano
watching Ophelia walk up and down the keys as Chloe
stormed in. Now he was turned to face her, and the kitten had run off to hide someplace.

"I got tired of this goddamn guy screaming at me,"
she explained, pacing. "He was senile or hard-of-hearing
or something, because I kept telling him the number and
he kept saying what what what? I said FR4-4876. I did
it slow. F. . .R. . .4. . . Still the idiot didn't hear. Finally
I yelled F. . .efff. . .efff as in *fuck*, R. . .4-4876."

"Jesus, you didn't. And the supervisor heard?"

"By then the old bitch was on me. I guess the whole
room heard it." And then she picked up the vase on the
piano and tossed it through the window with all her
might.

A woman Tom once knew tried to throw herself out

a window, but he caught her in time. Mitch did the crash routine once, but by accident: He tossed a tennis ball at Tom and it somehow went over his shoulder and through the windowpane and on into Tom's kitchen. Another incident occurred on Van Nuys Boulevard in Sherman Oaks. Someone flung a bottle through the stained-glass window of an "English Pub," and the flying pieces cut Tom's hand. And there was that terrible night in Glencoe, Illinois, the worst night of his life, and Kevin, how Kevin had—

But that night in Houston was the only time *he* tossed anything through a window. What he remembered most vividly were the sounds. Shattering glass. Hearing it tinkle on the pavement in the alley below. A voice shouting for them to "keep it down." And the needle of the record player, caught, stuck, maddening. . .

A chunk of glass had fallen to the turntable, which had been going around and around, Johnny Mathis finished but no one there to put the tone arm back in place. As the record spun, the glass made a harsh sound as it hit the needle. *Brrrrrup. Brrrrrup. Brrrrrup.* As he got dressed. *Brrrrrup. Brrrrrup. Brrrrrup.* In the living room as he stuffed the money in his jeans. *Brrrrr. Brrrrrup. Brrrrrup.* In future nights in future places, in his head, that nightmare of sound always came back to him. Still, to this day, he could not stand to hear a deep scratch in a record. It brought back Annie and the stink of Houston and he did not want that.

But he had no dreams that evening with Rachel. He had feared he would, after telling the awful tale which had haunted his mind on so many a dark night in the past. But now there was nothing but a gentle sleep. The nightmare had been talked out before he closed his eyes. He had spoken of demons, and thus they'd been driven out. They would never come again.

It relieved him. But as he sat there across the table from Rachel early the next morning, across from this woman who loved him so specially and easily, he could not yet tell her the major reason he was so happy, so relieved. He could not tell her he was overjoyed that he would never again have to wake Mitch in the middle of the night with his screams and terror.

Mitch.

It seemed he was always thinking of Mitch lately.

FOUR

He first met Mitchell on the beach. Tom had come out of the water to find a guy lying on a big red towel near his. He felt a little weak in the knees, for his first impression was that this was the most beautiful man he'd ever seen. He sat down and shook his wet head like a dog. The second impression was that he'd never seen legs like those on the man—long, slender, but muscular, the tanned skin covered with thick, wiry black hair. The third image imprinted on his mind at that moment was the bathing suit the man was wearing, and how it fit him: red, shiny, and tight. He wanted him.

Tom sat and stared. He lay down and stared. He stood up and stared. But the object of his driving gaze seemed oblivious to his existence. The man was soaking up sun, looking around only when he switched positions —which he did much less frequently than Tom—and seemed content to listen to the surf break, and sleep.

When he woke up, some two hours later, the sun had already begun to melt into the water, and the beach was almost deserted. Except for Tom, maintaining his vigil, which was certainly unlike him, but then again, he'd never seen anyone like this man before. Tom saw him stretch, rub his eyes with the palms of his hands, and then let out a gasp as if he were exhausted from sleeping.

37

It was then, as he turned his head on the blanket, turned it toward the shimmering ocean, that he saw Tom sitting and studying him.

They cruised for a long time. Eye contact. Look away. Back again. *He's still looking.* Stretch out a little more. Getting a hard-on. *Can he see it? Oh yeah, he sees it.* Long look out to the few boats left on the water, as if really interested in them. *Is he still looking?* Turn back. *Jesus, he's hard too. . .*

Finally Tom broke out a big grin, and the man got up and walked over to him. "Hi." The voice matched the fantasy—low and sexy.

"Hi." Tom looked up. He could see up the side of his trunks which were tented now that he had an erection. He thought he could die from pleasure. "How are ya?"

"Well, you got me turned on."

"Good. I wanted to."

The man squatted down. "I love your eyes. Robin's egg blue."

Tom smiled. "I love your everything."

"Hmmm."

"Listen, I've been sitting here staring at you for a couple of hours or more. I can't stand it anymore. Give me a break. I don't say this to many people, but you're too fucking hot for words."

The man looked a bit embarrassed. "Listen, sport, flattery will get you everywhere."

"No, I mean it."

"You're all right yourself."

"I want to fuck you."

There was no answer, but the erection stayed.

"Well, listen, not literally, if you don't dig it." Tom was flustered and he hated himself for it. This was unlike him. What the hell was happening here? "I mean, I want to get it on with you, that's all. Name it, a blow job in the car, sodomy on a surfboard. . ."

The guy cracked up. He ran his hand through Tom's

damp hair. "Hey, sport, you're incredible."

"Thanks. Do you live nearby?"

"No. Not at all. And I have to be somewhere in less than an hour. You?"

"I don't have a place near either. Can I call you?"

"Uh, no. It's a long story, just not cool." Tom was sure he had a lover. "Can I call you?"

"Sure." Tom reached into the parachute sack he used as a beach bag and pulled out a piece of paper and wrote his number on it. "My name is Tom."

"I'm Mitch." He extended his hand. Tom took it and their eyes met again and Mitch was kneeling down now and for a moment he pulled Tom toward him, to his chest, and held his head there. He gently kissed his air and then got up, grabbed his blanket and slid into his pants. "I'll give you a call," he said, and left the beach, running through the sand.

"Sure," Tom said, softly, knowing he would not.

And he didn't. For a few weeks, the man from the beach was a powerful masturbation fantasy, and every time the phone rang there was hope somewhere inside him it would be Mitch. But it never was. And after a while the man in the red trunks began to fade from memory, replaced by a boy Tom met in the super-market; soon he was forgotten completely.

Then, six months, three days and fourteen hours later, Tom found himself standing face-to-face with the out-of-mind object of his desire at a Christmas tree stand. Mitch was wearing a jogging outfit. Tom had on his University of Southern California sweatshirt. The air was brisk, the day sunny. Tom remembered; Mitch did not.

"You a student?" the man asked.

"Sometimes."

"You know anything about Christmas trees?"

"Some. I do know it's crazy to spend fifteen bucks on a dead one, when for only twice that you can get a living tree you can keep all year and use for all the Christmasses to come."

"I never thought of that. Don't I . . . listen, I have the feeling we met. Don't I know you?"

"You were going to call me."

The man looked embarrassed. "No. Really? Jesus, when? I'm sorry. . ."

Tom smiled. "Forget it. It was a long time ago. On the beach. Your name is Mitch, correct?"

"Right. And I have no idea—I'm sorry again—what yours is."

"Tom."

"Well, I remember the face."

Tom smirked. No, he wasn't going to gush all over, the way he'd done on the beach. He was sure that's why he never called. So he said simply, but with a certain tease, "And I remember a little more than that."

It had its effect; Mitch looked into his eyes.

Then a little round man with a red face—Santa?— came up to them and said, in a merry voice, "Okay, gentlemen, what will it be?"

Tom looked at Mitch.

Mitch looked at Tom.

It was obvious what it would be.

The man was bewildered. "Can I help you guys? You made a decision? We got a nice blue spruce over—"

"I want this one here," Tom said, his hand reaching out to touch the needles of a perfectly-shaped tree. "And he's going to get one like it."

"But I don't have a place to put it, not even a terrace," Mitch explained.

"Donate it to the parks," the round little man said, beginning to put a red sticker onto the branch of Tom's tree. "You can write it off. Or a church or something like that."

Tom found his eyes again. "Or you could give it to

me. I've got a little yard. I'd be happy to keep it till next year."

Mitch's dark eyes seemed to shine. "How can I be sure of getting it back?"

"I'll give you my phone number," Tom said, adding, *"again."* This time he had the feeling the man would call.

And he did. On New Year's day. Tom was recovering from his annual hangover when the phone began to echo in his head. He reached out from the bed, lifted the receiver, and dropped it right back on the cradle. But the ringing was back a moment later.

He put a pillow over his head. No good. He could still hear it. He stretched and shivered. He realized what day it was and was mad at himself because he'd missed the Rose Parade live on TV. He sat up. God, it was chilly. He'd forgotten to turn on the heater. He pulled his robe up over him and finally answered the phone. "Happy happy happy."

"Is this Tom?"

"I'm half-asleep. But yeah, it is."

"This is Mitch. The guy with the Christmas tree."

He brightened. "Hi. Hey, you kept your promise this time."

"Well, sport, I've got this goddamn potted tree taking up room here. I *had* to."

"That the only reason?"

"I'd like to see you. We're going to throw the tree out in a few days and I'd like to bring it over if I could."

We. He said *we.* Tom was sure he had a lover. "You name the time."

"What are you doing Friday night?"

You, hopefully. "I'll be home. Listen, let me give you directions. This place is kinda hard to find. . ." And Tom told him how not to get lost in the hills around the bungalow, how not to take the front drive up to the

Countess' Mansion, and how to park the car on the grass right next to the little house because there was simply no other place to put it.

"You sure it's not an inconvenience?" Mitch asked.

"I have a date with your Christmas tree."

When Tom hung up, he walked into the living room, sat at the piano, and slammed his fingers down into a very loud E-flat major chord. It said a great deal for Mitch.

FIVE

Tom lived in a guest house on an estate which had belonged to a silent movie star now long forgotten. The celluloid queen had the good sense to sink her money into real estate before talkies demolished her career. Now the Countess Oluspenskay owned the digs, the castle up at the high reaches of Bel Air with rooms no one had ever bothered counting. There was a Sparta like the one Old Man Hearst had built, and a less grand spa and waterfall, and one for the children which was filled with ducks since the Countess loathed all humans under the age of seventeen. Four garages held two Rolls Royces, a Mercedes and a Mark IV. There were gardens, acres of foliage, a forest of evergreens and tangled vines, and in the center of all that lush dark greenery sat a cottage. "Ze dacha," as the Countess called it.

Tom had been invited to an afternoon garden party at the mansion, and he'd wandered off and stumbled on the cottage. It was nestled into a canyon and had its own entrance apart from the gates surrounding the enormous estate. It was out of a storybook, and he was drawn to it.

It reminded him of a Swiss chalet carved into a music box Chloe had in Chicago. A vacation house in the Black Forest in Germany. A fantasy. There was a roof

43

of thatched shingles, walls of brick and stucco, and huge wooden beams. The windows were made from hundreds of pieces of glass, beveled in diamond-shaped panes. He found one open.

He pulled himself up over the kitchen sink and dropped to the floor. It was cozy and inviting. Such a stark contrast to the big white castle so imposing on the hill, with its palm and cypress trees flanking it.

The fireplace dominated the living room. It was in the center of the room and the hearth opened through to the bedroom. It was made from huge stones and had a mantle of solid oak. An old-fashioned popcorn shaker hung next to it, and copper pots, almost green with age and non-use, lined the outside wall of the chimney.

The kitchen came out of the stones, built around the corner of the room, with a serving counter of ceramic tile and stools flanking it. Tom wiped his footprint from the stainless steel sink and opened the refrigerator to see it had been rarely used.

There was a short hallway, bathroom with a big shower, and a bedroom nearly the size of the living room. The bed faced the fireplace. How marvelous to fall asleep with flames dancing at your feet. Tom felt the romantic stir inside him. And he knew right then he would live in this house.

Getting it wasn't easy, though he never thought it would be.

"Vat? Ze guest house? Ze dacha?" The Countess fluttered her fan in front of her heavily made-up face, as if trying to dry her lip gloss. She shook her head. "You go on and on about it, Tomas, but vat is it you *vant*?"

"Well, I. . ."

She turned to him. "Ve are blunt people, ve Russians. You vonder, darling, vill she let me live there . . . after all, vell, ze place is empty, collecting so much dust. Ya?"

"Yeah."

She tsk-tsked him. "But vhere vill I put my friends, Tomas, darling?" She called him Tomas and darling a lot.

Friends? He didn't know she had any. But he wasn't about to give up. "I just thought it would be so much easier if I lived on the land. I'm here all the time anyhow. And I've never seen anybody staying in there."

"Vell. . ."

"I know that Melvin, Jack and R.J. are sharing a beach house in Malibu, and they're not paying any rent. I'm still in a hole in Hollywood."

"Vell. . ."

"I know they've been with you longer. But I could do better with nice surroundings, you know what I mean?"

She did.

"I want something classier. I think I deserve it. I'm one of your most requested escorts. Don't you want to keep me happy?"

She cackled, rubbing her bejewled fingers together. They were so bony he was surprised they didn't bleed. "Vat a hustler you are, Tomas! Ze boy vorks for me three veeks and already is asking for Pickfair!"

"Just the guest house, it's only two rooms."

"Vell, you know, it vould be a tremendous sacrifice for me to make. Ze finest jewel in the crown. . ."

"You talking about me or the cottage?"

She jumped up and danced around the room. She sometimes thought she was Isadora Duncan, scarves and all, but in actuality she looked more like Ruth Gordon, and even moved like her, going nervously in twelve directions at once. Then she did her Czarina Bit, as Tom called it. "Oh, Tomas, you are no peasant! Zis glitter is not for you, but a cave is not for you either." She waved around the gilded room with its heavy Moorish furniture and velvet drapes. "A cottage at Petrodvoerts, perhaps, but never life in ze Vinter Palace.

Ach, yes, trees over head and pine needles under foot, a small dacha vhere you vill compose symphonies for me. . ."

Yeah, he thought, *and next comes a piano, you silly old bag.* But he wasn't going to press his luck all at one time; first the house, then the piano.

"Ach, ze dacha is yours, Tomas!"

And so he had his house. Then, three weeks later, he sunk his claws in and bit off another chunk:

". . .and to compose symphonies for you, dear Countess, I need a piano. That Yamaha up in the library sits unplayed. We could—"

"Next you vill ask me for ze crown jewels!"

"—move it in easily. Rolf and a couple of the guys could do it. I'd have to save forever to get one of my own. No one plays it here." Big grin.

"Vat a mover, vat a Sammy Gluck."

"Glick."

"Vat does it matter?" She tossed the flowers she'd been arranging into the air. "Oh vell, ze hustler hustles ze Madame. So things change. But you promise you vill vrite an opera for me one day?"

It's been written. Faust. You sold your soul to the devil long ago. "I have no desire to write opera. Just songs."

"And vat is Boris Gudonov but a bunch of songs? Vell, my Chopin, at least vun little tune for ze Countess?"

"Da."

And so he had his house and a piano.

The day they moved the big ebony instrument over to the cottage, Tom came back to the mansion and stopped by the pool. A muscular boy—Tom guessed he couldn't be more than nineteen—sat on a Brown Jordan chaise. "Where'd she go?" Tom asked. The Countess had been supervising the move, and then seemed to disappear. He wanted to ask her if she'd have the piano tuned, since it had been jarred in the moving.

The boy ran his hand through his dark red hair and pointed up to the third floor. "Some guy showed up, someone I've never seen before. She dragged him in and hasn't come up for air yet."

"Jesus," Tom said, with a smile. The guy who was cleaning the pool, the young man Tom had seen many times who walked with a limp and seemed self-conscious, seemed to be eavesdropping intently. "She's probably driving him into ecstasy with her vibra-balls—"

"Or her celery-sized vibrator," the red-haired boy laughed.

The young man cleaning the pool blushed.

"Oh, good old initiation," Tom said. "What did you have to do the first time?"

The boy howled. "She had me shoot marbles into her cunt."

Tom laughed out loud.

The pool boy dropped the hand skimmer right into the water.

"Real style, real class," the boy went on. "A whacko Russian contessa who likes cat's eyes rolled into her privates. Amazing. Fucking amazing."

Tom smiled, looking up at the shy pool boy who seemed to be getting vicarious thrills from the conversation, and said, "Well, one thing—it sure isn't boring."

Understatement.

Her name was Zena Matrinka Olga Oluspenskaya, née Anastasia Nicolaevna Romanov. Not that she was really serious about it, of course, but for a time in her outrageous life she got off on causing an uproar by claiming to be the notorious Anastasia. "Ingrid Berman impersonating me? Vat an insult!" It was in jest, was it not? She claimed to be serious. Her age, height, weight, blood type and just about everything else about her were wrong, proof that she was not a descendant of the infamous Tsar Nicholas II, but it did not seem to phase her when people pointed that out. When Dick Cavett told her he thought the only thing she had in common with the Romanov family was that they were both Russian and liked noodles, she threw him the finger and walked off the show.

She did make popular history, however. As a costume designer in Hollywood, where her Anastasia fetish didn't hurt her any in terms of publicity. No one may have taken seriously the testimony of just missing the bullets in that basement at Ekaterinburg, but it did get her on Merv and Dinah and Dick, and she was able to promote the "few designs I vhipped up in my spare time. . ." What made her choose a professional career even though she was a born princess? "I stopped my qvest for recognition when somevon did a Broadvay musical called *Anya*, vhich vas another insult to me, and at ze same time had ze vorst costumes ever to grace ze stage in my lifetime."

She was—to put it gently—theatrical. Where the phony accent came from, no one was quite sure, though it was thought she studied with the famous Jolie Gabor, who'd given three unassuming girls speech lessons which seemed to benefit them well in the end. Where the name —Zena Matrinka Olga Oluspenskaya—came from, no one was quite sure either, though it didn't really matter; that was her name. She told tales of her flight from Russia during the Great October Revolution, of her tormented life hiding in Poland and marriage to a count from Czechoslovakia, and his untimely death in her arms in the midst of ultimate passion. ("He vas qvite elderly and vonce vhile ve vere making love, he just vent *boom* on top of me and never got up again.") She then went to work as a seamstress in theatres in London and Paris ("I thank my mother, Tsarina Alexandra, for teaching me so much to sew ven I vas young. . ."), began designing on her own, and finally made a splash in the world of Seventh Avenue fashion. A noted Hollywood designer, miffed that this foreigner, this newcomer, had been chosen over him to design the gowns for major motion picture after only one year in the rag business in New York, told a gossip columnist: "That cunt was born in the Bronx and she talks like she was kicked out of Berlitz and what's more, she steals her sketches from the Sears Roebuck catalog."

That cunt, like her or not, had made a place in the world of fashion all her own. First she only designed women's coats and hats, but in the late Sixties, when the ladies of America stopped covering their heads with Jackie Kennedy pillboxes, she joined forces with a young jewelry designer who had burst upon the scene with marvelous enameled pieces; they agreed to put out a line of bangles to go with the clothes, and their names would be forever entwined.

But, alas, he drank himself to death at the age of thirty-three, after his lover left him for an usher at Radio City, and Zena quickly bought out his half of the business and excised his name from the logo because of its "scandalous" ramifications. Madame Zena had a line of jewelry all her own.

How she eventually became known as the Countess de Los Angeles is unknown; perhaps the real estate people dropped it on her when she bought the hillside hacienda —with the commission they got, she was indeed some kind of goddess in their eyes. Some said the title came from the marriage to the Czech count, and was thus justified. Others said she just decided to put it on her stationery one day. But many—those "in the know"?— were certain it was a kind of nickname she acquired when she began making inroads into other industries besides fashion, namely the successful marketing of a somewhat limited commodity: young men. And there was always the possibility she was just plain nuts.

Crackers or not, she was a shrewd and calculating woman, sure of herself and her enterprises. That she had

talent was obvious and could never be denied. She'd
been nominated for an Oscar for her first film; she did
three more films, then devoted her time only to her new
collections. "I am retiring from ze screen," she announced with a flourish at the Beverly Hilton, "vhich
saddens me greatly, but vill make Theadora Van Runkle
smile a lot. I must deal vit real life from now on." And
she did. Oh, how she did.

Her approach was different. Instead of a new Fall or
Spring collection, she offered a few new garments every
month, a continuing output which were copied by the
big clothing firms as fast as she could show them, and
soon found their way to the racks in Korvettes and
Ohrbachs, and subsequently into suburban clothes
closets. She was respected. And rich. And she was an
artist, so she had every right to be eccentric.

If that was the correct word.

She lived what people called an "outrageous" life, and
perhaps it was. The mansion was one oddity. Another
was her "shadow," Madame Platychivnik, the lush
always at her side, Vera Charles to her Mame. Another
was the never-ending line of gorgeous young men on her
arm; she fashioned herself a new Mae West, fluttering
her lashes for the photographers as she groped the
young man in the tuxedo just for emphasis and another
line in the column. Outrageous? It was to the readers in
Orange County.

The truth was it was not all in jest, the young men she
seemed to pull out of a hat. She had a passion for them,
and knew well how to benefit from their charm. She
learned people would pay for just what she had, an "escort" who was in his twenties, very handsome, and eager
to please. They would pay well. She started out with two
hopeful actors—a perfectly balanced business calcu-
lation from the start, one gay and one straight. She
counted the take and swore in Russian to Madame
Platychivnik how incredible it was what people would

pay for a roll in Tinsel Town hay. She ran an escort service, ran it quite surreptitiously. Five boys worked for her at any given time, but only five; Tom, when he became one of the five, was, however, her twenty-seventh discovery.

He met her on Santa Monica Boulevard. He had been to a trashy bar and then had gone to Drake's for coffee and a hoot and holler with the drag queens and silicone sisters. Bored, horny, he was hitching, looking for a car that spelled money, because the rent was due again and he was busted. When the Rolls pulled up, he sauntered over, hoping the guy wasn't *too* fucking ugly. When the window rolled down and he saw this Sylvia Sydney with rubies around her neck, and hair that looked like it had been done in a clothes dryer, he couldn't resist accepting a ride from her. He wasn't going anywhere, but for her, hell, he'd ride a mile or so. This was gonna be crazy.

He got more than he'd bargained for. She parked the car on a dark stretch of Genesee and went down on him right there. After her proposition, his mental justification was: She can blow me all she wants for a hundred bucks! He was used to getting twenty at the most. A hundred? Hell, she could fucking well bite it off for that amount.

But she did much more than give him a BJ in a Rolls on a hot Hollywood night. She changed his life. She got him out of his shitty apartment and put some decent clothes on his body. She enriched his experience with tales of her past. She told him what she had in mind for him for the future. But she only kept five boys at once, and there were no vacancies at present. Would he, in the meantime, like to be her gardener?

He couldn't tell a rose from a daisy, but he took the position, and as an assistant to a smiling, quiet Japanese man, did learn a lot about what makes things grow; before long he could tell you if a bush was a florabunda or climber just by the shape of the leaves. He liked his job.

He liked her. Life was evening out for him.

He also liked the boys who often sat around the pool. They seemed happy, fun-loving, well-fed and healthy. These were her "nephews," as she called them. Melvin, Jack, R.J., Sammy and Paul. One day Paul left the fold. She came to Tom and told him to throw down his shears, put away the rose food. His work was going to change. His ass for her rich contacts, an equitable business arrangement. Would he accept? He dropped his gloves and never clipped another rose.

Then came the house.

And the piano.

All in all, in a short time, he wasn't at all unsuccessful as a hustler.

SIX

Hustling. It was something that had crossed his mind long before he even met Den Mother Oluspenskaya. He had thought about it even before he met Chloe in Chicago and really decided he was going to hit the streets of L.A., and see how fast the savings account filled up. He thought about it soon after he left Houston, as a matter of fact. He thought about it that very same night he'd shut the door on Annie forever.

Oklahoma City was a lot like where he'd come from. Hot and dusty, the people cantankerous and backwards, drunk and loud and unmotivated. The women were cheap and the men all seemed like tattered versions of Marlboro ads. There were the same Cadillacs with rabbit fur seat covers and horns jutting out of the grille. Ten gallon hats and pointed-toe boots, fragmented badges of the Old West and money. The smell of oil refineries, gasoline and paint—Gary, Indiana, South—fumes which tightened the nostrils and made a person lightheaded.

It was a sorry place, too much a reminder of what he'd hated, too little an opportunity for a future. He wasn't quite twenty, did not know what he wanted to do with his life, but he was sure as hell positive about this not being the place in which he was going to attempt to find out. Another runaway at the bus station suggested he get a job on a ranch and make some money and spend his weekends in town getting drunk like all the rest of the guys. He *wasn't* one of the guys, he never had been. There had to be something more.

He moved on, but not by bus anymore. He only had eighty-seven dollars, and he was wise enough to know expenses would come up, clothes and food and a place to live wherever he finally settled. He didn't plan on going back to school. What for? He was sure he could learn as much from reading books and traveling and meeting new people. He wanted to work. He wanted to keep busy. There was challenge in that. He wanted to see the world and forget Annie and BJ's and that Texas even existed.

He got his first inkling of how to make fast money in a coffee shop outside Tulsa. The kid sitting next to him at the counter asked, "Enjoyin' your chili?"

"Yeah." Tom picked at it, moving it around in the bowl. He didn't feel like talking to anyone, but the kid was about his age and seemed pleasant. So he at least nodded.

"I'm Jake. You on the road?"

"Yeah. Don' know where I'm going, though. But I'm sure going. My name's Tom."

"I'm headed to Mexico," Jake said with assurance. "I got a job waitin' in Acapulco."

"That's a long way to go." Tom had read a lot about Mexico. South America. Brazil and Aztecs and Incas. Gold, conquistadors, Spanish ships.

"You hitchin' too?"

Tom nodded. "North. Chicago I guess."

"Shit, why you wanna go there? Winter's comin'! It'll freeze your nuts up there."

"Texas isn't the Sahara, you know."

"Guess it does get pretty cold down this way, too,"

Jake agreed. "Freeze your nuts just about anywhere 'cept Acapulco."

They shared stories. Places they wanted to see. Favorite movies. The first time each of them smoked grass. They talked for nearly an hour. The waitress poured two entire pots of coffee into their cups before she finally said, "Now, why don't you two darlin's move your butts on outta here? This ain't no hotel, ya know?" They didn't tip her.

They sat under a neon sign, near the road, and talked some more. Jake had been hitching around since he was only fourteen. He was twenty now, but didn't look it. "Movin' around keeps ya young," he said.

"You ever work?"

"You kiddin'?"

"How do you make money? You gotta have money for food. You had a big meal in there and you paid with a twenty."

"Good eyes, buddy." Jake hesitated a moment and then said, "Listen, there's lots a ways to make bread on the road. Guys give you money. Come on, you know that."

No, he didn't, and said so.

"You ever read the toilet walls?"

"What do you mean?"

"Buddy, you're greener 'n grass and you'd better wise up or you'll never make it *to* Chicago to freeze your nuts off."

"I guess I haven't been around much."

Jake turned and pointed his finger right at Tom. "You want some brotherly advice?"

Tom said he did.

"You're a . . . well, you're good lookin', ya know? You got a big dick?"

Tom's eyes widened. "Huh? Um . . . I guess so."

"Probably don't matter, 'cause you're good lookin'

enough and that's what counts. I ain't no movie star, but the size of my dick makes up for it. Everybody wants 'em big."

"What's it got to do with money?"

"That's how you make it."

"Someone pays you?" Annie suddenly danced through his brain. "Like a whore?"

"Sure. I'm a whore whenever I need some money."

"But you're a guy."

"That's why I make good money. Look, see that dude in the Ford over there?" Tom looked over to the far side of the truck stop parking lot. There was a man who looked like an accountant, sitting in his car chewing on his finger. "That's how I got the bread to go in there and hand out that twenty."

"He paid you?"

"Five minutes and I made five bucks."

"Five bucks for a BJ?"

"BJ? Oh, blow job, yeah. All you have to do is unzip and they're down on ya. Travelin' salesmen, truckers, they're all horny as hell. They always got five to spare for a kid. Lots a power in being' a teenager. Dick power."

"Yeah," Tom mumbled, staring at the man in the Ford whose eyes were glued to him. Male prostitution had never crossed his mind because it was his mother who got the money that way, not the men. He didn't know anything about it. But it interested him, on more than just a superficial level: his cock was getting hard. "Jake, do women ever pay for it? Girls?"

"Hell yes. But you don't meet 'em much on the road. That's why I'm goin' to Mexico. There's a big house down there and the guys service rich broads who are visitin' the fat farm or somethin'." He laughed.

Tom's cock was hard and he didn't know why. Or did he? He thought about the man in the car doing it to him, right there on the side of the road. It would feel like

Bobby. Good and warm and exciting. He saw himself lying on a beach in Acapulco, making a million dollars, women lining up for him. He was horny. He hadn't come since Houston. He'd been dropped off at the truck stop by a woman who'd smelled of a freshly mowed lawn. Delicious. Like the park he loved so much, like the bushes where he went with Bobby. . .

"Tom, why don't you come down to Mexico with me? We could have a good time. We'll be a team. Hell, we'll make a fortune off the broads. And you won't freeze your nuts."

Tom shook his head. An erection, fortunately, did not turn his brain into putty. "I've always wanted to see lots of snow and the stockyards and Marina City." He thought he sounded like Sinatra singing "My Kind of Town". "But I appreciate the tip, on getting the money."

Jake moved closer and talked in a fatherly tone now. "Listen, don't let it bother ya none. It ain't like you're queer or nothin' like that just 'cause you let a guy go down on ya. Hell, even when I got a fag doin' it to me, I think about screwin' some chick. That's how I get it up for 'em."

"I don't worry about being queer," Tom said. "I had a kid in my school who gave me BJ's all the time. It felt good. He wasn't queer either. He screwed girls."

Jake scowled a very manly scowl. "I don't know about that, buddy. I can see a guy gettin' it done to him, but I don't buy the same guy *doin'* it." The parking lights on the Ford turned on. Then off. Then on and off again. "See that? The International Sex Language of the Road. He's tellin' ya to come over and get your dick sucked."

"By clicking the lights on and off?"

"Either that or tappin' the horn a little or openin' the window and coughin' or starin' at ya for a minute. All kinds of signals. You'll see the more you hike."

"That's what I should be doing. Hiking. I wanted to get to Joplin tomorrow."

"Ain't you gonna let that dude give you five smackers? He wants ya, buddy. He probably sits there all night, the poor bastard, and blows ten or fifteen kids. I bet ya he owns a factory and has a wife and three kids in Tulsa. Life is crazy."

"Sure is." Tom got up and held his hand out.

"Take it easy, buddy." They shook. "Have one on me." Then Jake slapped him on the back, picked up his battered suitcase and started to walk away.

"Jake?" The boy turned. "You said five. But you got a twenty from him. What'd you have to do for that?"

"Specialty of the house. Stuck it up his ass. Cornholed him."

"Oh."

Jake went off up the road.

Tom crossed the highway and put his thumb out. No one picked him up. For ten minutes he felt the eyes of the man in the Ford staring at his swollen crotch. He wanted to be rescued by a passing vehicle. But five bucks, and he needed to come, and he was hard. It was different with Bobby, he knew him, it wasn't whoring. But where did he suddenly come up with a moral code all his own that said whoring was wrong? It was a way of life he'd known from the start. The man was still staring. He took a step onto the highway. He shivered. What would it be like to put his cock up a guy's ass. . .? And then a car pulled over and saved him from hellfire and damnation.

He was given a ride into Tulsa and dropped off near the bus station. He felt grimy. He needed a shower. He took his last few dollars and allotted just so much for the next few days—a dollar a day until Chicago—and that meant he had three days left in which he either got a job there or let some guy in a Ford blow him.

Fifty cents of his first day's allotment went toward a

shower there in the men's room of the bus depot. When he came out of the stall, feeling fresh and clean, he saw a man approach him just as he pulled on his dusty jeans. Tom saw a question written on his face. He expected the man to ask the time or question him about the bus schedule or ask for a light. Instead, he said, "Hey, hot little number, you gonna let me fuck you? I got a hotel room."

Tom swallowed hard. "No." He hoved his feet into his boots.

"There's ten bucks in it for that sweet little ass."

Tom got up and left in a hurry. He walked around the block three times until he was sure the man was gone. It started raining and he didn't feel like hitting the road again. Finally, he went back inside the station and fell asleep on one of the hard benches.

SEVEN

He learned soon enough to do what Jake had told him, becoming "trade," not knowing where it would lead. Strangely enough it led to the first meaningful heterosexual affair of his life, Chloe. But they never talked of his hustling, not once while they lived together in Chicago. They only talked about it when they were living together for the second time, after she arrived from New York, ready to take Hollywood by storm. They had parked the car on Selma and took a stroll down Hollywood Boulevard. The street was littered with hustlers. At the corner of Las Palmas, four young men dressed in Nazi regalia were lined up against the window of a coffee shop. "Macho city," Chloe muttered.

"That's trade," Tom said as they crossed the street.

"What's trade?"

"For a sophisticated intellectual, you don't know much, do you?"

"Tomcat, the only hustlers I know about are pool sharks. And the creeps on Forty-Second Street. It's a big enough shock to find out you're not selling sheet music, you know. So what's it like to hustle?"

"Just like selling sheet music, only the pay is better."

They stopped in front of a record store and looked at the display of new albums. "No fuckin' Janis in the window, man. No one remembers Janis anymore." She shook her head and turned sadly away.

They walked. Tom talked. "Trade means a guy lets other men do him, but he tells himself he's straight, so there's no guilt. He never lays a finger on the other guy and that way he doesn't have to fight his conscience about being homosexual."

"*I got dem old kozmic blues again, mama!*" Chloe sang. Then she asked him when was the first time he did it.

"What do you mean?"

"For money."

"Before I met you. When I got to St. Louis. I ran out of money to make it to Chicago. I did it again when I got to Chicago. That's how I got to Milwaukee, how I got the job in the dry cleaners. Then I never did it again until I got here."

"Say that again? No, never mind." She closed her eyes. "Never when we were together?" Her voice was softer suddenly, as if she were ready to be hurt.

He shook his head. "No. Never." They walked some more. Then Tom said, "You know, the first time I had a woman, I guess that was a kind of hustle too. She gave me some bread, though I didn't really think of it as payment for getting laid. But it was. We're all whores. All the time. Husbands and wives even. Give me a new toaster oven and I'll be real nice to you in bed for the next couple of weeks."

"Fuck for a toaster oven? Jesus, for a peacock maybe, or a trip to Paris. But a toaster oven?" She howled. They were back at the car. He opened the door for her and she pulled the feathers sticking from her hair down over her face so she could get in. "You still doing it?" she asked, looking up before he closed the door.

"No." He went around and got in. He knew she knew he was lying. "Well, sometimes," he said. He put the key in the ignition but didn't turn it. "Well, actually, a lot of the time. But you knew that."

"Yeah, well, fuck, who cares? I don't think there's anything wrong with it. I lived with a fag on the Lower East Side who used to make it with black transvestites. So—"

"I wouldn't call him a fag. *Strange* maybe, but he doesn't sound like a fag."

"Are you?"

"Strange?"

"A fag?"

"Chloe, you knew I was bisexual when we first—"

"No, I mean totally gay. Only guys now? You haven't made a move toward me since I got here. No women call. Just fags."

"Oh, come on."

"You trade?"

"I just explained that's what straight guys say—I mean guys who pretend to be straight—and I just said I'm bisexual. I know where my sexuality's at. I don't have a problem."

"Then why don't you just admit you're gay?"

"Jesus Christ." He started the car. "Listen, all I want to say is I hustle. I hustle men *and* women, okay? Don't label me with gay or straight."

"You just labeled yourself with—"

"—and sex is boring anyway, it's a boring subject. I don't want to talk about it anymore." He waited for a car to pass and then pulled out.

"You've always been a hustler. That's all you're good at, man. You take people. Suck their blood. When they can't give anymore, you take a walk. Fuckin' men."

"Shit, Chloe!" he yelled, slamming on the brakes at the light. "I don't want to hear that goddamn litany again!"

"Tomcat, you still love me?"

"Of course, dammit."

"Will we ever be together again?"

"You're living in my apartment right now. . ."

"That's not what I meant. Married, Tomcat. You were going to marry me."

He gripped the steering wheel so hard his fingers turned white. "Chloe, that was a long time ago. We've been through that. Things have changed. We're different now."

"That's what I hoped. I hoped you'd be different now. You were a bastard, you know. Leaving me without a fuckin' word, left me to explain it to my daddy and Sandy and mama, left me and Ophelia to figure it out, that damn short note. Oh, but I never once hated you for it. I didn't blame you. I accepted it—watch out for that fuckin' truck—and I took the shame and embarrassment and. . ."

"Come on, Chloe!" He was racing down the street, winding his way in and out of traffic, as if to hurry home to get this over with.

"Tomcat, listen to me. I'm saying that despite all that, it's still there. I still love you so fuckin' much, man. I'm a witch and I knew you'd hurt me, I knew it a long time ago when you stepped on me under the piano. You needed time to grow and breathe. You went about it in a pretty shitty way, I admit, but I'm over that now. But we're still going to be together, the way daddy wanted, the way he dreamed."

"Chloe, it's not there anymore, it's just not *there*. I left you the first time because I was scared, sure, but also because I was suddenly starting to realize nothing was left anymore. It wasn't idyllic anymore. It was dying. I couldn't change it. I couldn't make magic happen."

She grabbed his hand. "I can!"

"Chloe, I don't want to hear that mumbo jumbo. Go ahead, sprinkle the corners of the apartment with potions, read the tea leaves and coffee grounds, do whatever it is you do, chant and light all those candles and yell at the moon, but don't give me anymore of that witch talk."

She pouted for a moment and then muttered, "You're really a bastard. You really are, man. My mama was right the first time you left. She said you were full of shit. Man, you've been draggin' me down, down. You're doin' it again."

"You keep saying the 'first' time. I haven't left you again, you know."

"You will," she said softly, looking out the car window through tears which she refused to let fall. "You fuckin' will."

"Let's not talk about it anymore."

But she had to hit him back. "I'll bet you don't even get it on with girls at all anymore."

He wasn't going to answer. She didn't deserve it. He just drove. But she never liked the ammunition of silence and she was unrelenting. "Men! Fuckin' men, you're all alike. You're supposed to fuck women and they scare you and castrate you, so you fuck each other and women, women get the blues. You gotta be a dyke or miserable."

"Is that how it happens?" he asked with gritted teeth, looking straight ahead.

"Hell yes, man."

"You've got a lot to learn. And stop saying 'man' like some hippy chick from 1968."

"Fuck you."

There was silence for a long while.

Then Chloe asked, "Would you fuck me if I paid you?"

It was a preposterous question, meant to hurt and taunt, and it was effective; it put even more distance between them. It had started in that idyllic relationship in Chicago when marriage seemed so right and natural, like the next step. So fantastic. So average American and ordinary and acceptable—and *right*. He'd never known average. It was a fantasy, to do something truly middle-class, to live like ordinary people. It was simply the thing he never had, a romantic ideal of what "normal" might be. But when the fantasy started changing into real life, things didn't look the same. Responsibility. Hooked for the rest of your life. Two people could love together, but did that mean they could live together? Why suddenly did her drinking and pill popping come into such focus? Why did he start wanting men again all of a sudden, why did she seem so unsatisfactory, so unsatisfying now that normalcy—years of it, a future of it—reared its average head?

Yes, he'd left her, left her after he'd taken the good times and put them in his pocket. He'd hustled her, sure, but he justified it by convincing himself she had as good a deal; after all, had she ever known a lover quite as unique as him? Hadn't she told him that, that he was "unique" in all her experience? Wasn't it proof now, just the fact that she had come three thousand miles to be with him again after he'd been such a shit? Two years had passed—if only she'd stayed in New York, it was so much better by letter—and it was all wrong again. "I don't think we can be together in the same space ever again, Chloe," he said matter-of-factly.

"But we're part of each other, Tomcat." She was groping. And opening herself up for heartache again. But could she help it?

"It doesn't mean we can *live* together. We'll kill each other. We'll numb each other."

"So leave me another note and run away again! Or toss me out. Yeah, toss me out just like asshole Willie did in New York because I didn't approve of his damn black boyfriends stealing my underpants. Shit. I've been numb for years. I've been dead for years."

"I can't help that."

"You caused it." Then she laughed, loud, out of control. "I've been numb through everything that was supposed to be good. I was numb in Chicago because I was too much in love with you. I was numb after Chicago because I was so hurt by what you did. I was numb when I was a kid because my mama always beat me for no reason. I was even numb the first time I got fucked, by a teacher back at drama school, 'cause I had a tooth pulled that morning and the novocaine hadn't work off yet and I couldn't even feel him kiss me." She shook the eighteen bracelets hanging on her wrist and flung her shredded shawl over her shoulders. She seemed suddenly in good spirits again. It worried him, her schizophrenic moods of late. "Some first time, huh? Tomcat, what was yours like?"

"I never told you about that?" He turned onto the freeway.

"No. Tell me now. What was it like?"

"Wet."

"Wet?"

"Very."

"You did it in the bathtub?"

"No. It was raining. . ."

EIGHT

It was raining.

She picked him up just outside Joplin. She had long red hair and eyelashes to match, neither of which were real, he was sure. She was slim and older than him by a good ten years, maybe more, and her short skirt was hiked up to her crotch. He could see the garters holding up her stockings. He put his things in the back seat and then crawled in next to her. "Your suitcase looks mighty weatherbeat to me," she said. Her voice was high-pitched and her eyebrows arched when she talked. Her fingers sported red Fu-Manchu nails except for one, which had fallen off. She was chewing bubble gum.

"I'm really thankful," Tom said. "Drizzle's worse than a downpour."

"Where you headed, a kid like you out on an afternoon like this?"

"North."

"How far, the Pole? I mean what city, like it reads on the top of the Greyhound, you know, above the windows in front?"

He smiled. "Chicago."

"Ever been before?"

"To Chicago? No."

"Hey, you runnin' away from home?"

"I guess you could say that."

She seemed to love it. "What a coincidence. Me too." She slapped him on the leg.

"You? *You're* running away from home?"

"So's to speak. Just takin' a lil' vacation. Stayin' with my sister Sue. She lives here in Joplin. Her hubby ran off with a waitress three weeks ago Saturday. I come up to give comfort and get away from my own place for a spell. I live in Saint Louie. Didn't tell 'em I was goin' though. That's the only way I can get a fair vacation."

"Won't anyone worry?" He wondered if Annie was worried.

"Sure. I want 'em to."

He ran his hand through his hair and it felt as though he'd just stepped out of the shower. "Feels good to be in a warm car."

"My hubby bought me this claptrap thing from some junk dealer. But it gets me around."

Tom looked around. "It's a nice car."

"No Cadillac, honey. And besides, my little one, she pissed on the back seat a week ago last Tuesday. Can't you smell it? I even dumped Lysol on it and nothing works. Kids. Christ Almighty. You'd a thought I'd a learned my lesson after the first two."

"You can't be old enough to have three children," he said, hoping to flatter.

It worked. She blushed. "Oh, hush your mouth. And how old are you? You're just a kid yourself."

"Yeah. Eighteen. And I promise not to pee on the seat."

She laughed. "Listen, who you runnin' away from anyhow? Your girlfriend's daddy hold a gun to your head and say, 'Marry my ugly girl or clear outta the county?'"

The notion of a girlfriend amused him. He'd never had any. So he put it straight. "I left my ma."

"Ain't they just a pain in the old butt? You gotta love

'em, I know, but Jesus H., they're so much damn nuisance. Pardon all the cussin', but I get riled talkin' about my ma. She takes care of the kids fine, but she don't think much about me or Sue or my little brother, Jake, who's off in the Army someplace."

"He wouldn't be on his way to Acapulco right now, would he?" She gave him a look. "Never mind."

"What made ya run from your ma?"

He thought a second. What would be a good reason someone like her would understand? "Bible preaching. The Good Book in her hand all the time."

She screwed up her nose. "Yup. Yup, I know what ya mean. I read the Bible, don't get me wrong, but if there's one thing I can't stomach, it's religious. I believe in the Lord all right, but I don't take to religious being fed to you all the time like pablum. Makes you wanna choke and spit up. Your ma wear high-button collars and long skirts and wash your mouth out with soap when you say a cuss word?"

He had to laugh. Annie Brassen's first word had probably been *shit*. High-button collars and long skirts? She'd worn dresses cut so low that every time she bent over to put on her shoes, a breast would pop out. Skirts? Usually they were lying on the floor next to her or hiked up to her chest. But he said, "Yup. That's my ma." He liked it; he was creating a whole new life in less than five minutes.

She seemed pleased with her insight. She stopped for a light and checked her lashes in the rearview mirror. Her hair was accented with a dayglo pink scarf on her neck, and her vinyl boots were of a matching color, though splattered with mud. She put her hand on his thigh, and left it there longer this time. "Listen, I go only four more blocks. I can't see it, you standin' in the rain to get another ride tonight. Why don't you come spend the night at Sue's? She's got a cot on what used to be the back porch. Had it all done over real nice. Then you can get a fresh start in the morning when it's bright and sunny."

"No, I can't do that. Thanks, but. . ."

"Now, you listen to me. Vinnie's gonna take you home and feed you and tuck you in. Little tyke like you out in the rain, there should be a law. Now, I don't want to hear another word about it, hear?"

He heard. Yes. She was right. A free meal and a nice warm bed—cot—and maybe even a bath. She turned down a residential street lined with ramshackle white shingle houses. "Where you from, baby?"

"Houston."

"I knew a fella from Houston. Mighty romantic fella he was. Didn't have much of a brain, but that didn't count in them days."

"We have a shortage of them in Texas."

She laughed and slapped her own thigh this time, and then started twisting the garter. "I'm sure of that, but I know one thing they do give out mighty plentiful, if the fella from Houston was any indication!" She snickered and batted her eyelashes so hard one fell off and fluttered to the wet floor. She pretended it hadn't happened. "You miss your girl?"

He stared straight ahead, at the swiping windshield wipers. "I didn't have a girl."

"No girlfriend? Ever?"

Softly, he said no, never.

"I'm not one to pry, but you ever—?"

No, he said, he'd never had a woman.

"Baby, what's your name?"

He told her.

"Tom," she said, swinging a hard right and into a muddy driveway next to one of the houses. "It suits you, Tom. I'm Lavinia."

"Lavinia?"

She turned out the lights and pulled the key from the

dashboard. Then she reached over and fitted her hand between his legs and groped his genitals as she kissed him on the lips. When she finally pulled her tongue from his mouth, she said, "But you can call me Vinnie."

"I'll try," he mumbled, recovering.

She went around to his side and opened the back door and dragged out his suitcase. "Colder than a witch's tittie out here," she laughed as they hurried toward the door, "and I can smell somethin' on the stove already. Sue said she's puttin' a chicken up. I could devour it. . ."

As he followed her inside, he thought that wasn't all she could devour. In the light of the front room he could make out her nipples through her blouse, the curve of her buttocks and the even, pretty features of her face. He hadn't realized she was so pretty under the severe hair and make-up. This isn't going to be all bad, he said to himself. She kissed him again just before her sister entered the room and his cock started to rise in his pants. He was resigned to it, and wanting it. What fun was there in being a virgin anyway?

By the time the meal was finished, he was dying for her.

Lavinia was a sexy lady. She knew how to lick her lips with her tongue after a sip of milk and suggest she were licking something else. She could bend over the peas and onions in such a way that you could see all the way down her dress to her bellybutton. She had changed for dinner; Tom thought it looked more like she had changed for bed. She seemed to have the uncanny ability to get her nipples hard every time she took a bite of chicken.

She also was an expert at footsie under the table. She could turn her leg in what must have been a painful position and slide her toes right up the warm spot where the legs of his jeans came together. She knew her timing too, when to drop her napkin and bend to the floor for it, to give his erect penis a little squeeze. It was the first sexy meal he'd had in his life.

Things tumbled over in his mind before he tumbled into bed with her. This was exciting because it was playful, a game, the older woman coming on to him under her sister's nose. He wondered if Sue, a soft-spoken sweet drip of a creature, knew what was going on? If she did, was she in on it? Was he going to be the main course for Lavinia, and dessert for Sue? Sister Woman's sloppy seconds?

Sue talked of her missing husband and his brother's damn turkey farm. Lavinia ignored her and concentrated on driving Tom into an erotic coma. She blew him kisses, sucked on her fingers, offered her breasts with a look that drove him crazy. How often did she do this? Was she always running away from home to pick up chicken in Joplin?

Whatever, the chicken wanted the temptress. The barometer of his desire had been erect from the moment she'd kissed him in the front room. She picked her teeth seductively with the wishbone. Why had he waited for *her*? He could have had a girl back in Houston. Just because he didn't particularly want to lose his cherry to Marjorie's oversexed mother, he could have gone back at a later date for the daughter and her hot baton. Or any number of other girls who had made advances to him. Girls Bobby had told him about. He even had the phone numbers.

But here he was in the town where Bonnie and Clyde got all shot up and Annie and the Eyes of Texas were no longer upon him and if he had to beat off in another john in a gas station he'd go crazy. This was a real woman who wanted him. She really did. She wasn't drunk, stoned, nuts. She found him attractive and let him know it. He was tired of running, sitting under viaducts to get out of the downpour, bored reading Burma Shave signs and listening to idiotic truck drivers telling dirty jokes in cafes that sold hot mud disguised as coffee. It was time for a Coke after so much Pepsi. Time for the real thing.

Lavinia bade goodnight to her sibling and pulled the faded flowered curtain that separated the porch from the front room. It was only big enough to hold the cot, a table with a Christmas calendar on it from *Jaspur Samuel McCahan, Joplin's Foremost Lumber Man,* and a big old chair which was losing its stuffing because the slipcover had worn away years ago. She sat in the chair. Sat there and dared him. Stared him down. "Babypie, you think you can come close to that roast chicky back there? You gonna please Vinnie as much as that meal did?"

The challenge was a formidable one; here was a woman with experience, and it had definitely been a good chicken. What did he have? Experience? Memories of BJ's and some dirty pictures. Knowledge? Lots of well-read pages in dirty novels. Love? What did he know about that, and did it even have anything to do with this? Not at all, and he knew it. He had youth. And passion. And adventure; discovery would be his. He learned fast. Hadn't he driven a car perfectly without taking any of those dumb courses? Didn't the piano come easy? What could be so difficult about making love to a woman?

"You got me all hot and bothered the second you set foot in the Buick," Lavinia whispered.

"Will Sue mind? I mean, she'll hear."

"Susie-Q's gone beddy-bye, and anyways, she minds her own business." She turned and closed her eyes. "Unless you don't *want* Vinnie."

"Oh, no, I do, I do." He sat down on the cot across from her. "I wanted to all through the meal. I thought I was going to—"

"Shoot in your drawers?" She giggled.

"Yeah." His face was aglow. "I thought I was going

to die when you grabbed me."

She pretended to be hurt. "How come you never touched me?"

He seemed embarrassed. "God! I couldn't do that! Not in front of your sister."

"You can now. She ain't in the room as I can see." She leaned back in the chair and kicked off her slippers.

He got up, bent over her, and put his hands on the soft arms of the chair. Then he let his body come down to hers, feeling her knee against his thigh, his penis pressing between her legs, pushing the skirt higher than it was in the car, his chest touching hers now, those hard nipples poking at his flesh through the top of the dress. Their lips met again and this time it was his tongue that moved through her mouth and sent shivers down his spine.

He bent his knees and felt the floor come up to meet them. He knelt there looking into her eyes. The rain hit the window. He cupped his hands very gently over her breasts just as thunder struck overhead; he rubbed the exposed flesh of her neck with his fingertips. She was hot, steamy to the touch; if the rain hit her, she'd short circuit, he thought. He moved his index finger to her mouth and she pulled it in, sliding her tongue along it just as she'd done with the wishbone at the table. He pressed his groin into the chair between her legs and felt a pulse of stimulation which frightened him and told him to stop everything—to think about horseshit and Betty Friedon and dead people so he wouldn't ruin it all and come in his pants.

"You gettin' too excited for your diapers, hun?" she purred.

"Ohhhhh." He sat back on the floor and recovered.

"Well, Vinnie's gonna get more comfortable, so you have a little more to work with, if you catch my drift." She stood up and peeled off the dress, panties, pink garter belt, the stockings with dark seams, and then planted her hands firmly on her cushy buttocks and offered it to him. Her pussy. Three inches from his face.

My God. Nothing had prepared him for this. Suddenly he was part of the porno pictures he'd looked at so reverently every night for years; if there had been anything religious about life in Houston, it had been the way he'd revered his pornography. The same zeal infected him now, the same holy passion. He looked at what was before him in the dim light from the alley which came through the rain-spattered window and thought, here goes. . .

He surprised himself. He immersed himself in the sensuality of the situation. He knew from the onset he was going to be a willing participant, but from a watchful point of view, from the grandstand. It didn't work out that way, however. He succumbed, dove into the sea of new pleasures, the whirlwind experience, the truly marvelous torture of it, and ended up rising to the surface, panting for breath, and going back down for some more delicious drowning.

He buried his face there for the first time in his life. His head spun and he felt a tingling everywhere. Grass had never done this to him. Booze had never come close. Not even the verge of coming while beating off, a state he had perfected over the years of experimentation. This was new and marvelous. He didn't like the odor because it was unknown. But it made him even more excited simply for that very reason—it was different, sensational, new. And it made him . . . it made him feel feminine. It was the only way his brain could voice it. Yes, feminine. As though part of his make-up, his being, his soul was represented here in this woman, and making love to her would be the fullest expression of his power as a human being, for he was both the man and the woman. It was an odd sensation and it jumbled his mind. Masculine and feminine had meant something totally different in the past. Now, suddenly, in the first act of sex with a woman, he felt everything about her that was attractive —her softness, the curves of her body, the ease with which she seemed to breathe, move—was also part of him. In the past, with Bobby, he'd always felt like some kind of emperor, looking down at the slave at his feet, better than him, always in control, directing every move. This was the opposite. He wanted to worship her. He had lost all control. She was showing him how, guiding him along. A simple, plain, uneducated woman from St. Louis was at once a goddess. She pushed his face to her with her hands. "Yes, yes, baby," she muttered, "harder, harder." And he did, until his tongue was raw.

Lavinia ran her hands through his hair, yanking on it at times, pulling it and his head away from her, just long enough to look down at his delighted boyish face, and then shoving it back to the spot so hard he thought she wanted to see him crawl right up there and into her. She cried out finally and fell back in the chair, spreading her legs over the arms. She told him to sit on the daybed for a minute while she played with herself with her fingers, just staring into his eyes. She drove him crazy.

Then she got up and moved to the daybed and spread her legs wide again. Tom knelt between them and un-zipped his pants and pulled them down to his knees. He brushed his hand over his cock and felt the head wet already. She was moaning for him, no longer the voice of authority. Suddenly he felt masculine, strong, in charge, winning. The emperor again. He positioned himself and guided with his hand. Her cunt was heating the tip of his cock and he gasped. He knew he was going to come fast. All the visions of horseshit and Betty Friedan and concentration on dead people couldn't stop what was going to happen now. He plunged into her, madly, slamming down with such force he thought the cot would fold up beneath them. She clawed his back and he stiffened and that was it.

He came for what seemed like an eternity, ten, eleven,

twelve separate shots of semen—he counted them—and shudders of anger and pain and delight and wonder. She let out a scream and yanked some hair out of his head and slapped the hell out of his buttocks until her orgasm had subsided, and then she started to cry real tears and he pulled away and sat there, trembling. What had he done wrong?

She said nothing to him for a long time. He listened to the rain. He realized he'd felt feminine again, once he'd entered her, and wondered what it was all about, bouncing back and forth like that. The she touched him. "You done real swell, Wonder Boy."

"Honest?" He couldn't conceal his pride.

"That woulda won a prize at the County Fair, blue ribbon special." She dabbed her eyes. "No man's made ol' Vinnie cry in a coon's age."

"Gee. Thanks."

She reached out and held his hand for a moment. The goddamn teenager had done what no husband or any other man had been able to do in years, bring her off; the tears were very real, the satisfaction intense. "I'm still a woman," she moaned, smiling and crying at the same time. "You know what that done for me, Blue Eyes?"

He just sat there. He didn't quite understand. All he knew was he'd done well and it had been very nice. And it had done a lot for him too. Made him feel different from any sensation he'd ever experienced—the feeling of being "feminine." And he didn't even know what it was all about, what it meant. He knew only that it had been wonderful and it had made him feel somehow complete.

"You're gonna make a lot a ladies happy, Tom," she said to him.

He looked at the window, at the splash of rain. He thought about the other guys like him out there in the night, on the road, huddled under trees, soaking, shivering, too cold to even raise a thumb into the glare of headlights of the passing van. He smiled. He was the lucky one, at least for a night. Life wasn't going to be so bad after all.

Lavinia finally stood up, pulled herself together, and left the room for a minute. When she returned, she was wrapped in a tattered pink chenille robe, running a plastic brush through her carrot hair. She took Tom's hand and pulled him up from the daybed, bare naked, and led him into the kitchen, where they got themselves some cold chicken and milk.

"And that, dear lady, was my first lay, as they say." Tom laughed. "They say you never forget the first one. It's the truth."

"Yeah," Chloe muttered, fishing in her bag for some kind of pill. "What did you do then? When you left there?"

"Hitched to Chicago. Bitch of a winter—but you know that. You were there."

"But we didn't know each other yet."

He smiled. "Yup. I was letting guys go down on me in the bathroom of the State Lake Theatre for ten bucks a shot and you were playing Ophelia at the Goodman. I guess you could say we were both in the theatre at the time."

She didn't smile. She had her eyes closed. "Oh, Tomcat," she said languorously, "how wonderful it all was then."

"It was rotten for me that winter," he muttered.

"No. When we met." She lit up suddenly, turning to him, her hand on his shoulder. "Remember the day we met?"

He smiled. Yes he did. Of course he did. How could he ever forget. . .

NINE

He stepped on her under the piano.

He'd moved in with two guys in Chicago. They had a large apartment with an extra small bedroom and bath, and needed another roommate to share the rent. Tom met Dan at the zoo in Lincoln Park one afternoon and tricked with him. Dan introduced him to his lover, Larry, that night, and a week later Tom moved in. The apartment was on Burton Place, a lovely tree-lined street in Old Town, and boasted of a fireplace in the living room, big back porch for hot summer nights, and a Wurlitzer spinet, which Dan never played.

So Tom got his own room and a piano to boot. He spent more hours in the little music room than his own bedroom. One wall was glass to the floor and looked down at the street. It reminded him of the Paris he knew from photographs. He'd sit at the piano at night, playing in the dark, as lovers walked hand in hand under the trees. He'd play Chopin and melodies from *Irma La Douce*. He found solitude, and began to write songs which fit his mood or expressed what he was feeling about life.

He had started playing the piano in Houston. After an energetic and promising start as an amateur plunking away at the keys of the beat-up upright in the school meeting room, a spinster down the hall in their apartment building started giving him lessons. Annie objected at first—what did he need lessons for, he picked out the melodies of popular songs easy enough. But the old lady —Mrs. Jensen, who'd taught piano all her life—convinced Annie it was necessary, and where was the harm? She wasn't charging.

"You could really do it some day, you know that, Tommy, don't you?" Mrs. Jensen asked him one evening.

"Do what?"

"Really play. Concert halls. On the stage. Records."

The little boy's eyes sparkled. "You mean I could make a record album?"

"Yes. You really are that good. Now, you know I'm going to be moving to Atlanta in a few months. When I go I don't want you to stop. I'm going to talk your mama into getting you a real fine teacher, someone who will be able to understand the talent you have and guide you toward a glorious future."

"Wow. I'd love it. But I want *you* to teach me. You play so great."

Mrs. Jensen sat down on the bench with him. "You know I don't want to go and I'm going to miss you terribly, however, my brother's family has offered, and I'm getting on in years. But I want a promise from you that you'll keep practicing and really become someone someday."

He promised.

But he didn't keep it. Annie had been talked into the lessons and Tom was a welcome pupil at a reputable teaching conservatory, but after three visits Annie cut them off. They were costing too much in the first place, and the expense for practice rooms was more than she could handle. And Tom had been depressed from the start; he was the only kid there who didn't have a piano at home. Annie said she wasn't going to get into hock to a finance company for the rest of her life. No piano. Tom said, all right, then the hell with the lessons. Mutual decision.

But he still played, mostly at school whenever he could sneak into the music department and pound away. He studied fundamental technique and the basics of theory in regular classes, but the desire for private lessons remained strong. He would occasionally bug Annie about them when she was in a good mood, but the reply was invariably: "You play fine enough as it is." So he had to make do. He found a church to sneak into. It had been several denominations over the years, with the Baptists in the lead (it had been a Baptist church four times). For a few months it was called Church of the Blinding Light, and Tom always expected to find seeing eye dogs parked out front. He played the organ in there, an electric Hammond of ancient vintage, hating the fifths in every tone, but it was a keyboard and that's what counted. And Bobby the BJ boy introduced him to his neighbors, who had a piano, and Tom sometimes played there.

Every time he got the chance, in the trek from Houston to Chicago, he would put his fingers on a keyboard. He played in several taverns, dance halls, even a funeral parlor in St. Louis. He had natural talent, in Mrs. Jensen's words. He could make the keys sing. She always told him, "You may be playing a very unimaginative song like *Mary Had A Little Lamb*, but if you play it faithfully ten times a day, you're developing technique." He loved music stores in shopping centers, where he'd test the merchandise and draw a crowd; often the managers asked him to stay all day. His dream was to own a baby grand of his own.

So the piano in Dan and Larry's apartment got a workout because Tom never let it rest.

He came home one night from work at Lyon-Healy, Chicago's largest music store, where he sold sheet music and played the grands on his lunch break, and ate a sandwich in the music room, sitting in the dark watching the street. It was early fall and the trees had just started turning. The air was crisp. You could smell chestnuts and drying oak leaves and candied apples in the air. He loved nights like this. They were romantic. He decided to write a song about the street.

He turned around, in one fast move, his ass sliding on the polished bench, his fingers ready to hit the keys, his feet moving to the pedals. But instead of the hard metal of the sforzando pedal, he felt something mushy. In place of the sound of hammers hitting strings, he heard a voice mumble, "Goddam . . . what the fuck?"

Lights. He reached up and flicked the switch. And there she was, curled in a blanket under the overhang of the piano keyboard, a girl he'd never seen before. She looked up at him with angry eyes, which wasn't surprising given that he'd stepped on her face. He began to apologize and she started to laugh.

She explained she knew Dan, needed a place to crash for the night, and wanted to be near music. "They got the stereo locked up in the bedroom with themselves, so I figured ah, a piano, never slept under a piano before. You're Tom Brassen, huh? They told me about you. I'm Chloe."

"Hi. I'm really sorry."

"It's all right, I wasn't going to use that eye tonight anyway." She got up and dragged her blanket over to the window and curled up again. "Play me to sleep. Dan says you play wonderfully."

"Any requests?" She did something to him. She moved him somehow. He didn't quite know what it was, what was happening, because it had never happened before. A new feeling. *"Fascination? Misty? Stardust?"*

"What's this, a bar? How about *People*."

"People it is, Miss Brice." He played the song, slowly, softly, with feeling and love, and when he turned around

after the last chord, she was sound asleep.

He stood up, stared down at her for a moment, and then walked quietly to his room. He stripped off his clothes and crawled under the covers and lay there with his arms folded on his chest, watching the light of the moon reflect from the mirror onto the ceiling. He liked her. He really *liked* her. He hoped she would be around in the morning.

And then, just as his eyes started to close, the apartment was filled with something that resembled singing. *"Tom Brassen, Tom Brassen, Tom Brassen,"* she howled, doing her best Streisand, *"what a beautiful beautiful name."*

He laughed out loud. *Chloe.* He'd never known a Chloe before. *It* was a beautiful name. And he had the feeling it was going to mean more to him than that. The start of a beautiful friendship? A love story? A song? He wasn't sure. It was something, though. How could it not be, with someone who slept under pianos?

"I know all about you," she said to him at the sheet music counter.

"How?" he asked.

"Dan told me."

"Dan doesn't really know a lot about me."

"Larry told me more."

"Larry knows even less."

"You're from Texas."

"How'd you ever guess?"

She nodded. "You're trying to get rid of it, the accent, and I can help."

He blushed a bit. Yes, he did want to get rid of the slight drawl. He'd done a lot already, softening it, concentrating on his speech. "How can you help?"

"I'm an actress. I used to be La Duse in another life. I'm a poet and a director. I play a fast game of cards and can wash a car in fifteen minutes, no hot wax. I'm also a witch. A white witch. Good energy. Black witches, man, they're fucking up the world."

"I couldn't agree more. And my supervisor is watching so I'd better pretend to show you some music."

"Oh, yeah . . . *ohhh, I love that song, but it looks tooooo hard for my little fingers! Oh, Simon and Garfunkel, they're my favorites*!" Yes, she was an actress.

"You don't have to overdo it," he whispered. "You really want to help me with the accent?"

"Why do you wanna get rid of it? You Texans are supposed to be proud of all that, the Lone Star shit and Texas Rangers and LBJ and everything."

He looked at her with a serious expression. "I'm hoping the whole place will secede from the Union one day. I'd give it away, but nobody would take it."

She shrugged. "Never thought much about it myself. Do you like steak? Got any Valium? Speed? Can anyone as straight-looking as you really be homosexual? Can you play *White Rabbit* on the piano? You don't have to answer now, I'll see you at home. I moved in. We can listen to the Rotary Connection and burn coconut incense and I'll read your palm. Bye."

She turned and left. His supervisor came up and smiled at him without lifting the bifocals up from the chain that held them under her left boob. "Mr. Brassen, we can't be spending our time chatting with friends when there are customers in the store who deserve our attention, now can we?"

"The store is empty."

"Oh."

"Anyway, I never saw her before. She's nuts."

"That was apparent."

He took a deep breath as the woman walked away. *She's nuts.* It was a statement he would make again regarding her, some years later. Only that time he would truly believe it.

* * *

They made love that night. He hadn't planned it. Maybe she had, he didn't know. He came home and she'd taken over the kitchen, an attempt to cook for him well-intentioned but poorly executed. There was smog in the air, something that looked like black chimney soot. "Goddammit!" she screamed, flinging a Revere Ware sauté pan against the wall.

"Chloe, stop." He grabbed her hands. "What are you doing?"

"I tried to make you a fucking dinner and the steak burned when I was making the salad because I turned it to broil after I already broiled the damned thing and I was supposed to put it on 200° to keep warm, but I turned the fucking dial the wrong way. Shit."

"Don't worry about it." He looked around at the incredible mess. "Where are the masters of the house?" He knew Dan and Larry would kill her if they saw it.

"Went to a movie. Damn. I wanted to make you dinner."

"We can have the salad. And maybe we can rescue the steaks. . ."

Paul Bunyon's axe would not cut through the meat. They fed the charred T-bones to Larry's big Afghan, who normally ate anything, but even she turned up her nose at them. So they tossed them over the balcony on the porch, into the alley, hoping some starving bastard of an animal or wino would find them. "Maybe someone can use them as bricks," Chloe suggested.

They poured wine and ate toasted garlic bread and salad, facing each other at the kitchen table. She told Tom about herself. She came from Chicago, over on the West Side, a Polish neighborhood where her parents still lived. Her mother had been the original Bohemian beatnik rebel, now living a disguised life as a middle-class housewife. "Some day she'll break out and become Pope or something. She teases hair in a funeral parlor. My dad works in a factory, and my sister Sandy is still in high school."

She told him she'd had a normal childhood, except for the times her mother beat her. Her parents never got along well (daddy was big on clobbering Mama Chloe with lamps), and the woman always seemed to take it out on little Chloe. When Sandy came along, it seemed only right that she'd get some shoes thrown at her too, but it didn't work out that way. She was praised and pampered because she was turning out to be a normal child. Not artistic and outrageous, high-strung and intense like Chloe. Being different had its price and she paid it; she was the brunt of all her parents' frustration.

She called herself a mad genius, and he came to believe her. He saw her at a play at the Goodman Theatre; she was utterly brilliant. Offbeat and unique. She could write breathtaking poetry. She sang with force and determination, if not proper pitch. Years later she would insist she was the reincarnation of Janis Joplin and move into the building where Janis died on Franklin Avenue in Hollywood and consume a fifth of Southern Comfort a day right about the time Tom met Mitch. But early on there were few signs of such chronic madness. That night with greasy garlic on their fingers, she seemed fresh and alive, different from any person he'd ever met, and wonderfully attractive.

She wasn't beautiful. She wasn't homely. She was Chloe. There was no other way to describe her. Her hair was naturally brown, but it varied over the years from Lucille Ball red to mousy yellow to pitch black and back again to brown, when it all started falling out. She had a big frame, but she hadn't yet gained all that weight; back then you could have even called her slim. Her breasts were large and sagged if she didn't wear a bra. Her legs were of good Polish stock—thick—and a little heavy around the thighs, but her arms were long and thin, and she used her hands expressively. Her face was strong-featured, lips red and luscious, eyes filled with ambition and a desire to do so much in a very short time.

From what Tom could discern from that first conversation on the floor, she hated her sister, loved her father dearly, and felt her mother was an amusement. There was a mountain of guilt to tunnel through regarding Mama Chloe, and he didn't want to start digging; but she seemed to be learning to live her own life and shed the pall of "what my parents wanted me to be."

Tom opened himself to her slowly. Bits and pieces about Houston, Annie, living on the road, staying "with some friends" in Milwaukee, finally drifting to Chicago. She asked about his relationship with Dan and Larry and he told her they were friends. She said Dan told her he'd been one of the best lays Dan had ever had. "That was only once," he cautioned. "I couldn't live here if that was going on."

"He also said you make a lousy faggot—that from Dan, who'd love to see the whole world gay. You hate queens and calling guys by girls' names and bars and cruising johns. And that women respond to you all the time but you don't turn onto them much."

"Jesus, you know what size underwear I wear too?"

She smiled. "I know you don't wear *any*."

He had to laugh. "Listen, I like girls, and I like guys, but I'm picky or something. If there's a person I want to go to bed with, I'll do it. I don't want to be pegged as gay or anything, I don't want to be called a faggot just because every once in a while I sleep with a guy. Dan's right. I don't like that stuff." He put his legs out and shook his head. "I really don't know anything about that world anyhow," he lied.

"I do. Straight men bore me."

"Really?"

"Yeah. Listen, do you want to go to bed with me?"

"Yes, I do."

She called it a mystical experience; he said it was a good lay. But what they agreed on what that they were meant for each other. They were young and in love and nothing else mattered. "Tomcat, don't you feel we're in a big playpen and we can have any rattle we want?" she asked him one night. He agreed, never really thinking about the implications of that line. But later, when he gave it some thought, he realized just how correct she was, and what children they'd been.

Life was a big game, and the playpen was Chicago. They were determined their lack of finances would not inhibit. They sneaked into the exit doors of movie theatres, second acted plays which were in town (Tom saw Act Two of *Hello, Dolly!* twelve times with three different Dollys), skipped out on checks in restaurants, shoplifted everything they could get their hands on. Chloe got bored with their record collection one night and the next afternoon went to Rose Records on Wabash Avenue with a large shopping bag which held a used Rose Records bag, an old Rose Records receipt, and a staple gun to use in closing up the bag with the receipt just the way Rose did at the counter. Nine albums later, she walked out the door with the security guard holding it open for her, smiling smugly. Tom shuddered as he sauntered by the man, but she'd pulled it off, and they had new music for a week. Out on the street, he jumped for joy, and kissed her.

Chloe attended the Goodman off and on, taking acting classes and working part-time as a secretary, an operator for an answering service and then for Ma Bell herself, as a babysitter. She always got fired. She wasn't cut out to work a regular job. She was meant to be an artist.

So she wrote and she danced and she did plays. Mama Chloe would come to visit with Vladimir and ask her daughter when she was going to grow up and get a job and get married, blah blah, and what a disappointment you are to me and here's twenty dollars but don't tell your father. Vladimir would then slip her another twenty and tell her not to tell her mother. It was a fairly steady income, considering.

Tom liked them both. After he tasted Mama Chloe's pierogi and kilbasa, he wanted to spend every Sunday at the Kosenkowski house. He stayed slim, no matter how much he ate, but Chloe put on pounds easily. She exercised every night as Tom played the piano, doing her bends and push-ups and sit-ups in her tights, putting on Janis when he finished, singing along till the people downstairs rapped the broom on their ceiling.

They moved away from Dan and Larry, into their own apartment just around the corner on LaSalle Street, and again the downstairs neighbors pounded on the ceiling with their broom. But they didn't care. Tom just changed the tune to match the beat of the thumping, and Chloe howled like Joplin through the wood and plaster. With each day, they became closer, in the laughter and fun, in the quiet moments, the reflective times as well. It was something new for Tom. He'd been solitary all his life and suddenly now he was released, he was discovering the world with someone he cared about. Sometimes he thought he and Chloe were one marvelous talented crazy person with four legs and four arms and two heads which were much better—or at least more fun—than one.

They shared a little of each other's souls. He let her in on his fantasies; she told him he was "a force in my cosmic aura," which meant he was part of every breath she breathed. When he had a cold, she sneezed with him. When she lost a job, he felt just as depressed as she did.

And they read together. They had Scott Fitzgerald in

common (she fashioned herself another Zelda) and she introduced him to Edith Sitwell and Sylvia Plath and books about horoscopes and mysticism, but *Linda Goodman's Sun Signs* was about as far as he cared to venture in that realm. He turned her onto adventures and Jane Austen and fairy tales, and gave her a copy of *The Little Prince*. Together they devoured the *Rings* trilogy and passed each other the books as they finished. Tom loved reading about politics as well, mostly the Kennedys, anything about the Kennedys, and now and then he'd interrupt her occult story with an anecdote about Bobby or Teddy.

Tom bought his Rambler, and during the winter, they went to the country every chance they got, to play in pure white snow, not the gray slush of the city, the blinding new snow Tom loved so much. Getting the Rambler stuck was half the fun. He'd gun the motor until they slid and sunk down to the pavement or the dirt, and then he'd give her the wheel and he'd lift and push and rock and when the car started to move, Chloe usually steered it right into another snowbank. She never did learn how to drive very well.

When spring came, they took Sandy with them for a vacation to the Wisconsin Dells. The motel owner didn't want to believe they were brother and sisters, but accepted their money anyway. They rode the boat ride through the dells and in the midst of it Chloe felt an attack of paranoia coming on and began to throw a fit. In the process of popping a few pills into her mouth, she knocked a woman's purse into the water, which caused the husband to dive overboard in daring rescue of the car keys and credit cards, ruining his Bermuda shorts and white Corfam shoes in the process. "What a goddamn excuse for a tourist attraction," Chloe muttered as they left the boat. They got out of town that night, afraid they were going to be run out with torches.

That first winter, in the early time of their relationship, was glorious for them. Tom had a girl, a cat, an apartment, a job and a piano. He wrote songs while Chloe memorized lines while Ophelia dashed from corner to corner chasing a tin foil ball. They watched all the bad movies on TV and listened to music at full volume on the record player he'd gotten from the Columbia Record Club. They discovered Frango mints from Marshall Field and jams from Honey Bear Farm. They ate popcorn every night from a big bowl in the middle of the bed; they got comfy at either side, and Tom devoured Faulkner while Chloe explored the new underground experimental plays. Three times a week, on his way home from work, Tom went into Krock's and Brentanos, and picked out a title for himself and one for Chloe, and then walked out of the store with them in his arm. He never bothered stopping at the register.

He had epitomized his secret formula for successful shoplifting—tell yourself it's yours, and it's *yours*. All in the mind, all a matter of believing. Chloe compared it to a theory of acting in Charles McGaw's book, *Acting Is Believing*. And she learned so well, in fact, that three weeks later she toddled out of Carson, Pirie, Scott and Company not in the tattered cloth coat she'd worn on the way in, but wrapped in a beautiful brown wool number trimmed with fox. With the price tags hanging from the left sleeve.

But he was the king. "Tomcat," Chloe told him, "you could put a Maytag washer on your back and walk out with it." Not quite, but he came close. Her favorite was the time he got the headphones from the stereo store. He'd walked out with a pair of Koss Pro 4-A's on his ears, with the spring cord dangling along at his side, bouncing as he walked up the street. She nearly choked with laughter. Again, no one batted an eye.

One night, the night of her birthday, they read together in bed, after eating half the cake Tom had baked for her. From opposite sides of the bed, they touched toes, and he put his book down and looked at her. He was overwhelmed. This was his family, his home, warmth and encouragement and a future. It was so . . . so normal. Softly, he said, "I love you. I think when I'm on my deathbed, you should call the priest and get us married. I want a Mary Hemingway around after I'm gone to take care of all the songs left unsold." He was joking, and yet he was serious; he surprised even himself.

She was silent for a long time, looking at him with adoring eyes. Then she giggled. "Hah! Our kids would be brilliant, but the boys would probably all be nuts like me and the girls would be tall and have hair on their chests like you."

"So we'll have cats."

She smiled and went back to her book.

He put his head down and continued with his.

But neither of them could concentrate. She was the one to finally voice it: "Tomcat, would you?"

"What?" He didn't look up, but he knew, oh how well he knew, and he tried to make light of it, tried to be flip. "Get you more cake? I'd love to. . ."

"Would you marry me?"

He said nothing but his eyes met hers.

"I love you so much, Tomcat. It was meant we would always share each other's lives, grow old with Ophelia's kids at our feet."

"Well, they say it's terrific for income tax reasons."

She smiled. "Then we will?"

"Only if we can do it quietly and secretly. And not right now, somewhere in the future." His head was spinning and he wasn't sure of what he was saying. Or was he? Wasn't he filled with emotion that had been building strongly in the last few minutes, that feeling of family and solidarity—a feeling opposite everything his life had been up to that point? "We'll do it and one day just announce to the world that we're man and wife."

She jumped up and kissed him and they laughed

about it and went into the kitchen for more cake and wine.

Later, in bed, Tom felt the alcohol doing funny things to his bloodstream and brain. "It would be wonderful, you know," he mused dreamily. "Married and maybe a son—if I didn't have to change diapers—and a house with a picket fence. . ."

"And a garage we could turn into a theatre."

He hugged her and they giggled. The dream was delightful, and they were suddenly very young and anxious and hopeful. "Tom," Chloe said in a near-whisper, "ask me."

"What?"

"Ask me to do it, please? I just want to hear the words. I know it's corny, but please?"

"Will you . . . will you marry me?"

"Oh, yes," she sighed, and snuggled up to him and closed her eyes. He stroked her hair and she fell into a happy sleep.

They did not talk about it again for a long time, until it was forced out into the open in a loud and glaring way at the Kosenkowski dinner table. Vladimir said, while carving the chuck roast, "So we understand you've proposed to Chloe."

Tom gulped and swallowed his salad, about to protest, but Chloe kicked him in the leg under the table and he just smiled and nodded, telling her with his eyes that he'd kill her later. He explained yes, he loved their daughter, wanted very much to be her husband, but was wise enough to plan for the future, and right now he couldn't provide for a wife and family very well. Mama Chloe snorted and said he was the best boy she'd ever met, they should rent the hall already. But her husband understood. "Leave the boy alone, it's a sign of maturity that he doesn't wanna run into something he can't handle. There's time. Plenty of time. Tom, you've got common sense, good to see that in kids this day and age.

You're gonna make the best son-in-law a family could ask for. Pass the beans."

The talk of a wedding ceased for a while, and it was during this time that Chloe started taking large amounts of speed. They'd discovered spring and summer together like the kids in the playpen still, watching their kitten grow into a lovely lady of a cat, reading and stealing and living life together as usual, but as the leaves turned, so did Tom; he began to question what love was all about.

Their sex life was practically non-existent by October. It just didn't seem to happen; Tom's interest had waned, and the pills Chloe took seemed to satisfy hers. He increasingly felt the urge to move on, to go someplace different. Something about being tied down was getting to him, and thoughts of marriage seemed suffocating. He knew he didn't want to spend the rest of his life in Chicago. He was sick of sheet music. And he was again finding men more attractive and growing increasingly unsure of a future with a woman. And Chloe was acting very very crazy.

She was suddenly filled with tremendous energy. All day, every day, going like mad, nonstop. Memorizing lines and cleaning windows and floors and taking showers and attempting to bake pies and read plays and write poems and talk to her mother on the phone for hours all in ten minutes. She was flying, never resting a moment, never settling down. Tom didn't know what was causing it at first; it couldn't have been those same little yellow pills she'd been taking when he found her under the piano, could it?

It could, but by the handful.

One day she came home at two in the morning, after a long rehearsal, turned on all the lights and pulled him out of bed. "Tomcat, we need two new songs for the show and you're going to write them!"

"What!"

"I got Robert to agree to let you do the songs we

need, where we've got holes in the script. Told 'em the thing shoulda been a goddamn musical from the start."

"You're kidding?"

"Goddammit! Would I kid about the theatre? Listen, they have to fit in here. . ." She showed him the script, described the mood, explained what they had to accomplish and do for the play. One was a ballad, the other rock. She needed them a week from tomorrow.

Six days later, there still were no songs. "I don't know what it is," he moaned, sitting at the piano with an empty Dr. Pepper bottle resting next to his hands. "I can't find it. It isn't coming. I've never written a song *for* anyone before. I just can't—"

"Shit, man!" She ranted around the room, throwing things, breaking glass, and he didn't even bother stopping her. He deserved it. Here she had counted on him and he'd promised and this could be the start of dreams come true. And what did he have to show for it? Lots of balls of staff paper on the floor.

They argued for an hour. She called him lazy and lousy, afraid to take a chance and disappointing, and then left the apartment and didn't return till very late. "Where were you? Tom asked. "I was worried."

"Out."

"Chloe, come on."

"I was at Dan and Larry's."

"I got something on paper."

Her eyes lit up.

"It needs work. . ." He played her a few bars and sang some of the lyrics. She was enchanted. "But I can't have it ready tomorrow," he cautioned. "I'm just too tired."

And then she got a screwy look in her eyes. She had a plan. She was going to get the songs on time if she had to wring them out of him. She reached in her bag and dug for a prescription bottle. "Just a little helper for you to write all kinds of good things."

"Oh no, I'm not taking any damn pills."

She held the bottle in front of him, rattling the pills around, teasing. "One of these and you won't be able to *stop* writing. . ."

He protested for a long time, but finally agreed on an experiment. He would work on the song until he was beat. Then he would go to sleep—but after taking one of the pills. She would wake him an hour later. "That's how they work best, you feel like you've slept for twenty years. And the energy you have, Tomcat, the energy is vital and organic and wonderful!"

He found out. It was beyond energy; it was as though someone had wound him up and his spring had to untwist before he could stop moving. There wasn't anything organic about it, and nothing very wonderful either. He went to bed at three, after taking two little white pills, and she woke him at four, her Judy Garland eyes seeking approval. He gave her more than that. He danced, sang, slammed his fingers down on the keys until the upstairs neighbors did a little early morning time-step on the floor themselves, but he found their thumping to be music to his ears.

Every noise reverberated in his head and came out on paper as song. He not only finished the numbers for the show, but four more as well, frantically jotting down lyrics, working to get them on paper before they left his head, for his mind was racing and his brain couldn't keep up. His fingers ran over the keys faster than he could follow them with his eyes, and his heart seemed to pump so madly he felt hot, his blood boiling and rushing and bubbling. He thought he was having a heart attack. He thought he was a tennis ball being rocketed through the air. He had the sensation that the piano at which he was seated was an extension of himself, that his cock had the amazing capability of playing a concerto. He thought he was losing his mind.

He ran around the apartment in cut-off jeans, slapping his hands at the walls. He ran around the block like that two times, slapping at male and female buttocks alike with wild abandon. He did the laundry and took three showers—"To see what it's like to be Joan Crawford!"—and three more pills. He thought he was an airplane.

When Chloe went to rehearsal with the songs tucked under her arm, he went to the State Lake Theatre and saw a James Bond film, but spent most of his time changing seats. He went up to the balcony and let four guys go down on him, but he couldn't come. He rode a bus home and then walked all the way back downtown and rode another home again. He found Chloe there the second time and they dropped another pill together. She told him the songs were hits, perfect, everyone loved them. He lifted her dress and ripped her underpants away with his teeth and didn't let up until she squealed with laughter on the floor and they collapsed into a convulsing heap. He suddenly got an erection and pushed into her on all fours, shoving her across the room until her head cracked into the side of the piano. He couldn't come, so they went out for a walk, but they skipped and jumped, ran and danced, everything but walk.

When they got home they were still rushing. Chloe said she had to come down, so she got out the sleeping pills. They went up to the roof—Adolph and Eva atop the bunker—and took them together, the suicide pact. They babbled on and on about the stars in the sky and the lights of the cars on LaSalle Street and a lot of nonsense. Then their hearts stopped beating so fast. Tom felt dizzy. They went downstairs and were comatose for the next twenty-seven hours.

Ophelia woke him, biting his nose as hard as she could to get him to feed her. Tom stood up, opened a Nine Lives for the starving animal, and set it down near her water. Then he pulled the curtains and it was dark outside—funny, what happened to the day? He looked at the clock and was confused. Then he opened the door and grabbed the paper in the hall and looked at the date. He couldn't believe it. Two days gone! He sat down again, moved a little towards Chloe, who was stretching and smiling now, and then everything went black; he flopped face-first to the floor.

It was the first and last time he did speed.

"Do you love me?" she asked him in a lucid moment. It was getting cold again. Winter was coming. They both feared it. She had her pills and liquor to keep her warm, but what had he? He hated Chicago. It was boring him. He dreamed the dreams he'd had in Texas, visions of Paris and Hollywood, new people, excitement. He felt guilty about thinking of leaving her, but he knew it was the end, simply because all she talked of now was marriage, and there was desperation in her voice.

In one breath she would tell him she wanted a big wedding so they could get all that loot relatives give you, and then she would seriously discuss their going to New York so she could get into guerilla theatre on the Lower East Side. One day she'd play the role of the young Midwestern bride-to-be, registering at Fields for silver and Spode china, and then she'd lock herself in the apartment, skipping breakfast, lunch and dinner for a couple of diet pills and a slug of whiskey.

Tom wanted to think he was enough to keep her together, that just his presence was all she needed, but he was being presumptuous. She wanted a wedding, bridesmaids and rice, the smile of her parents, dancing into the night, and now she feared, because she could read his mind so well, that she would never see that day. She was fighting deep-seated problems of an emotional childhood and past which had nothing to do with him, but affected him strongly. Her psyche was made up of the mad artist fighting the straight girl from the suburbs: one wanted to destroy the other. He had promised her so much, and now he didn't know what to do to help her.

"Do you love me?" she asked again.

He had to answer her sometime. He couldn't just sit there and be mute, pretending he didn't hear. "Yes," he said. And he did, it was true. But he wasn't *in* love with her, as he'd thought he'd been; he doubted that he even knew what that was. If anything, he thought, it was a sensation of the soul, and that had not come to pass.

He knew now he had to do something else. He needed to be somewhere else, someplace new, unchartered, undiscovered. He didn't want to shovel snow again this winter. Selling sheet music made his skin crawl. Ever since that night in the balcony, he wanted men again. But he'd made her a promise, he'd made a commitment. . .

"Tomcat," she moaned, curling up at his side. "I love you so much."

"Chloe, we'll always be part of one another. Don't be afraid." What was he saying? He was probably more frightened than she was.

"I am, Tomcat. I feel it. It isn't good. I'm scared."

"No," he soothed, "everything will be all right."

But everything was not all right.

It culminated the following Sunday at dinner on the West Side. When Mama Chloe announced, over the stuffed cabbage, "Chloe told us you finally set the date," the shit hit the fan.

Sandy said, "I'll be maid of honor, won't I?"

Vladimir Kosenkowski said, "Tom, *son,* I'm glad you made the decision. You've got a good head on your shoulders. You've got a good job. And we'll help you out as much as we can."

Chloe avoided Tom's piercing eyes. "But I. . ." he tried, but they just kept talking.

"The church hall is available in January, last two Saturdays, and the wedding could be ten o'clock, either week." Mama Chloe passed the bread to Tom but he no longer had an appetite. "Then there's the VFW, but the drapes in there smell like the smoke of the Civil War and I think the church hall is better because Marsha Safranski's wedding was there and that was a real nice wedding. Pass the salt, Chloe."

"How about a shower?" Sandy asked.

"I'll give Tom a stag party," Vladimir added, winking in Tom's direction. "No babbling females allowed, hey?"

"Chloe, where you gonna get your dress?" her mother asked. "Downtown or one of the little shops here? There's a nice one in the window at Dorothy's. And you let me do your hair. I'm not gonna have you coming up the aisle looking like a drowned chicken like you do today. . ."

And so it went. Through dinner. After dinner. Right up until they got into the Rambler. Just before Tom shut the door, Mama Chloe inquired where they planned to honeymoon. "Oh, California, I imagine," Tom said. "Especially since it will be winter." Then he slammed the door and drove off.

On the Stevenson Expressway she said, "I'm sorry. It just had to be. I mean, they're *living* for it, for us. We have to, Tomcat."

He said not a word. California was indeed in his mind, but not as a honeymoon retreat. Stories from movie magazines danced in his head and thoughts of streets paved with gold compelled him. Stars. Palm trees. Sunshine.

The next day when Chloe woke up, Tom was not there. She looked for him, thinking he might have gone out early for a walk before breakfast. But he did not show up. She called Lyon-Healy at ten and was told he hadn't arrived. Then she went to the closet and realized most of his clothes were gone. Why hadn't she heard him? She'd only taken two little Seconals.

She ran out back and the car was not in its parking place. She searched the apartment for a note, but found nothing. She called her mother and screamed and hung up when the woman told her she was making no sense. She even kicked Ophelia when the cat tried to rub up against her leg.

And then she found it. Sticking out of her yellow legal pad, the envelope with her name on it, and she read it and realized where he'd gone, that he'd taken the honeymoon alone, that there was no place in his life for her anymore. She grabbed his photograph and clutched it, and then screamed, threw it on the floor, stomped it, and finally tore it up.

. . .*and what's in California? he wrote. Something. Something I can't explain, a feeling of destiny, something that isn't here.*

So many times he would remember writing that to her. And he knew he'd been right. There was something waiting for him in California, and it was part of his destiny: a man named Mitchell.

TEN

The bell rang. Tom opened the door. His first thought, looking at the handsome man standing in the light of the porch, was, *Jesus Christ but he's beautiful.* "Hi," he said, cooly, however, so as not to give himself away too much.

"Hello. I'm late. It wasn't easy finding this place."

"No, you're on time. It's a little obscure, but it keeps the tour buses away."

Mitch laughed. "You wanna help me get the tree out of the back of the car?"

"Oh, yeah, sure." Tom stepped out of the cottage and followed Mitch around to the street, down the narrow little path between the shrubs and ivy. He studied the backside of him. It was as good as the view from the front. He was wearing tan pants and a dark red sweatshirt. Over that was a tan windbreaker, not really protection enough for the chilly nights of Southern California, but the guy looked the type who'd never had a cold in his life. Tom was still amazed how athletic he seemed. Making it with him, he thought, must be the summer and winter olympics combined. He looked at the tight buttocks as the guy bent forward to tug the bottom of the tree from the back of the hatch. Then he remembered he was supposed to be helping, not observing, and he grabbed the other side of the redwood pot.

They got it out and Mitch locked the hatchback. "The damn thing's bigger than the car. Coming over here I thought I was driving a Christmas tree."

"There's still some tinsel on it," Tom remarked.

They bent forward to grasp it again. "Jeremy put the tinsel on. He's a shiny silver freak."

Tom was right, he had a lover. Shit. Shiny silver *queen*. "I hate tinsel."

"What do you like?" They were lugging the tree around the back, to the patio. It wasn't easy; Tom was panting.

"I like lights and bulbs and a golden garland. You'll see mine when you come inside. I still have it up."

Mitch caught his eyes and smirked. "Oh, yeah?"

They set the tree down. "One thing's sure," Tom said, "yours is heavier than mine."

Mitch grinned even more. "Prove it, baby."

"Can't. Not till it's time for mine to come down."

"Your *what* down?"

"I think this conversation is getting us in trouble."

"So ask me in and change the subject."

Tom ushered him in the door.

Mitch looked around and smiled. "Feels like a mountain cabin," he said, staring at his reflection in one of the big copper pots hanging on the stone wall. He knelt down in front of the roaring fire and warmed his hands. "It's terrific, Tom. I like the tree too—yeah, it's better than tinsel." But it was the cottage that marveled him. "I *really* like this place. It must be you, huh?"

"Me?"

"It must *reflect* you. Yes, it does."

"But you don't even know me."

"I will. And this is a start. Earthy and honest. It tells me a lot about you."

What bullshit. "Something to drink?"

"Beer, if you've got it. From the can."

How butch. "Michelob okay?"

Mitch nodded and looked through the hearth to the bedroom. "Can I ask what you pay for this?"

"Nothing. Comes with the job." Tom handed him a beer.

"What do you do?"

"Lots of things. Work for the lady who owns the big house. She's a dress designer. I accompany her collections around." He made it sound convincing enough. "And I kinda act as a gardener around the place."

"Can I take off my shoes?"

You can take off your pants if you like. "Sure." Tom kicked off his own shoes and sat next to him.

"Do you play?"

"Pardon me?"

Mitch pointed to the Yamaha. "Would you play for me?"

"You serious?"

"I love the piano. I'd very much like to hear you."

Tom gazed into the dark brown eyes. How could anyone resist a request from someone who looked this good? The man could have asked him to leap into the sea and he'd have done it. "Sure. Anything special?"

"Anything you want to make special."

Their eyes lingered for what seemed a very long time, and then Tom got up and sat at the piano. For the next ten minutes, Mitch was enraptured with some of the most romantic music he'd ever heard. A strain kept repeating itself. It was simple and catchy. When Tom finished and turned back to him and brought his feet up to sit cross-legged on the bench, Mitch asked who'd written the piece, what was it?

"Me. I wrote it."

"What's it called?"

"I don't know." Tom shrugged. "I just made it up as I went along."

Mitch got up. "You're kidding me. But there was one

part that kept being repeated. . .”

"I know. I make up a melodic theme and just do variations on it.”

"It was marvelous.”

"I know.”

"Humble.”

"Not at all.”

"Sexy too.”

"Yeah?”

Mitch nodded. "Very.” He ran his tongue over his lower lip. "I love looking at you, sport.”

"I'm glad.” He could feel his cock hardening. "You're hot.”

Mitch set his empty beer can on the stack of music books. The shine of the polished ebony reflected the fire, and outlined Tom's head like a kind of orange halo. Mitch ran his fingers through Tom's hair, moving his steady, strong hand down to his neck, his shoulder, and then brought his fingertips up to his lips. Tom kissed the flesh of his hand.

"I want to fuck you,” Mitch said. He took Tom's hair again and pulled it a bit and then pressed Tom's head against him until it rested against his stomach. "I want to make love to you.”

Tom felt the muscles, the heat of his body, the scent of his cologne and his sweat and his crotch, the murmur of his heart. He wrapped his arms around him and grasped his buttocks. He could feel the man's cock growing against his chest.

Mitch bent down and kissed his soft hair. His voice was gentle and kind as he whispered, "You're beautiful, Tom. I've been wanting to kiss you from the moment I saw you. . .”

Tom offered his lips as their faces met and they were drawn into one another. They fell to the floor and rolled over and over as lips opened and tongues tasted. Tom slipped Mitch's sweatshirt over his head and brought his lips to his chest, his teeth to his nipples, and he kissed his arm and licked his armpits and ran his tongue down to his navel and bit the top of the khaki pants, pulling them apart. Mitch reached down and pressed the outline of Tom's penis. He shuddered. He finally got the zipper open and freed tt. Then he pushed Tom away from him and knelt down to look at him from a distance in front of the fire.

"What's wrong?" Tom finally asked. Mitchell was kneeling there for what seemed an enternity, consuming him with his eyes, not allowing him to move.

"Nothing. I just wanted to look at you. You're the dream everyone has once in a great while and never gets to realize."

Tom raised his head. "I thought that of you. But it's more than that. I feel something . . . God, you must think I'm nuts . . . but I've never been this excited."

"Yes. I understand." The voice was full of knowledge and caring. They kissed again and then began a battle, each trying desperately to know every inch of the other's body, to take every morsel of flesh into their mouths and taste it, lick and kiss and bite it, chew it off and have it forever. Tongues dragged over eyelashes, lips swallowed toes, hands fought for cock and balls. They took a crash course in each other, and graduated with honors.

They twisted around and around on the floor, drinking in the scent of each other, kissing, rimming, moaning, sucking. Mitch forced Tom down on his back and took his penis in his mouth and refused to let go, even when Tom cried out that he was going to come. Tom grabbed his shoulders and dug his nails into his flesh. It was unbelievable. He was going to shoot the sperm, the physical essence of his manhood, into the mouth of this person he thought he would die for. Something moved in him on his way to climax, some sensation of the soul which had not been in his experience before, and as he crashed with a might he'd never known, he thought, *I love you. I love you. I* love *you.*

The spasms subsided and he looked into the blazing fire without blinking. He hadn't been wrong; somehow he knew this was what it felt like to be in love. They had been two bulls meeting in the clearing, locking horns; there had been a struggle for domination. He knew it didn't matter who won the match, the passion is in the battle. It isn't who is fucking whom, it is who's in control. Love is a balance of that struggle, that fight. He'd never made love with his equal. Women always had let him know he was in control from the start. And even with the best of male tricks, it never was an even match. But this had been unlike anything that had ever happened before. It was intensely masculine, and precious.

Mitch lay next to him, breathing into his hair, chewing on it a little. "I saw you on the beach and I thought you were nothing but another good-looking tease. And then it caught me, grabbed me somewhere. I wanted to run. That's why I never called you that first time. I would dial and then hang up. I never felt that—this—before. Scared the shit outta me." He reached down and placed his hand over Tom's softening penis. "I wanted to taste your eyes and feel your mind and cuddle up with you in a big brass bed on a mountaintop. I wanted to hold you in the rain." His soft words were like a gentle breeze warming Tom. "Then I knew it *would* happen, the second time we met. All of it. It was inevitable. As much as I fought it, I knew it was destined."

Tom looked at him and asked, "Are you still fighting it?"

"Yes."

"Why?"

"Now's not the time to discuss the negative aspect." He kissed him, hard and passionately. His fingers felt Tom's cock move again, rising, and he was on top of him, pressing his body to his, the bulls back in the pasture, back in combat of a sensational kind, and this time Tom was the victor.

He made love to Mitchell with all the expertise he knew, but it was more than sexual technique. Tom himself was pleasured in a way that was unusual in his experience. This was what he'd been preparing for; all the others had been practice, training. This was the first time he made love to a man—to *anyone* really—because he felt *love*.

Mitchell gasped and held his breath and did not cry out as he neared. Tom thought his head was going to explode as his heart beat wilder and his spirts soared higher than ever before. It was as if he were coming himself; never before had he felt so much satisfaction in bringing a man to orgasm. Lightning crashed in his skull and waves broke on the wall of his emotions and a magnificent music deafened him as his passion moved to a blinding fury of kaleidoscope colors in his soul. And then Mitchell came and everything was soft and golden and peaceful.

After a time of stillness on the floor, Tom opened his eyes. The fire was low now, still dancing over Mitch's body. The room was strangely quiet. Funny, but he thought they'd ripped up the carpeting and knocked down the walls. Their fingers were intertwined and they sensed that something more than physical had been joined together in that room, in that passion, now in that peace, that could never be taken from them in their lifetime. They knew that something had begun.

It started the way so many affairs begin, with sex, and it was idyllic. It has been said that two people in a love affair get to know the worst about each other, but people who merely trick together know only the finest things about one another. It was that way with them; they had certainly witnessed the other's finest moment. It had been incredible, and whether it was the beginning of a love affair or simply one special night, they knew the emotions had been honest and rare, and the glow would last always, even if they would come one day to know the worst about each other.

After what seemed like hours, Tom said, "Are you thinking what I am?"

"I think so."

"How do you feel about it?"

"It scares the shit outta me."

"Me too."

"Baby," Mitch said lovingly.

Then Tom moved closer to him and locked his head in the pillow of his shoulder as a protective arm came around and held him tight.

"You're in trouble," Rachel said, running her finger around the rim of the wineglass.

"Nope." Tom shoved his food from one side of the plate to another.

"I've never seen you like this. In Bloomingdale's you finally see the shirt you've been whining about for three months, and it doesn't phase you. You've been after me forever to get a Bunn coffeemaker because the Countess has one, and we find it at Zabar's marked down to $39.95, and you don't even react. I make you incredible coffee, Jamaican High Mountain, for which I paid an arm and a leg, and you just nod. That's a pork roast in front of you—my mother should only know—which is your favorite food, in case you've forgotten, and you just pick. If you're not in trouble, you're sick or you're in love."

"Both. I feel weak, paralyzed. I've never been like this. I don't know what to do. It's so wonderful, so incredible, I think it's too good for me. I feel guilty about being this happy. I think I don't deserve it. I walk into walls and nearly drown in the bathtub and I think I don't even resent my mother anymore. See, I am sick."

"Goyish guilt? No such thing. You're infatuated."

"I'm in love."

"I've heard it before."

"Not from me."

"No, not from you, but at twenty-four, people tend to fall in love easily. Who is it? Mitchell?"

"Yes."

"*He's* the one who should feel guilty," she laughed, poking at the juicy roast with her fork. "He's the one who's Jewish."

"I always did have a thing for Jewish men."

"You always had a thing for all men, darling." She chewed the meat with a smile. "And all men always did have a thing for you."

"Does it upset you?" He asked it with honest concern. He had been afraid to tell her.

"I've known how you felt since the first time you mentioned him, when you called me after your first night together."

He looked surprised. "I gave that much away?"

She gave him a look he understood well. "You underestimate me."

"I forgot. You're the smartest woman who ever lived."

She shook her head. "Wisest. Not smartest."

Suddenly, he slapped his hand on the table and yelled, "I don't know what to do!"

"Enjoy it," she said calmly, downing the last of the wine.

"What?"

"En*joy* it. Go with it. I'm not going to tell you what you want to hear. I just tell you what I think. Now, eat your pork and shut up."

He speared some meat and shut up.

When she cleared the dishes, she paused at the sink, where he couldn't see her, and closed her eyes. Oh yes, she wanted him to enjoy it, but she also really believed it was nothing more than infatuation. She didn't want to lose him. Let him be crazy with infatuation, but she prayed the love be reserved for her. She wound the dishrag around in her fingers and wished to God she didn't love him so damned much.

She came back with dessert and as they ate, Tom talked of Mitchell. Then they watched television, and through the news, weather and sports, Tom talked of Mitchell. He talked of Mitchell over Johnny Carson's monologue. Rachel was beginning to tire of the very mention of the name, so she began to stroke Tom's fur, massaging his scalp, moving her hands down to his chest, and finally to his groin, where his penis was standing hard. It shut him up.

They made love and Tom felt something happening to him which had not occurred before. He was suddenly confused. Because he began to *compare*. Rachel and Mitchell. Before, men were men and women were women and when he slept with a man it was simply different from sleeping with a woman. But Rachel was very special, she attacked something in his heart which no female had ever done before. And special was the man, so far away in California at this moment, and yet still so close, there inside him. The man reached in and held tight to something in him no man had ever done before. And as a result, to make love to Rachel meant dragging Mitchell into their bed. Tom hated himself for it—could she sense what was going on in his brain?—and tried to put the man out of his mind. But nothing he did would remove Mitchell's presence. Holding her breasts. Feeling her lips on his ears, on his chin, on his toes, on his penis. Running the back of his hands over her white thighs. Moving slowly inside her. He felt wrapped in her sensuality, in the softness of her body, in the undemanding gentleness of her lovemaking, but the string holding the package together had a man's name on it.

Tom tried to think it out as they paused and rested,

holding hands, listening to one another breathe, kissing lightly, playing with their lips and eyelashes. Rachel was the only woman who did not force him to be something other than himself in bed. He could play the cowboy from Texas riding her with a force that nearly frightened, or he could be totally passive, lie there and be loved and cared for and cuddled like a little boy. Tom had come to believe all persons had elements of masculine and feminine in them (he learned it from Rachel). He felt the femininity of Rachel—not only the soft curves of her body, but the very nature of her personality and aura—brought out the same in him, tapped the female elements in his soul. He even toyed with the theory that because she was so in touch with her own masculine side, it was the thing that allowed her to accept the fact that he slept with men as well as women without her ever being threatened by it. She was the sexiest, most desirable woman he'd ever known, and perhaps it was her inherent masculinity that caused that sensation, for it enticed the homosexual urge in his makeup.

Oh, for Christ's sake, wasn't he getting just a bit too deep? Come on, Tom, what was it? What wasn't there? Sizzle? Spark? Fire? Another dick? Something was . . . missing.

Missing? Was that the word? Or was it that sex with Mitch, with a man he loved, was incomparable next to sex with a woman he loved, with Rachel? He tried so hard not to compare, to keep each in separate parts of his mind, as they were in separate parts of his life, a continent apart, but it was impossible. He could not explain what the difference was between the male/male and male/female experience, but the nature of his mind was such that he demanded an answer of some sort, a theory, an understanding of how and why he was thinking this way. *Bisexual* seemed to him a clinical term, some stamp on your forehead that said you were certified a physical lovemaker to both sexes. USDA

Choice. Dumb. What Tom thought important was being able to truly love—on all levels, emotional and spiritual as well as physical—another person, male *or* female. In that sense he was "bi" or "dual" because he felt equal emotion for Rachel and Mitchell, equal love, equal satisfaction. But even that wasn't quite true. He knew it now. No matter how wonderful sex with Rachel was, it lacked the true rock-bottom intensity of Mitchell.

Again they made love and when it was over, and Tom and Rachel had both achieved glorious orgasms, they rested and cuddled some more. They were both aware *then* that previous orgasms had been a touch more glorious. Tom knew it had been terrific, he'd loved it, but all through it his mind had been playing pingpong. He knew he would touch her one moment and then his mind would flash to the strong hairy arms and the hard chest pounding against his and the sound of the deep passionate groans so like his own. He had fantasized about Mitch while making love to Rachel. And never had the situation been reversed. That told him a great deal. And scared him.

She could tell he was greatly disturbed. Oh, she knew Mitch wasn't out of his mind when she shushed him by playing with his cock. No, she may have silenced the soundtrack, but the movie was still running. He had been talking of Mitchell all evening, what would make her think his mind wouldn't be on him all night long? Good thing they kept kissing. He might have shouted out the man's name when he came. . .

She too hated thinking like this. It detracted from the pleasure she'd just experienced. She should have stopped him, she shouldn't have accepted his love under such circumstances. He had cut into what was her time. It was a violation. But the excitement had been too great, her passion much too roused to suddenly halt and think clearly. But now her urges were fulfilled, and her mind was clear. What he'd done was rude and unforgivable. There was always room for him in her bed, but for his male lover as well? *That* much understanding would have been unrealistic; it would have been stupidity.

It was the first night they spent together where Rachel got up after Tom fell asleep and went to the living room to curl up on the couch. She just couldn't sleep next to him that night. Not when she was sure he was dreaming of lying next to Mitch.

"Can you spend the night?" Tom finally asked him when the fire had dimmed to ashes with tiny red hot spots.

"No. I want to, but I can't."

"I understand."

"I must go, but I want to make love to you all night long."

"Kiss me."

Mitch kissed him, took him in his arms and lifted him from the floor. It took strength to lift Tom Brassen and carry him from one room to another, but that's what Mitch did, easily. He set him on the bed and said, "It's cold in here." The window above the bed was open.

"I'll warm you," Tom said, pulling him into bed with him.

They felt the urge rise again, another battle to be fought with all the manly strength and determination and pride they had in their souls, and Tom turned over and stretched out on the bed as Mitchell knelt between his outstretched legs and ran his hands over the smooth cheeks of Tom's ass.

Their lovemaking in the living room had been frantic and sweaty, two athletes in the stadium, the olympiad of the masculine in its fiercest intensity, the bulls matching horn for horn. But now, in the bedroom, on the old-fashioned quilt, in the light from the moon and glowing embers, it was a lingering, slow, romantic and sensual kind of lazy love. The basic femininity in Tom was rising to the surface, and he was beginning to understand the quality and use it; indeed, he knew it was a trait which made him attractive to both men and women.

He'd first discovered it the night in Joplin with Lavinia. But Rachel had brought it out in him when she told him he truly was a pussycat in bed. He asked her what she meant. She explained that one of his cat-like features was the ability to curl up and purr, a feline trait which was neither particularly male or female. He could be docile. He could lie back and allow her to service him, pleasure him, and he didn't feel he had to repay the favor. He could assume a passive role in bed, and not worry whether or not his manhood was being threatened. He even found that he didn't necessarily have to reach an orgasm to be sexually satisfied during a session of lovemaking; sometimes it was enough that he was able to make *her* see stars. There was something imperceptibly feminine in such thinking, and it came from his blood. He began to feel he was born not so much the cat as the chameleon. He could be passive or active, masculine or feminine, whether he was with man or woman. And sometimes he could be both at the same time.

He was both now. He was the breathing, moaning essence of a man, muscles shining and taught, shoulders and nape of his neck musky with sweat and cologne, legs spread as if about to do push-ups on the gym floor. But another man entered his body as he lay there, penetrating slowly as a man would a woman, moving with tenderness and caution, moving down toward him gradually, bending forward to lick the fuzz on the back of his neck, then to kiss the wet shoulders, run strands of his armpit hair through his teeth.

Tom was docile. No screams, no shouts, no passionate lurches or movements, but the whole concept of maleness flooded his mind. He was a man. The man he loved was inside his body. That joining was feminine in nature, in feeling, but they were two men and Tom felt shudders of exquisite pleasure just from thinking it. He knew it was something that could never fully be explained, something that would never really make sense since it was so very emotional and implicitly personal, and yet something—the one something—which would excite him more than any other feeling in life. Man with man. As one.

Mitchell was inside him and it was to be savored, this moment, this sensation, like a fine sauce or smooth brandy or delicious piece of chocolate. Mitchell was inside him and Tom accepted him with pain in the marrow of his bones, and a joyful noise in his head. He felt the man deep within his bowels and felt his belief reinforced: he *was* in love. He had never felt this way. He wanted to say it, whisper it, breathe it, but he didn't dare; just to think it seemed more than he should be allowed.

Mitchell began not to thrust, but to knead, pull, push, undulating to the point of release and the relaxing afterglow that made lovers feel they'd been joined as one. Tom accepted and responded, savoring every move. And when the orgasm came, it seemed to happen in agonizing spurts. Mitchell's body rested upon his and the beads of perspiration on chest and back came together as they held onto one another.

They lay silently on the bed, soaking up those last few moments of contentment as all lovers do before the real world again begs to be remembered.

Mitchell finally got up and kissed Tom's cheek and went to the living room and dressed. Tom couldn't move. He was still on his stomach when Mitch came back into the room. He sat next to him, car keys in hand. "Thanks for taking care of the tree. Promise I'll get it back next year?"

Tom looked up and said, "Only if you promise to come back soon and check on it."

"You free tomorrow afternoon? I want to see you again."

He nodded. He wasn't but he would arrange it. "I'll be here all afternoon."

"See you then."

Mitch stood up and there was a long, awkward pause. Tom finally said, "I can't move. I'm dead. Do you mind if I don't—"

"I'd rather remember you just like that." Mitch bent down and kissed his ass.

"Tell me something," Tom said.

"Sure."

"What do you do? I've fashioned you an athletic coach, you know."

Mitch laughed. "Jesus, and I thought you were on the USC basketball team. Looks are deceiving. I'm not much of an athlete. I'm a corporation lawyer in Century City."

Tom's expression admitted his surprise. "No shit. And I'm not much of a student."

Mitch gave him a slap on the ass. "Sport, you could teach the goddamn class. Tomorrow at two. See ya." And he was out the door.

When he'd thought he was in love with Chloe, it all seemed so corny. And now that he was sure he was in love with Mitch, it seemed just as corny again. It was absurd. Dreaming of being with him in a snowbound cabin with lovesick words being whispered in the ear. *Sergeant Preston Of The Yukon Goes Gay.* All right, he had no control over what he dreamed at night, but wanting Mitchell's semen never to leave his body the evening before, that was right out of all the paperback porn he'd read when he was fourteen, and it was *corny*.

He sat there, nonetheless, filled with anticipation of the arrival of the young lawyer who looked more like a quarterback. He was naked, sprawled on the couch, his cock hard, picturing Mitchell naked, his sinuous muscles holding him tight. He tried to see him in a business suit with a briefcase in hand, but the image wouldn't focus. He kept seeing the black hair against the bronze of his thighs.

He was a goner. He'd read about it in countless books. People had told him, cautioned him about falling in love. It never made sense and it was painful because it was almost always one-sided and it held no reason whatsoever and made everything else that was happening in your life at the time seem totally meaningless and insignificant. It was the worst possible of situations to be in, and yet it was the most wonderful state of being in the whole damn world.

Mitch showed up shortly after two. Tom was still naked when he opened the door. Mitch was pleasantly surprised, and he wrapped his arm around Tom, placed his hand firmly on his ass, and kissed him. "I only have an hour. I want to spend every minute of it in bed with you." Tom kicked the door shut behind him.

They made love, whispering nothing but sounds of passion, and hurried breathing that comes with foreplay, half-words, exclamations, moans. They memorized each other's bodies in the light of day, taking time to adore, to penetrate with excited eyes, to touch with tenderness and wonder. They climaxed together, just holding one another, their bodies digging into each other's groin, chests heaving as one, mouths pressed into the nape of each other's neck.

The hour passed quickly. Tom lay beside Mitch, his head on his hip, his eyelash touching the man's penis, and again he thought how remarkable this was, how strangely different. He'd always felt a quest to *know* people, know all about them, quickly, questions and more questions, yet here he was giving heart and soul to this man on a Monday afternoon and all he knew was that he had a fabulous body and worked as an attorney.

Sure, he was curious, but he felt no need to press, no need to hurry the process; this was meant to be different from anything which had come before. It would set its own pace. Things would happen the way they were meant to happen. He was content with little this time, but the little was so much, and that's what astonished him.

"When will I see you again?" he asked as Mitch was getting dressed.

"I'm not sure. Rotten week for me." He was silent as he buckled his belt. "Thursday night?"

"I can't. The Countess is having a soirée and she'd cut my balls off if I didn't show."

"Countess?"

"She's a character. The bananas lady I work for. Hey, would you want to come?" Tom asked only because he was positive the man would say no.

"No. I can't. Saturday would be good—no, shit, I'm taking Jeremy to a movie in the afternoon and there's a family thing we're going to at night. How about Friday?"

Tom didn't hear the last question. He felt fire rushing through his brain. Jeremy? To a fucking movie in the afternoon? How sweet. How middle-class romantic. What's Jeremy, some chicken high school queen whose big day of the week is Saturday? Shit! Family thing? What family, who's family? *And there's a family thing we're going to at night.* Terrific, you and Jeremy have a ball with his family, or your family, or whoever it damn well is. Do his mom and dad call you "son?" or maybe their "son-in-law?" Goddammit. Here's a guy who's affecting me like no one ever has in my life and it turns out he's got some punk lover he takes to the movies on Saturday and then to din-din with ma and pa and the cousins. God damn—

"Tom! What the hell is wrong? Hey, where are you? Earth to Tom!"

—my luck. Jeremy. Pretty faggy name for—

"Tom, for Christ's sake, what's wrong?" Mitch shook him.

Tom came back to the planet. And felt like a fool. "I . . . I'm sorry. I was just . . . just trying to remember what I have planned for the weekend."

"Well, how's Friday?"

"Friday's fine with me."

Mitch tied a full windsor and looked in the mirror. "Do I look as though I had a nice quiet lunch at La Serre?"

"Absolutely."

Mitch came back to the bed and sat down. He brushed the hair from Tom's forehead and pressed his hand to his face. "Tom, you're beautiful. Thank you for this." His voice was like soft velvet. "I know it was hurried, but it had to be. I'll find a way to stay out late Friday. We'll have all the time in the world."

"Would you like to come for dinner?"

Mitch seemed amazed. "You cook too? Jesus, he's a gourmet, plays the hottest piano I've ever heard, fucks like he must have done his graduate thesis in it, he's an expert on live Christmas trees—is there anything he *can't* do?"

"He can't whistle."

"Thank God, he's human."

"Very."

"I've got to run. Pick you up at, oh, seven, okay?"

"Don't you want dinner here?"

"Next time. I've got a plan for Friday, something special. Dinner at a place I love and never get to anymore."

"Okay." Tom watched him get up, and then Mitch

bent down and they kissed again. "Mitch . . . I really . . . I really like you."

The man winked. "Ditto."

Then, just as Mitch was going out the door to the bedroom, Tom called, "When you talk about this, and you will . . . be gentle."

Mitch turned around and laughed. "Listen, kid, get yourself a new writer. That's a very unoriginal closing line."

ELEVEN

It was an uneventful week. Tom thought of nothing but seeing Mitch on Friday, and spent most of what was left of Monday reading *Tender Is The Night* for the seventh time. Tuesday was bright and clear. The rain had knocked whatever crap had been hovering in the Los Angeles sky all to hell and you could see forever. He went up to Griffith Park and hiked for five hours. All sorts of humpy guys were lurking in the trees on this beautiful day, but he didn't have the inclination to trick with any of them. He felt strangely unpromiscuous. In a few days he'd have Mitch again. Why settle for less?

He banged away at the piano that night, practicing for hours, and it relaxed him. He worked on a song he'd been at for nearly three months and was pleased to finally get something decent down on paper. Then he decided to tackle the dishes from dinner the night before. He was standing at the sink when he heard a noise on the patio.

He went out to see what it was, and found a boy standing there, looking sheepish and embarrassed. It was the boy who cleaned the pool. "Kevin. What are you doing out here in the dark?"

"I'm sorry. I was . . . well, I was listening to the music."

"Huh? Why didn't you come in? Jesus, I didn't even

know you were up at the house today."

"I wasn't. I . . . I drove up to listen to you play. I have a confession to make: I do it a lot."

Tom couldn't believe what he was hearing. "You come up here and sit in the dark and hope that I'll be playing the piano?"

The boy nodded.

"That's nuts. I'm flattered, but that's just nuts."

"I know."

"Want some tea?"

"Yeah. With some brandy, if you got it."

"Hey, why are you shaking?" Tom put his arm on his shoulder. "Kevin, what the fuck is wrong?"

"Nothing. I just hope you're not too pissed at me for doing this."

"Pissed? Come on!"

"No, I don't mean that. I mean, I hope you don't think I'm some kind of creep, like a peeping-tom or something."

"Kevin, you asshole, come on in and have a drink."

They went inside.

Tom had begun to notice the kid who cleaned the Countess' oversized swimming pool. He was there three times a week, and he seldom talked to anyone, but Tom figured that was because nobody ever talked to him. The Countess seemed to ignore his existence, treating him the way she did all servants, as slaves, peasants, the rabble, the *dreck*. Tom was swimming one afternoon when Kevin had to ask him if he'd get out of the water while he vacuumed the pool. Tom did, but he hung around, asking more and more questions, until Kevin finally opened up a little, which led to their becoming friends.

Kevin wasn't stunning the way the boys who surrounded the Countess were stunning; his beauty was in his eyes—they sparkled. He was a native of California, one of that rare species, born and raised in San Diego.

His parents moved up to Sherman Oaks three years earlier and his father started a pool service company. Kevin still lived with them and worked for his dad, though he'd wanted to get out on his own for a long time. The reason he didn't was the reason he didn't do a lot of things—he didn't like himself very well.

He'd had polio as a baby. Unusual and unfortunate as it was in the early 1960's, he was stricken with the disease and suffered for years. It left him permanently scarred for life, though less on a physical level than an emotional one. His right leg dragged behind him because it was slightly withered, but in his mind he was a cripple, grotesque and doomed to go through life without friends, without love, without happiness.

"You're really full of shit," Tom said to him the first time Kevin came down to the cottage to see him. "I know you're shy and I know you're only twenty-two and I realize you had a rough time as a kid, but don't you think it's time you forgot all that and opened up a little."

"I've tried. People can be really mean. Especially kids your own age, all through school, they really were ugly. I just kinda stay at home and get frustrated."

Tom sat him down and faced him. "Now listen to me. I've got my own problems, but it's always easier to deal with someone else's. And I like you. I just do. You're nice, Different. Quiet and good-looking, gentle, easy. I think you're probably smart too, a closet intellectual or something. You ever had a girlfriend?"

"I'm gay."

"Yeah?" Tom was actually surprised. "Well then, you ever had a boyfriend?"

"You kidding? I've had sex, some, but nobody's going to want a lover who—" He stopped cold.

"What were you going to say? Limps? What did they call you in school—*Peg Leg? Long John Silver?*"

Pain flashed through the boy's eyes. But then he

smiled as he realized Tom was looking at him with caring, maybe even affection, and no one had ever viewed him in that way, ever. "They called me *The Blob*. I used to weigh a lot too. I knew there was nothing I could do about my leg, but if I wanted to get my cock sucked, I had to lose weight."

"And you look terrific."

"You don't have to do that."

"Do what?" Tom asked.

"Patronize me. I know what I look like."

"No you don't! You walk with your head facing the ground, you know that? Yeah, I've watched you around the yard. And don't say it's because you have to keep looking down into the pool. You carry yourself like you've got a sign on your back that says LEPER. Why not tie a rattle around your leg to let people know you're coming?"

Kevin had to laugh.

"See how ridiculous it is? The last couple of times we talked, I really was impressed with you. I haven't met a guy since . . . well, ever, that I just liked talking to. Honest, never in my life. I've never had a buddy. I want one. I want you to be my friend. But I won't have a friend who puts himself down, who walks around like he's a fucking Quasimodo. If you only realized how sharp you are on the inside, you'd stand up straight and start to smile. Listen, I don't go for just anyone, and if I think you're worth it, then you have to think you're worth it yourself, or I'm the asshole. Jesus, Kevin, you're a lot more interesting than those Mr. Americas she's got scattered around the pool."

Kevin said nothing.

Tom stared at him. Were those tears forming in his eyes?

They became good friends. Kevin didn't transform overnight, but he did become more sure of himself because Tom seemed sure of him, and he began to glow because he'd found a friend, someone who cared about him, someone who wasn't related to him, someone who hadn't been told they *had* to be nice to him. And he did seem to stand taller, and walk less self-consciously.

They were as different as night and day in some respects: their background, the kinds of family situations they had experienced, experience itself, with Tom in the lead in just about every category, for he was older, had traveled more, had never been sheltered and was years ahead of Kevin sexually. But Tom had never known pain and suffering, and he longed to understand the sensitivity that disease and anguish had nourished in his new friend.

They were also much alike. They each buoyed the other's spirits because they both wanted a good life, money, fame, importance, falling in love with the White Knight forever and ever, silly dreams that were fun to talk about as if they were school kids. They liked roses and chocolate and animals and going to the movies together. They were good beach partners, though Kevin always kept his jeans on because of his leg. Tom would say, "The crowning achievement of my Henry Higgins days with you will be the moment you strut down Will Rogers sandy shore in an Ah-Men bikini."

Kevin had a talent beyond skimming a pool. He was a fine photographer. His sense of color and composition was acute and he shot endless rolls of Tom. Tom in trees, rolling on the grass, swimming in the ocean, sitting on rocks. Tom in bed, black and white sensual shots which came out looking extremely erotic. Tom posing next to his car, glaring color which for some reason turned out looking like a silly Low Rider queen and his prize GMC chariot. Tom finally turned the Leica on him, and when the prints turned out dreadful, Kevin was able to announce he was justified in labeling himself as "a grotesquity." Tom blamed it on the camera and his inability to use it to any advantage. He finally pulled out his Instamatic and photographed Kevin on his own turf, and the result was twelve very handsome photographs of a very good-looking young man. Tom had caught the eyes. It was all in the eyes. And even Kevin, though he would not vocalize it, had to agree; he even signed one and beamed with pride when Tom framed it and put it on the mantel.

"You know what you do for me?" Tom said to him one night after they got home from a movie.

"What?"

"You make me feel less lonely."

Kevin was touched. "You do the same for me. But you always seemed so . . . I don't know . . . glamorous or something. I can't believe you were ever lonely."

"Sometimes, very. At least lonely for a friend. I've had enough lovers and tricks.

"I'll always be your friend."

Kevin went to his car and waved as he drove out through the trees. Then Tom went inside the house and played the piano for a couple of hours before going to sleep.

"I did it the first time that night you told me you'd been lonely," Kevin said, sipping tea into which Tom had poured Jamaican rum. "I drove down the hill a little and stopped and ran back and just sat and listened."

"Why didn't you tell me?"

" 'Cause then you'd play differently. I don't want you to perform. I just want to listen to you practice. I envy the talent you have."

"You envy me? You think I like it that I can't learn to work anything more than a goddamn Kodak I got for six bucks and fifteen soup labels?"

"You played different tonight. I've never heard you sound like that before. And all classical stuff, before you started working on your song."

"I'm feeling high."

"I could tell."

"I'm having an affair. I think."

Kevin's ears perked. He wanted all of it now, every last detail, for one of the things they did best together was gossip.

Tom told him about Mitchell. About their love-making—Kevin's eyes bugged out—and about their feelings for one another. He described him in detail, as if he were being quizzed. He told him of the passion he felt, the hope that it would last. He told him he was very sure he was in love.

"I'm jealous," Kevin said, a bit sadly.

"He's not your type."

"I'm jealous of what you feel. I don't even know what love is like. I don't think I'd recognize it."

"I love you and you recognize it."

"That's different. We're friends. I'm talking about—"

Tom cut him off. He knew well what he was talking about. The thing which had been missing from his life before Mitch. "I once thought I was in love with Chloe," Tom explained. "I even believed it for a while. But this is so different, I mean, my tongue goes dry thinking about him and I shake and I can feel the blood running in my veins—*feel*, feel my heart, see . . . it's going two-forty. It's zonking me. Coming back from the park today, I missed the exit on the freeway. I've never done that in my life. I'm like in space."

"God."

"We're going out together Friday night."

"You know something, I can see it on your face, just like I heard it in the music. It shouldn't surprise me, though, because you're easy to love. You deserve love."

"Is that supposed to mean you're not? You don't? Do I see you regressing right in front of my eyes?"

Kevin looked away. He felt a bit ashamed; he'd really convinced Tom he had conquered the self-pity. But he wanted so much to be like Tom, so much to be as free as he seemed, to be in love the way he was in love, to be as happy. "It means Mitch had better be good to you. And you tell him I said so. I won't let anyone hurt you."

Tom realized he was serious. "You really wouldn't, would you?"

"That's what friends are for." He seemed to want to say more, something else, but he hesitated, then suddenly got up and said, "I've gotta go. Got an acid wash to do at eight in the morning in Beverly Hills. I'll call you tomorrow night, okay?"

"Okay."

Kevin went to the door. "Tom," he said, turning back, "I'm really happy for you."

"Thanks, Kev."

TWELVE

On Wednesday morning Tom had a client, a woman of obvious means, too much Estée Lauder, and Jane Russell full-figure bazooms. She was over fifty, not a candidate for *Penthouse* by any stretch of the imagination, and really rather dull on top of everything else. He closed his eyes, convinced his wild mind that this was Mitchell here with him, feeling him, touching him, tasting him. The fantasy exploded pleasure in his mind. And he came violently.

Madame Zena of the mansion made the trip down the little path herself that afternoon to tell him how much the woman had loved him. "Vat a cock ze boy has, Fannie tells me. He is so strong, ven he comes he holds my hands down and pounds into me like jackhammer! She tells me, Oh, Zena, I inzist you give me him every time. I vant no other boy but him."

"Zippideedoo."

"You did not like her, Tomas?"

"You wanna know the truth? Yecch."

"Vell, she loved you and zat is all vhich counts. Ve have a little bonus for you for being so good." She pulled a roll of bills from her cleavage and stuck them in his jeans, and then gave his crotch a gentle pat. "You take care of zat baby, darling. Ve vant it in good shape at the ball.''

"Oh, no, come on. I was the attraction last time. I don't want to—"

She stuck a few more bills in his pants. "Just a little show in the library at midnight, darling. For select guests.''

"I'll soak it in rosemilk so it's all nice and soft and fresh," he said sarcastically.

But she did not understand sarcasm. "Oh, no, God forbid such a doing! Ve vant it hard, not soft!'' And she fluttered away, humming like a demented bird.

Tom dialed Kevin and got his father. "When he comes in, will you have him call me right away? Yeah, thanks.'' Kevin called an hour later and asked what was up. "How'd you like to go to a party with me tomorrow night?''

"Where?''

"The house.''

"The ball the Countess is throwing?'' Tom could hear the enthusiasm in his voice. "Jesus, you think she'd say it was all right?''

"You're gonna be my guest, not the hired hand. You be here at eight. And if you don't have a jacket, buy one. It's a classy affair. But it might be fun.''

Kevin hesitated. "You . . . you sure you want me along?''

"Sure I'm sure, dummy. Who knows, you may meet someone and fall in love.''

"I'll be there, I'll be there.''

Tom didn't sleep much that night. Mitch walked through the corridors of his mind and he was alternately elated, sad, horny, mad. He listened to music, beat off, read *Time* cover to cover, and wrote a letter to Mrs. Jensen, his old piano teacher who was probably dead by now, but he figured he'd chance it all the same. What kept creeping back into his mind was Mitchell in the arms of another man. And he tried to fight it, tried not to be a faggot and simmer with jealous tremors, but he found himself fuming, walking around and banging on the piano, drinking wine and eating Fig Newtons as the sun came up.

He decided to reason with himself. He might be anticipating too much, taking too much for granted—after all, neither of them had even told the other they felt they were falling in love. But Tom knew they would, so he had to deal with this: Would Mitch leave his lover? What if he one day found someone else? Wasn't there always another pair of buns lying on a blanket in the sand? Would Mitch use him the way clients did, toss him out, the sex toy they tired of in a few hours?

He told himself it was more than sexual, that he had to trust his emotions. What point was there getting upset over self-inflicted nightmares of anguish? Wasn't he the one who told Kevin, months before, "Faithfulness is outmoded. There's no reason getting uptight just because your lover tricks. Loving someone is so much more complicated than that." He said it, but did he believe it? Could he share Mitchell with someone named Jeremy? Did he have a double standard in his thinking, was his open and hip speech to Kevin just so much hot air?

And on top of that—while we're at it, Tom, let's hit all angles—where did he get off not telling Mitch about his tricks? Would he *ever* tell him?

No. He knew it would take superhuman effort for anyone to understand and accept that his lover was making a living getting it up for other guys. 'Hi, Mitch, home from work early? What did I do today? I got fucked in the ass by a trick from Seattle, and there's a number in the bedroom I still have to suck off, so could you make dinner?' Shit.

He flopped on the bed. He thought about the women.

How would Mitch take *that?* God. He wanted the genie in the magic lamp to grant him one wish at that moment: a blank mind. He wanted to get some rest.

He took the phone off the hook and stuffed his head under the pillows and slept until five in the afternoon. Then he got up and showered, shaved, splashed himself with Imperiale, and donned the only suit he owned, the green corduroy he bought at Dickens on Madison Avenue in New York. He looked in the mirror and smiled.

Kevin showed up looking as eager as a teenager on prom night. He had on a tweed sport coat with a tan shirt and sleek brown pants. Tom had never seen him in anything but a T-shirt and jeans. He had to admit he had never come close to realizing how really attractive Kevin was. "You look terrific," Tom said.

"Thanks." Kevin didn't even say, "Oh, come on, I do not, not really." He was changing. He accepted the compliment graciously, and walked up the hill with Tom to the sound of a mariachi band playing in the yard.

The mansion was overflowing, and most of the guests looked right out of Central Casting. The rich, the genteel, the jaded, the bred, the boring. But the Contessa liked to keep a balance, and there were enough interesting people to keep the ennui at bay. Faces anyone would recognize, the Hollywood names, rock stars, the Allen Carr contingent, television personalities, and others whose names were well-known, if not their faces, people who wrote books and advised presidents and conducted orchestras. There were a couple of surfer-types who had been imported from the beach to loll around nude in the pool, Zena's idea of "outrageous," at least, she thought correctly, in the eyes of some of the bankers and society butterflys she'd invited. And, wandering around among the others, Madame Zena's own explorer scouts, her small army of beautiful young men.

She squeaked, with a wave of the hand, "Ach, my

boys!" She was talking to a commodities trader and his prune-faced wife. "Ven I die, zey vill carry on for me in spirit." She said it with all the theatrical Russian guts, growl, and love of the Motherland she could muster up. "My boys are ze most beautiful in ze vorld, except perhaps ze Crimea."

"Oh, where is the Crimea?" the prune asked.

Zena blinked. "A suburb of Cleveland, darling." She had no patience with idiots.

"Oh," the woman said with a smile.

Tom and Kevin had overheard it and broke into laughter.

The man said, "I was chatting with Madame Platychivnik on the patio earlier, and she tells me your nephew just arrived from the Soviet Union."

Zena put her hand to her breast, swooning. "Ach, my heart soars. See zere?" She pointed to a dark-haired, heavily-moustached hustler sitting alone in a big wing chair, looking morose. "See ze unhappiness on his face? Oh, ze horrors he has had to suffer! But ve got him avay from ze dirty communists and he is vit me now forever."

Tom wanted to throw up. The truth was she'd picked him up on the corner of Hollywood and Cahuenga, five minutes after he'd stepped off the Trailways bus from Des Moines.

"Does he speak any English?" the wife asked.

"Yeah," Tom said to Kevin behind Zena's back, "with a flat Iowan twinge."

"Oh, no no no," Zena gasped. "The silent, brooding type. Ven he adjusts, he vill speak better than me even."

Kevin thought he was going to pee in his pants.

Tom tapped the Countess on the shoulder and she turned around and made with the hugs and kisses. "Tomas, my Tomas, as ve vould say in my youth, ice skating on ze frozen Neva, Tomas like a brilliant star in ze Czarist sky. . ." Melodrama suited her.

"Countess, you know Kevin."

"Vat?"

"Kevin."

Kevin held out his hand. She looked for some sign of recognition. "I clean your pool, ma'am."

"Oh, yes, vell!" She took his hand, and graciously, with a deep bend forward, he kissed it. She was impressed. She looked to Tom, bewildered. "Are you sure ve have ze same boy here?"

"I polished him up," Tom said, smiling. "Excuse us, we have to mingle."

"Oh, yes, yes, by all means," she said, giving both of them a pat on the back. Then she pulled Tom aside and said, "Don't forget, ze library at midnight."

"Is that when we find out if the butler did it?"

"Vat?"

"Never mind." Tom walked away and Kevin followed.

The commodities trader asked, "Who was that, Countess?"

"Tomas, a magnificent cloud in ze glorious sky over Dubrolyubova Prospect, an icon in Blagoveshchensky Sobor. . ." She disappeared into the sea of people, chanting the praises of her favorite young man.

They made an attractive couple, the tall blond in his green suit, the red-haired boy all in brown and gray tweed, Tom sparkling because he was in love, Kevin bubbling because he was too, whether he knew it or not. They circulated amongst the guests, met new people, talked, ate caviar which the prissy waiter assured them came via Aeroflot jet from Estonia just for the occasion, but which Tom knew had actually come by Chevy van from Chalet Gourmet on Sunset Boulevard. Chunks of bright green broccoli sat on huge shining trays. Gilded samovars dispensed coffee and tea. And everywhere, from the pool to the third floor, waiters handed out glasses of champagne. Tom was careful to make them last, but Kevin downed one after another.

Tom struck up a conversation with a girl he'd seen in a play on PBS recently, and they talked about Lanford Wilson, one of Chloe's favorite playwrights. After a while, they joined other couples on the dance floor, and Tom caught a glance of Kevin, over the girl's shoulder, looking anxious suddenly, unsure. When the dance was over, Tom excused himself and asked Kevin what it was. Kevin said he thought maybe he'd had too much champagne, that he'd better sit down and rest. "I'm going out to the patio for a while. Don't worry. I'll be fine. Go back and dance. I'll see you later. This has been more fun—I mean, I've never been to anything like this before. Thanks for bringing me."

Kevin went to the patio and Tom danced another slow dance with the girl. He wondered what had upset his friend, and suddenly he knew. Tom was waltzing around like Fred Astaire, and Kevin couldn't dance. Tom knew he'd embarrassed him, made him newly aware of his deformity. Determined to give Kevin one of his lectures on self-esteem, Tom excused himself from the girl and went to the patio. But he was too late. Kevin had escaped into a gentle sleep on a lawn chaise. Tom decided to let him be. It was eleven-thirty. He had to be the old gal's Paul Newman in half an hour. Playing lots of famous parts this night. He hoped she'd only make him masturbate like the last time. He had no interest in having sex with anyone, not when tomorrow night he'd be with Mitchell.

He went back inside and talked to the ambassador from a country he'd never heard of, and started up the big staircase where a very chic woman and a man in black tie were having a loud argument. The Countess fluttered past him, mumbling something in Russian. A woman slithered down the steps behind him and sudden-

ly took hold of his shoulder as if it were a crutch. He'd
never seen her before. "What *is* this?" she asked in a
husky voice, her hand sweeping in a gesture to encom-
pass the entire main floor, eyes squinting at the decadent
scene. "Tell me, what *is* all this!"

Tom said, "The fall of the Roman Empire."

She fell back, relieved, sitting on a step, looking on
the verge of death. "Thank God. For a moment I
thought it was just another of Zena's parties."

He went upstairs. He walked into an empty room, a
small sitting room overlooking the backyard and
gardens, and he looked out to check on Kevin. He was
still out cold on the lounge chair. Tom could see the roof
of his storybook house from there, nestled tight in the
trees. He wished he could have been there all night,
alone with Mitchell. Could he possibly get it up for the
voyeurs upstairs? Yes . . . if he thought of Mitch.

In the private library, select guests had gathered for
the performance, the highlight of the evening which
always made Zena Oluspenskaya's parties "unique."
The room was lined with books and filled with deep,
comfortable sofas and arm chairs, set up toward a stage,
something like a private screening room. Oriental lamps
and tables accented the dark green drapes, and a new
grand piano sat in the corner next to a small bar.

Someone was playing the piano when Tom entered.
Everyone turned toward him; all the sofas and chairs
were already occupied. Zena closed the massive carved
oak doors and gave a butler orders to make sure that no
one disturbed them. The room was dimly lit. Cigarette
smoke rose from long holders and diamonds glistened
under the lamps. Tom saw a famous actress and a leading man known best for his having married four times in
less than two years. And he recognized a Pulitzer Prize-
winning novelist and his boyfriend. Standing near the
piano was a stunning black girl he'd never seen before.

Zena introduced the girl as Solange. Her lips were full and sensual and she licked them and they shined. She was light-skinned, almost mulatto, with very small breasts and long fingers. She was nearly as tall as Tom. Exotic. Rare. She unfastened a clasp on her floor-length, clinging dress. It fell from her shoulders to piano accompaniament—lousy trills, Tom thought—and dropped to a heap on the floor. Then all the lights went out, except for a spotlight on the stage. And that's where they went.

All eyes were riveted on them. Tom did nothing. Solange also did nothing at first. She let everyone drink her in, feast upon her sexually austere body. Then she helped Tom off with his suit coat. And his tie. And his vest. His shirt. His shoes, socks. Everything but his pants. She sat him on the chaise under the light. She knelt down. And she took his toes into her mouth. There were gasps from the audience as well as from Tom.

Then she opened his pants. As she pulled them off, she kept his penis hidden from the spectators. She pressed it between her breasts and looked up at him, telling him with sweet eyes that she was enjoying her part of the scenario. He felt her lips slide down the skin of his prick and he closed his eyes as people bent forward to watch intently. The piano tinkled. Solange moved her head up and down. Tom lifted his feet to the cushions of the chaise, spread his knees wide, stretched out. She teased him and kept him hard, cupping his balls, fingering his anus and pricking at him with her nails.

She showed the audience nothing but the movements of her body, her soft-skinned brown ass shining in the light, her head jerking up and down wildly, hands coming around and up every few moments to touch his hard nipples and reach for a lick of his tongue. He put his hands on his knees and held tight. He groaned and bucked his hips into the air.

Someone yelled that he was coming.

A woman's voice moaned, "Oh, I don't believe it!"
Someone near them said, "Show us, show us. . ."
Another voice gasped, "Oh, he *is,* he *is* coming!"

And he was. He saw himself on a horse in his fantasy, a cowboy with spurs and turquoise belt, and the horse bucked up and hit his cock and each time, semen spurted out. It was painful and erotic, the bronco dancing under him, and he gushed into her mouth to the shuddering moans—and some applause—from the audience.

Solange moved away and everyone finally saw Tom's penis. It was full and tumescent, but not hard anymore. It hung down over his balls and over the edge of the chaise as he turned with his feet down on the floor to give them all a better view. Solange got up, her lips sealed shut, and walked around the back of the lounge to find Tom's moist lips. She put her head above his and looked into his eyes. She wanted to kiss him, he guessed. He opened his mouth. She opened hers. And a torrent of semen and saliva fell from her mouth to his face. He reflexed in shock and surprise by pulling away. He realized what it was when his eyes suddenly began to burn.

The audience went wild, cheering, applauding the Countess for outdoing herself this time, and Solange walked into the center of the spotlight and smiled— smirked?—as white still trickled down her nutmeg skin. But she wasn't finished; the Countess had another trump card.

Solange reached down and undid the little snap on the side of the bikini-like G-string she was wearing, and she exposed a small penis and hairless testicles. A piano roll accompanied her, as she rubbed her silicone breasts for emphasis. The audience let up a collective gasp.

Tom sat bolt upright, a stunned look on his sticky face. He suddenly felt himself getting sick. He felt dirty and cheated and dumb. The audience howled. They knew Tom had thought she was a real girl; the bizarre joke was more on him than on them. He had to get out of there.

He picked up his clothes. Solange was trying to force her hideous penis in his face. The audience was mad with laughter, jeering. Tom thought he was suddenly in Berlin just before the war. "Damn you!" he screamed. *"God damn fucking all of you!"* The room was suddenly silent.

He stared at them. The lights came on and hit his eyes. He gave a little moan, like a sick child, wounded. He rolled his clothes into a ball and began to shove his way to the doors. "But Tomas, it vas all. . ." the Countess said; he ignored her. "No hard feelings, man," some guy said as he passed. "You were wonderful, honey," a woman called to him.

He ran down the hall and locked himself in a bathroom. He dressed and went back into the hall carrying his tie and jacket. He wanted to hit someone. Or scream. Or throw something. As he dashed down the main staircase, Kevin saw him and began to follow. "Tom, what's wrong? Where have you—"

Tom ran outside. Kevin followed, trying to keep up. "You okay, Tom?"

"No." He ran through the trees, jumping rocks and branches until he was at his door. He stood there with his heart beating in his throat. He steadied himself and told himself not to vomit, it was going to be all right. He heard his phone ringing, but didn't care. He sat down on the brick walkway in front of the door and put his head in his hands.

Kevin came through the trees. He hesitatingly put a comforting hand on Tom's shoulder. He asked, "Want to talk?" Tom shook his head as his body trembled. Kevin sat down next to him and said, "I'm your friend. I love you. Tell me. It's good to talk things out, you taught me that. What happened?"

Tom wiped his ear, which was still wet with his own semen. "Kev, you know, I don't think anything is sick or unnatural or wrong or demented or disgusting or anything like that. Some of the guys who work for the Countess participate in a lot of weird shit, but pretend they don't and put people down who do."

"Yes." Though most things "weird" were beyond Kevin's experience.

"I don't pretend not to do some far-out things, stuff a lot of people would call depraved and sick."

"What *happened*?"

"There was a little performance up there in the library."

"So that's where you went."

"You were sleeping. And I promised the old lady. Some chick went down on me for the private guests."

"Oh."

"It was okay, I got into it and I like to know people are getting off watching me. I'll admit to being an exhibitionist now and then. There's nothing wrong—"

"Tom, you don't have to justify it to *me*."

"She . . . she whipped out a cock."

"Huh?"

Tom felt his stomach tighten again. "She was a black transsexual. I came apart. I couldn't handle it. I saw how they laughed at me when they realized I was shocked. It was filthy and revolting and ludicrous."

"Humiliating."

"Yes," Tom said, turning to face him, holding his hand tightly, "it was. I ran out like a crazy man and I feel ashamed suddenly." He took a deep breath and then muttered, "Oh, shit." He got up and walked over to the big pine tree at the edge of the patio and leaned against it. "Why do I feel this way? Because of Mitch? I never felt guilty or ashamed before. I could always handle it before."

"Are you sure?" Kevin asked, coming over to him.

Tom thought for a moment. "It's like for the first time I asked myself what am I doing? I don't belong here, I don't want to be here. I just want to be with Mitchell. I want to be his. I don't want to be a hustler. I thought how hurt he would be if he saw what I was doing tonight."

"You're right, Tom. I've thought about it many times. You're *better* than the rest of them. It's too easy for you. You've got the talent to do things, real big things in life. You could set the world on fire. . ."

Tom saw his breath in the cold night air. Then he moved away, laughing, giggling, twirling under the branches in a sudden ballet of nerves. "Jesus, Kev, this is like out of *Zhivago,* standing in the birch forest near the big Russian mansion, talking of love and passion. Shit, Kev, it's so dumb! Guys aren't even supposed to feel this way about each other."

"You sound like a redneck in a singles bar."

"I just wish none of this were happening. It would be a whole lot easier."

Kevin looked him straight in the eye. "You're wrong, Tom. See, you said it again, *easier.* Is that all you want? I really respect you and care about you because you're my best friend in the world. My life was rotten until you came into it. I want to support you because I care. You felt the right thing. I would have thrown up on her if it had been me. You were right to think about Mitch and feel guilty. It's normal. It's healthy."

"Boy, I never thought I'd get a lecture from you." Tom turned his head away and sighed.

Kevin moved closer to him. "It's only because I care so much, Tom."

Tom reached out and wrapped his arms around his friend. "Kevin, I'm so fucking in love with him," he whispered against his warm neck, "and I don't ever want to lose him."

Kevin had no reply. Tom waited for him to pull away, to move back, but he did not. Was he waiting for Tom to initiate it, to pull away from him? Neither one moved, and the silence of the cold was overwhelming.

They stood there, each in fear of what they might be feeling on some level they did not want to discover. They held each other and felt the other's heartbeat. They——

Suddenly, a loud laugh filtered through the trees from the mansion. Tom moved a little. So did Kevin. It was the excuse they needed. "Well, someone's still having fun," Tom said, dropping his arms.

Kevin held his hands loosely in front of himself, the boy with the hard-on who'd just been asked to go to the blackboard and face the class. "I'd better get back up there."

"What for?" Tom was startled he wanted to go back.

"Well, while you were gone, I . . . I met this guy. I decided this was the night I'd allow myself to be dazzled. He was bored and blond and we met in a sea of people we hated. . ."

"Kevin, hold the syrup."

"He wants me to go home with him."

"That's . . . that's wonderful." Tom didn't sound convincing.

"Thank you."

"Me? Why?"

"You made me feel really special tonight, just by asking me to go with you. I felt, well . . . good-looking."

"Bravo."

Then Kevin sounded sad again. "But I wish I had a Mitchell waiting for me, then I could feel rotten and guilty, all those healthy natural feelings."

Tom smiled. "Go and fuck your brains out. *You're* the lucky one; no strings attached."

"You going to be okay?"

Tom nodded. Then: "Did you mean what you said before? That you . . . loved me?"

"Yes, dummy, you know I do." He put his hand on Tom's shoulder and held it there.

"Kevin. . . can I kiss you?"

Kevin looked stunned, and slowly nodded.

And Tom kissed him. With emotion. It was the only way he could tell him he felt the same thing, love for what really was a friend.

THIRTEEN

Mitch picked him up in a black BMW. "You got a new car?" Tom asked.

"That was the second one. The hatchback for groceries and stuff. This is my first love. The neighbors think I'm nuts. I've always got it out in front of the house, washing it, waxing, sometimes just kinda petting it."

"House? I thought . . . I thought you had an apartment the size of a doghouse."

Mitch grinned. "I needed some kind of excuse to see you again."

"You mean you really did have room for a Christmas tree?"

"For ten of them. Listen, it says something for you."

Tom smiled. "Wow." He settled back in the leather seat. "I've always wanted one of these."

"Don't you like your MG?"

"It's fun, but I get bored with toys. I want something better. Bigger."

Mitch glanced at him. "Mmmm."

"Faggot. Is that any way for a proper Century City attorney to act?"

"No. But right now I'm not very proper."

Tom put his hand on Mitch's shoulder. "God. Where are we going?"

"Malibu. Hungry?"

"Famished."

"How was the soirée at Catherine the Great's?"

"Don't ask.

"I really want to know."

"Dull. Oh, the Countess is eccentric and unique, but her parties are just the run-of-the mill rich, jaded, coked-up Hollywood crowd out for a joyride. Hey, what's your last name?"

"Birney. What's yours?"

"Brassen."

"It was Bernstein but my dad changed it before I was born," Mitch said. "He had a fight with his brother and they split the business and he didn't want to be known as Abe Bernstein's brother. So I'm Mitchell Birney, fourteenth down on the list of attorneys in the upper left hand corner of the letterhead stationery. It's a start."

"It just occurred to me, what was a Jewish guy doing with a Christmas tree?"

"Jeremy wanted one this year."

Tom's smile disappeared. "Oh." He didn't want to hear about the tree sitting on his patio that had belonged to Mitch's lover; he changed the subject. "The best thing about a BMW is the dashboard. I know a girl who has plants growing in hers."

"Best thing is the handling. You've got to drive this some time. It's unlike anything else on the road."

They reached Pacific Coast Highway and Tom began to feel more at ease. After all, Mitch was with him, not with anyone named Jeremy or Bob or George. What right did he have to be jealous of anyone? "I missed you," he said.

"I swear to God," Mitch said, wheeling around a van covered with JESUS SAVES stickers, "I counted the minutes."

"You can stop counting. Time's up."

At the stoplight, Mitch turned and bent forward and

kissed Tom on the lips and let his hand slip down between his warm thighs for a moment. Then he looked out the window and saw the disgusted glare of a woman in the car next to them. Mitch waved at her. She tsk-tsked him. He yelled out, "It's okay, he's my brother." And sped up the coast.

"Have the house dressing," Tom said. "It's great."

"How do you know? You've never been here before."

"I read about it in *Los Angeles* magazine."

Mitch made a face. "Ugh. Joyce Haber telling you which side of town is currently *the* chic place to live."

"Where do you live?" Tom asked.

"Westwood."

"Joyce says it's very *in*. What do you do for fun?"

With a sly smile, Mitch said, "You."

"Besides that."

"Work out, play tennis, jog, go to movies, walk on the beach."

"Have you been here long? I swear I hear the East in your voice."

"I grew up in Boston and my parents still live there. Born in Connecticut actually. Got my law degree out here, Stanford, and the firm picked me up right from there."

"Because you're so handsome?"

"At Goldberg, Gould, Mutnick and Korf, who should care how you look? The criterion is, 'Will he grow up to be the shyster we already detect in him?' "

Tom laughed and chomped on a breadstick. "Do you go to court sometimes?"

"Rarely. I sit at a desk working out contracts to get people fifty times more than they're already making, which is already fifty times more than they deserve. And I take very long lunches."

"Yes, I know."

"Tell you the truth, sometimes you can get a better

deal sealed and delivered on a tennis court or in a restaurant than in any office situation."

"How old are you?"

"Thirty," Mitch said. "And I like it."

"That's funny."

"How so?"

Tom shook his head. "I always thought you had to be a doddering old man before you could call yourself a doctor or a lawyer."

"Forever an intern, never a physician? And straight as well, right?"

"Took the words right out of my mouth."

The waiter approached and they ordered. They feasted on salad and steamers and freshly baked sourdough bread. After dinner they shared a piece of pecan pie and sipped Amaretto on the rocks, and Tom explained, to Mitch's question, exactly what it was he did for Zena Oluspenskaya. His lie was convincing. Mitch said, "That sounds like the easiest job in the world. What do you do when the actual showing's on?"

"Hang around. I go to New York mostly, the garment center."

"Design them in Paris, cut them in New York, I know." Tom suddenly feared Mitch was secretly a couturier and was going to blow holes in his story. But Mitch's words soon put him at ease. "I had an uncle Solomon who worked in the garment district his whole life. Dressed like a bum, but he knew fashion. We used to say he was born with a thimble on his thumb."

Tom smiled. "I don't know much about the business. It's not my job. I play while I'm there, visit with Rachel, go dancing and boogie all night. Then I make sure the clothes are back in the trunks and I bring them home."

"Who's Rachel?"

"My best friend in the world. My pal, my confessor, my surrogate mama, my—" He almost said "lover," but stopped himself. "—ice skating partner. We met skating at Rock Center."

"She's not another Chloe, is she?"

Tom laughed. "You don't mention them in the same breath. Rachel is an incredible woman, self-sufficient and together, with the most amazing mind I've ever known. She's always so right about things. She helps me a lot, Mitch. I can tell her anything and she doesn't judge, she just listens, and gives good wise advice only when I ask. She's quite a lady."

"You're quite a guy."

Tom smiled. "Thanks."

"Do you ever go to bars?"

"No. Do you?"

Mitch shook his head. "The few I've been in depress me. And I'm always worried because the office is super-straight, and there's that image thing to think about."

Tom didn't want to get into a discussion of *that*. He knew it could lead to an argument. So he said, "Thanks for the dinner. The clams were super."

"Let's go walk by the water," Mitch suggested.

"Okay."

They stood on the pier overlooking the ocean. The magical lights from the sweeping curve of Malibu reflected on the enormous pool of the Pacific. In the center of the still sky was a full moon. "The kind of night," Mitch said, "Cole Porter would have put into a song."

"Romantic?" Tom asked.

Mitch took his hand. "Very. Listen, let's go up to my favorite place on the ocean, Coral Beach. I want to share it with you."

They drove north on Webb Way, past the beach houses, and stopped where the buildings ended. The breeze cut through them. "It's always windy in this cove," Mitch explained. He zipped his jacket up, and Tom did likewise, and then, hand in hand, they climbed down the path leading to the sand.

When they were down there, Tom realized why Mitch loved the spot so. It was a world all its own, with only the soft roar of waves pounding against the wet sand. No reflecting pool here; the ocean was booming, calling, compelling. The highway was above them. There wasn't another person in sight. The deserted lifeguard stand on which they sat seemed made for them, a perfect spot to watch the moon over the water, to be close to one another and the wonder of nature, completely alone on the edge of the world.

"There's something awesome in being on the last few feet of land, at the edge of the map," Mitch said. "It seems the farthest away from life I can get. My troubles all melt into the waves. I used to sit here all alone and wonder when some beautiful man would come up from the sea and reach out to me . . . I'd be riding a great white horse along the shore and he would lure me into the water and I'd know a new life."

"I felt like that one winter in Chicago. I walked down by the lakefront and the wind whipped the water into my face and snow was blowing and I was soaked and freezing and it was the most exhilarating feeling. I was the only person in the world. I was special. And I thought, how easy it would be to walk out on the ice and drop through, and no one would really care, it wouldn't make a dent in what was going on back in the real world across Michigan Avenue. Fatalistic, huh?"

"Existential." Mitch put his arm around Tom. "But I'd care."

"Really?"

"Are you warm enough?" He pulled him to him so Tom's head rested on his shoulder.

"Yes."

There was a pause. They both looked out at the dark waves. Then Mitch whispered, "Tom, I'm very much in love with you. I can't help it."

"Do you want to?"

"Help it? No. But it's hard for me." He sat up straight, and Tom lifted his head and listened to him. "See, I talked myself into conforming long ago. I was supposed to fall in love with a nice Jewish girl and have nice Jewish children and lead a nice Kosher life. *Fegalim* had nothing to do with my frame of reference, even though I knew I was one. But I subverted it. I said I'd wait a while, after the kids got older, then I'd have some tricks on the side. And now I'm sitting on a beach in the middle of winter with my arm around someone who has a cock and balls like I do and all the promises I made to myself are vanishing. I feel my heart cracking in two over you. God, but I love you. I love the smell of you, the look of you. Your hair is cold. . ." He held Tom's head in both hands.

"But what about Jeremy? Aren't you in love with him?"

Mitch looked perplexed. "What?"

"You even said it was *his* Christmas tree. You must have been—"

Mitch shook his head and tried to keep from bursting into laughter. He slapped his hand on the railing of the lifeguard stand and howled. "Oh, Jesus, Tom, no wonder you frowned every time I said his name. Oh, it's too funny to . . . I never even. . . !"

Tom pulled away, hurt. "What the fuck are you laughing about?"

"Jeremy is six years old."

"What?"

"He's my son, Tom. Jeremy's my son."

Tom closed his eyes and leaned back against the railing. "Holy shit." He'd never felt like such a fool in his life.

"And Christine's my daughter, she's two. Paula is the girl I married almost seven years ago, when I convinced myself the thing to do was lead a straight life."

"Married? To a real woman?" Tom sounded as though it could not be possible.

"It's still done, you know."

"It . . . it just knocks me out. Shit, I never even looked—" He glanced to Mitch's hand and saw the wedding band. "Boy, am I dense."

"The question is, how do you feel about it?"

Tom shook his head. "That's a loaded one." He hesitated, then: "You want to know? Well, right away, I'm thinking it gives her power over me, being tied to you that way—would you choose to fuck me before her? —the bitch, how can you compete with a cunt? Oh, shit, I'm sorry. I'm being a jealous fag."

"It would throw me for a loop too," Mitch assured him. "But don't hate her, Tom. She's a wonderful person. I was really afraid to tell you. I thought I'd be running the risk of losing you. I was right, from the look on your face."

"No, hey, I just didn't expect it. I think it's a relief. See, I can't compete and won't even try. With another guy, that's *all* I'd be doing." Tom suddenly laughed at himself. "God, I've been jealous of a six-year-old."

"You should be. I love him a lot."

"I thought he was your lover. I really did."

"I've never had a lover," Mitch said, taking his hand, "only a wife, and that's not the same thing. I haven't had a guy since we were married. Well, once, with a guy on campus the last year of law school, but I was so drunk I hardly remember it. You're the first. You're pretty special just for that reason."

Tom looked into his eyes. "Mitch, I love you too. I feel so childish all of a sudden, but relieved, really relieved of all the competition I thought I was going to have to face."

"You thought a wife and two kids weren't *competition*?" Rachel exclaimed.

"They're not. And they won't be. We've been together a while now and it doesn't take anything away from what he gives me."

"You read that line in some hip self-help book?" She stopped walking and leaned against a post. "Have you still not told him?"

"No."

"You say you're madly in love with him, and you go on letting him think you're being faithful to him? That's abhorrent."

"Hell, no one made promises of fidelity. Should I expect him not to sleep with Paula? It doesn't bother me."

"But what if he got it on with another man?"

"Why do we always get into these talks right after I get off a plane and I'm so tired?"

"It's the only time when you're susceptible. Come on, answer me."

"Well . . . that might bother me."

"And you don't think he believes you're being faithful to him? Does he know about me?"

"Yes." That was true.

"Does he know we make love?"

"Yes." That was *not* true.

"Does it bother him?"

"No. He's mature. What should I do, be celibate in New York? Anyhow, I met you long before he came into my life. I'm not going to change something I find very satisfying."

"What about the trick you were with last time? The one you're probably seeing tomorrow?"

"Business. I don't even think of it as sex."

"That's the point I'm making. *You* don't consider it sex, but you're afraid he might. Don't you realize it's what *he* thinks that counts? Don't you believe that if he loves you enough, he will accept anything, that he'll at least try to understand? If he's as good and thoughtful and smart as you say he is, he's going to respect your truthfulness more than he'll feel jealous. And even if he finds it difficult, you can work it out. He's bound to find out anyway. I did. He may know already and he's just giving you time to bring yourself to tell him."

"I will when the right time comes. I just don't know if he can accept it as easily as you or I can."

"As *you* can!" She whirled around and took a deep breath. "You're a mass of contradictions. Haven't you admitted to me that you hate it, that you can't stand that part of your life? If you can't accept it, how can he?"

He looked at her for a moment, and then walked on up the street. She followed. She put her arm in his and finally he leaned on her shoulder. "Tommy, cat, I'm only trying to help you make that terrible transition from boy to man. It's because I care. This is the perfect time to do it, with your feelings for this man, in this relationship with him. Don't you owe *yourself* some honesty, as well as him? He told you about his wife and children. That took real guts. A lot of guys don't want to be lovers with a man with a family and a straight business life because, face the music or not, that's one hell of a major stone in the path of an affair, and it will one day present some kind of problem for you, even if it isn't doing so right now."

He still said nothing. She kissed him on the forehead as they stood on the curb, waiting for the traffic to pass. "I want you to grow up to be a big, strong tom, not a kitten all your life."

"It isn't easy."

"I know, I know. But give it a try. If you can't do it for yourself or for him, do it for me. I don't ask much of you, but I'm asking this time. *Do it for me.*"

It finally got to be too cold for them. They walked back to the car with their arms around one another. Mitch stopped at the top of the incline and kissed Tom roughly, pulled his hair, held him as if he wanted to mesh their bodies into one. Then, silently, they got into the car, and Mitch turned on the heat, slipped a tape into the player, and headed back to town.

Streisand sang and Tom closed his eyes and put his head back. Mitch undid Tom's zipper, driving with one hand on the wheel. He eased Tom's penis out and held it. It did not grow. It was already stiff. And it stayed that way all the way home.

They were in bed faster than they could park the car. They did not make love as furiously this time, perhaps because they were secure there would definitely be a next time, this wonder would would not disappear like some mirage. The love had been verbalized, and they didn't have to show it by physically assaulting each other.

It was not gentle, however; it was strong and intensely male and whole, filled with ecstasy that only manifests itself when you are with the one person you feel more complete with than anyone in the entire world. The power was overwhelming, as if a force over which they had no control lifted them into another consciousness, and they were filled with joy.

They climaxed and lay still. The bedcovers were wet with perspiration and sperm. Tom put his head on Mitch's chest. "With other guys," he said softly, "I'm always the one who lies there and puts my arms out and lets the other guy lay on my chest. They always curl up against me. But with you, I like putting my head here and feeling you breathe with your arms around me."

"You're incredible. You say what you think."

"Know what? I'm really happy that's Jeremy's Christmas tree out there on the patio. I wanted to hack it down when I thought he was your lover."

"Would you be *that* jealous?"

"No. Not after a while. Early on is the time people get really crazy, I think. Because there's so much to lose, so much you don't know."

"You won't lose me."

"Can I meet him sometime?"

"Jeremy? Sure. He'd take to you like mad. He says he wants to grow up to be a Texas Ranger. This week at least. Paula's mother took him to see the Rose Parade and he saw a float with Texas Rangers on it and he's hooked. He's a cowboy nut. I told him you were a real one, from Texas."

"You told him about me?"

"Well, I didn't tell him I suck your cock, but yes, I told him about you. Paula too. She understands I need to have friends just the way she has girlfriends, pals. We can't limit ourselves to each other."

"Does she know about you?"

"No. Absolutely not."

"What would she do if she found out?"

He didn't answer right away. He thought about it. "I'm not really certain. I don't think we could be together any longer if that happened. She wouldn't be able to accept it."

"So she should never know."

Mitch smiled at him. If things could forever be that simple. "Listen, I have to go. Walk me out."

Tom put on jeans and a jacket, and walked him to the car. "Thank you for a beautiful night."

"I'll never forget it." Mitch got in and rolled down the window as he started the car. "Tell me something. You're happy, you have a terrific place to live, a job you like, your piano, everything you seem to want. Now you have me too. And I have you. But if you had your choice of one thing that's missing in your life, what would it be? One thing in all the world?"

"A pasta machine. No. A long roll of postage stamps so I wouldn't have to stand in those hideous lines with all the derelicts at the post office every time I run out, because I hate that zoo more than any place on earth. Nah. I'd want a cat. I've *always* wanted a cat of my own."

"When I first came over here last week, you said cats are what your life is all about."

"And the lack of one too. Rachel says it's obscene that I don't have one."

"You know what I'd like?"

"What?"

"To be free to run off to some mountaintop with you for the rest of my life."

"I'll settle for a weekend trip to the foothills."

Mitch held out his hand. "Deal." Tom took his hand. "I love you, baby. Now get your ass in there because you're freezing."

" 'Bye," Tom said, teeth indeed chattering.

Mitch sped away.

The next afternoon, Tom and Kevin drove to Westwood in the MG. Kevin was looking at a Los Angeles street map, trying to locate the street on which Mitchell Birney & Family lived. Tom had talked to Kevin about it all night, and had come to the conclusion that Mitchell probably didn't have a wife at all, it was just a way of covering up his lover. Kevin told him he was being ridiculous and insecure and reacting like a stupid jerk, but it was understandable under the circumstances. So Tom had dragged Kevin along for a look into the private life of the man he loved.

"Turn right at the next corner," Kevin said.

Tom did. "Perfect, just perfect, nice little houses all cramped in next to each other, so goddamn suburban."

"So maybe they don't like apartments. What's *wrong* with you? Okay, slow down, it should be that . . . that house over there, the cream-colored one. Stop, yeah, that's it."

Tom pulled over. The house was pleasant enough, small and well-kept, a big palm tree towering over the front walk. The garage door was open and he saw the small hatchback which had delivered the Christmas tree to the patio. It was the right place all right. "Jeremy is probably a twenty-two year old blond dishrag who stays home all day, doing the laundry and clipping coupons."

Kevin snickered. "You amaze me. Sure he is. Of course he is. As opposed to a *twenty-four year old one such as yourself.*"

"Fuck off."

"What are we gonna do?" Kevin asked. "Sit here and keep a vigil?"

"I just want to see if anyone comes or goes. It's almost three. If he has kids they should be out playing at this time. All kids play in the streets after three o'clock."

Kevin laughed, not really sure whether or not his friend was kidding—he seemed so obsessed with knowing. He'd tried to tell Tom to trust Mitchell, surprised he didn't because he had sworn true love and devotion to him. But then, as Tom said, if he would lie to Mitch about his hustling, why wouldn't Mitch lie to him about his wife? It made some kind of silly homosexual sense, the kind of gay bar menatality Kevin found so loathsome. He racked this escapade up to Tom's temporary insanity due to cupid's arrow up his ass.

They sat there for fifteen minutes, and then it happened. A car drove up, a station wagon, stopped, and out jumped a little boy of about six or seven. He dashed across the yard and called out to someone, and the door opened. The woman came out and waved to the other mother driving the station wagon, calling, reminding her not to forget the bake sale on Sunday, and the station wagon drove away.

Tom sat mesmerized. There she was, in a skirt and blouse and apron, her hair pulled back in a scarf, looking like the typical young housewife, her complexion light and her skin dull, as if she hated the sun and had hid from it most of her life. But she was pretty, he could see that clearly from the car, and the little boy, the happy looking little kid who was jumping up and down telling her some seemingly dramatic story, looked just like her. Mrs. Birney and son. And then a little girl toddled out the door and the woman picked her up and took the boy by the hand and went back inside. The door closed.

"Seen enough?" Kevin asked sarcastically.

Tom felt like a heel. And he looked it as he slumped down in the seat.

"Some hunky lover, huh? You think her cock is bigger than yours?"

"Shut up, Kevin. I admit I was wrong. I feel like an asshole." He started the car and floored it, squealing rubber as he tore out of there. Kevin let up on him because he could see that he really was ashamed. He'd learned a lesson. And he knew he would never doubt Mitchell's word again. He didn't even bother to think about how nice it would be if Mitch could say the same for him.

The first time Mitch brought Jeremy to visit Tom, he said, "Hi, my daddy says you'll teach me how to play songs."

Tom smiled and pretended he'd never seen the kid before. Oh, he liked him right off the bat, he was Mitch's son, after all, but the fact that he looked like his mother seemed to produce some kind of absurd resentment deep inside him. "Sure will, little buddy," he answered, lifting the boy high into the air. It was hard for him to believe that he was holding his lover's flesh and blood in his hands.

"My daddy says you're his best pal. I have a best pal. He lives next door. His name is Peter."

Probably in the brick house to the right, Tom thought. "That's a good Russian name, Peter."

"I like your name," Jeremy said. "Texas Tom."

"Where'd you get that name from?"

"My dad says you're from Texas."

"Yeah, that's the truth, but I don't like to remember it. I don't like Texas much."

Jeremy pondered it. Then he announced, "Okay, I'll just call you Tom then, how's that?"

"That's me."

"I wish I was a Tom."

"Listen," Mitch said, with a laugh, "you're lucky we didn't just give you a number and let you choose a name when you got to be twenty-one. What if we called you Four-Seven-Nine all the time?" Jeremy giggled. "You stick with Jeremy."

Jeremy contemplated what he'd said. "Okay, daddy, but if I wanna change it to Tom when I grow up, I get to do that. I have the option to do that."

"Where the hell did a four-year-old learn a word like *option*?" Tom asked, startled. What was this, some precocious genius?

"Paula and I were arguing about it yesterday. She was reading a book—it was written by that woman whose whole family was on TV on PSB some years back. . ."

"Pat Loud."

"Yes. And Paula said she agreed with her that you have to leave yourself some options in life and we got into a hassle about what those options should be. Jeremy has big ears."

"That's terrific. He's adorable."

"He's a good kid. I love him a lot. It meant a lot for you to meet him and know him." And they turned to find him climbing one of the Countess' trees.

After that, Mitch brought Jeremy by often. On sunny days when nothing was happening in the Countess' yard, they played catch or chased each other around the pool. One Saturday Tom took him to the movies while Mitch worked on research for a case. Another time Tom taught Jeremy how to make a pizza, which ended up pretty much on the floor. And a week after that, Mitch told Tom he had to go to Lake Tahoe for business reasons and Paula wanted to go with him. Tom felt a little disappointed that he wasn't going to be the one going off to that mountain cabin after all, but when Mitch told him Jeremy didn't want to go to Paula's parents' house, he was very happy to invite Jeremy to stay with "Uncle Tom".

Mitch said it was fine. "Paula says so too. In fact, she keeps asking when she's going to meet the great guy Jeremy keeps talking about."

"Oh." Tom felt his throat suddenly go dry.

"It's inevitable, Tom. You can't avoid her."

"Does she know, does she sense?"

"No. Not at all. There's no reason in the world to tell her. If it were causing problems, then I would. She just thinks you're a friend I've come to know from the gym."

"The gym?"

"You're muscular enough to pass. Say we play tennis together. Listen, I'm in a hurry. You sure it's okay?"

"Great. I love that little creep."

"I'll talk to you tonight then. 'Bye, baby."

And so Tom got Jeremy on Friday night. He met Paula at the same time, when they dropped the boy off. She was much prettier than he'd been able to tell from the car. Her hair was still tied back. She looked healthy, strong, an outdoors-type. Mitch had told him her two passions in life were skiing and poetry. He could picture her on the slopes in a bright red outfit, her long hair blowing in the wind around big sunglasses, Jackie O style, curling up at night by the fire reading Erica Jong and Rod McKuen, while Mitch poked his head through law briefs. Tom wondered what had been the attraction —then he knew. It must have been physical; they did make an attractive couple.

And the thought made him happy and sickened him. She had a part of Mitch that he'd never have, and he had a part she would never know. They both were losing at one of the greatest gains in the world. Neither could really ever win, but did it matter? He thought the most important factor was whether or not either one or both of them could go on forever being satisfied with the part they had.

To dwell on that would make for a lousy time for Jeremy, and Tom wanted it to be the boy's best weekend ever. And it was. They went to the circus and had big greasy hamburgers and shakes and watched monster movies in bed. Jeremy slept there, curled up next to his teddy bear, while Tom moved to the couch. On Sunday morning, After Jeremy had jumped on Tom's head and dragged him by one foot from the couch, they watched cartoons and then went to the beach to throw stones in the water and make a sand castle. It collapsed before they were finished, but it had been fun. They walked on Santa Monica pier and ate corn dogs on a stick and watched the men fishing. Then they drove back to the house and baked cupcakes together, after Jeremy won a wrestling match on the living room floor.

Kevin called and Tom told him about their weekend and Kevin told him he wanted to puke. They argued. "What are you doing playing surrogate mother?" Kevin asked.

"What?"

"Tom, you're only doing this because in your mind you're competing with her, and you hope Mitch will see you do just as good a job."

"Bullshit, Kevin!"

"What's all this gook about monster movies in bed together? Such buddies. I never heard you say you even liked children. And I don't believe you like this one. You don't care about him, you're only showing off."

"I'm not going to listen to this. And he's still awake and I don't want him to have to hear this."

"Tom, wait a minute, don't hang up. Listen, I'm saying what I think simply because I don't want to see you fuck it all up with Mitch. Don't pretend you're two daddies when you're really assuming the role of the mother here. If you want that role now and then, great.

But do it because you really want it, not because you want to show him you're as good as she is."

"I'm not. I'm really not. I honestly love the little creep. I had a great weekend with him. Jesus, Kevin, do you have to analyze my every move? Can't I just do something once for the fun of it."

Kevin sighed. "Okay, maybe I'm wrong. I have personal motives you wouldn't understand. Maybe I'm a little ticked I didn't see you all weekend. I don't know. You told me I had to learn to assert myself. I'm asserting. I'm sorry."

"Christ. I created a monster."

Jeremy was sound asleep when Mitch came for him just before midnight. Tom watched him scoop his son into his arms and carry him out the door without even waking him. Tom brought out the teddy bear and kissed the father goodbye.

Then he went back into the house, smoked some dope, and wrote to Rachel, letting loose, telling her all kinds of things he'd never told anyone. His desire to have a son someday. The loss he felt in never having had a father, how spending time with Jeremy filled some of that void in reverse. How chilling and awesome it was to see Mitchell holding his kid, his child, part of himself Tom fantasized the three of them living together on that mythical mountaintop forever. He didn't know how he felt about Paula. He wondered if she hadn't sized up the situation already. *There is something between us, it's in the air, no matter what we do to hide it,* he wrote. *I guess I now understand what they mean when they say there is electricity between lovers.*

But he also wrote, *I think I'm facing myself for once. You told me not to deny the basic femininity of my nature, that it was one of my attributes. I think it's coming out with Mitch's son. Kevin got on my case about it, because I wouldn't admit it. But I do. It's true. I'm playing mother. I like having a kid.*

She wrote back, *Get yourself a cat instead.*

Then, a week later, he got three surprise visitors. It was Sunday afternoon and he was supposed to be in New York but he had caught a cold which had become the flu, and he'd been in bed for three days. Madame Platychivnik brought chicken soup. Kevin took his temperature. Rachel was disappointed, for she had looked forward to seeing him, but she was concerned about his health. The Countess was raving that she had to send another boy to New York and how could he do this to her because the john didn't take to replacements. Tom felt so lousy, he didn't really care what anyone was thinking.

Not until Sunday afternoon. There was a knock at the door. He thought it was Sandy, who was living in California now. She'd called and told him she was going to bring over some herbal drink Mama Chloe always made when she was sick. He asked her not to drag her sister over, please, and she promised. When the bell rang, he called out to come in, and Mitch surprisingly appeared in the doorway. "You decent?"

"Under these blankets rests a dead body wrapped in pajamas. Sexy, huh?"

"You in pajamas? Where'd you get them?"

"You won't believe it, but Madame Platychivnik brought them over. I think they belonged to her late husband, Ivan the Terrible. You alone?" He sensed there was someone in the next room.

"Nope. You have a visitor."

"Uncle Tom?" The voice came through the fireplace.

"You shouldn't have brought him," Tom said. "I don't want him getting sick. . ." But before he could protest too much, Jeremy was in the room. He had something inside his jacket. "Hi, Jer," Tom said, "and don't you come any closer or you'll catch the bubonic plague."

"I brought a present to make you feel better."

"Huh?"

Then a fourth voice was heard. It was a distinct *meow*.

Tom's eyes widened. *It couldn't be!* Little Jeremy opened his jacket and a kitten jumped out, right onto the bed. It sniffed around a little, checking things out, and then gave its coat a few licks to be presentable for its new master. Then it walked up to Tom's chest, plunked itself down and purred like a motorboat.

"Daddy says we should call him *Blizzard*. But you can change his name if you want. He's six-months-old. My friend Peter's cat had cats. Her name is Mabel. This guy is the prettiest one. I asked for him for you."

"Oh, God," Tom sighed, looking into the green eyes of the happy kitten. He was the most wonderful cat he'd ever laid eyes on. Black with one white paw, and a patch of white on his face, between his eyes and on his nose. A shining piece of black coal on which someone had dropped a snowball. Blizzard was the perfect name. "I don't know what to say," Tom whispered.

Jeremy said, "I hope you like him. We got a litter box and food bowls in the car. I'll get them, daddy." And he dashed out.

Mitch sat on the bed and stroked the cat. "He's you, you know. You said you wanted a cat and I knew this was the right one because Jeremy seemed to sense it. He's going to be the tomcat you wanted with Chloe."

"I take it you're sure he's a male." Tom rubbed his nose against the cold of the kitten's.

"Look. He loves you already. He's as healthy as they come and he's had his shots and he should be neutered soon and he's in need of a good home."

"He's got it." Tom kissed the kitten and licked his nose. Blizzard licked him back, then jumped off the bed to start getting the feel of his new abode. Jeremy ran back in and told them the box was in the bathroom and the bowl of water in the kitchen and some dry food was already in the other bowl, so Tom didn't have to worry.

"Thanks, Jer."

"Do you really like him, Uncle Tom?"

Tom fought back tears. "You little creep, are you kidding? I love him almost more than you!"

They left and about half an hour later, after Tom listened to paws getting to know the lay of the land—piano keys being struck, things rattling in the kitchen, the thump of little feet in the bathtub—Blizzard came back in and jumped up on the bed again. He seemed pleased. He deemed it a suitable place for him to live. He leaped over Tom's head and checked out the sight from the window. Lots of trees, little animals to chase, lizards and birds and moths. Maybe even some mousies. It would be just fine.

Then he curled up by Tom again and he lay there petting him, staring at the precious, beautiful animal. He felt very loved. And the cat would feel just as loved. It had finally happened—he had his own cat. All his life he'd wanted one. The cat finally had a cat.

The flu miraculously disappeared that night, and he was down on the floor in front of the fire playing with a crunched up piece of cellophane and his new roommate, a kitten named Blizzard.

FOURTEEN

The only thing to mar Tom's happiness and anticipation with Mitch was something that occurred between
him and Rachel, something that left a scar that would
never fade even though they pretended otherwise. It
began with a phone call.

"Tommy?"

"Rachel?"

"Oh, Tom, you're finally there."

He looked at the clock. Almost three. Six New York
time. He and Kevin had gone to Studio One to see
Charles Pierce and then to a restaurant for sandwiches.
He'd just gotten in. "Rachel, what's wrong?" He could
hear the terror in her voice.

"Barry. My son is missing."

"Missing?"

"He went on a camping trip in the mountains. They're
missing, two others from school and the instructor. Oh,
Tommy they've been lost out in the snow for two days
and—"

"Rachel, my God."

"—they told me to stay here because there's nothing
I can do, but I feel so helpless." She started to cry. He'd
never heard her cry before. "Oh, Tom, I need you so
badly."

171

"I'm coming. I'll get on the first plane. I love you."

"I know you do, Tommy."

"I'm coming."

But he never went.

She called him twenty minutes later. He hadn't yet packed his suitcase and he was drinking a cup of tea. He was thinking about his date with Mitch the next night, contemplating putting off the flight until at least after that. But she rescued him—temporarily—from any guilt he might feel by calling to tell her that, or to lie to her that something earth-shattering had come up and he'd be there in two days—but what could shatter the earth more than the pain of not knowing what has happened to your only child?

"Tom," she said, "they called from the school and told me they think it's a good idea if we—the other parents as well—go down to the resort where they were camped. I'm leaving in a few minutes."

"Where? I didn't even ask where Barry had gone."

"To the Adirondacks. They're flying us to Mount Marcy. At first, they said not to come, there was nothing we could do, there was a big snowstorm. But they just called me. It's better if we're there. I feel so helpless here."

"Do you want me to meet you there?"

"I don't . . . I don't know. I must go. I'll call you from there. Say a prayer." She hung up.

He did; he walked up the canyon and said a prayer and walked back down and waited for the phone to ring. Kevin joined him and they played canasta and cribbage and the phone did not ring until late in the afternoon.

Rachel was beside herself. Barry and his companions had set out for an overnight in the snow. The instructor was excellent, and had done such easy expeditions hundreds of times in the past, but when they did not return after an entire day, a search party went out; there was no trace of the four campers. They had food only for two days. And a blizzard was raging.

Tom said he would come, but he offered knowing she would ask him not to. She told him it was crazy there, people confused and hurt, the other parents in shock, authorities questioning them, she needed some rest and wanted to be alone. They would find him before Tom could even get there. She would call back when that happened. Yes, it would be soon, she was sure. He told her he was too, and promised to call and check if he didn't hear from her.

He didn't. And he didn't call right away. He had to figure things out in his mind first. Damn. She didn't deserve it. Why was it the people who seemed not to deserve it were always the ones who got the shaft? Why did the bad guys win so often?

Kevin left and Tom took off his clothes and dumped them into the closet. He shut off the lights and drank hot tea in the dark, walking around the house, looking out the windows at another still, cold night. He knew he needed sleep, he hadn't had any for over twenty-four hours. He finally got into bed and pulled the quilt to his chin. He thought of Rachel having Barry back home with him tucked in his bed in his room. Rachel with the air conditioner and a bed twice the size of his and the noise of the fan and the shelter of her arms and the gentle warmth of her body. . . .

He did not sleep well. He kept thinking of her, and thinking of himself as well. She was alone, terribly alone in a strange and horrifying situation. He was just the same as always, maybe better. She needed him—despite her denials—and he should be going to her and he knew it.

But he was selfish. He had a date the next day with Mitchell, and he didn't want to miss it, not for anything in the world. Not even for Rachel and her honest, loving need. Oh, he ached for her, he felt his heart breaking for her, but not enough to cancel a date with Mitch, and not enough to make him face the question of whether or not he could adequately deal with someone else's trauma.

He called her and there was no news. She told him she had finally gotten some sleep and didn't want to talk. He promised he'd fly up the next day, after he saw Mitch, and be with her. She told him she'd just gotten off the phone with Barry's father and it had been a difficult conversation and she was worn out emotionally and physically and she would talk to him in the morning, or before if she knew something.

All through the week, he called several times with concern, but also with excuses. Mitchell on Saturday. A headache on Sunday. Monday brought an audition and he did well and another was scheduled for Wednesday. It was for a pianist to fill in for someone in an orchestra on a TV game show for a week, but it could be the stepping stone to more. He would fly up on Thursday. By Wednesday night she was beside herself with grief—anxious hope had changed to fear to an almost numbing inevitability—and weeping so hard he could not even understand her. He hated himself for not being there. But he justified it by asking: what could he have done?

And then the call came that same Wednesday night. "Oh, Tommy, they found him . . . they *found* him!"

"Oh, God, how, where?"

"He's all right, he's in the hospital here, he's got frostbite and he hasn't eaten much and exposure and—oh, God, he and little Greg Kaplan, they made a sled from bark to bring the body back—"

"Body? What body? Who?"

"The instructor—oh, Tommy, I'll tell you everything later, he's all right, I just wanted you to know." And she hung up.

They talked about it only once after that, several days later when he called her to find out why she hadn't been in touch. "What did you want me to do," she asked, "beg you to come?" He'd told her he hadn't been sure she needed him, that he'd been unable to "deal" with it. "You really don't know me at all, not at all, Tommy."

"I'm sorry. I really am. I feel terrible."

"You should. When are you going to understand the needs of the people you say you love. Your not being able to deal with it should not be the overriding concern; your assessment of the other person's problem and need should be the important thing. I'm not blaming you, I'm not scolding you. It's over and done with. I've never known such fear in my life, you can't imagine what it is like to think you've lost your only child. I needed your arms around me to help out."

Tears welled up in his eyes. "I'm sorry, I'm so sorry."

"It's all right. I do understand. I'm just asking you to try, with everyone you care about, with Mitchell especially right now, to put their needs up high on your list of priorities. And sometimes that means above your own."

"It's hard."

"Of course it's hard. But the rewards are simply unlike any others."

"Rachel, you've never really told me what happened. I really want to know."

"No you don't. You feel you're expected to ask me because you feel guilty for having been so selfish."

Silence. He didn't know what to say.

She continued. "Oh, what the hell? The instructor fell while climbing and could not continue. He died and the boys holed up in a cave for two days while the snow raged until they could make a kind of sled to bring him down and hopefully be rescued. So that's the story, but don't pretend to 'ooh' and 'ah' because sometimes I don't think anyone's suffering penetrates your thick skin. I really don't care to talk to you anymore." And she hung up.

"I'm sorry," he said. A day later, he was standing on

the stoop of her apartment building as she walked up carrying two bags of groceries. "I can't stand it. I'm sorry. Give me a chance."

She eyed him without visible emotion for a moment, and then broke into a smile. "Scrappy little cat, hasn't anybody fed you lately? Come on in and I'll fatten you up."

"I'm forgiven?"

"Only if you carry these damned things." She handed him the bags and then kissed him on the cheek.

They went inside, but the cleaning lady was scouring the kitchen and the plumber was working on a drip inside a wall in the dining room, so they went to Kegon, their favorite Japanese restaurant. And before the green tea was poured, Tom began to tell her about Mitchell. "We got to know each other, just like this, over fish."

Rachel smiled. "Only it was cooked."

"Right." Tom gulped down a chunk of sushi.

"Oh, Tommy, you're so young sometimes."

"Yeah?"

"You're panting like a schoolgirl. Not that it's unhealthy, but it is amusing. Did you tell him what you do for a living?"

His eyes grew wide. "You kidding? He'd shit."

"Is he living in the 1950's perhaps?"

"A little."

"But you said that night on the beach you told each other all about your lives."

"I gave him an abridged version."

"You lied, in other words."

He averted his eyes and said nothing.

"Tommy, listen to me a minute," Rachel said. "I once asked how was it that you got to New York all the time, and you recited the right-hand-man speech for Madame Oluspenskaya. Okay, it made sense, you could be working for Halston just as easily, accompanying designer originals *is* a job. But you're not a very good liar. You started to tell me about a typical day's work, and it was clear you didn't know the first thing about the rag trade."

"But she *has* two guys who do just that for her."

"So what? Look, this is Rachel you're talking to, not Chloe or the landlord or a bank officer you want to con. The only thing I expect of you is honesty. I've had to pull it out of you, but lately you've been offering it up front. It's getting easier with me, isn't it?"

"Yes."

"Well, so why not with Mitchell? Doesn't he deserve at least that much?"

"You *care* about him?" He was astonished. "I thought you'd be jealous."

"Why? I'm sure of us. He isn't a threat to me. If he makes you happen, I love the guy. But don't play games with him, Tom."

He tried to explain. "I was . . . scared. I thought he'd think less of me. But I know what you're getting at. Hustling itself, right? I'm always saying it's a good thing and doesn't harm anyone and all that shit. And yet I'm afraid to admit I'm a hustler."

"Maybe down deep you don't really believe what you say. Maybe you really don't think it's all that respectable."

"I never said respectable." He shook his head vehemently. "No, that's not it, honest. You *do* help people, you fill a void in their lives, sometimes *save* their goddamn lives just by being there because they're so lonely. Give them a moment of tenderness and passion and it keeps them going, because they say, 'Hey, maybe I am worthy of that guy being nice to me.' It does more good than harm. But it isn't *respectable* any way you look at it, because it's sexual, and that's why Mitchell wouldn't understand."

"What is he, some kind of monk?"

"He leads a very straight life. He's not the kind of guy

to have casual sex. I mean, he's married. He doesn't fool around. It's like he's married to me too. Rachel, he just doesn't think like we do."

"What makes you so sure? For all you know, he could be going to the baths every night. Maybe he hangs out in public johns on his lunch hours."

Tom was angry and silent. He shoved his tempura around the plate. His eyes finally grew red, as if the time bomb were slowly ticking away. Finally he blurted out, "I'm a goddamn good hustler. But that's like saying Julia Child is a good customer at McDonalds. Think what a good pianist I could be. Or what a good composer."

"Then why aren't you?" she snapped.

"I don't know. It just hasn't happened yet. Speaking of that, did you mention me to Jarvis?"

"Don't change the subject."

"I'm not. You promised," he whined.

"Tom, he's the president of the label, he *owns* a record company. I'm not close to him, I just can't walk in and pull up a chair and chat. When the timing is right, when he's particularly receptive, I'll do it."

"I brought you another tape."

That pleased her. "And have you sent it out to producers?"

"No. I thought I'd have better luck through you. You've got the connections."

That was precisely the kind of thinking that depressed her. "You know why it hasn't happened yet? I'll tell you. You don't want to do anything more in life right now, at least not badly enough, otherwise you'd be out fighting for it, beating the doors down with tapes and copies of songs and lots of charm. But no, you're comfortable where you are, why take chances? If you fail, blame it on Rachel's connections being lousy. You rely only on what others are willing to give you."

He pouted some more.

She took his hand. "Tommy, I'm not trying to be mean. You *are* a hustler, and I don't mean in a sexual sense. You know how to work things to your advantage. A cat is the most self-absorbed animal there is, but cats make their own way in life, and are totally self-reliant. You hustled the Countess for a house *and* a piano, my God. You hustled Chloe for a family life and used her while it suited your purpose. You're hustling me for—"

"Wait a min—"

"—for my contacts in the recording industry, and you should be doing the same with Mitch as well."

"Huh?" He was thoroughly confused.

"I'm saying you know how to get things for yourself in other ways, why don't you put some of that energy into getting your career moving? How long will you be content to sit home on your ass while everyone pimps on your behalf."

Tom got up and tossed his napkin down. "I don't have to listen to this." And he started to get up.

"Sit down," she snapped.

He looked at her, hurt and anger vying for dominance in his expression. He waited for her to go on.

"I'm only trying to encourage you, Tommy, to show you some of the potential you don't see in yourself. Sure, you have your satellites revolving around you, but they burn out eventually, you know. They've got to be moving around some strong force or they'll just fly away. You've got to believe in yourself and work as hard for yourself as the people who love you are willing to work for you."

"Now you sound like Kevin," he muttered.

"Is that so bad? My God, Tom, he seems like someone who honestly and deeply cares for you."

"But he thinks I shouldn't hustle. And I get tired of his preaching, always telling me I'm opting for the easy way out. Christ, everything I do is wrong."

"You *do* take the easy way out!"

"Sure, gang up on me," he muttered. "Kevin also bitches that I'm really not happy because I'm not doing what I was put on the earth to do, so thus I'm fooling myself pretending I'm happy. I think that's a crock. What do you say to that?"

"I say I think I could learn to love that boy."

"Let's go," he suddenly said, and was out the door before Rachel could argue. She paid the check, found him outside kicking a rolled-up newspaper in his path. He shoved his hands into his pants pockets and seemed to be seething as he walked. Rachel followed at a steady pace. "Tommy, stop acting like a child and talk to me. . ."

He whirled around. It all came out. He shouted, "I hate it! You know that? I fucking hate it! I grew up dreaming about the end of the rainbow, and I know the pot of gold isn't being a whore for the Madwoman of Bel-Air." Rachel could see the ache in the creases in his forehead. He leaned against a building. "You know how it sometimes makes me feel? Can you imagine having to go to some tract home in Pomona to screw a woman who looks like Attila the Hun while her husband in a wheelchair sits there beating his meat because he can't get it into position to fuck her anymore? And then going home and sitting down at the piano and writing a song? It's fucking *horrible!* I know I'm better than that."

The anger was there in his eyes, the pain and conflict, the unrest. She finally saw raw honesty rearing its head and wondered how long this war had been going on within him. Not for very long, she was sure; it was only recently that such questions had been brought to the surface of his conscience, prodded by his love affair with Mitchell and friendship with Kevin. "Tommy, you come from strong stock. It takes guts to do the things your mother did, just to survive on that level. I want to see you survive, and you're the only one in control, the only one who can decide to get out and do something with

your talent, or lay on your back and take fifty dollar
bills for your orgasms until your looks give out. And
then what? Take a choice: pianist or prostitute."

He didn't speak, couldn't. He pulled her to him and
held her for a moment. He was trembling and fighting
back the agony of truth. . .

And she knew he was trying.

FIFTEEN

"Yeah?" he said, picking up the phone.

"Tommmmmmcat?"

Oh no. He had a feeling it was her calling. The tone was low and dense and loaded with self-pity and Southern Comfort. "Okay, Chloe, now what's wrong?"

"It's that fucking bitch Citronella." She was screaming at the top of her lungs now. He held the phone a foot from his ear. "Nobody's gonna knock my talent, Tomcat. Nobody, especially that bitch who can't even tie her fucking shoe laces without consulting a guide book on how to do it first. I'm gonna kill her!"

"That's a switch. You're always trying to kill yourself."

"How could she do that to me?"

"Do what to you?"

"I'm in the kitchen, right? In our new apartment. Now, I admit I'm not the greatest cook in the world, but I'm better than her, she can't even pour salt. So I'm in the kitchen and I made this big pot of stuff, right, and I cooked over that goddamn stove—almost burned my tits off—for about three hours, peeling fucking potatoes and watching a timer and all that, and she sits herself down at the table and asks me how come there's no garlic bread. No garlic bread! I fix her a fucking feast and she can't even thank me, she wants garlic bread. She won't eat 'cause there's no garlic bread and then I got so fucking mad, Tomcat, I threw the whole pot against the wall and the cats ate it all off the floor." She started to cry. "Oh, Tomcat, I need to get out of here, I need some air, I need to get away from that dike bitch before I kill her. I shoulda dumped the pot over her dumb fat head. Oh, Tomcat, come get me. Let's go for a ride."

"Chloe, listen, I can't come over now. . ."

"Well, shit, man! You got time for my sister and you got time for your fuckin' tricks but you don't have time for me. *Meeeeeeee! Chloe!* You were gonna marry me, remember? Tomcat, we're one, we're parts of the same person. Why are you throwing it all away?"

"The only one who's thrown anything away is you with the stew or whatever it was you made."

"Spaghetti."

"With potatoes?"

"It's a new kind."

"Anyhow, what's this got to do with knocking your talent?"

She settled down a bit. "After the bitch went upstairs —I chased her up with the rabbit ears from the TV set —she screamed at me that I would never be a filmmaker and the play I'm directing is gonna close before it opens and I'm a lousy actress. I'm a fucking great actress, Tomcat, you know that." It was less a statement of fact as it was a plea for reassurance.

"Yes, you're a great actress, Chloe."

"Tomcat, we're losing it, man. We're losing it all fast."

"Chloe, you can't expect me to . . . you can't hold onto every moment."

"Fuck, man, I'm dying here, I'm really *dying* here and I need help! I got no money, no food, the cats have to eat, the show is a mess 'cause I got this insane actress in the part I should be playing and she's not taking direction, she thinks she's Sarah Bernhardt, the bitch. And then there's that little dyke upstairs and you're so far from my energy field now—"

"Chloe, what are you really asking for?"

"Could you spare twenty bucks?"

"Christ."

"I need some bread, man. I need food."

"The last time I gave you money for food you spent it on pills and liquor. No more. I'll take you out to dinner, so I can see you get some nutrition, but no money. How'd you make spaghetti if you don't have money for food?"

"Sandy gave me a few bucks. Honey, you don't know what it's like being broke. Broke, fucking broke. I was eating cat food last week." She sighed and sounded forlorn. "Oh, Tomcat, where did it all go? Remember how we read together? We can't even talk now. I want to be back at Dan and Larry's. I want Ophelia back. I want my life! Someone stole my goddamn *life* when I wasn't looking! Just like Janis, they got her life too."

"Chloe, I'm sorry, I gotta go." He hung up. Then he lifted the phone off the hook and stuck it under a pillow. He walked around the room for a while and then went outside and sat in one of the lawn chairs. It was twilight. Ten minutes that occur each night in Southern California before the sun drops into the ocean like a heated rock. It sizzles and steams and is gone. Now you see it, now you don't. Night falls like a curtain. You can blink and miss twilight.

He didn't blink. He just sat there, numb. She could still pull guilt strings in him. Why? Old time's sake? Because he loved her? Sure he had, at one time, but did he still? No, hell no, he was sure of that. He loathed her. No he didn't. He loathed her heavy phone calls which always came at the wrong moment. He hated her helplessness and the helpless feeling she inspired in him. He pitied her because he knew she did not want to save her own life, and he couldn't help her anymore. He'd done too much already, tried too often, and had always been rejected or hurt in the end. She was beyond him now. And he felt guilty.

He picked up the garden hose, turned on the water. He took his time, watering Mitch's Christmas tree and all the other plants on the patio, his own tree, hosing down the red tile squares and wetting the ivy so it glistened. His head drifted back in time. To so many places, so many occasions, through so many emotions and incidents involving Chloe. They'd been through a lot in a short time. . . .

Tom had left Chloe in Chicago and moved to Los Angeles. She packed up and went to New York. They kept in touch through letters. In the two years that they were separated, Tom lived in a variety of places, from rented rooms to the YMCA to a big old house in Venice where some thirty or forty young people "hung out" and tossed a few bucks each into the hat when it was passed at rent time. One day, Chloe wrote him that she was leaving the Big Apple. She said she'd forgiven him for what he'd done to her—"they call it desertion, you prick!"—and she was on her way to live with him again. He didn't take her message seriously, and a few days later he got his very own apartment in Hollywood. He moved in on Sunday. Chloe showed up on his doorstep on Monday afternoon.

The landlady explained she'd been under the assumption she'd rented the place to one tenant, and one tenant alone. She threatened to toss them both out. "If you don't get rid of that . . . that feather duster," she said, in reference to the exotic bird feathers forever sticking out of Chloe's tangled hair, "I'm putting you *both* on the street." But she never went through with her threats after she saw Chloe chanting a spell against her under her balcony.

Life with Chloe was going to be different from what it

had been in Chicago; Tom figured that out the very first day. She was going through her gypsy phase (thus the feathers, trinkets around the neck, bells on her ankles) and taking to chanting mantras only she could dream up. Sitting, for instance, in the corner of the bedroom and wailing, "Fuuuuuuuuuuuuuuuuuuuuuck."

They tried to make *something* work, but nothing did. She was on the rebound from an affair with a boy in New York, an actor/singer/starving artist/jerk named Stephen Murk. She told Tom about their assorted trials and tribulations, how she washed his socks in the sink of their dump on the Lower East Side, how the refrigerator used to slide across the kitchen floor right up against the bathroom door and once pinned her on the toilet for seventeen hours, how Stephen beat her over the head with his guitar when frustrated with a song, how she slung hash or was it egg foo young for two months while Stephen used the money she made to buy dirty comic books and a Broxodent toothbrush. She described high times on acid and health foods, how they fought and later made up at Phoebe's, the gathering place of all the Chloes and Stephen Murks in New York City, to kiss and drink to the future. Tom told her it sounded pretty normal. For her. She said only one thing had been missing: sex.

He never made it with her. He made it with Jim and Bobby and Paul Vincent and some black guy who used to come by to collect the rent once a month, but he never touched her. He told her he loved her too much. She was a goodess of purity and he couldn't violate her aura. She finally told him to take a flying leap at the moon and kicked him out into the hall, guitar and all, and told him to go sit on his Broxodent toothbrush.

But he came back. She fell for him again. They tried sex. He couldn't get it up. She grew terribly frustrated and masturbated in front of him. He threw up watching. Then he left for good after she, in a rage, smashed his guitar into some fifteen hundred pieces on the rail of the fire escape. The pinging sound of the breaking strings was, she told him, the best music that had ever come out of the thing. He slugged her and when she came to, he was gone.

When she told Tom that story, she said, "Well, Tom-cat, you've heard it all. What? Tell me. What was it all about?"

He shrugged. He didn't know.

"There's gotta be *something* you can say!"

"Sounds pretty Murky to me."

She made a face and walked away. He thought she knew then it wasn't going to work with him either. He would never be as cruel as Stephen Murk, but he couldn't be the warm and loving partner he'd been to her in Chicago either. She wasn't the same person. And he had changed as well. He didn't even shoplift much anymore. The excitement was gone. He thought it just bored him; Rachel said it was a sign of growing up.

Chloe was pale. Her eyes were tired. She was drinking more than he'd guessed from her letters, which had always mentioned she and Janis had one thing in common besides talent and gravel voices: a passion for Southern Comfort whiskey. Sometimes in a glass of milk, no less. She was dropping more pills too. Speed as usual, and then half a dozen tranquilizers at a time to bring her down. She had what she called "stomach attacks" often. She said it was Mama Chloe's gall bladder trouble interrupting her energy waves. Another theory was a punishment by all black witches because she was one of the last of the Great Whites. She thought the change of climate would help; it didn't. The Witch of the East became the Witch of the West and it was the same on each coast. Tom tried to warn her that Southern Comfort and Valium and bennies made the same poisonous brew everywhere, but she wouldn't listen. The medication *helped* her stomach, she insisted.

At first, she at least *did* things. She started an experimental theatre and lived off the money her father left her. He had died never to see his strange but beloved daughter walk down the aisle of Saint Stanislaus Kostka and out the church doors as Mrs. Thomas Brassen; but he died believing it would one day happen. He suffered a heart attack shortly after Tom had formally asked for Chloe's hand in marriage, with Chloe twisting the knife in his back. He spent four months in difficult recovery, and then, on the first day back at the plant, he was run over by a fork lift. Died instantly. All that recuperation for nothing, Chloe said.

Mama Chloe wired Tom money for a plane ticket as soon as she heard of her old man's death. She wanted her "son-in-law" there at the funeral. So Tom went to Chicago, via Kansas City, where a raging blizzard grounded him for nearly a day. When he got to O'Hare Field, the funeral was already in progress and he rented a car and drove to the house, where a relative in mourning greeted him tearily with, "Oh, you must be the Tomcat." He admitted as much and asked how late he was. "They should just be leaving the church! Hurry, you'll catch them!" She told him how to get to St. Stan's.

He missed them. The church was empty but smelled of incense, tears and Mama Chloe's relatives. He got back in the car, his nose red in the freezing air. He turned onto a large thoroughfare and saw a funeral procession. He lucked out. It had to be them, right? How many funerals could you have in a Polish neighborhood on a Wednesday morning? His car didn't have the window sticker, but he tagged in at the end anyhow, lights on, head bowed in profound sympathy.

They turned into the Catholic cemetery and any worries he'd had were gone; God had been on his side. But as the cars were circling near a tent flapping in the Chicago wind, he wondered why so many of the people already getting out into the icy air were not Caucasion? It seemed strange that so many blacks would be paying their respect to a man he distinctly remembered was known for his prejudice. Chloe's father's voice rang in his head: "Only thing I can't stomach in this world is those niggers thinkin' they own the whole stinkin' place." Would so many niggers indeed mourn a man of such persuasion? Perhaps to show their glee that he was now out of the way, yes. But Tom had the sick feeling that he'd made a very big mistake.

He parked the car and got out. He started walking behind a black family, still searching desperately for a face he recognized. Then he turned his head and caught his name being called. Through the trees. Crisply. The voice of an angel, albeit an overweight one, Chloe herself. Up a little hill, around the trees, across a frozen creek the size of a healthy piss he had to run, and as he did so he thought how absurd it all was, getting the wrong funeral in the right cemetery and then over the river and through the woods, to grandmother's mausoleum we go.

They were there. Chloe on one side, Sandy on the other, each propping Mama Chloe up, all two tons of her—one ton for the body, half a ton for the hair, half a ton for the fur coat. She sobbed, "My boy! My little boy is here!" Tom kissed her and said he was, indeed, there. Better there than mourning the black man down the hill, since he at least had known Mama Chloe's husband.

The service in the little building was interesting. Tom stood next to Chloe. They whispered to one another as the friends and relatives filed in from the cold. "Where the fuck *were* you?" she muttered.

"L.A."

"I mean yesterday. Today. Were you in church?"

"Yeah. Too late."

"Jesus, Tomcat, we needed you so badly. Mama needed you."

"I'm here, dammit."

"I got a dress. A real straight people's kind of dress."

"Where is it?"

"On me."

"Where?"

"Under this coat, idiot." She nodded to a man who came up and made the Sign of the Cross near the casket.

"How are you?"

"Becoming a superstud takes time. Especially in L.A."

"What's that supposed to mean?"

He was about to tell her he'd been thinking of becoming a hustler, but he was stopped short by the entrance of two grey-faced undertakers in grey suits and grey gloves. They even had grey eyes. And a priest. A young priest. A young and handsome and very attractive priest. With big blue eyes Tom thought you could die from just looking at. He started to pray. They all bowed their collective head. Mama Chloe swooned and gasped and Sandy stuck something under her nose and then the priest continued. Everyone was looking at the floor except Tom and Chloe; they were cruising the priest.

"I know what you're thinking," she whispered.

"Shhh."

"He's mine, goddammit. He taught my sister religion in high school and I saw him first."

"What's he doing being a priest?"

"Confession can be fun."

"Oh, Jesus."

"Stop thinking about going to bed with him."

"Who, Jesus?"

"He should be marrying us. Not burying daddy."

Requiscat in pace. Amen. Heads up, then one of the grey-faced undertakers handed Mama Chloe a gold thing that looked like a lethal weapon, a round metal ball with little holes in it on a handle, and she sprinkled the coffin and then collapsed to the floor with the ball thing, screaming, *"Oh, Vladimir! Vladimir! Dear God, give my Vladimir back to me!"*

It came to Tom at that moment that the wrong woman in the family was aiming for a career on the stage.

Sandy sprinkled. Chloe sprinkled. And then Tom sprinkled and said a silent prayer of thanksgiving that this charade was over and they could leave. Mama Chloe made him ride to the house in the big limousine. She told him she needed him at her side and some relative would drive his rented car home. She stopped weeping the minute the car doors shut, worked on her makeup, and then began crying again about four minutes before they arrived at the house.

Mama Chloe was the belle of the ball. The food was plentiful and the relatives seemed to be in good humor. Tom enjoyed seeing Sandy again and was pleased to find she was developing into quite a woman in her own right. He began to think of her not so much as Chloe's little sister any longer, but as a friend.

Old Vladimir had left more money than anyone had figured on, and Chloe, Sandy, and Mama Chloe became the rich Kosenkowski ladies. Chloe used hers to leave New York and move in with Tom in Los Angeles. For a time it seemed to be working out—she had her own little theatre on Melrose Avenue in Hollywood and she seemed actually sane with responsibility; Tom deluded himself into thinking it would stay that way. When the theatre folded because of artistic differences with the woman who acted as producer, Chloe holed up in the house eating frozen egg rolls for a month. Then Stephen Murk dropped in. For a month. They fought night and day, and Tom tried not to get involved, but it was his apartment after all, and it was he who suffered the threats from the landlady. The fights usually ended up with Chloe and Stephen screaming at him for being a lousy host.

Tom finally tossed Stephen out, but he broke in one night and ripped off Chloe's prize possession—the tap shoes which Maria Montez had really worn in some musical—so she got pissed and went to the place he'd moved into on Cheremoya and not only bashed his second guitar to smithereens, but bent his flute as well and walked on the tone arm of his turntable.

Then Sandy and Mama Chloe dropped in from Chicago for a little visit and that was the last straw; Tom moved out of his own apartment and back to the "Y," and waited until they'd gone. He adored Sandy and felt close to Mama Chloe—some moments with her were warm and motherly, when she cooked especially for him, told him her million troubles and woes and how much he meant to her—but he could not bear their fighting all the time. And fight they did. Mama Chloe slapped her oldest daughter across the mouth and Chloe slapped her right back and Sandy ran in between them to stop it and they knocked the shit out of her. It was a horror movie, the Creatures from the Polish Lagoon, and Tom ran from the theatre.

When the visitors departed, Tom came back long enough to tell Chloe he'd rented a room in Hollywood and he was moving in there—alone. It was a coward's way of throwing her out. He never had much guts when it came to her. There were times when he should have killed her, or in the very least, walked out of her life forever. But he didn't. He moved and accepted the phone calls, the cries for rescue and attention. "I just took a bottle of sleeping pills." He would go and walk her around and pour coffee into her or get her to a hospital if the pills were stronger than Sominex. "Tomcat, I'm putting my head in the oven." He went to her and talked her out of it and told her to get a microwave. One night she called and said, "Tomchat . . . Ivvvvvvmmmm been . . . lishten. . ." He rushed over. She was living in a room down the hall from a hookers' lair which fronted as a Notary Public. The place was filled with mangy cats and empty Southern Comfort bottles. She was drunk.

But he stayed with her while she cried, while she vomited, and while she slept. He gave her money. He gave her food, which she poked at, nibbled a little, and washed down with whiskey. He even tried getting her a job, but it was hard enough finding one for himself.

They drifted apart.

Mama Chloe rented out the house in Chicago, and moved with Sandy to a trailer court in Pacific Palisades. If the Palisades was good enough for Ronald Reagan, it was good enough for the ladies Kosenkowski. It got Chloe out of Tom's hair because she moved in with them. They invited him out often, as one of the family, but he never went. Mama Chloe was understandably hurt, Sandy more so because she needed a big brother since the loss of her father. All the burden was on her, with a sister who was stark-raving mad and a mother who was depressed more than usual because California made her remember she had wanted to be a chanteuse and wasted all those good years teasing hair on corpses.

But Tom had to stay away to keep his own sanity, as he explained to Sandy a year later. He needed to break with Chloe, needed to erect a firewall, and that meant putting the whole family out of his life. Of course they would be back after Mama Chloe choked to death on the 727, when Chloe and Sandy moved from the mobile home to an apartment in the Hollywood Hills. They would call him, the mediator in all the fights, suicide prevention, dial-a-hope. Sandy would move in with him for a day or two just to get away from her sister, which only enraged Chloe more, and then Tom, as well as Sandy, would suffer her wrath.

One day, Sandy called him at the breaking point: "I don't know what to do, Tom. She grabbed me and you know how fat she's gotten since Mama's death, she's just sitting around all the time eating chocolate and watching the soaps and saying she sings better than Barbra Streisand and she pinned me to the floor and started hitting my breasts. She just kept hitting my breasts and screaming that I got everything from Mama and Daddy and she got nothing. And that's not true because she got all the furniture and the Wurlitzer piano and the tree ornaments—"

Funny how Christmas trees kept popping up in his life.

". . .and she never understood what I went through all those years while she was off writing her lousy poetry in Chicago and New York and I had to listen to Mama and Daddy fight all the time and I had to take all the shit when I saw them sending her money for her pills and her dope and I was the good one, I was the one who stayed home and took care of them and worked and made my way in the world. She was the one who was out having a good time on their money. And now she beats my breasts. Tom, what am I going to do?"

He told her to pack up and move the hell away from her. Fast. "Save yourself, Sandy. No one can save her anymore, it's too late, but you've got a whole lifetime ahead. You have to get away before she pulls you under for good. I did."

Sandy moved out and found a good life for herself. So, Chloe then sent for Citronella. She came out by moving van. Hopped on in New Jersey and covered three thousand miles on a crushed velvet sofa. Shortly after her arrival, the Countess inquired whether or not Tom knew some "honest-to-God freaks" who would pose in the background of an ad for her new line, to show just how far life had come since the sixties. Tom had the perfect specimens: the two "C's," Chloe and Cinch, as they called her.

He liked Cinch. Oh, she was strange, but he liked her nonetheless. She was a little dwarf of a thing, about bellybutton height. She had lots of long greying hair and rotting teeth and she wore two pairs of glasses, one taped over the other, the outer pair having a purple tinge to them, which made her eyes look like violet marbles. Her tits sagged and her ass dragged and she was unforgettable. She *looked* like a Citronella. How did she get the name in the first place? "I was conceived on the patio and my parents named me after a bug candle."

She had a good disposition and cared about people and animals and never said a bad thing about anyone. It was obvious that she loved Chloe very much, for she had taken care of her many times in New York, where she'd been renting the apartment next door to Chloe. Tom felt she was a good influence on Chloe, and she was there to help. Chloe needed someone with her all the time, and Tom had had it with the late night rides to the emergency room to have her stomach pumped and get yelled at by nurses in Spanish about how he should take better care of his girl and then having to ransom her back before they could leave. He hated everything about hospitals.

He wondered if Chloe and Cinch were lovers. Once, when he said something about their "relationship," Chloe went into a tirade. "You too?" she screamed. "You think we're dykes too? I'm a separate entity, goddammit. You got any idea how hard it is to be a straight woman today? If you don't ball guys from singles bars, they think you're a dyke. Shit."

But just last week, Sandy had told Tom, "Chloe's got Cinch and I think it's going to work for them." Fat chance. Here he sat, in the darkness on the patio, looking at the wet ivy and foliage, watching a rose petal fall to the ground. Her words rang in his ear: *"I'm gonna kill her!"* He hadn't gone to her in months. Maybe this one time she wasn't kidding. . .? He didn't want to see Cinch dead. *Who knew what Chloe's mind was capable of?* He got up and went inside and grabbed his car keys.

When he got there he found Chloe sitting in the middle of the living room floor, surrounded by twelve cats of every shape and color and size. The place smelled like one big litter pan. "Chloe?" he said softly.

"Tommmmmcat." She groaned his name and turned with big red eyes. "Oh, Tomcat, you came."

He went over and bent down and put his arm around her head and held it tight. "I'm here."

"It hurts, it all hurts so much, Tomcat."

"I know, I know."

"It hurts, life hurts. I don't think I can take it anymore. Joplin sang about it man, the blues. I got the blues and I ain't never gonna get out."

"Let's go for a walk."

"Tomcat, please drive me up to the mountaintop to look at the lights. Please."

They sat on a blanket on the side of Mulholland Drive, and looked down at the Sheraton Universal sign and the rest of the twinkling San Fernando Valley. He told her it wasn't Cinch she hated so much as what she'd done to herself, what she'd let herself become. She admitted Cinch was good and kind and she needed her, even though she still had no right to ask for fucking garlic bread, especially when Cinch knew garlic gave Chloe a stomach attack.

He laid into her about her attacks, her stupid illnesses, her excuses for avoiding the dark side of life. "Who told you life was going to be easy?" he asked her, echoing Rachel's exact words to him.

"But I've suffered so much. I'm in such pain, Tomcat!"

"You're feeling sorry for yourself. You're so wallowed out in self-pity you can't see any problems but your own."

"I gotta get rid of Citronella. She's pulling me down, Tomcat, down, down. Shit, man. There's an apartment in the building where Janis died, on Franklin, and I think I can get it, but I gotta get rid of Cinch. . ."

Tom shook his head sadly. "Perfect, just perfect. You finally made it, Chloe. You're finally up there in the big league. The apartment where Joplin overdosed, your National Shrine." Christ, he felt depressed.

She pulled a bottle of liquor from her bag. "Oh, Tomcat, marry me."

"I almost did once." He shook his head. "But I won't ever marry anyone, I know that now Chloe. I was a kid then."

"But even so, you were willing to marry me, that's enough—"

"I was young and never thought about what it *meant,* about the responsibility. I was caught up in our 'family' —Ophelia and your parents—and I said things I didn't really mean. Fantasies."

She started to weep. "Oh, Tomcat, Tomcat, at least you asked, and you meant it for a while! Oh, God, no one has ever done something as beautiful for me. Oh, Tommmmmcat, I love you."

"Chloe," he said, rocking her in his arms. "Chloe, mother of Ophelia, goddess of. . ."

She put her hand over his mouth. "I want to go home," she suddenly said. "I want you to play a Janis tape in the car. Just take me home. I want to sleep. I'm so sleepy."

He took her home and helped Cinch put her to bed. She'd swallowed three sleeping pills before he'd gotten there. Now they were working. He wished Cinch well and when he left the house he hoped he would never see either of them again.

But he knew he often hoped for too much. And that one of the truths about himself was that he was really very weak.

SIXTEEN

Everything went well for a while. Later he would look back and view it as the calm before the storm, but it was a good time for him, one of the best times of his life.

He was seeing Mitchell regularly, no longer in hiding, not only in his little house for clandestine trysts by candlelight. They lunched together in Century City. "Hank, Martin, this is my buddy Tom, the tennis partner I told you about. . ." They went swimming and took Jeremy. They went to the movies, to the health club together, even to a party the law firm threw when Paula happened to be sick. Tom was Mitchell's best friend, a man's man, and, after all, "We've known each other since we were kids. . ." Mitch even added on one occasion, "Tom was engaged, but his fiance was killed in a plane crash."

Kevin told Tom he was a "liberated homosexual who thinks that means you pretend you're straight to keep a lover."

But it was good to be with Mitchell so often, out in the open. Their love was their big secret—as they rubbed knees under restaurant tables like schoolkid lovers, as they held hands in movie theatres, as they snaked a few moments of BJ rapture behind the lockers at the ever-so-straight health club. Tom felt as though he were being courted, and he relished it, for it was new in his experience; Mitchell felt happy and alive with this beautiful boy who satisfied him in every possible way. They loved each other, deeply. The affair was working, and working well.

Tom finally did approach Mitchell about the music business, and Mitch gave it a shot and Tom sold a song. They broke out the champagne the night the contract was signed, and Kevin joined them for the celebration party. It was a song called "Wonderland" and it eventually turned up on a record album for kids, and sold well enough to earn some royalties. But most importantly, it was a credit, a tangible beginning. Tom was a published composer. The satisfaction when he realized hundreds of kids would be listening to the music and lyrics he wrote was immense, and Jeremy told him it was his "most favorite song in the whole world."

He was becoming increasingly fond of Kevin. They seemed to argue more than ever, but it happened because they expected a lot from one another. Tom had tapped a hidden source in the boy, a well of determination to help Tom just the way Tom had helped him, making him a better person. Rachel called once while Tom was in the shower, and Kevin talked to her for several minutes. He promised her he'd keep Tom in line on his end, laughing that "he needs all the help he can get."

After the record had been made, Kevin had all the more ammunition to use to get Tom off his ass and make a success of himself. Tom fought back, but it was a weak fight. The reality of what was going on inside him at that time in his life was the bleak cloud in an otherwise clear sky: it was becoming harder and harder for him to function as a paid hustler. He was refusing clients often, and Zena was beginning to get upset. It didn't seem as bad with women as with men; he didn't feel he was cheating on Mitchell so much when he was in bed with a female. But with men it was nearly impossible. He tried his damnest to erase his lover from his mind when he was with a trick. It worked to an extent: as long as the situation was sexual, he could make it through, but if it turned to the romantic, if a man wanted to kiss him, hold him tenderly, he freaked and ran.

And then something happened which forced him into getting out of hustling.

Rachel came to town. She gave him a day's notice. Tom didn't know what to do. He'd never told Mitchell anything about her other than she was his best friend. Could he risk allowing them to meet? What if Rachel let Mitch know she was sleeping with him? He'd never told Mitchell anything remotely near that. And he'd told Rachel the exact opposite, that Mitch knew all about their affair. He felt his nerves tingling. What would he do?

There was only one answer—lie some more. He told Mitch he was going to Atlanta for two days. He told Rachel *Mitch* was going to Atlanta for two days, the same two days she was going to be in town, wasn't that a shame? He warned Kevin not to slip up, but Kevin said he didn't want to get involved, and promised to stay away, despite the fact that he was dying to meet Rachel.

She arrived and Tom said, "I want to spend every moment with you, just the two of us. We're locking ourselves in my house, away from the world." It would be just his luck to bump into Mitchell in a restaurant or something. He wasn't going to take any chances; they'd be hermits for two days.

Which wasn't an unattractive idea to Rachel. She reminded him she had two business meetings to attend, but other than that, yes, they would just relax and play with Blizzard and make love.

She brought him a care-package from Zabar's: pungent cheeses and fresh dill and coffee beans. A copper colander to hang on the fireplace wall. Little scarlet tiptree strawberry preserves. The first night, they had a picnic on the floor in front of the fireplace. They toasted and ate and got drunk and giggled alot. "Are you and Mitch getting on?" she asked.

"Very."

"How about his wife?"

"Thinks I'm his best pal in the world. Doesn't suspect a thing."

"She must be awfully dense. How's Kevin?"

"Impossible. He's in San Diego with his folks for the weekend. Sent his love."

"Darn. I wanted to meet him."

"Chloe's in town."

"No thanks."

He poured more wine. "How's Barry?"

"No more nightmares about the snow. Saw him last weekend. He's swell."

"Did you happen to talk to Jarvis yet?"

"No, but I sent him a copy of the children's album with a big circle around "Wonderland." Play me a song?"

He got up and chugged down his wine and sat at the piano. He played "Send In The Clowns" and "Losing My Mind" from *Follies*. He loved Sondheim, the intricate chords, the sweet and easy sound. Then, he went to her. She was stretched out in front of the fire, eyes closed.

He fell to his knees and ran his hand over the outline of her breasts. He put his hand under her skirt. He ran his finger along the elastic of the silk underpants, along the legs, and massaged the raised mound until the silk was wet. She was breathing heavily, moaning from the back of her throat.

Tom pressed his head to hers and licked her lips. She sucked on his tongue. His lips were on her nose, licking her eyes, biting on her chin. She did the same to him, taking his chin into her lips, sucking on the stubble of his beard, the blond beard that was never visible but certainly there.

Still kneeling, he unzipped his pants and his penis found its way out of them. She opened her eyes and looked at it as he pressed a finger into her. He was ripping her panties with his hand, but she didn't mind. She opened her mouth, begging for his cock without saying a word, asking for it with her waiting tongue. He moved his pelvis close to her face, slowly, and teased her lips with the head of the organ, teasing and touching.

He grasped his penis in his left hand and held it down to her. She came up and took it in her mouth. He slid two fingers into her cunt and she lifted her buttocks from the floor and twisted in passion. He pulled his hand out for a moment, lifted a leg and straddled her, knelt above her face, one knee on each side of her head, anchoring her long hair to the carpet. He gave her his swollen cock with his hand, and then reached behind him and found the spot between her legs again and began to finger her as expertly as before. She moaned for him to make her come.

She was seized with a feeling she had often tried to explain to him, wondering if he experienced it when he was with a man: the feeling of cock. Nothing but cock, all over her, everywhere, as if she were powerless under it, a slave to its might. Cock, the essence of a man, what he was all about. She had said you never really know a man until you've licked his balls and smelled his asshole and drunk his cock.

She felt his penis grow and swell until it was suddenly bigger than his body, bigger than the room, the house, the world, and it was pressing her to the floor. Smothering her. Hurting her. She moaned with his cock down her throat and he hurt her more with his fingers, but it was an exquisite hurt, just the way she taught him, just the way she liked, the way she came best. He massaged her into a shattering climax which lifted her feet into the air and filled the room with anguished cries of passion. Tom felt his balls tightening. He looked down and saw her eyes staring up at him, pleading for his sperm. He felt it moving already, as if the orgasm were starting down in his bowels somehwere, as if—

He froze. Perked his head toward the window.

She pulled her lips off his penis. "What's wrong?"

"Shh. What was that?"

He was whispering. He looked frightened. Startled. She had never seen him like this. "Tommy. . .?"

He lifted a leg, squatting with his rapidly-shrinking cock at her shoulder. He looked at the window. He knew it, sensed it; someone was out there. The noise he'd heard was the sound of a car door closing.

Mitchell's eyes met his through the glass pane. The cat had pushed the curtains apart while Rachel and Tom had been making love. Tom didn't move. Mitchell bought a hand up to the glass, scraping it with his nails as his face turned ashen. Then he was gone.

Tom grabbed his jeans and pulled them on and ran out the door, never once looking at Rachel. He ran to the car and pounded on the windows as Mitch started it and refused to look at him. He jumped on the hood when it started to move, screaming, "Mitchell, don't, don't, please don't go like this!" Mitch backed up. He stopped. Tom slid against the windshield. Then the car moved forward and Tom shouted, "Goddamnit, you fucker! *Stop! Stop and talk to me!*"

The car jerked to a halt between the trees there in the drive. Tom flew off the hood and rolled in the cinders. He lifted his head—the car lights blinded him—and everything was swaying; he lay back, feeling cold, thinking he was dying. But he felt someone lifting him. Mitchell was asking him, "Are you all right? Tom, are you hurt?"

"No." He sat up on his own and waited a moment until everything stopped spinning. Then he saw Mitch kneeling there, in the lights of the car. Tom began to cry. "I didn't mean to hurt you. . ."

"Why? Jesus, Tom, why?"

"I don't know. I fucked up, that's all. I was afraid. I couldn't tell you."

"Who the hell is that?" Mitch asked.

And Tom suddenly realized he didn't know. *Oh, Jesus Christ.* "Rachel," he said, softly. "That's Rachel."

The pain and confusion in the man's eyes was unbearable. He groaned as if stabbed with a sleek knife, and turned his head away. He stood up and stopped for a moment, tried to speak, but then he jumped in the car and slammed the door.

Tom got out of the way. If the passion in their love-making was any sign of the intensity between them, he imagined Mitchell was capable of running him over at that moment with little thought as to the ramifications in the future. Tom jumped into the trees as the car roared down the drive. And then he ran to the MG, grabbed the spare key from the glove compartment, and took off in pursuit.

They squealed around bends in the road through Bel Air, seemed to round curves on two wheels, and just missed a collision on Sunset. Tom took his chance on Beverly Glen. He downshifted and passed the BMW, and then slammed down on his brakes, forcing Mitch to stop. When he did, he leaped from the car and ran to him. Mitch was slumped behind the wheel, out of breath. "Leave me alone," he moaned.

"Yes, I will, but not until we talk. I know I let you down. But I won't let it end like this." Tom was gripping the door of the car, as if hoping to hold it in that spot forever.

"You don't care about my feelings," Mitchell said.

"We can't stay here like this. I want to go home."

"No. I'll park my car and you do the same. Please, Mitchell!"

The man looked up at him. He finally nodded.

Tom moved the MG to the side of the street, and got into the BMW when Mitch pulled up behind him. It was dark, almost black. They were under a huge tree which hid the street lamps down the block. Tom just sat there with his eyes closed. Mitch said nothing, put his elbow out the window and stared off into space.

"You know what it's like to come upon a scene like that?" Mitch's voice was trembling with anger and hurt. "Especially when I was coming to you because *I* was already upset and needed to—"

"You knew I was gone," Tom snapped. "But you didn't believe me, you had to snoop around."

Mitchell grabbed his hair and yanked his head around so he faced him. "You fucking little bastard! How dare you try to turn it around and make *me* look like the one who didn't trust?"

"You're hurting me. . ."

Mitch let go. "I feel like killing you," he said, biting on his thumb, bashing the steering wheel with his fist. "I've never been so angry in all my life."

"You fuck women too."

Mitch screamed at him. "Jesus, what's *wrong* with you? Where do you get off playing dumb with me? I don't give a good goddamn if you fuck sheep, but don't tell me otherwise. I was never suspicious about Rachel, though, thinking back now, you gave me every reason to be because how many times did you tell me, 'She's *only* my friend, we don't have *any* sexual attraction for each other'? What hurts is I never doubted you."

"It isn't sex like . . . well, like it is with you."

"I don't care about the *kind,* that has no bearing on this. You told me it was all maternal and I walk up and find your cock in her mouth. Terrific. Shit, you should have lied some more, told me the woman was someone else, that might have made it easier . . . I wouldn't have known you're such a . . . oh, fuck it, who cares? Never mind. It won't make a difference.''

Tom wanted to scream, run, hold Mitchell and make love to him, die. He started to ramble, tears being fought back, knowing this was it, the edge, teetering there, it would either be fixed now or never again. "Mitch, I'm sorry . . . so sorry . . . love you . . . I don't know why . . . easy, it was easy . . . I didn't want you to worry every time I went to New York, thought you would be jealous . . . it's different, you're married to Paula . . . just didn't understand, thought part of my attraction to you was being totally gay, not having women . . . oh, Mitch, please, please, give me another chance . . . I didn't mean to hurt you, I didn't, I didn't. . ."

"I had a fight with Paula," Mitch began when Tom finally stopped. "It was horrible and stupid. I mean, over who forgot to pick up milk earlier. *Stupid!* That wasn't it, though. It's the strain I'm feeling, the tension that's there. She's picking up on it. She says I'm lying, there's something I'm keeping from her. She told me to go out for a few hours, she didn't want me around. She threw me out of my own house! I needed somewhere to go to think, a place where I could relax. I knew you were away. I figured I'd go to your house and visit with Blizzard and get my head together. In our bed. And then I find you in it with that fat—"

"We weren't in bed. I'd never sleep in that bed with anyone but you. She wanted to go in there, but I refused."

"I didn't mean literally." Mitch wiped his brow. "Tom, you'd better go back home. There's nothing more to be said tonight. I don't . . . I don't feel good. I need some sleep."

Tom turned and took Mitchell's cold hand. "I'll never lie to you again, ever. I swear on my life."

"There's no reason for it. There *wasn't* a reason for it. It only fucks things up. It's just what Paula and I were arguing about tonight."

"Forgive me."

"Yes. The hurt will wear off in time."

Tom tried to kiss him, but Mitchell pulled back. "Mitch, please don't!"

"I can't, Tom. Go home now, please go home. Nothing has changed, I love you still. But I need to be alone."

"Mitch!" Tom yelled, grabbing him by the shoulders. "I love you!"

Mitch tried to pull away again, but caught Tom's eyes, and he shuddered, reached up with both hands and pulled his hair, tightening it in his fingers, and he suddenly smashed his face to Tom's, biting his lip. Tom moaned and cried out and felt blood run down his chin. Mitchell sucked the warm trickle into his mouth and tears came down his cheeks again. Then he began to bite on his neck, on his shoulder, hurting him, giving him pain, doing what Tom had done to him emotionally.

"God," Tom moaned, hurting everywhere, cock hard, heart racing. "Fuck me, Mitch, hurt me . . . I'm sorry . . . love you . . . kill me . . . don't leave me, don't ever leave me."

Mitchell moaned as Tom frantically dug into his pants. He felt his lover pull his cock out, felt the fingers tug on it, felt it hit the steering wheel, felt it as it slid down Tom's throat. He still held Tom's head by his hair, held it and moved it up and down, slamming his thick cock all the way into him, choking him, gagging him, fiercely trying to ram it down his belly. When he came he groaned like a wounded animal and held Tom's head so far down on his penis that he heard Tom's teeth rubbing against the metal of his zipper. He came and lay his head on the windowsill and ached all over.

Tom lifted his head up. His lip had bled again, all over Mitchell's undershorts and pants. He looked bruised, puffy. His eyes were hollow sockets. He tried to kiss Mitch, but an arm came up and held him back. Again, Mitchell asked him to go. Tom opened the door and got out. Mitch started the car. Tom got into the MG and watched as Mitch drove around him, barreling down the street and out of sight.

Tom turned the key. The car started immediately. He clicked the lights on. But then killed them again. He turned the engine off. He couldn't move. Rachel was there, at the house, waiting for him. He'd not even said a word to her. What would she be thinking? How could he face her tonight? Did he have the strength? Could he take more of it, being called a liar and hateful? Could he show more remorse this evening?

If only he had told Mitch. If only he'd told Rachel. If only she hadn't come to town. If only that cunt Paula hadn't picked a fight with her husband. If only he hadn't gotten so drunk and decided to have sex with her. If only—

The car stopped behind him. The light went out. He heard a door open. Then he was aware of the man standing next to him. He looked up, half-expecting to face a policeman or a gun. But it was Mitchell. "Can I get in for a few minutes?"

"Ye . . . yes."

Mitch got in and looked at Tom. "I had a feeling you'd still be here. I had to come back. I can't go home yet and I can't figure things out. We left it all so uncompleted. I've never been hurt like this before. Never. Never loved so much to allow it to happen. You may not understand this, but I see you as so much more than my lover. I see you as an out. A whole new world, a new crack at life."

Tom held his hand.

"You're the break I've wanted for years, don't you see? You're my release from the straight world that I've locked myself in. The closet, if you will. I'm so sure of you—of us—that I'm beginning to see I really don't want what I told myself I wanted. I really don't want to be married and be a father. I really *do* want to live with you. I really *do* want to say I'm gay to the world and live honestly for a change. I really do want to be able to kiss you good-bye in front of anyone's eyes without worrying if it would ruin me someday. You've been the only person to get to me, to allow me to break down and really see what I want, see the truth . . . and tonight I saw it all falling apart because I thought I didn't know you suddenly, that I had trusted too much, that you were just an illusion."

"Oh, God, Mitch, I'm not an illusion. I want it all too. You're an *out* for *me,* from the life I lead now, the people I work with, the things I do. I'm not a lie, just a liar sometimes. I always had to do it, when I was a kid. Always pretending to others that things were okay. Lying to my*self.* It's so easy—Kevin keeps knocking me about this—that I just find myself doing it and doing it, and I don't even *know* I'm doing it."

"It's got to stop, or it'll ruin you, and us."

"I know, I know. Jesus, we've got so much going for us. So much to anticipate, to live for. A future, a real future."

"I want you, nothing more or less. Just you, my lover, the man I love." Mitch took him in his arms. "I want to be free one day to be only yours, and you mine."

"Yes. . ."

They kissed and were silent, sitting in the dark car for almost an hour, Tom almost asleep on Mitch's shoulder. Then they realized they'd best go home, separately. Paula would certainly be sleeping, and Rachel deserved an apology.

Before he got out of the car, Mitch said, "Tom, part of my anger—my surprise—was because this was the first time you were unavailable to me. You've always been there, waiting, whenever I wanted, to fit my schedule. Then I pick a night to fight with Paula when you're traveling for the Countess and it threw me. I needed to be around you, even if I couldn't have you with me. So I . . . well, I already told you why I came over. I'm sorry I came apart so. I never knew I could feel such raw passion. It tells me a lot about us. Now I'm really sure."

Tom said nothing. He touched Mitchell's lips with his fingers, and then they parted. He drove back up to his house wearily, unable to face what was waiting for him, but knowing it was inevitable.

She wasn't there. "Rachel?" he called outside after he'd checked the bedroom. "Rachel, you here?" But then he saw that her bag was gone. He sat down on the bed and groaned. Maybe it was better like this. He wasn't sure he could handle another scene. She couldn't have left town, she had a meeting scheduled the next day, and he knew where it was. He would find her there. Yes, this was the right thing to do, sleep now and deal with it later. . .

He slept fitfully. He kept waking up seeing Mitch's face filled with hurt and hatred. He made himself some tea at eight and drank it in bed, wondering just what he would tell Rachel. What *could* he tell her? The truth? The truth had been obvious. He knew she hadn't left because she'd been embarrassed or anything like that. She left because she'd been lied to.

He waited outside the 9000 Building on Sunset for over three hours. Finally, he went inside, to the office of the record company where she was involved with producing a series of liner notes, and asked the receptionist when her meeting was scheduled. The girl told him it was a luncheon meeting, but she thought Rachel would be coming back to the office with the others. Would Tom care to wait?

He sat down on a purple sofa and waited. Five minutes later a man entered, white-haired and distinguished of face, but disheveled of clothing. "Oh, Mr. Douglas," the receptionist said, "Sheldon isn't back yet. I'm sure it will only be a few minutes."

"I'll wait, thanks, Sue." He sat down next to Tom. "Hi, young man, how are you?"

"Okay." Tom didn't want to tell him how rotten things really were.

"You waiting for Sheldon too?"

"No. Well, I don't think so. I'm waiting for someone who doesn't really work here."

"You in the business?"

Tom put down the copy of *Billboard* he'd been looking at. "No. Want to be, though."

"That so? What do you do?" The man seemed sincerely interested.

"I write music."

"What kind?"

"You name it. Lyrics too."

"Can you score for piano?"

"Yes."

The man reached in his pocket and pulled out a card. "I'm Richard Douglas and I've got something coming up that I need new talent for. We're auditioning tapes now. You got anything to send, just put it in the mail. My assistant will get it back to you if we don't think it's right." He handed Tom the card after he'd scratched out the printed phone number and inserted the new one. "We're out at Burbank now."

"Th . . . thanks." Tom looked at the card. *Richard Douglas.* Jesus, he was a big-time film director.

"What have you done in the past?"

Tom started telling him about "Wonderland," but the door opened and in walked the man Douglas had been waiting for. "Sheldon, good to see you," Douglas said, getting up, but turned back to Tom to add, "Good luck now."

"Thanks."

Then three other men came in the door and the receptionist told one of them about Tom, and the man walked up to him. "Sue said you're waiting for Rachel. I'm sorry, but I think she's on a plane. She went directly to the airport from the restaurant."

Tom bolted out the door and ran down the hall to the elevator. All the way down, he wondered if he should chance it, should he try to catch her at the airport? He knew she always flew American. But if they didn't have time, would it not be more frustrating than the night before, and what if there were a scene? What did she want, just to be away from him for a while, or never to see him again? He had to find out.

But he didn't go to the airport. He drove home and called American Airlines and had her paged. She was already seated on the plane, but he swore it was an emergency, and they pulled her off and gave her the courtesy phone. "Yes?" she said.

"It's Tommy."

She held back obvious anger. "I have nothing to say to you."

"I know, and I understand. But I have to tell you I'm sorry . . . I'm . . . well, that's all I can say. There's no excuse, nothing you don't know. It just . . . happened too fast. But I learned something from it. I'm changing completely. I'm never going to hustle another day of my life. I swear it. I'm going to tell him all about it. And I'll never hurt you again, ever."

"Tommy, I must get back on the plane. Please don't call me. I need some time to think. I'll write you."

"Rachel. . ."

"Good-bye."

"Rachel, I—" She hung up. He put the phone down. Kevin was standing in the door, in his jeans and white T-shirt, his pool clothes. Tom looked at him. "I know, I know, I look like shit. It's a long story. When you're done working, come back and I'll tell you all about it."

"You okay?"

"Yes. If I'm sleeping, wake me up."

Kevin nodded and went up the hill to the big house.

He returned later in the afternoon and found Tom wide awake, reading a letter. "Hey, Kev, this is crazy," Tom said. "I just witness Rachel walk out on my life and today get a letter from her in the mail telling me we'll be together forever."

"What are you talking about?"

"Where's the Countess?"

"She's out of town. Europe I think."

"You're kidding?" Tom looked pained. "Shit!"

"What the fuck is going on?"

"I'm quitting. Not another trick, not another day. I have to end it." He could see that his friend was totally confused. "Kevin, Rachel and I were getting it on last night when Mitch came up, looked in the window, and saw us."

Kevin sank to a chair. "Oh no."

"Yes."

"What happened?"

Tom took a deep breath and related the whole story. Kevin told him it would work out, maybe it was good that he learned a lesson. "What did he say when you told him about hustling all this time?"

Tom looked surprised. "I didn't."

"Why not?"

"Jesus, he almost left me the way it was. You think he could have taken that kind of shock?"

"Wouldn't that have been the best time to tell him?" Kevin thought for a moment. "You know what? That was the *only* time you could have told him. You can't now, not while he's reeling from the other lie. Oh, Christ, Tom, now you can't *ever* tell him!"

Tom nodded. "That's why I'm getting out. So I won't be lying from this day on."

Blizzard jumped into Kevin's lap, licked a paw and curled up. "If this works out with Mitch and Rachel—

and it will—are you really happy right now? Is that all that's screwed up?"

Tom nodded.

"You're lying again. It's the piano there. You won't be complete until you get the inspiration—no, a reason, a force behind you—to do something about the talent you've got."

"Kev, this isn't the time to get on my case about becoming another Horowitz." Tom got up and grabbed a banana from the counter. "Can't it be just a hobby?"

"No!"

Tom threw the banana into the sink. "Goddammit, you're all on my back and I'm sick of it! Chloe screamed at me that I had to spread it around, I had a duty to do that, like Dolly Levi and her manure speech. Rachel never stops telling me how I'm selfish keeping it to myself, and that I only do that 'cause I find it easy. I know, I know, there are a lot of people running around who'd give their right arm to play the piano or paint a picture . . . *or take a good photograph.*" He glared at Kevin.

"Now's the time to confront it," Kevin said. "You taught me to confront my image of myself, and I feel like a new person. What about you?"

Tom sat down. He tried to explain without shouting. "Listen, I know what everyone thinks. But it's what *I* think that counts. Right now I don't care a damn about a career or anything like that. I only care about saving my relationship with Mitch."

"Oh, come on, you're not *that* small-minded. You're pouncing on him and Rachel all the time. But you don't believe inside yourself yet. You're just the way *I* was when we met."

Tom reached to the piano and grabbed Richard Douglas' card. "See this? You know what I did today? I made a contact, *on my own.* Yeah, I've been working at it for a long time, and I finally got to him, and we talked and he's going to listen to a tape of mine." Kevin's eyes lit up. "So you're wrong, I do believe, at least enough to go to one of the biggest men in the whole business and tell him I want to write music for his films."

Kevin got up, Blizzard dropping to the floor, and grabbed Tom close. "Well, I'll be goddamned."

Tom let his friend hold him. He was depressed again, and angry with himself because he was aware that he was lying—he didn't make the contact on his own, he hadn't tried to reach Douglas. He hated his own need for having to please everybody. "I love him, Kevin," he said softly. "I never want to see again what I saw in his eyes last night."

Kevin stroked his hair and whispered that it would be fine, his life was going to be new from now on, everything would change. Then Tom lifted his head and said, "Have you ever heard anything about the Countess being into drugs?"

"How do you mean? There's always bowls of grass up at the house."

"Yeah, I know that, and her medicine chests are like pharmacies. I mean heavy stuff. Listen to what Rachel wrote in this letter." He got the letter and read. ". . .and I know a girl here in New York who says Zena is one of the big connections in the country. This source is usually stoned out of her skull, so it may be all talk, but nonetheless, I'd check it out. I don't want you getting involved in anything like that. I think you should consult Mitchell about it. He's an attorney, after all. He may be able to give you some advice." Tom looked at Kevin again.

"With Siberia Susie, anything is possible," Kevin remarked. "How's Chloe, speaking of the insane?"

"Bananas. Now there's one I would welcome walking out of my life, but I can't seem to shake her."

"I think *she's* the dangerous one."

"Oh, come on. She's harmless. She just hates herself for being attracted to homosexuals, pretends she's Janis

Joplin, thinks she invented the Women's Movement, and likes to believe she's a witch."

"She's going to hurt you someday," Kevin insisted quietly.

"She can't. Not any more." Tom shook his head. "I don't feel anything for her like I once did. So she can't."

"But you still run when she calls."

"I wish Mitch would call," Tom said, changing the subject.

"Want to come for supper? Mom's making a veal stew that's delicious."

"No. I want to be Garbo tonight."

"I'll call you later. 'Bye." Kevin hesitated a bit and stopped in the doorway. "Hey, if it's any consolation, *I* still love you."

Tom smiled. "Yes, it is, as a matter of fact."

Kevin waved and left.

But he returned three minutes later. Out of breath. "Tom! She's still here! Zena, she's not leaving for another few hours . . . she's in the house. You can catch her if you want to."

Tom jumped up and ran to the big house.

He walked into the sitting room where the Countess and Madame Platychivnik were already seated, Auntie Mame and Vera Charles receiving visitors. Court was in session.

"Vell, darling, vat is it?" she said. "I know for veeks now. Clients say, 'Countess, something is vrong with Tomas.'"

"I don't want to hustle anymore." He said it steadily, in one even breath.

She fingered her brooch nervously. Madame Platychivnik glared at him. He faced them without expression. The Countess jumped up, suddenly, and fluttered around the room, jabbing the air with her bony finger to make points. "I give you everything. Money, ze dacha, best customers. I bend over backvards for you,

Tomas. Is this vat I get in thanks?"

Madame P. piped in with her humor. "Don't bend too far, darlink, or he'll steeek eet een you." When she was drinking, her accent varied as though she couldn't decide which country to be from. Sometimes it seemed Chinese.

"Zena, I'm tired of it." And he looked very tired. "I know you've done everything for me, and I appreciate it. I don't want to leave, I just want to change jobs for a while."

"I vill lose a million dollars vithout you!" she exclaimed, falling backwards into a convenient chair.

"No you won't. I need a rest. I'm wearing out."

Madame P. said, "Pleeeeease, who are you kidding? Zat ting of yours vill never vear out."

"I would like to work the exhibits."

"Vhy?" Zena's eyes were penetrating.

"So I could still work for you. So I could still travel. So I'd still have a job."

Madame P. said, "Throw zee two-bit hustler into zee street," but Zena wasn't taking advice from her. "Ungrateful putz," Madame P. said, downing her sherry.

"If I vere to agree, this vould only be a temporary arrangement, a temporary situation?"

Tom said yes, that's all. He'd go back to turning tricks in a few months. Of course, he had no intention of doing that at all, but it would give him time to plan for the future. Maybe he'd have a job in music. Maybe Mitch would leave Paula by then.

Zena thought it over, pondered it with theatrical sweeps of the hand, wipes of the brow, looks out the window. "Vell, you realize ze other job is dangerous? You must defend yourself and ze jewels and designs, ya?"

"Sure. I can handle myself."

"I know, I know. I remember you nearly put Mister Todd in zah hospital on one occasion."

"He wanted me to! It was his greatest day, he even

sent me a card *thanking* me! A masochist's dream is to be banged-up enough to be hospitalized someday."

She thought about it and nodded. "Vell, he did kick in a good tip zat time . . . I'll have to tell von of the boys to do it again to him soon." She thought some more and then made an announcement. "Vell, it vill cost me—ach, the moaning I am going to hear from so many—but ve all need a holiday now and then. Vill you still meet vith tomorrow's client?"

Oh, God, if only he didn't have to make that decision. He looked her straight in the eye. "No."

"Hmmm. Vell, all right. Ve vill talk about your new duties vhen I get back from Roma. There vill be a jewelry convention in Palm Springs, I tink. Vell, you can go now."

Tom thanked her and as he walked by Madame Platychivnik, she mumbled, "You're crazy letting zat body to go to the rocks. Ungrateful schmutz should be out on zah streets."

"Shut your mouth!" Zena snapped. "Tomas, tell me, vat vould you have done if I had said no dice?"

"Quit for good."

Zena nodded politely. Then she turned back to her sidekick and yelled, "Silly old cow! Vat? I should lose him all together?"

Madame P. growled.

Tom ran out of the house, across the yard, dancing through the trees until he saw Kevin. He grabbed him, lifted him into the air, hugged him, turned him round and round. "I did it, Kev! I did it! Nothing's in the way anymore! It's over!"

"Tom, I'm so glad."

"I can't wait to tell Rachel. . ."

SEVENTEEN

Tom didn't get to tell Rachel until three weeks later. He'd tried calling again and again, but she hung up at the sound of his voice. He even sent a Mailgram, but there was no reply. Then one night the phone rang. Afraid it was Chloe, he let it ring twenty-seven times. Finally, he answered it. "Tommy, it's Rachel."

"Oh, God."

"I'm coming to California. I told myself I would do it without seeing you, but I can't. I'm going to San Francisco for a few days. I've always wanted to see San Simeon. Could you drive up to Santa Barbara and meet me? I'll fly down."

"Yes, oh yes."

"I'll call you tomorrow with the flights and times and all. How are you, Tommy?"

"Fine. Really fine. I'm not hustling anymore. I'm waiting for Zena to come back from Rome and then I start doing what I pretended I was doing for so long, traveling as a bodyguard for her designs."

"I'm so happy." And she sounded it. "How are things with Mitch?"

"Wonderful."

"I'm glad. I'll call tomorrow night. 'Bye, Tommy."

"'Bye."

Things *were* wonderful, but it had been difficult, and it had taken time. Mitchell found he was putting up his guard, finding it hard to trust anything Tom said, but Tom convinced him he'd learned from that one indiscretion. Now that Tom was going to see Rachel again, he knew he had to tell Mitchell. And it wasn't going to be easy.

"Are you going to sleep with her?" Mitch asked when he heard it.

"I don't know. She'll expect me to, I guess."

"That's why you do it? Because she expects you to?"

"No. Well, sometimes. I always had this thing about not being labeled, like I didn't want to be called bisexual. But I'm gay. I know it and you know it and she knows it. Sometimes I really want her, because she's unlike other women, she's not demanding, not threatening. I don't know what to tell you. If I feel like I want to, then I guess I will. Does that hurt you?"

Mitch shook his head and ran his hand across Tom's chest. They were sitting outside on the patio. "No, I'm over that. As long as you tell me how you feel up front."

Tom closed his eyes. "Gay. What a word."

Mitch nodded. "My coming out was really difficult . . . hell, I'm still coming out. Even now I have to play games for my parents, for the partners in the firm."

"You chose it that way."

"Right. And I'm complaining about myself." He put his head back. "But at least I'm not telling myself I'm straight or anything as absurd as that. Tom, it isn't easy, gay lib and all that, it still isn't easy. Sometimes I wish I worked for a firm like a couple I know where the lawyers are out, open, and no one thinks it's so bad. If I had guts, I'd start a firm of gay lawyers for gay clients and call it The Gay Bar."

"That's funny."

"Thank God for the young kids who are saying it outloud today, the teenagers who know they're homosexual and don't think it's any big deal one way or the other. Maybe Jeremy's generation will really be happy, content."

Tom reached for Mitch's hand. "What's hard are those terms—is gay 'faggy gay', or is it simply that you're a homosexual? Everyone has a preference, even the most bi of bisexuals. No one feels evenly divided. Rachel really helped me see that in myself, because she made me admit nothing with a woman had ever given me the kind of pleasure and true satisfaction as making love with you."

Mitchell pulled him up and kissed him gently. "You're the most wonderful thing about my life. I never knew how much I needed you. You make me complete, whole. I'll never let you go."

Tom smelled the faint odor of his cologne as he put his head into the crevice of his shoulder, the spot on this man's body which had been chiseled just for him. "This is what the dreams I had as a kid were all about. This is why I came here. You're the street paved with gold. I told Chloe it was my destiny, that someone was waiting. It was you."

Mitchell's arms enveloped him and they made love in the chair on the patio, and slept there half the night.

Mitch left at four, promising he and Jeremy would come feed Blizzard while Tom was away. The phone woke Tom at four o'clock. He picked it up and heard Chloe screaming for him, and he hung up. Twenty minutes later, the ringing started again. He picked up the receiver and shouted, "Damn it, Chloe! I can't listen to suicide threats tonight. I have to be on the road in three hours and I need some sleep."

But it was Citronella this time. "Tom, you've gotta talk to Chloe, just for a minute . . . please."

He couldn't do it. He hung up, then took the receiver off the hook and left it there until he heard the alarm at five-thirty. Blizzard was on top of him, kneading his claws gently through his hair, biting his nose, purring like a steamboat that had just been stoked.

Tom got up, opened a can of tuna, set it down. Then he put the phone back on the hook, and it rang almost immediately.

"Yeah?"

"Tomcat, please! *Pleeeeeease!*"

"Aw, Chloe, have a heart, huh?"

"Tomcat, my mama died."

"Yeah, sure, and you want five hundred bucks to throw a funeral, huh?"

"Tomcat, I'm not kidding!"

Something in the way she was shouting told him she was telling the truth. "Chloe . . . oh no."

"My mama's dead. Sandy was with her. She died on an airplane."

"But they went back to Chicago three weeks ago."

"She wanted to see the fuckin' Everglades and Disneyworld. They were on vacation in Florida."

"Chloe, you're not putting me on, are you?"

"Tomcat, my mama's *dead.* My mama and daddy. They're both gone." She began to sob.

"What happened? How? Did the plane crash? What about Sandy?"

"No crash. Mama choked on a fuckin' olive, man, and they wouldn't land because they said she was already dead but I know she was alive and they just didn't want to bother landing the plane, you know?"

"What can I do?"

"Come to Chicago with me. Sandy's okay, but she needs you too."

"I'm leaving town in half an hour. I . . . I can't come with you. I can't change my plans, it's impossible. God, Chloe, I feel terrible. I hadn't been out to see your mama for so long. . ."

"I want my mama back!" she wailed.

"Chloe, I'm sorry," he mumbled, and hung up, for

she was crying her heart out now, not listening to him any longer. He took a shower, wondering if he should cancel his plans with Rachel and go to Chloe and Sandy. He dressed, and again considered it—but stopped himself. No. He had to do what he had to do. What he wanted to do. And he wanted to see Rachel. She was more important.

He felt sorry for Sandy. She'd devoted so much of her life to taking care of the rest of her screwy family, and now she had to be the one to see her mother die. She'd have to arrange the funeral. She would have to put up with Chloe sobbing how much her mother loved Sandy and hated her, how the woman never understood her genius. Sandy would have the burden of having to sell the house in Chicago before she could come back to California to care for her sister. Oh, yes, it would go on. He knew it. Sandy would devote her time to Chloe. And Tom wished he could change that, but there was nothing he could do. Mama Chloe was dead and there was *nothing he could do.*

He thought of his own mother as he put his suitcase in the car. Where was she? What was she doing? Did she wonder the same about him?

He stopped himself from thinking about the past. It held no surprises, it could not be altered. Only the future was interesting. And the only mother in the future was a mama cat. He'd be curled up with her in a motel room before the day was over.

That made him smile.

They met in Santa Barbara and drove up to San Simeon where Rachel had reserved a room with a fireplace at the Cavalier Inn. The surf broke on their patio. They lay in bed in the late afternoon, relaxing, talking.

Rachel was on a high from San Francisco, where she'd interviewed the Rolling Stones for *Esquire*. Tom was down about Mama Chloe and still depressed about how he'd treated Rachel the last time he'd seen her. She told him she wanted this to be a happy trip, that it was all done and finished, that he had learned a big lesson and she trusted him never to forget it. "We're not to talk about that ever again, Tommy. Life is only going to be honest and good for us from now on." Then she crossed her arms and laughed. "You know what I'm going to do one day? Write the liner notes for your album."

"I don't sing that well."

"Does Carole King or Neil Young?"

"I'm not sure I want to make an album."

"You'd give your ass to do an album!"

"No. I think I'd rather write scores for feature films. I want to be Max Steiner."

"Tell me," she said seriously, "what would you do this very minute if you could do anything you wanted with your music?"

He thought about it for a long time. Then he sat up, faced her, and crossed his legs on the bed. "I'd write a musical play."

"Honestly?"

"Honestly. You know *Follies?*"

"Yes, of course."

"Well, picture that same kind of thing. But with all the president's wives. Call it *First Lady.*"

"Tommy, you're crazy."

"Listen," he said, jumping up to his feet, acting out the story in the middle of the room. "You've got the White House and they're tearing it down, the government's moving to Hyannis port or Salt Lake City or someplace, and there's this one last party for all the former First Ladies. Do you realize they're all alive?"

"No, they're not."

"I mean the recent ones. Bess Truman, Jackie Kennedy, Lady Bird Johnson, Pat Nixon, Betty Ford and Rosalynn Carter, all alive, all breathing. At least we think."

"You're insane."

"So was Shakespeare, they said. Listen, there's this opening number in the decaying mansion and they sing, *'Hat's off, here they come those beautiful girls. . .'* and they all show up in their inaugural ball gowns. Jackie is very late, of course, and Pat Nixon moves around in her motorized wheelchair, crying all the time that 'He didn't mean it, he's not a bad man, really.' And they have these poignant moments about each administration, about their famous husbands, and Lady Bird is pushing a barbecue grill around the place and Betty Ford is popping pills, still trying to figure out which room is which, Jackie's forever giving her tour of the place and can't imagine where all the pretty French furniture went and how all that Orange County modern got in from San Clemente.

"And there's a big production number just like "Mame," with four hundred chorus boys dressed like Senate pages. He acted it out, strutting and kicking. Bess knits and ignores everyone and couldn't care less what all the fuss is about, she liked Blair House better anyway. Jackie is redecorating and Lady Bird plants a tree in the catered Swedish meatballs. Rosalynn gets them all square dancing . . . ho down, lo down, left and right, swing your partner down one flight. . ."

Rachel was howling with laughter as he danced around the room, telling her this silly, brilliant, idiotic and wonderful idea for a show. "Stop, stop! Let me out of here, I'm locked in with a maniac!"

He fell to the bed and playfully wrestled with her hair, and then he settled down and she asked, "How long did you work on that?"

"Work on it? I thought it up a few days ago. It's just a dumbass fantasy."

"Yeah, and I wish I could produce it tomorrow. Your dumbass fantasies could well be winning Tony Awards. Someday, I hope you have as much faith in you as I do.

I love competence in people. I love people who do things well, like this idea."

His juices were going. "I've been feeling very creative lately. I put more on tape. And I sent a copy of the best to Richard Douglas, the movie director. He's looking for untapped talent."

"Good."

"And I wrote a song for you."

"Me?"

"Don't worry, no lyrics yet, nothing you couldn't play for your mother."

"You don't know my mother!"

"I'll play it for you when we get to town."

"Tom, I can't stop at your house. I have to be in New York the day after tomorrow. If we spend tomorrow night in Santa Barbara, then you can take me directly to the airport in the morning."

He sensed something more than that. "You don't want to go back there, do you?"

She shook her head. "No. The memory is too unpleasant. But I said we were not to talk of it."

"Okay. I understand."

They toured the Hearst Castle the next day and drove to Solvang for dinner. Tom bought a bag of Danish pastry, which he ate in the motel room they took in Santa Barbara. They walked on the pier and held hands. It was like old times. The hurt had worn off. She loved him still. Everything was going to be fine.

They got up early the next morning and Tom parked the car at the LAX terminal exactly forty-five minutes before the flight she wanted was scheduled to leave. She had reservations on a later one, but preferred to get home earlier. She walked to the long line at the ticket counter to see if she could change her flight, when Tom suddenly shouted, "Hey, Kevin! Kev!"

Kevin turned his way, astonished. "What are you doing here?"

"What are *you* doing here?"

"I dropped my granny off. She just left for Seattle to visit her sister. I was going home and call to see if you were back yet. What. . .?"

"Come here," Tom said, and dragged Kevin over to the ticket line. "Kevin, this is Rachel."

He held out his hand. "Well, hi," he said, a little shyly.

"Hello, Kevin. I've wanted to meet you for a long time. I feel as though I know you so well." She watched him blush. "You're my West Coast counterpart."

"Did you have a good time up the coast?" Kevin asked.

"It was wonderful," she said. "The tour guides make Hearst out to be a saint! He sacked and pillaged Europe and stored his cache up on that hill, and now he's revered as this great humanitarian for his salvation of fine art. Hah! Monasteries died for that house."

Kevin laughed. "I've never seen it. I'd like to."

"Take the tour of the kitchens. It's really the most interesting."

"My mom and dad have been up there, they—"

Tom interrupted. "Hey, remember me? Listen, you two go to the gate. I'll change the ticket and meet you. I know you're dying to talk behind my back."

Tom stood in line for nearly half an hour. He got the ticket changed, even though he knew she'd die having to sit in the smoking section for six hours. When he got to the gate, Rachel and Kevin were seated in a corner, talking with such vigor that they seemed oblivious to the world around them. When Tom got closer, he saw that there were tears in Kevin's eyes. He started calling to them from afar, giving them time to break it up; he didn't want to embarrass them. "Hey, you two, how dare you desert me!"

They got up. Tom told Rachel it was all set, and she'd better get moving or they'd close the doors on her. Then she took Kevin in her arms and whispered something to him, and he hugged her for a moment, and then kissed her on the cheek. She kissed Tom, and was off down the ramp.

"What was that all about?" Tom asked. "Looked pretty heavy."

"No," Kevin said, looking at the plane through the dark window. "Not heavy at all. Wonderful. Just wonderful. What an incredible woman."

"Yeah."

"You hungry?"

"If you are."

"Let's go eat lunch," Kevin said, but not moving.

"Sure. Come on." Tom saw that he wasn't going anywhere. "Kev, what's wrong?"

"I just want to watch the plane leave first." He stood there like a little boy watching his first jet as it taxied away from the terminal and disappeared. "Bon voyage," he said, with a little wave. "Okay, lunch. Oh, Chloe called me and told me to tell you you're a bastard. What did you do now?"

"I'll tell you all about it over a cheese sandwich."

There was only one time after her mother died that Tom actually had a good time with Chloe. She called one evening, when he was in the mood to talk, shoot the breeze, to reminisce. "Hello?"

"Tomcat, this is Citronella."

"Hi, Cinch."

"Chloe wants to talk to you. Don't hang up."

And she was on. "Tomcat? Don't hang up!"

"I'm not going to hang up."

"Well, you make me paranoid, man. Can you get me any dex?"

"No."

"Downers?"

"No."

"How about a Royal Crown cola?"

"No."

"Tomcat, you're not much fun anymore. Can you lend me twenty bucks? I want to get my fur coat out of storage in Chicago."

"It's July, Chloe."

"I plan ahead. Remember that coat?"

He did. He remembered not only the time she stole it, but when they'd used it as a blanket when the heat went out.

"That was the night Ophelia pooped on your face."

"Since when do you say *poop* for shit. And it was my chest, not my face," Tom reminded her.

"Poop is elegant. I do things now with a certain amount of élan, you know? It was your fault, you hadn't cleaned her cat box for a week."

"Real lady, crapping on my chest. I learned. I keep Blizzard's box spotless, but he usually goes outside anyhow."

"Who keeps your box clean, Tomcat?" She howled.

"I have a woman come in once a week."

"Fuck man, it's so good to talk about cat shit again. Remember when we wanted a pet clam?"

"*I* wanted a clam. You wouldn't let me have one."

"Ophelia would have eaten him. You wanted to put him on a roller skate and walk him with the dogs in the neighborhood."

"No, I thought he should be allowed out of his shell now and then. But leashed. Slop slop, squish squish. Good protection too, keep him in a bowl by the door and the burglar comes in and *ka-chunk,* off with his foot."

She was laughing from deep inside, like old times. "Tomcat, what's it like to go around seeing the world from six inches off the ground? I'd give anything to be a cat for a day. I want to be the one that gets mistaken for a meatloaf."

"The Kliban book."

"How *do* you tell a cat from a meatloaf?"

"I guess," he said, "you know it's a meatloaf if you bite into it and it doesn't jump."

She roared. "I was singing "Ball and Chain" yesterday and I thought of you."

"Great songs you always pick to think of me."

"Janis knew how to say it, man. Tomcat, when are we going to go to Paris? You promised we'd go to Paris."

"We already did," he said, softly. "Long ago, in our dreams." She'd once given him a diary with photographs of Paris on each page, and they made a promise to see it together. They tacked a map of the Paris Metro to the wall. Chloe wrote love poems to the city. She said it was a good omen that Jim Morrison was buried in Père-Lachaise because she felt such an attachment to the Jim/Jimi/Janis era and possessed a death wish which was almost supposed to be taken for granted at the end of the age of acid rock and psychedelics. Chloe wanted to be buried there as well, even though Janis was not. "Who wants to be buried in Texas, man?"

Yes, who indeed? Tom thought.

"Tomcat, do I sound more together tonight?"

"Yes. What happened?"

"I ran out. You sure you ain't got no dex?"

"How's Sandy?"

"She ain't got no dex either. Fuck man, what's life without some dex? I'm trying Royal Crown, but a quart of caffeine won't give you the buzz of one little white pill. Tomcat, I wrote a brilliant screenplay on Safeway bags last night. I'm gonna be a filmmaker and writer. Directing ain't that fulfilling. You gotta put up with actresses all the time."

"I love this song."

"What song?"

"'Imagine.' John Lennon. It's on KNX right now."

"My radio broke. I threw a Royal Crown bottle at

Citronella and missed and hit the fucking stereo. Tomcat, when I'm getting my theatre together, let's collaborate on something. I do the dialogue and you do the music."

"What will you do? How about a splashy musical called *Gidget Goes To Juarez?* Actually, I want to do a film, *The Sound Of Music* of pornography. It's called *Ding Dong!* and it's about three horny Avon ladies, Patti, Maxine and Laverne, balling their way through Canoga Park."

"Tomcat, you're too crazy to live without me."

"But still too sane, I fear, to live with you."

"We're still gonna get married one day. You were my fiance, you know."

"I gotta go. Got a date."

"Ask him if he can get me some dex."

"I'll be talking to you."

"No, you won't," she said sadly. "You won't call, but I understand. That's cool. Cats gotta be independent."

"Rachel told me the same thing."

"Who's Rachel?"

"A woman I know in New York."

"She hang out at Phoebe's?"

"I'm afraid not."

"Shit. If she did, she could get me some dex there. You know what? It was rough getting drugs in New York 'cause they always said they come from California. Like this was the magic land of medicine, Librium growing on trees, you know? And you get to California and you find out they come from Iowa or someplace. It's depressing. The universe shits on you every time."

"Chloe, stick to Royal Crown."

"Tomcat, let's go steal a pound of hamburger soon, like the good times, huh?"

"Sure, Chloe. We will."

After he hung up, he went for a walk, alone, through the trees. He thought of those Chicago days in a new light; he viewed them with clarity and sharpness of mind, taking a close look at himself then and now. He'd been a seller of sheet music, and until recently a seller of his body. He had been in love with a girl then and now was in love with a man. The changes were not that great. What stood out was the change in his music.

He had always been at the piano, from Mrs. Jensen's to the Steinway he played on his lunch hour at Lyon-Healy, to the Yamaha sitting right there, inside the little cottage that was his home. He'd never been serious then, not really. He played and played well, but the depth of meaning wasn't there, the strength of purpose. Now it was beginning to build in him, and it showed in the songs he wrote, in the way he played—as if performing rather than simply playing, understanding the power of his music and letting his feeling, love, awareness of it come through the piano.

He went inside and wrote a ballad. It was slow and melodic, filled with impressions and wisps of thoughts he believed in. He scribbled onto staff paper, hit chords, listened, sang with them, erased them, put new ones in their place, recorded it, was pleased, played it again and again, and finally the song was finished:

> Sometimes I sit and wonder,
> Talk to myself and ponder—
> Let me be what I am. . .
>
> Trying to hope and pray,
> That soon there will come the day
> That I can be what I am. . .
>
> A big butterfly, soaring high in the sky,
> With brilliant black and golden wings!
> Flying around, from the clouds to the ground,
> Summer, Fall, Winter and Spring. . .

Landing here, landing there,
In a flower, in your hair. . .

I don't understand
Why in this wonderful land,
I'm not allowed to be what I am!
Birds can be birds,
And the bees can be bees,
Being what they are, feeling free. . .

So let me be what I am,
And I'll do what I can,
I'll make you smile, make you laugh, make
you sing.
Singin' so high, reachin' up to the sky,
Being you, being me, being we!
Then I stop, and I think,
And feeling sad I say:

I really don't think that I hope for too much,
And I can't be happy this way. . .
So if I can ask for one wish in the world,
Please let me be what I am . . . today.

He changed the last chord to E flat with a D flat bass
and seemed satisfied. Then he re-recorded the song on a
new cassette, and added the best of all he'd accumulated
in the last years onto that same tape. He found Richard
Douglas' card on the piano where he'd left it and copied
the address on the envelope into which he put the tape.
He licked the stamps, put them on, and set the envelope
on the little table near the door. He finally was doing
what he'd told Mitch, Kevin and Rachel he had already
done. He wanted it now. Success, a future in music. He
really wanted it. And he made up his mind he was going
to hustle all the harder for it. It was time to pounce. He
closed the fallboard and went to bed.

Kevin called before he fell asleep. "Zena comes back tomorrow, or did you know that? My dad told me Madame P. called to ask me to be sure to give the pool a good going-over. Where do you think she'll send you with the rags?"

"I'm hoping for Leningrad," Tom joked.

"Probably something more exotic, like Anaheim."

Not quite.

She first sent him to Palm Springs as promised. Then to New Orleans. Then San Francisco. San Francisco again. To New York twice, which he loved because he was able to see Rachel. And to Denver, Atlanta, Miami, Seattle, Salt Lake City.

The work was easy. He delivered her duds and came back with them. Between flights he played, roamed new places, felt new winds on his face, tasted foods he'd never tried before, met people he hadn't dreamed existed. Many of his boyhood wishes were coming true. He was sure that sooner or later he would be sent to Paris.

In Miami, however, a woman recognized him on the beach and called out to him. "Thomas! *Tom!* Don't you recognize me, lovie? Grace Rosenbloom. Olga Oluspenskaya introduced us. . ." A former client. Oh, he remembered her well. She was the one who liked to sing "Tie A Yellow Ribbon 'Round The Old Oak Tree" as he diddled her with a vibrator. He felt a chill run up his spine. What if he were with Mitchell some day and a guy came up and said, remember me, I used to fuck you regular, every Monday night for about a year. He ran.

He had more free time now, and most of it was devoted to Mitch, but problems came up. Mitch was rising fast, devoted to the firm, and seemed to have less time for Tom. When Mitch was busy, Tom was with Kevin. His relationship with him was still different from any other; they were not lovers, nor was it a mother/son kind of arrangement as it was with Rachel. They weren't gay "sisters"; there was no hint of Mitch or Rachel or Chloe or Sandy or Annie. It was brotherly. If it was anything else, they both suppressed it.

He found more time for his cat. They chased each other in the forest. And he was forever ridding the bed of half-deceased snakes and birds and mousies that Blizzard loved to eat, the bed being the spot Blizzard thought would be most pleasing to Proud Papa to receive his catch.

He read Russian history, spurred on by Anastasia up there on the hill, and all the nature books by Edwin Way Teale. He learned to play chess and backgammon, though not very well. Scrabble was his forte, and he and Mitch played it incessantly. He refused to attempt it with Rachel, however; she made words he'd never heard before, and they always showed up in the dictionary when he challenged them. He began to really study classical music, perfected a recipe for honey wheat bread, grew what seemed like tons of zucchini in his own garden, and bought the best tape player he could find for his MG. The months passed quickly and happily.

And then one night, the phone rang.

"Tommmmmcat? You got any Darvon?"

"Huh?"

"I need some fucking Darvon. I'm in pain."

"I'm asleep. What time—?" He looked at the clock radio. "Chloe, it's four-thirty."

"I've been in excruciating pain since ten o'clock and no one cares, man. Fuckin' Citronella tries to rub my head, but I need some fuckin' Darvon, not a cold rag. Goddamn Sandy took her phone off the hook."

Smart girl. "Chloe, I can't help you." He hung up.

An hour later he was awakened by car lights in his room and the sound of a horn. He heard a door slam, another, followed by the bark of a large dog. There was a hard rap at the door and a cry in the night: "Tommm-mmmmcat!"

Dear God, what did I do to deserve this? He slid his jeans on and opened the door. She came in screaming. "Tomcat, you gotta help me—not a bad place you got here—I need help, Tomcat!" And there she stood. Pale, washed up and wiped out but still functioning, which he thought unfortunate at that hour of the morning. She was dressed in a caftan which was ripped down the side, revealing her frayed panties. Over her shoulders was the tablecloth she used as a shawl, and her hair looked as if it lived somewhere else and only visited on weekends.

Citronella followed her in, looking none too much saner herself, and gave the place the once-over. "Hiya," she said. Then a huge dog stuck his head in the door. "Phoebe, this is Tom. Tom, Phoebe."

"Oh, no—" Before he could get out another word, the giant animal was in the room, on the leash on Cinch's arm, and little Blizzard—very little, now—was atop the counter, his fur standing on end, hissing at this beast for all he was worth, frightened to death. Tom wondered if he wasn't more scared of Chloe than the dog.

Phoebe barked and barked and Tom finally yelled, "Get that fucking animal outta here!" So Cinch opened the door again and dragged him out. It was probably a mixture of every large dog on earth, and it started to run, dragging Citronella behind it. She didn't feel like skinned knees, so she let the leash go and the dog ran howling up the walk, into the Countess' backyard.

In a minute the flood lights were on and the bodyguard, Rolf, the Nazi Zena employed at nights, was charging around the house with his club and flashlight, just as Tom and Chloe ran up to the patio area to hopefully fetch the animal before Rolf shot him. "Rolf, it's me, Tom! It's okay, my fault, really!" The man looked relieved in his toothless grin. Tom looked up and saw the Countess in her window. He shrugged. He knew he'd have some explaining to do the next day. Then he saw a face appear next to her, and he realized he would have more than explaining to do; he'd probably messed up the great fuck of her life. Oh well. There was a dog to retrieve.

In the commotion, Rolf went to turn on the pool lights but hit the wrong switch, turning the yard lights off. The area was suddenly pitch black. At that point, Chloe had been chasing the still-barking Phoebe near the pool, and immediately there was a loud splash and the sound of an animal frantically paddling. "Jesus, no," Tom muttered. He watched as Chloe, at the side of the red brick coping, tried to pull the wet hound out—but of course the wet animal instead pulled her in. An even louder splash filled the night air and then screams, barking, Rolf shouting, Citronella screaming, "Man overboard!" and the Countess rapping on the window with her diamond-encrusted knuckles.

Tom had had enough nightmares for one night. He turned and walked back to the cottage, past Citronella, who told him, "Think of it this way. It coulda been worse. It coulda been a horse." He went inside and found Blizzard cowering behind the sofa and pulled him out and stroked his fur. The cat looked at him as if to ask, who *were* those people?

He heard them finally getting the dog into the car, then coming back into the house. Blizzard took another flying leap and hid under the bed. Chloe was drip-drying. Cinch opened her bag and pulled out a fifth of Southern Comfort. "Here, drink. It'll warm you."

Chloe drank and then spit at Tom. "Can't even offer me a towel?"

Tom gave Cinch a towel and the hairdryer, and she started blowing Chloe back to the mess she'd been when she'd arrived. She finished off the bottle. She moaned about the pain in her mouth. Her teeth had been killing her for years. That's why she drank all the time, she could only stand liquids on her teeth. She had been too embarrassed to tell anyone.

"Yeah," Citronella said, standing there like a poor man's Vidal Sassoon, "her teeth are really fucked-up." Tom snickered; Citronella's mouth was a dental student's dream or nightmare, depending on how far along he was.

Chloe said she'd been to a dentist the day before and was in great pain since. Tom asked why she didn't call the man. She did, she said, but he told her to take codeine and sleep it off and he'd see her next week. "The fuckin' jerk doesn't want to have to give up his golf game," she moaned. "Cinch, goddammit, you're burning my ear."

"Sorry."

And she went on and on, Tomcat this, Tomcat that, you're the only one who can help, you don't understand, you're the *only* one who understands. She had to borrow the car from Sandy and she couldn't drive with the pain anymore and she needed to find a dentist who'd take her now and get me there, Tomcat, please, I need that tooth pulled, it's got to come out and Cinch can't drive and I've been up for three days, honey, taking all that dex and I need to crash but I can't with the pain! He'd heard it before, all the many versions of this same story. He was falling asleep as she told it.

The phone rang and it was Sandy, in hysterics. Her car was missing. A neighbor saw someone driving it out of the garage! Ah, worry not, Tom said, your dear sister has it and I have your sister. He handed the phone to Chloe. And the Kosenkowski sisters fought it out. Chloe apparently had had a key made and when Sandy took the phone off the hook, refusing in that gesture to drive her sister to any more hospitals or parapsychology clinics (when Chloe claimed she was suffering from "psychic overload"), she left herself open to car theft. Sandy realized Chloe was drunk and she didn't want her wrapping it around a tree, so Tom got back on the line and promised he'd get the car safely back to her.

While Tom was on the phone, Chloe tiptoed into the bathroom and opened the medicine chest, silently, almost reverently. The pilgrim on her knees before the tabernacle. Finding nothing stronger than Tylenol (she swallowed the entire contents of the bottle in one gulp), she went to the cabinet under the sink. He caught her as she was digging through toilet paper and Kleenex and condoms and bars of Zest. She begged him for just one Darvon. He said he didn't have any. She knew he was lying. She could smell pills, any kind of drug, miles away. Citronella had once said, "They should leash her. She could make a fortune for herself and a million busts for the narcs."

He finally gave in. The sun was coming up and he was tired. He pulled the bottle of Darvon out from under a pile of clothes in the corner of the bedroom, opened it, and handed her one. Then she took her life into her own hands, which wasn't very precarious, considering what was left of it. She brought up her knee and jammed it into Tom's crotch. He doubled back in pain as she fell to the floor with the red and gray capsules, flipping one after another into her mouth. Tom moaned on the bed, "Take them all, you cunt, and I hope you choke to death, if you don't OD on them first."

Cinch dragged Chloe out of his bedroom, but five minutes later she crept back in, apologizing, asking him to try to understand. He couldn't comprehend such desperation so said nothing. The knee in the balls hurt, but it was more than a physical ache, it went deeper than that. He loved her once? This, this animal? She repelled him! He'd lost her a long time before; with that kick to the groin, she'd finally lost him.

He knew there was no way to get rid of her without carrying her out bodily, which was physically impossible. She was going under from all the Darvon. They made coffee, and began to walk her around. When a pot of black coffee and miles around the living room did nothing, Tom called the Emergency Dental Clinic, which turned out to be an answering service, which in turn referred him to a dentist on call, who in turn asked him to stop bothering him at the ungodly hour of six in the morning, and call his office number, where a girl on another answering service would give him a referral, "to one of my crazy colleagues who takes cases in the middle of the night." Tom did get the crazy colleague and explained the situation. "Can't she take a few more painkillers and wait until the regular office hours?" Tom told him another painkiller would do just that, kill her. The dentist agreed to see her in half an hour at his office in Hollywood.

"How are we gonna get her in the car?" Tom asked Cinch.

"Well, I saw a wheelbarrow out there on the path. We could dump her in that, sorta."

"Jesus. Yeah, I guess we have no choice."

"I'll get it. You keep slapping her." Cinch went out to get the wheelbarrow, and while she was gone, Chloe vomited, and Tom had the unpleasant task of having to clean her. Then she started crying about her father, saying it just wasn't fair to get run over by a fork lift the very first day of work. And Mama Chloe had always hated him for confining her to the suburbs of Chicago when she—

Citronella slammed the wheelbarrow against the door frame and said, "Let's dump her in backwards."

"Can you help lift?"

"In Kansas somewhere, in the moving van, a walnut buffet fell on me when we hit a bump and I had to push it off. I got muscles."

"Come on then. Heave-ho." Together they lifted the mass of caftan, hair, fat and beads into the wheelbarrow. Then Tom grabbed his wallet and slid it into his jeans and pulled a T-shirt over his head and locked the door. Blizzard perched on the window, looking perplexed.

They carted her around the cottage to the car, where Phoebe was again barking. They rolled her into the Pontiac Sunbird and fastened a seat belt around her middle. One breast fell out of the caftan and Tom pushed it back in. Citronella got into the back seat with the dog, who pressed his nose between her legs. She bashed him with her fist. Tom fleetingly wondered why they called a male dog Phoebe, but wasn't about to ask.

They got to the office at six-thirty. They sat out front for forty minutes before the good doctor showed up. The dentist took a look at them—this hustler in ripped jeans looking dazed and sleepy, a Mama Cass with electric hair and a shredded table cloth wrapped over her shoulders, groaning, and a dwarf with purple glasses holding onto the biggest dog he'd ever seen—and cursed himself for ever answering his phone. Then he put his hand on Citronella's shoulder and said, "Come along, dear, let's see what we can do."

Aha, Tom had been right. She *was* a dentist's dream!

Unfortunately for him, Cinch steered him to the correct patient. They all helped the semi-comatose Chloe into the office and then the doctor asked Tom and Cinch to stay in the waiting room. They sat in silence; Chloe was making enough noise for all of them:

"My mama died on a stupid goddamn plane, on a fucking olive, man, an olive! *Owwwww!* Please make the pain go away. Everything's going wrong, man, my fiance is fucking my sister—"

Tom dropped his head on the couch on that line.

"—and my roommate doesn't understand me and I don't have any money left and these fucking teeth are killing me and the cats don't have any food and everyone thinks we're dykes and my mama . . . my mama died on a *fucking airplane* over the *swamps* someplace. . ."

"Please be quiet when you open your mouth," the dentist pleaded.

"Fuck man, she didn't *like* it in California, they stole her life just like they're stealing mine and— *Owwwwwww! God, don't do that! Nooooooo! Help!*" She coughed and spit and he shouted at her to sit still or he'd have to gas her and then she cried some more and let out a terrifying scream. *"Heeeeeeeeeeelp!"*

Cinch looked at Tom and said, "Heelp?"

Tom shrugged. This couldn't be happening. It was a bad dream. But when she cried, "Tomcat, it's all his fault!" he knew he was awake. Cinch took his hand and told him not to listen, but it was overpowering:

"He promised to marry me! I was gonna be his wife, his fuckin' *wife!* My daddy died believing he was gonna marry me . . . and my mama knew he wasn't and she was hurt. He started it all, he just walked out, left me a fuckin' note and left me with our cat in the snow and cold. . ." She coughed and spit and begged the dentist to stop hurting her, and then she continued. "I told myself it would still happen. He would marry me some day. I went to New York and I was a fuckin' great actress there and then I got fucked over by that asshole Stephen and—" She seemed to choke. The dentist asked her to please stop shouting. But she kept on. "Goddamn *men*, fuckin' charming men, Tomcat, that bastard, *fuckin' fag bastard!* Goddamn fag's afraid of something normal, something real—shit, man, I didn't want a split-level house and kids, all I wanted was a man who would marry me. *He stole my life, man!* He did it and I hate him. *I hate him, the rotten lying son of—*"

Tom jumped up and ran out the door.

He was standing near the car when Cinch called to him to come and help. He went back inside the waiting room and watched the dentist write a prescription for

codeine—*more* codeine?—and the man told them he
never wanted to see Chloe again in his life, and he was
sure she'd never want to see *him* again once she got his
bill. He slammed the door after them.

Tom drove them home. Cinch apologized for Chloe.
"She didn't know what she was saying." Tom nodded
and told her he understood that; he had needed to get
some air. He dropped them off and had the prescription
filled and brought it to the house. Cinch pushed a pill or
two down Chloe's throat, over in the corner of the kitch-
en where she'd collapsed. Three cats were nestled up
against her warmth. The big dog licked Tom's crotch; he
turned and left in disgust.

He drove to Sandy's apartment and gave her the car
keys and told her what had happened. "It's the root of
it all, Sandy. She's never forgiven me for not marrying
her. She's never really understood. Cinch said she didn't
know what she was saying, but she knew *exactly* what
she was saying. I feel helpless and to blame. I know I
shouldn't, but I do."

"She's real sick, Tomcat. She's real sick and my
mama knew it and I know it. You can't feel bad."

He shrugged. "I'm falling out. Can I sleep here and
you drive me home later when you have time?"

"I can take you right now if you want."

"Yes, oh, please. I just want to pull the covers over
my head and forget."

She took his hand. "My sister's real crazy, Tom. Stop
blaming yourself. You can't feel so bad."

"Okay, I won't." But he was too smart not to. Somewhere deep in his soul he faced the truth of what he'd
done to her, and knew the guilt would always be with
him.

EIGHTEEN

"Do you realize Christmas is here?" Tom said to Mitch, sipping champagne, smiling at him. "It's been a whole year since we met."

"The best one of my life.",Mitch was standing next to Tom in the midst of some fifty attorneys and their families and friends. The firm was throwing a Christmas party, and Mitchell Birney brought his lovely young wife, Paula, and his very best friend, Tom Brassen. Paula had been pleasant to him all evening, but had spent most of the time chatting with other wives and friends. That was fine; it gave Mitchell more time to be with Tom. "If it hadn't been for Christmas, we'd never have met."

"When do you want the tree? Will you help decorate mine on Tuesday or Wednesday?"

Mitch shook his head and took another martini off a gleaming tray. "I won't be needing the tree this year."

"Why not?"

"It's going to be a kosher Christmas for us. My parents are coming from Boston."

"Oh." Tom looked disappointed.

"They love the holidays, but having a tree in the house, that would be going too far."

Tom felt sad. He'd been taking care of the tree all year, knowing it would be standing guard over the presents for Jeremy on Christmas morning. "Jer's gonna be mad."

"Pissed. He is already. Not only can't he tell his gram and gramps that we had planned to have one, he can't mention last year's. Paula's parents loved it, but they're not Jewish, of course. Mine keep a religious house." Mitch looked over at his wife, talking with friends, looking sleek in a long black dress. "She's going to miss it too. She was brought up a Catholic. She's a convert."

"I didn't know that. Why?"

"She studied religion her first two years of college and just picked the one that interested her most."

One of the senior partners of the firm came over and Mitchell introduced Tom. "Herb Mutnick, I'd like you to meet Thomas Brassen. He's an up-and-coming composer. And my tennis partner."

"How do you do, Brassen. I think I met your wife over there on the other side of the room."

"No, I don't think so. Haven't tied the knot yet." With a glance to Mitchell.

The big fat man laughed heartily. "Give you some free advice—don't ever. All they do is bitch at ya. Merry Christmas, Birney, you too, Brassen." And he walked off.

"You know, Tom," Mitch said, "with my folks here, I won't be able to see you."

"Not at all?"

"Maybe for lunch now and then. They're staying the whole week. Their first time out and they want to do it all, Knott's Berry Farm, Dizzyland, San Diego Zoo—"

"Hey, that's mine! I promised Jeremy I'd take him down there after the first of the year."

"I didn't know."

Tom looked resigned. "It's okay, forget it." He picked up a canape and popped it into his mouth. "Blue bread with pickles and shrimp on it. How Christmassy." He ate another. Then he asked, "Can you still come over one night and do the tree with me?"

"Of course. Maybe we'll have our own little holiday together. I'll spend the night."

"Just leave it to me." Mitch looked around. "Hey, let's sneak out to the balcony." The lobby was filled with people, but the terrace was deserted and dark. Outside, Mitch dragged him over behind a pillar and ran his hand over his cheek. Tom felt his cock getting hard in his green corduroy suit pants. "We'll decorate both trees and have our party together under them. I want to fuck you for Christmas."

"You're nothing but a dirty old Santa Claus."

Mitchell pulled him to his strong frame and kissed him lovingly, running his tongue through his warm mouth, holding his head in his hands. "I love you so much. You've given me more pleasure in one year than most people experience in a lifetime."

Tom reached down and put his hand between the man's legs. "I want you. Now."

"But we can't—"

"Sure we can."

"No, not here. . ."

"Mitch, be quiet."

Tom pulled him by the arm and they went over to a corner of the terrace where huge philodendron leaves obliterated the space. Mitchell was nervous, protesting softly, but Tom forced him into it. The truth was Mitchell had never done anything so daring—hadn't he always told Tom the thing he hated most about his life was that he'd always played it safe, never took chances? This was certainly not safe.

Tom did it quickly. He fell to his knees and took the hard penis into his mouth, and with his hand and his lips and tongue quickly brought his lover to the peak of a violent orgasm.

Mitchell held his breath. It was cold and he could feel it on his face and hands, but his cock was hot, wet and

hot, and he was dressed in his best suit, and Tom in his,
and his wife was right behind those doors where the music was playing and this was the spot he sometimes ate
his lunch from a little bag with a couple of the secretar-
ies and now he was being sucked off by his—

"Oh, Jesus!" One cry, only one sharp sound in the
night, and it was over. He fell back against the stone
wall of the towering building and panted. Tom got up
and put him back into his pants. He said nothing, only
wiped Mitchell's brow and nuzzled his chin until he
smiled. "You freak me out," Mitch said.

"You need it."

They walked back inside when they looked fairly
sedate once again. Mitch noticed a long questioning
look from his wife, but he said nothing about it. He
seemed deep in thought as he and Tom filled plates with
roast beef and potato salad. When they sat down, he
said, "Why don't you go away for the holidays?" His
voice was bright and enthusiastic.

Tom's immediate emotion was hurt. "Why? Where?"

"If you stay here you'll be unhappy, I know you will.
Why don't you go away with Kevin, maybe, or to New
York and see Rachel."

Tom was amazed at how unpossessive Mitchell was—
it was as though he were so sure of his position in Tom's
heart, so secure in his role in Tom's life, he didn't have
a suspicion in the world. But then too, maybe he just
didn't really give a shit, way down at the bottom line.
Tom felt his head beginning to pound with the thought.

But what was there to be suspicious about? Maybe the
guy was simply being smart. Smart enough to be sure
not only of his position, but understand Tom's needs
and desires as well, smart enough to know when and
where to hold on, when and where to let go. They'd sur-
vived a year together, a year and a wife and tricks and
friends and strong forces on both sides, children and
women lovers and a great deal of time.

"Rachel did ask if I wanted to go to Jamaica with her," Tom remembered. "But I think she bowed out herself. It was a charter thing with friends. Kevin's family is going to San Diego to be with his grandparents. They invited me along. I like his parents, but. . . Maybe I should go to New York and stay with Rachel."

"She'd love it."

Tom thought about it for a little while as they ate. Then he announced, "I've made up my mind. I'm going."

"Where?" a woman's voice asked from behind them.

Mitch got up and helped Paula sit down. She had a plate of food the size of a mountain in front of her. "I'm famished. Where is it you're going, Tom?"

"New York for the holidays. To see my friend Rachel."

"Just a friend?" Her voice had lovely overtones.

"Friend, lover, sweetheart, mother sometimes. She's the most incredible lady in the world." Tom avoided Mitchell's eyes.

"Oh, damn. Mitch always told me I was."

Tom gave her a phony grin and excused himself to get some more roast beef.

Wednesday came and Mitch arrived on time and it was the beginning of their Christmas together. They dragged both trees in from the cool night of the patio and decorated them. Sparsely, because Tom only had ornaments enough for one, but their hearts were in it and that's what counted. Christmas carols played on the stereo. A fire roared. They popped corn over the burning logs and drank cinnamon cider. Mitch gave him a Cartier tank watch and Tom's gift to him was a leather-bound gold-stamped rare copy of the works of Tolstoy, Mitchell's favorite author.

They made love in the living room with only the glow of the embers and little colorful tree lights to illuminate the room. They came together and basked in the afterglow, their bodies masculine and feminine at the same time, strong and hard, soft and giving. They slept there with Blizzard curled in between them, but then the room got chilly and they woke up and drank some more hot cider and put more logs on the coals and made love another time, slowly, luxuriously. And they slept soundly in each other's arms.

In the morning they held onto each other until the last possible moment, until it was time for Mitchell to leave the dream for the reality of the office. No good-byes were uttered. Only a simple, "Merry Christmas, I love you," from Tom.

And a kiss and embrace from Mitchell which contained all his feelings.

Kevin invited him to spend an old-fashioned Christmas with his parents, Zena asked him to join her at a famous novelist's Christmas gathering at Lake Arrowhead, and Rachel wanted him to come to New York. He opted for mama cat. But not in New York; he had changed his mind about that.

They holed up in—of all places—Santa Fe, New Mexico. Rachel had been offered the use of a house owned by a musician she knew, who happened to be on tour in Europe. Tom loved the idea from the start. "We'll be all alone in the hills, and we'll visit the adobe Indian villages and go to Old Town in Albuquerque and I think there's a real Zuni pueblo down there and we can buy all kinds of jewelry and find real Mexican places to eat. . ."

Tom was drooling.

They met at the Albuquerque Sunport the day before Christmas Eve. They rented a Mazda and drove to Santa Fe and found the house after winding blindly through a canyon for an hour. "Look for a dusty road to the right," an old-timer told them. Dusty translated to mucky since there was snow on the ground in spots. When they finally got settled in the small white adobe cabin, they were exhausted. "I feel as though I've traveled three thousand miles," Rachel moaned.

"You have."

They checked out the town on Saturday. Small, quaint, almost primitive in parts, hard to believe this was a state capital. There was something refreshing in that. They found what seemed like dozens of little arts and crafts shops on Canyon Road, and Rachel made it a point to return, getting Tom to swear they'd treat themselves to some of the homemade wares. They bought a scrawny Christmas tree from a bearded fellow for a dollar—it was the very last one in the lot—and decorated it with tin foil ornaments they made from a roll of Reynolds Wrap in the kitchen, and cranberries they'd bought from the market.

They had dinner—Rachel made a mushroom soup, very bitter and delectible, some Christmas sausage, red cabbage and butter and caraway seeds, and flour tortillas—and then dressed warmly and went into town and parked the car. They strolled around the city for almost an hour, amazed at the simple beauty of what was truly a Spanish Christmas, the houses and lawns and walkways in the town square lined with *luminarios,* candles stuck into sand inside brown paper bags, burning as if glowing stars dropped from the heavens, hundreds, maybe thousands of them. And Christmas trees with their red and green and blue and gold shimmering in the frosted window panes of the houses. An icy mountain wind howled and strains of Christmas hymns filled the air at the same time as they walked near the Capitol building. Townspeople wished them a Merry Christmas wherever they went, and one couple even invited them to a large family gathering, to feast, to drink to happiness, to raise their voices in good will.

Then they went to Midnight Mass. They found a small adobe church built by the Spanish missionaries in the 1700s, and it was lit by nothing but candles. The musty old walls echoed with song and spirit. Franciscan priests in their most dazzling garments and altar boys in red and white cassocks and a choir in the deepest of green robes formed a long line in the aisles. The bishop carried a statue of the Christ child, leading them in procession to the manager. The congregation sang "Oh Come All Ye Faithful" and then "Silent Night" as the bishop knelt before the crib, joined by the other priests, by the nuns, in their forbidding brown robes, their faces radiant, by the angelic altar boys, the choir members and everyone in the pews, everyone from the faithful who turned up at Mass each Sunday, to Tom and Rachel, who'd never turned up at any Mass before in their lives.

Snow flurries were coming down on their heads now as they walked to the car. Church bells pealed all over the city. It was Christmas. They got into the car. "Whew, it's cold," she said, rubbing her gloved hands together. "Tommy, tell me, how did you feel in there?"

He started the engine. "There was a sense of—what would it be called—serenity I guess. Christmas should be uncomplicated and serene. It's never been like this for me. It's always been wild and party-time and let's-get-drunk and stuff like that. It never meant anything. I've never been in a church like that before. It was so . . . basic. Yeah, down-to-earth. I think I—this sounds dumb, but I mean it—I think I really had a spiritual experience."

She turned the heat on as he pulled out of the parking place. "I feel the same way."

They drove back to the little house and lit a roaring fire and they exchanged gifts. Tom gave Rachel a hand-printed note which read:

> Tomorrow you can pick out anything you want in the world and I'll buy it for you for Christmas (providing it is under $25.00 which is all my budget can afford right now). XXXXX Tomcat

Rachel gave him a silver heart to wear around his

neck, a silver heart filled with deep red coral; it suited him and he loved it.

The sun was coming up as the fire burned its way down to the bricks and they went to bed and hugged under the big goose-down comforter, but they did not make love. It would not have been right; it would have been imposing something on a special time that just wasn't there. They felt happy in one another's arms, peaceful. That was enough.

They held hands in bed as they settled into their places for the night, sleeping on their sides, facing each other, comfortable and relaxed deep inside. Outside the little house, the clear New Mexican sky was still filled with light snow, the flakes of glimmering crystal falling gently to whiten the red tile roofs.

In the morning, Rachel cooked up some muffins and put up cinnamon coffee. Then they set out to climb the hills around the house, hiking until they were wet and muddy and silly with childish laughter. They threw snowballs at each other. They went inside to toast their bodies by the fire and then they retired to corners of the room for solitude; hours passed easily as Tom read a book and Rachel did needlepoint. They went to town to a restaurant for a delicious old-fashioned Christmas dinner of turkey and cranberries and yams and cornbread with honey and a hot pepper or two. After that they went for another walk around the town, talking to kids, old folks, anyone they met. People were kind and loving, unlike so many they'd become used to in the big cities. Back at the house, Tom called Kevin and Mitch and even the Russian Countess, wishing them all a merry day. Rachel called her mother, and her son at school, and a few friends back home. And they spent another quiet evening in the pleasure of each other's company.

On Monday they ate breakfast, looked out at the snow piling up on the hills, and decided to stay in. The house had a closet filled with games, and they played

them all, checkers, Scrabble, Boggle, Clue, and Risk.
And Tom lost them all. They made love. They built a
little snowman in the yard and brought in more fire-
wood from the shed. Then they went to a freaky artsy-
fartsy party given by some sculptor named Betty and her
lover, also named Betty, who created erotic life-sized
sculptures out of melted-down automobile tires with bits
of turquoise and Indian silver stuck on at the end of the
process. "And they say New Yorkers are weird," Rachel
whispered to Tom. But they had a good time.

Tuesday was the last day. They drove to Albur-
querque and checked out the big sprawling city first
from up on a mesa, from the campus of the University
of Albuquerque, then into the city itself, buying desert-
scented perfumes in Old Town, Tom's gift to Rachel,
eating more Mexican food than they could reasonably
justify, watching in amazement at the families careening
down the streets in beat-up and battered-all-to-hell pick-
up trucks, stopping to look at some marvelous homes in
more residential parts of the city. They ate it up, every
moment of it, and after crossing the Rio Grande, which
was little more than a trickle, they once more made their
way back to Santa Fe and to the adobe house atop the
canyon road.

He looked thoroughly satisifed after dinner, as he sat
stirring his coffee.

"Happy?"

"Happiest cat in the alley."

She bent forward and kissed him on his nose.

They did nothing that night. Relaxed and talked and
watched some kind of animal—they thought it was a fox
—come up to the door and sniff and go away. They put
their jackets on again and went for a walk in the middle
of the night. The air was fresh and crisp and dry even
though it was so cold. "It doesn't go through you the
way it does back east," she said, holding onto his arm as
they made their way up the hillside.

"Careful, you'll slip on a patch of snow and I'll have to leave you with the Zuni witchdoctors," he warned.

She laughed. Then she asked him to stop climbing. She was huffing. "I'm an old lady."

"Hah. I've seen you shlepp the streets of Manhattan. You could outrun me."

"On Thirty-fourth Street, sure. It's flat. But this is too much." She turned around and looked behind him and then she saw why he'd led her up that far. "Oh, Tommy, it's gorgeous. It looks like a Wyeth painting."

And it did. The colors were dull in the night, muted yet expressive, understated, magnificent and cold. Chimneys pouring smoke into the icy air, billowing, spiraling into the chunky clouds high in the deep black sky. White adobe houses stark and still, all the roofs with patches of white snow at the foot of the canyon. Few lights at the edge of the city, far away.

"You *see* things, Tommy," she told him. "It's one of your best qualities." She gazed at the serene sight for a moment longer, and then faced him. "If you had to choose one thing about me that is most important to you, what would you say?"

He said nothing for a moment. He folded his arms and held his head high, breathing into the woolen scarf on his chin. Finally he answered: "Your wisdom." His teeth were chattering, and he pulled the scarf up higher and talked through it. "Rachel, why do you love me?"

She knew he was serious, not fishing for some flippant Mother Cat reply. "Because you're big and beautiful and bright like a star. When I'm with you I feel just as bright, just as youthful and glowing. I need you."

That surprised him. Needed him? Wanted him, yes. Desired him, sure. But needed him? "Honestly?"

"Very much so. You make me more complete. I don't go around for boys in their twenties to pull into bed, a guy half my age and gay on top of it."

"Are straight men really boring?"

"Only by comparison. I'm turning to ice. Let's go back."

"But it's so marvelous up here."

"Marvelous is one thing, frostbite is another."

He took her hand, and they started down the hillside.

"Tommy, I've known women who look for gay men as a mountain to climb. But they always come down alone. I'm coming down *with* you. It's a very popular thing right now—in the big city—to conquer a homosexual, especially a young one who is supposed to be repelled by a woman's body. So the woman seduces him and the gay boy says, "Oh, it's so easy, it wasn't so bad at all." And the woman thinks she's done it, pin on a medal, just like a man taking the virginity of a teenage girl. Such self-patronizing, such ego-massaging.

"But those women are never happy in the end because the boyfriend isn't going to suddenly be transformed into the lover, the forever bed partner. He's going to be off doing it with Bruce the next night, just like before . . . oh, it's too complex, it goes too deep, Tommy."

"Tell me."

They reached the door of the house. "I don't feel like wasting our last few precious hours talking about the ladies who go down on twenty-three-year-old fag cabdrivers at lunch time. You know it isn't that way with us. It would never have lasted this long had it been; one of us would have tired of it. Remember Susan?"

"Yes."

"She thinks you're the hottest thing since hot pants."

"If I wasn't so frozen, I'd blush."

She opened the door and they went inside and sat by the fire with their coats on. "Susan said to me, Oh, Rachel, you *sleep* with him! as if it were dying and going to heaven. She thought it was about sex and nothing else. I told her you were a swell lover, but you don't have a platinum cock, thank you very much."

Tom laughed. "I thought it was worth its weight in gold."

"Gold maybe, platinum never." She kissed him. "I find that your homosexuality is part of the myriad things that makes you you. That talent you have in those fingers, your feel for conversation, for making me laugh, the way you talk and walk, dress and think and feel and smell, oh, I love the way you smell, the scent of you." She buried her head in his collar. "You are one of the great gifts of my life. I ask nothing of you but to be yourself always, and to grow. When you stop growing, I want nothing more to do with you."

"I'll grow, I'll grow," he laughed. Then he unwound the scarf from her neck and kissed her tenderly.

She took her coat off and put another small log on the fire, and then sat looking at him, the big frame all covered with the winter jacket, jeans wet at the bottom with snow, blond hair looking dark now, eyes brooding. "I want you to know something. You come off as this big hulk of a hot stud, the whole number you do, the faded jeans and Western belt buckle and flashing those robin's egg eyes, the low voice, sexy ass and all, but you don't fool me. It's easy to take you for that and nothing more —I mean, I'm the first one who'd admit she loves to fall asleep with a hand on that sexy ass, right?—but there's so much more to it. Not your being young and gay, I'm not talking about any of that. It's the femininity in you. The sensitivity, the part that cooks and cleans and appreciates good music and plays with Jeremy—though the 'Uncle Tom' stuff is a little nauseating—and is another kind of wife to Mitchell. No man has ever been able to curl up in my arms and let it all out the way you do, his fears and anxieties, frustrations, bad dreams, memories of a terrifying childhood. And of wanting to be loved, his passion for men, cocoa and brownies. And of your dreams and fantasies of the future.

"I want to see you succeed and get ahead in life. I want to help you do it. But you must rid yourself of the childish aspects of your makeup and concentrate on the sophisticated part, the mature side."

He blinked. No one had ever said things like this to him. He blushed and yet felt proud.

"Yes, you've got a sophistication you won't even admit to yourself. It's been developed just from the mere fact that you've traveled so much and met so many different kinds of people. So many varied experiences. You're still a kid, but you've been forced into growing up in ways some kids never see—getting out on your own when you're sixteen, keeping your mom out of jail for years, burying your head in fairy tales to right the grim reality around you. Plugging away at the piano against all odds, constantly telling yourself the world was waiting for your talent. So many things, a life in Chicago, one in Milwaukee, another in Los Angeles . . . my God, *three* lives in Los Angeles—"

"I'm using up my nine pretty fast."

"You've got at least eighteen. You're twice the cat than most. But do you understand what I'm saying? I want your estimation of yourself to be as fine as mine, as high, as objective."

"I don't think you're very objective."

"You should hear the praise I'd give you if I weren't, you'd throw up." She laughed and stretched in front of the heat of the fire. "We must give ourselves credit, all the time. I see the inner you, a you that is rarely shown to others. I think you must show the same to Mitchell, or I hope you do. I see the person that is lurking there under the smooth-talking, sexy blond man. It's that you *allow* me to see that side of you that counts. Anyway, even though you act it sometimes, you're not sixteen any longer. Want some tea?"

"Yeah. Can we try the black currant stuff on the shelf?"

"Absolutely." He followed her into the kitchen. "No, darling, you're not the little Ken doll that so many hungry, middle-aged women want, the doll you wind up and it fucks you and then you put it back in the playhouse till the next time you're horny. You're not a vibrator, you're a person. Age means nothing as long as everyone remains as young as possible in spirit. If an eighty-four-year-old man made me feel young, I'd be with him."

She put the kettle on the stove and lit a match to get the gas started. "And I know that nothing is forever," she said quietly, shaking the match in the air. "That's why I want to savor every moment."

He leaned against the door frame as she rinsed the cups. "Don't you ever feel competition with Mitch?"

"I know I can't compete with a man. That's a whole different kind of pleasure. So I choose not to even try. I trust myself. And you."

"What would I do without you?"

"Be miserable," she said with a laugh.

"No kidding, I would be. Maybe you're wrong. Maybe some things are forever."

"Well, my love for you will never die," she said softly, letting him take her in his arms.

He held her close, his fingertips pressing into her shoulder blades, his muscles taut, his entire body trembling. "I'll make sure we will always be together. From New York to San Simeon to the Sangre de Cristo mountains. We'll never be without each other."

She waited until he released her. She wanted to tell him she knew better, that more experience and years taught her more than he could know at his age. She knew people grew and changed. But what sense would there be in pressing the point, reminding him she was what he said he loved about her, wise. The kettle was whistling and she tended to it.

And he went back to the living room.

She brought the tea and they drank together and lay

on the floor, watching the flames dance on the ceiling. Oh, how she wanted to protect him, buffer him from what lay ahead. The shocks and the bumps. If only she could keep him there on that hillside, but that would be unfair, for she'd be forcing him to remain the boy she loved, not the man she wanted so much to respect.

She thought about her life with him and she felt herself shining. And then she thought of life without him and it brought tears to her eyes. No. She would not allow herself to think about that. Maybe he was right, maybe she'd met her match; maybe he was wiser. Maybe he *would* make sure they'd always be together.

NINETEEN

The New Year came and he found himself on another plane, riding back in time, a capsule jetting him back through the years.

He was on his way to Dallas, and he was rereading *The Wind In The Willows* for the sixteenth time in his life, nervous and nostalgic. Why, of all cities in the United States of America, did Zena have to send him to Dallas with the collection? Dallas. That's where Annie lived now, so he heard. Would he see her or would he not? He talked with Mitch about it before he left, and the conversation depressed him.

Mitch asked, "What made you leave and try to wipe her out of your mind all these years?"

"Heavy question. She hurt me. I was ashamed of her. No kid should be ashamed of his mother. She *hurt* me and that's the part I can't forget. See, I loved her for a long time before that. Loved her even though I felt so much . . . disgust. I prayed so many times, in daydreams at home and at school and by a big tree in Houston, that we would have a family, be one. Not even with a father, just the two of us. It was never like that. I envied all those other kids. I never got to know other kids very well because they had mothers and fathers and brothers and sisters and they had hot meals and did things together and went to church and bought different houses and moved in and they even went on vacations together, they traveled, and it was so threatening!"

"Tom, hey, take it easy. . ."

"Mitch, hold me."

"I'm here, baby. You have to realize you may have ended up better off than those other kids with real families. Sometimes they give the illusion of love and togetherness, but there's really not much there . . . and they wonder why they got married and—"

"Mitch?"

"Sorry. I just wandered."

Tom ran his hand through Mitch's hair. "No, tell me. Something's wrong. I can feel you tightening up. What is it?"

"The *illusion* of being together. Paula and I don't do much together anymore. She finally mentioned it."

"She mentioned *me,* in other words," Tom said.

"Yes. I spend every moment I have free with you and the kids. I'm a lousy father to Chrissy. She's always at Paula's parents' house or with a sitter. Jeremy talks about you constantly. Even when Paula and I are together alone, my mind is on you. I sit and count minutes until I can get away and see you. I think if Jeremy had his way, he'd pick you over his own mother and that is wrong and it's all my fault. I allowed it to happen, I fostered it. She feels it. And she's changing, dropping projects she once gloried in, staying at home more, withdrawing. We haven't slept together in months. I'm not happy there as long as I know you're here, in this bed, alone, and I could be here with you if I hadn't made a few wrong decisions earlier in life. I said this situation would work out fine. Tom, I *want* it too, I don't want to lose either, I want you and I want Paula and the kids."

"Who's asking you to choose?"

"No one, no one is making demands, but I'm the one who feels responsible toward the two ends of the rope.

My wife and my children, and my lover. I want it all. I want to take a magic pill that will make it all fine. Oh, hell, it can't be as bad as I'm making it out to be."

"It's worse."

"But we'll work it out," Mitch said hopefully.

"I think it's your decision.

Reading *Willows* was an escape from that too. Should he pull away from Mitch to save his marriage? *What* marriage? It wasn't his responsibility, he wasn't making any demands. Mitchell had, by the fact of marrying Paula, taken on a commitment he had to work out on his own. If he found himself a lover and it interfered with his marriage, that was his problem to work out. Only Mitch could make the decision. And Tom seemed sure if one had to be made, it would be for him. Mitch could still visit his children if they lived together . . . maybe they could even raise Jeremy themselves; maybe Tom could really step into the role of—he hated to think the word, much less say it—mother.

Mother. He sat in the Dallas/Fort Worth airport, that cold and monstrous place, waiting for Zena's trunks and the truck which was to meet him. *Mother*. Somewhere within miles, Tugboat Annie Brassen was living and breathing. Unless she too had met her maker. No, she'd probably live forever, giving BJ's and playing old Patsy Cline albums and entertaining drunk dumb cowboys and truckers until the world came apart. He looked around. A man walked by, sporting a stetson hat. A woman in Dale Evans boots dotted with pearls. Another in pink hot pants, her fanny sagging sadly out of the dacron seat. If the world ended, Dallas would be the place to go first. It deserved it.

Right until the minute he walked into Twisters, he kept telling himself he wasn't going to see her. He wasn't going to seek her out. How did he explain, then, his actions that afternoon as he drove some hundred miles in search of one person and another, anyone who had a guess as to where Annie might be? What a way to find your mother. Most kids just walk in the door, and come upon their parents sitting there in the family room watching TV. He had to go from bar to bar, from tips and guesses by big-breasted whores, managers of sleazy hotels.

He sat in the rented car for nearly an hour in front of Twisters. Something told him she was in there, for sure. It was intuition. He saw guys and girls come and go in that hour. He watched a fist crash into a guy's jaw and two drunks stumble down the steps together with their arms around one another. Friendship. A girl came up to the car and lifted her skirt to adjust her panty hose, flashing her cunt in his face. When he didn't open the door or roll down the window, she hissed at him and threw him the finger.

Finally he got his strength together and walked into the bar. It was dusty and smoke-filled and looked like all the places he'd pulled Annie out of when he was small and hungry and she hadn't been home for days at a time. He looked around. Lots of eyes hit him but the country music continued to blare and eventually no one paid any attention to him, except a young lady who stared at his zipper. He'd half expected the place to go silent when he entered, the Red Sea parting, Annie in the center, arms wide. *John Wayne pushed open the bar door and hush, they all turn.* But John Ford wasn't directing this one. Nothing happened. The bartender kept sliding foamy beers down to the far end of the bar.

Tom went to the end closest to him. "Gimme a beer."

"What kind, sonny?" the old cattle rustler asked.

"Any kind."

"Mexican?"

"American."

"Ah, imported." He filled the glass with Budweiser.

Tom inhaled the foam off it. His eyes were getting used
to the black light and garish posters with love symbols
and peace signs, to the smoke and tinny noise. He
glanced at the tables. No one looked like her. They
looked like a collection of extras on a set for a grade-B
Hollywood movie. Bored, peaceful but with the hint
that they were all sitting on firecrackers. He'd never seen
people like this. A guy with white fringe all over his
body, money, a roll of money, clipped to his watchband,
flashing it all around, a whore on each arm. At a table
in the corner, a skinny woman, skinnier even than the
old woman who'd played Bonnie Parker's mother in
Bonnie and Clyde. She was talking to herself or singing
along with Charlie Parker, he didn't know which. If she
was singing, she didn't know the lyrics. Near her were a
couple, his hair long, hers short, both of them
overweight and pimply and barely post-adolescent,
making out. Tom took a deep breath and gulped the
beer, wanting to get out.

And then he saw her. Oh, he knew she was over there
at the other end of the bar. He'd seen them clamoring
around the fat woman, the guys all holding beers in their
hand, bottles, no glasses for them, and laughing and
slapping her on the back and carrying on, hooting and
hollering almost loud enough to drown out Charlie.

He fixed his eyes on her. She was the center attraction,
a kind of hostess. She was dressed in a tight white sweater and her tits seemed more enormous than he'd recalled. Her fake suede whiskey-stained skirt was hiked
up to her buns and she wore high boots with platforms
to make her taller, or maybe she thought them stylish.
The hair was piled atop her head, pushing under a kind
of yachting cap, the cap he remembered her wearing
long ago, long before the Captain and Tenille had even
been invented. She had too much lipstick on her. It
crawled up into her nostrils. He used to tell her—as

young as seven—that it was silly-looking to fake your lips like that, going that high. But she never listened; she still did it.

He finished his beer and the bartender looked at him and he answered the look in as Texas-macho a way as he knew how: "Hit me again, partner."

"Sure 'nuff. Bud, right?"

"Right. Imported."

The bartender smiled.

"Hey, who's the lady over there, the one causing all the laughs?"

"Ain't she got the best jokes this side a Big D?" Then he stared at Tom. "Hey, sonny, I ain't never heard nobody in here ask me who she is. You ain't never been here before, have ya?"

"Nope. She just looks so popular, I wondered if she's your entertainment you advertise out front."

"*Sheeeeeit*. That's Tugboat Annie, boy! That ol' tub's what keeps me in business, not the blondie I got singin' in here on the weekends. Everybody knows ol' Annie. Don't have to advertise her none."

Tom nodded and the man went away. The blondie he'd referred to was standing in a glittering Annie Oakley outfit, holding a mike in her hand, waving to the bartender that she was ready. He snapped off Charlie Pride in the middle of a vowel and a garish pink spotlight hit the girl and she thanked them all for "showin' up here in God's junkyard tonight." She told them she was going to sing the "fav-o-rites you all've been askin' ever so much to hear. . ." She started to sing. And Tom's eyes drifted back to Annie.

Her eyes were heavy and she looked tired, but not older. Fatter, rounder, her hair—what he could see of it —a little grayer, but not older. Through the cigarette smoke and the pink spotlight she looked happy enough. Maybe going up to her would make some of that happiness vanish. Why risk that for her? She was in her world,

and he wasn't part of it. He didn't belong with these
people, nor they with him. She was loving the bad
singer, nodding her head in time. He wondered if she
would nod like that to something he would play on the
piano. Probably not. He was sure she preferred the
guitar and the singing cowgirl.

She probably had convinced herself of something,
some story, that he was a movie star or maybe he was
dead in a terrible plane crash or he was a hippy living in
a commune in Canada or he was a banker on Wall
Street, wasn't that a hoot, Annie Brassen's kid in a coat
and tie? She had some tale and she had probably come
to believe it herself by this time, and what right had he
to destroy her fantasy?

The singing cowgirl revved up for the big finish.

The lights changed, brightened.

She ended it with a bang.

He was staring at her as the audience applauded the
end of the first song, applauded and stomped the floor
with heavy boots and six-inch heels and filled the air
with the kind of whistles he'd only heard at rock concerts. Then the girl began her second number and he
realized Annie was looking across the bar, staring right
back at him. His eyes focused on hers and he blushed,
startled, feeling his feet giving under him and his back
getting wet with sweat and his stomach churning. But
then she gave him a big "Welcome, handsome!" smile,
as if greeting a new face in the old crowd.

He grinned and nodded back. *Please, God, don't let
her recognize me.*

He was sure God existed then and there because she
turned back to the singer and started nodding in time
with the music again, with the horrible twanging guitar.
He dropped three dollars on the bar, took one last look
at her and left. He drove fast, back into Dallas, back to
the hotel.

And he got rip-snorting, filthy drunk, but he wasn't

used to drinking and threw it all up before he could find comfort in sleep, and then he took too much Alka-Seltzer and threw that up too. Finally, after a cold shower in which he sat on the floor of the shower stall, he felt the dizziness leaving and the numbness of approaching sleep coming over his body.

He thought of her once more before he dozed. He thought how she looked in the last glimpse he'd had of her, just before he went out that door. He thought she looked mighty happy.

He was glad he hadn't asked for much. This way he was happy too.

What was most upsetting about the trip to Dallas was not contact made across a bar with only a smile to a stranger. The thing that bothered him most was what he overheard through the walls of the hotel: men arguing. It started him wondering and worrying, questioning whether or not he was just paranoid. He ran to a phone booth and called Rachel and told her what he'd heard. Her advice: "Call Mitchell. I told you that once before. He's a lawyer, he can help. I don't know what to tell you. You could be all wrong or maybe you've hit on something very real and frightening. Get Mitchell's advice."

But he didn't. He held it all in until he got home and drove to Kevin's apartment and nearly beat the door down. "You overheard *what?*" Kevin asked.

"A conversation and they kept saying 'the shit' and they weren't talking about bowel movements." Tom flopped in a chair, looking distraught.

"Drugs?"

"I don't know. But it has to be. There was a big fight in the room next to me."

"Who was fighting?"

"The guy who met me at the airport, the one with the truck who was handling the old bag's things for the showing. And some voice I didn't recognize. He was a Texan, had the same Houston drawl I used to have."

Kevin shook his head in confusion. "So what if they were arguing about drugs? What's it got to do with you?"

"Everything! If she's behind it, then I'm involved."

Kevin sat down by him. "Tom, you need proof, and you need to show how you're involved. Are you taking the money for the stuff to the supplier? I mean, how does it involve *you?*"

"I don't know. All I know is the Texan kept yelling about the 'stuff' not being as good as the last shipment and his people were going to be pissed because they were spending a lot of bread for quality merchandise. And that *she* better get her standards back up or he'd find another source. The guy running the fashion show said, 'You think you'll find a system as foolproof as this? You got no risk here, no risk at all. This is ingenious.' He said if the Texan didn't like it he could go back to selling golf clubs at Sakowitz like he used to do."

"A system?" Now Kevin seemed interested. "The trunks with the dresses, does anyone ever inspect them?"

Tom shook his head. "Only once in Toronto, and there was nothing wrong."

"It doesn't make sense. She's making a fortune with dress designs and has the biggest call-boy operation on the West Coast under her belt. At least the most successful. What the hell would she be doing playing around with drugs? It's dangerous enough for her with prostitution."

"Bullshit," Tom said. "It isn't dangerous, she's paying off half the town, probably half the country. And she's nuts, she's a total loon, everyone knows that."

"Bullshit to that," Kevin snapped. "Everyone *thinks* she's eccentric, being Anastasia and all, but it's completely calculated. She's a shrewd lady. Her cunt has teeth. She's good to us, but we're not in the line of fire.

I'd hate to really tangle with her."

"Yeah."

Kevin said, "something's been bothering me. I was up at the house last week when Zena was yelling at someone on the phone—it was in Mexico, because she kept swearing about the Mexican phone connections—and she told someone not to bring 'it' into the country for a while because the heat was on. I just took it to be grass. No big deal."

"But the guy I heard said 'shit' and that's heroin."

"When's the next trip?" Kevin wanted to know.

"Tomorrow. That's why I'm so panicked."

"Where to?"

"San Francisco."

"Just keep your eyes and ears open. Watch the trunk as much as you can. I'll nose around with the guys up at the mansion and see what I can pick up. Call me the minute you get back. And be careful."

He was.

He went to San Francisco with one trunk filled with winter coats, stayed an entire day, and returned without incident. Nothing had been out of the ordinary, nothing suspicious, and there had been no mention of drugs by anyone. He met the same man he always met in San Francisco, the coats were taken from the trunk and displayed privately to some buyers, then neatly packed away and again entrusted to Tom for safe return to Los Angeles.

But.

Tom checked the weight on the air freight scale going to San Francisco, and he checked it coming back. He had never bothered to pay attention to the scales before, never thought about the weights. But here was proof—the trunk was lighter coming back. Something was in there going that wasn't in there coming back.

When he got home, Tom called Kevin. He told him in

an excited voice what he'd discovered. "What the hell should I do?" he asked.

"Did you see them being packed?"

"Yes."

"Did you see them coming back?"

"I always count them. Sure. Exactly the same amount, same number."

"Did you mention it to her?"

"Are you crazy? Of course not."

Kevin thought for a moment. "Listen, do this. Go back up there and tell her. Be very la-di-da about it, but like you're concerned too. Blame it on the guy at the air freight thing, like he made it real clear the weight difference was there and you swore the same stuff was in it . . . I don't know, just bullshit. Watch her reaction. You may get fired, but that might be a blessing."

Tom hesitated. "I don't know. . ."

"Do it. What's there to lose? I'll be over by the time you get back."

So Tom went up the hill to the big house and found the Countess chewing on roast chicken. "Vat is it, Tomas?" she asked from the end of the long dining table.

"Zena, I completely forgot, the girl at the baggage scale at the air freight terminal told me the weight of the trunk was less returning than going. She wondered if I was aware of it and I said it didn't make a difference, it was probably a mistake because I had counted all the valuable coats in it and they all were there. But I thought you should know."

She seemed to choke on a bone for a moment, but fully recovered and did a little dance in quite the other direction, pretending not to care less. "Oh, Tomas, you interrupt my dinner for that? Vell, of course, Joseph kept a number of the fur collars, they detach. He is showing them in another collection. But thank you, I'm very proud you are so diligent."

"I thought it could be important. I don't want anyone ripping you off."

She smiled. "Vould you vant some vine?"

"Sure." He sat down. This was the perfect time, she was in the place he wanted her. "When is the next trip?"

She poured him a glass of red wine. "Chicago. But not for two weeks. You are free until then."

"Could Kevin go along with me?"

She was aghast. "Kevin? Who is dis Kevin?"

"The pool boy. I'll pay for his flight."

And the Shmatte Queen shook her head.

"I get bored," he told her. "I want to have someone to play with." He added a wink for good measure.

She cackled. "Oh! Vell, vhy didn't you say dat? You and ze pool boy fall in love, vell, that's amazing. Vell, of course he can go with you. Have fun on ze honeymoon, darling."

He finished his wine, got up and pecked her on the cheek, and left. *We'll get you, you hypocritical old bitch.* He ran down to the house. Kevin was there.

Tom told him everything that had just happened. "Me? Kevin asked. "*I'm* going along?"

"Yeah! Don't you want to do a little sleuthing?"

"What if we get in trouble?"

"We won't. All we have to do is find proof and then we get the fuck away from here, for good. Maybe we can blackmail the old bag. Maybe—"

"Could the fur collar thing be true?" Kevin asked.

"Hell no, every coat had a fur collar, coming and going. I'm not blind."

"So we wait until Chicago, huh?" Kevin said, feeling a slight sense of anticipation and excitement.

"Joe and Frank Hardy, on to the Windy City," Tom laughed.

TWENTY

"God, I couldn't wait till you got here!" Tom pulled Mitch into the house and hugged him, danced him around the living room. "It happened, it finally happened!"

"What happened?" Mitch pulled his tie apart and plopped to the sofa to relax. "You sounded hysterical over the phone."

"Richard Douglas, you know, the director?"

"Sure."

"Well, he called me this morning and asked if I could get my ass down to Burbank Studios in an hour."

"You sent him a tape ages ago, I remember."

Tom beamed. "Yes. And I jumped in the car and went out and he showed me the rough cut of this film, just the two of us in a screening room."

"And?"

"And when it was done, he turned to me and asked if I had a feel for the music that should go with it."

"Oh, Tom, that's terrific!"

"Wait. He said, 'I'm tired of the same old shit you hear as background for everything on TV.'"

"And you agreed like crazy."

"Sure did. He asked if I thought I could take a stab at it. I very cooly said yes."

"When does he need it?"

"In less than a month."

"Jesus, Tom, you think you can do that?"

He nodded. "Best under pressure, you know? It's bull, but I have to, I don't have a choice. The film is good, full of impact even without the music. There isn't much dialogue. It's very lyrical, a love story in the wilderness, and it makes a statement that's biting and sad at the end, like what happens to them is paralleled by what's happening to the environment."

"I read about that project. He finally got the network to go for it, huh? He'll lose money, but win an Emmy."

"He's a swell guy. We're going to use only piano and organ where there are some majestic mountain sequences."

"Rich Douglas is known for giving newcomers a chance, especially with writers and actors. He's always up against union problems and whatnot, but he usually wins."

"I'm going to have that problem. I don't belong to anything and I'm going to need your expert help."

"Expert, hell. I just screwed up a million dollar deal today."

"In your business, that isn't a big problem, is it?"

"Only if there's no way to rectify it."

Tom looked concerned. "Is there?"

"I think so."

"I have a contract to sign I want you to look at. It promises him a finished tape, the whole score, on the dot one month from next Friday, which is when he expects to have the final cut. I'm pinching myself to see if I'm sleeping."

"I want to see that contract. You're not signing anything until I go over it." He reached out and tousled Tom's hair like a puppy. "Wow, your voice sounded strange on the phone. I thought you were sick or something."

Tom knelt down and sat between Mitch's legs on the floor. "It's just the right timing. Rachel said something would come along sooner or later. It always happens when you really want it and work for it."

"I'm proud of you," Mitch said, bending forward and kissing Tom's blond hair. "Now how about making me dinner?"

Tom was surprised. "You don't have to go home?"

"Nope. I told Paula I had a lot to do at the office, and then I was stopping at the gym."

"Doesn't she ever wonder about all the time at the gym? You should look like Charles Atlas by now. Or at least Arnold."

"Nope. But do you?"

Tom got up. "Huh?" He went to the kitchen. Mitch followed him.

"I mean do you wonder? I am there a lot, you know. It isn't all lies to cover up my being with you. Do you wonder if I'm *doing* anything there?"

Tom grabbed some butter and then the wire basket filled with eggs and set them on the bar. "Cheese and spinach souffle?"

"Fine. Answer me."

"Well, of course, sometimes. But it doesn't matter."

Mitch watched him as he started cooking, breaking and separating the eggs, heating the oven, melting the butter, chopping the spinach. "You really meant that, didn't you? You're really not possessive at all."

"No. Look," he said, waving the whisk for emphasis, "sure I wonder, who wouldn't wonder with a guy as stunning as you wandering around a locker room filled with other naked guys? Whether you're celibate or if you're gang-banging them, it makes no difference, ultimately, as long as it doesn't affect your love for me. And as far as I can see, it hasn't."

"Were you always so free from jealousy?"

"Move over, I gotta put the yolks in the sauce. I never

was in a situation to get jealous before. So I don't know how to answer that. Fidelity is an outmoded notion anyhow."

"I tricked with a guy last week."

Tom stiffened for a moment. Then he dumped the five round golden globs into the white sauce. He said nothing, but felt a cold shiver run up his spine.

"It just happened. I've felt guilty about it. I had to get it off my chest. It meant nothing. It wasn't even very good. All we did was—"

"Spare me the details." Tom stirred the sauce and turned off the gas under the spinach. Now was the time to see whether or not he believed the theory he'd been spouting. He said nothing, but his mind clicked away like crazy.

"Say something," Mitch begged. "I mean, yell at me or something, throw me out, tell me it's all right, anything."

Tom finally folded the sauce into the beaten egg whites. Then he dumped the mixture into the souffle dish and put it into the oven after running a knife through it.

"Tom, please, are you angry?"

He finally faced Mitch. "No, I'm not angry and I'm not hurt. It just surprised me, that's all. Something ran through me, some pang of jealousy and insecurity. I'm okay now." But his face didn't seem to mirror what he was saying.

"I'd be out of my mind to ever leave you," he whispered and then went into the bedroom to change into the jeans and T-shirt he kept in the closet.

Tom set the table for dinner, but his mind was on what Mitch said. *Out of his mind to leave me? Why in hell did he say that?* Was he contemplating it?

They ate and Mitch read the contract Tom had been given by Richard Douglas. "It's okay, standard,"

Mitch said, "but I want to put in a few changes for your protection."

"Be my guest."

"Larger screen credit for one. . ." Mitch penciled it in. Tom beamed. "You should own these rights, no way you should give them up. . ." He penciled in another few words. "I'll have Peggy type them in tomorrow, and messenger them on to Douglas for you, okay?"

"Sure."

"What's wrong?" Mitch asked, realizing Tom wasn't quite there suddenly. "On and off all through dinner you were gloomy. You were so high when I walked in. What's the matter?"

Tom stirred brown sugar into his coffee. "Why did you say that?"

"Say what?"

"About leaving me."

Mitchell squinted. "What?"

"When you went to change clothes. About being out of your mind to ever leave me."

"I would be. Anyone would be."

"But why did you say it?"

Mitch shook his head. "It wasn't anything. I was just caught up in how unselfish you are. I thought to myself, this is the best person in the world. I thought about how free you are, with no one else to answer to—"

"And you have Paula and Jeremy and Chrissy."

"Yes. But I—"

"I understand."

"No, you don't!" Mitch jumped up and walked around. "You don't understand because I don't understand. I don't understand why it has to be the way it is, why I can't be with you all the time. I don't understand myself, why I made that decision in the first place, to get married and live a straight life, such bullshit. Oh, I understood why I had children only after I had them— there's something I can't explain about that, like it's perpetuating yourself, and a union between homosexuals won't go beyond that because they can't produce children and only someone who is a father or a mother can fully understand that—but I don't want to get into that because that's a whole other fight for some other time. What I'm saying is I'd have no qualms about leaving the kids with their mother or keeping them with me if we separated, except that there's this thing inside me that keeps saying you have to keep a *home* for them, you have to keep up the façade for them. . ."

"Don't you think they'd find out anyway? Don't you think Jeremy knows already, senses it? Kids are really smart, Mitch, they have intuition and imagination and know when mama and papa are terribly unhappy. I sometimes think the worst thing you can do is keep the marriage going for the kids' sake. Thanks but no thanks, they'd say if they could. Jesus, *you* come first! You *have* to come first. How can you really love your kids if you don't love yourself enough first? How can they respect you if you don't respect yourself? You keep it going for the kids and one day they'll tell you they wish you would have ended it—for their sake. You have to be happy too, not only your kids. You think they're gonna smile away their lives growing up in a house where husband and wife don't enjoy each other, don't love one another, don't get it on, don't talk—"

"Christ, Tom, are you telling me I should divorce Paula?"

"I'm not telling you anything. I'm suggesting you do what you have to do. It isn't killing me. Maybe it isn't even killing her. But it's killing you. How long can you go on being pulled by each arm before you start to hurt all over? Until one breaks off?"

Mitch sat down by the fire and put his head in his hands. "I hurt everywhere already. It's too much for my head . . . and on top of it the pressures at the office are monumental and my parents are trying to get me to do something . . . but I don't want to talk about any of it tonight. Another time. I have to go." He got up and went into the bedroom and changed clothes again.

Tom didn't move. He was on the floor with Blizzard, watching the fire burn. Mitch came back into the room and thanked him for dinner and said he'd call him in the morning. "Mitch," Tom said softly, "I know you don't have to leave. Please don't go."

"But I do." He bent down, kissed him, and was out the door.

Tom looked at Blizzard and licked his cinnamon nose. The cat licked him back in the same spot and yawned. "You've got it made, furry little bear," Tom said, envying him. "Just lie there without a care in the world, get up and eat, sleep some more, crap in the azaelas, spend the morning dragging mice out from under the house, the afternoon chasing big butterflies who usually outsmart you, lick yourself so clean you get hairballs in your tummy that make you throw up after a gluttonous tuna binge, and then just turn around and eat more tuna and more fur. Dumb. So dumb sometimes."

He rolled Blizzard over on his back and rubbed his stomach. "What a life. A new flea collar every three months. A car to hide under in the driveway. Grass to chew to make you throw up. Flowers to whack with your paw. Trees to climb. I envy you." He picked him up and cradled him in his arms, holding him to his heart.

Kevin came over the following evening and they gobbled up a big bowl of popcorn and a bottle of Gallo rosé. They sat on Tom's bed in their jeans and socks, two kids on a schoolnight saying the hell with homework, they were going to talk. And they did. Tom told him about Mitch's statement the night before, about his unusual behavior, and Kevin said, "I could have told you so." Why was it that people always tell you that when it was too late? If they could have told you so, why didn't they do it when the telling could have made a difference?

The phone rang as they were arguing about fidelity and lovers and what it all meant. It was Sandy. "Tom, Chloe's freaking out, she's really freaking out. She busted up her house yesterday and tossed bottles and cans through all the windows. Citronella put up cardboard everywhere. Then she pays Cinch back by locking her out of the house last night and she had to climb through the cardboard. Then this morning, she tried to steal my car again and she smashed up the front end. Went through the back of the garage and my landlord says he's gonna sue me. I told Chloe I'm gonna call the cops the next time instead of the insurance company. So today I told the insurance guy I did it, my foot slipped. And I had a hard day at the shop and I came home and the traffic was terrible and I'm in a rotten mood and I find this note on my door, written right on the door, like the Manson people wrote on that refrigerator. She wrote *JANIS DIDN'T DIE FOR NOTHING, MAN!* With a Bic Banana. I washed it off. Tom, I'm scared of her."

Tom told her not to worry, and to call him if she came over, and not to let her in. When he put the phone down, he said to Kevin, "You know, it's strange, but I have this feeling that I'll never see her again."

"Such blessings we don't all get in a lifetime."

"No, Kev, I'm not kidding. I have this sensation I'll never see her again."

But it didn't include hearing from her; the next phone call was her. "I know that bitch sister of mine's tryin' to get you to turn on me," she screamed. "Well, I'm not gonna take it anymore, you hear me? Not from you or her or Cinch or anybody, you got that? I'm somebody just like Jim was somebody and Jimi was somebody and

Janis was somebody and you're not gonna fuck me outta my life like they got fucked outta theirs! I'm an *artist,* man, a talented writer and a poet and filmmaker and—"

He hung up on her.

"Leave it off the hook," Kevin said.

"Sandy may call back if she needs me. I'd better not." He left the phone as it was. "I'd never forgive myself if she did something that I could have prevented. She's capable of anything at this point."

They talked about madness. From mad housewife madness to Son of Sam madness. About crazies and geniuses, the truly insane and the brilliant people who seem it. And the phone rang again at midnight.

It was Chloe again. This time she was soft and almost controlled, but her voice was icy and it chilled Tom's blood. "You listen to me, Tomcat, I know I tried to kill myself many times, man, but I always knew something. I knew that I'd never go without *you.*" How amazing that in her moment of ultimate insanity she should sound so lucid, and how for the first time in all her threats, he finally believed her. "Man, we were gonna live together, so we're gonna fuckin' die together and you better be ready. *I'll get you.* Tell your lawyer lover to come visit the cemetery. You're gonna be with me and mama and daddy and Janis." She hung up abruptly.

Kevin tried to ease his worry. "She's nuts, bananas, just berserk and whacko. She's finally certifiably insane. She can't do anything to you. She won't."

Tom sat wondering how someone he'd loved and cared for and had given so many moments of laughter and happiness to could turn into such a monster. She was beyond the point where she could help herself any longer. What was there to do now? He just sat there, immobile. And he wondered how she knew about Mitch?

Kevin picked up the receiver and called Sandy. "What are you doing?" Tom asked. He didn't want him to get involved.

But Kevin refused. "Sandy, you can have her committed legally," he said. "Tom can talk to Mitchell about it—he must know someone who can tell you how to go about it."

Tom took the phone. "I never really thought about it, Sandy, but maybe it's the only way of protecting her from herself—and you and me too." Sandy, crying, agreed, and told Tom she had already discussed it with Chloe's psychiatrist, who recommended it over a month before, and their aunt in Chicago, who was ready to sign anything. Tom was close and dear, like a brother. He also could sign and help put her away. He promised to talk to Mitch about it in the morning.

Kevin soon went home and Tom put Visine in his eyes because they seemed to be burning with worry, and then got into bed. Blizzard found a spot at his side and settled in for the night. Tom opened a book and the phone again disturbed the peace.

It was Sandy and she was hysterical. *"Tom! The cops got her! She was running down Hollywood Boulevard with a hammer in her hand, smashing all the windows! Tomcat—she's in jail!"*

Tom saved the front page of the *Los Angeles Times,* the picture of fifteen store windows on Hollywood Boulevard which had been shattered by a young woman identified as one Chloe Kosenkowski of Hollywood, who had startled even the most jaded Hollywood Boulevard types as she ran down the street screaming obscenities and feminist outcries, striking glass with such force that some pieces landed in the street. She was wearing only a bathrobe at the time. But she had on knee-high boots which had protected her feet through the hurricane. Her arms and hands were severely cut and slashed, and there were cuts on her face which required stitches at Hollywood Presbyterian Hospital.

Tom helped Sandy through the ordeal. He even helped Citronella, who had tried to stop Chloe when she left the apartment after taking a handful of uppers, another handful of downers, then washing them down with Southern Comfort and a cup of Ginseng tea. Chloe, in turn, had managed to stop Cinch from stopping her by throwing the teapot at her. In it was boiling water and Ginseng root, and Cinch herself spent part of the night in the emergency room just down the corridor from Chloe, having the burns attended to.

In the days that followed, Tom gave Cinch a ticket to New York, on an airplane this time; Bekins had no reservations on cross-country sofa. Cinch thanked him and admitted she was worn out and she'd been wanting to go home for a long time, but felt she had an obligation to care for Chloe. "She's going to the right place," she admitted, when Tom told her of the decision to put her into a hospital where she could get some care. Cinch said she didn't ever want to be told what happened to her in the future, she wanted to leave it with knowing she was going to get help. The prognosis was not good, she knew, and she'd seen *Snake Pit* when she was young. Her fantasy would do, thank you.

Mitchell got to a lawyer who got to the psychiatrist Chloe had been seeing, and together they talked to Tom and Sandy. The aunt in Chicago agreed. The decision was that she was in a psychotic state, schizophrenic as well, it was drug-related, and she would have to be put into a state institution immediately with the hope that rehabilitation was possible.

When Tom signed the papers as a witness, he knew, as Citronella had known, that she would never get better. Something inside him told him she would get worse until they finally gave up and simply put her away. Where would she go? Camarillo? Some horrible place like that?

He thought of it and wanted to go back to a time long ago when the snow fell in Chicago and they slept with their little cat in a kind of playful madness that had enveloped them both. But it could not be. He had to face life head-on and be strong for Sandy and for himself.

He suffered greatly from guilt, though, and spent a lot of time stewing about Chloe, remembering, blaming himself. And worrying about Mitchell, about that something that didn't seem exactly right with him, about how he could get their rightness back. They saw each other several times the last few days before Tom and Kevin went to Chicago, and there was an intensity about their relationship, as if they were clinging hard before having to let go.

They made love passionately, roughly, hurting each other as much as they pleasured one another. They did not talk of the problems building in their minds; instead they took out the energy on each other's bodies.

The night before he and Kevin went to Chicago, Tom asked Mitchell, "Are you worried about our future together?"

"I'm worried about my future. I have to make a decision.

"Let me tell you a story. When I first started college, I got propositioned by a professor, an ex-jock who'd come back to teach physics or something. He really came on to me. But I was scared of my image and all. Then he offered me money. . ."

Tom gulped.

". . .and I hid for a week. A couple of times after that, up in San Francisco on weekends, I was offered money, unsolicited. And how I wanted to do it! But I never did and now I wonder why? Because it would have meant I wasn't cautious, I wouldn't have been playing it safe. Play by the rules, Mitch. Oh, yeah, you end up beating off alone, wishing you'd done it, fantasizing you'd done

it, only to realize you blew the chance to do something
a little *outrageous*."

"Hustling couldn't be that terrific," Tom said, thinking God would strike him dead any minute.

"But you don't understand—it doesn't have to be
that. That's only an example that comes to mind. I'm
talking about breaking free from convention, from what
you've been told is the right or wrong thing to do. It can
be anything, taking a trip, quitting your job, moving to
the mountains to farm turnips, climbing a glacier. Anything that's a little risky. Facing yourself. Doing what
you really want to do."

Tom let that sink in. "Then there's hope for us yet,
huh?"

Mitch pulled him into his arms and held him tight.
"Oh, yes," he said with confiction, "there's more than
hope."

Tom closed his eyes and felt more at ease about his
lover than he had in months. And so he opened up to
him more than he had in the past. "Mitch, Rachel heard
that the Countess might be behind a drug syndicate."

"What?"

"No one knows for sure. But on that trip to Dallas,
well, I wasn't going to tell you because I thought you'd
worry. . ."

"I want to worry, dumb ass. That's part of what loving someone is all about."

"I overheard this conversation that made me think
Rachel was right. And then I found out all this stuff on
a San Francisco run. I think . . . I think maybe I'm cart-
ing the stuff for her."

"You?" Mitch was astonished. "How?"

"Dunno. Kevin and I are going to Chicago to find
out."

Mitch shook his head. "Are you nuts? To find out?
What does that mean?"

"It means we're just gonna look around. I don't know what it is, heroin probably, but it could be nothing, you know? I just think I'd better try to find out, because I don't want to be hooked up with her if that's what's going on."

"Absolutely not. Jesus, why didn't you tell me sooner?"

"I told you. And I wasn't sure. I'm still not sure. But I have a feeling I'm going to find out this trip. It's a big one, four trunks more than usual."

"Filled with shit that could get you a nice prison term."

"Look, I can't find out by staying around town. And if I'm wrong, I'd be giving up a good job and this house for what? For nothing, for some paranoid idea I had. I want to find out."

Mitch said nothing, thinking over what Tom had said. Then he took Tom's hand. "Okay, go to Chicago, and look around, but don't do anything foolish, don't get yourself into any trouble. The minute you're sure, the minute you think you've had enough proof—if you overhear something, see something—I want you to call and tell me. If you're right, you two get your asses on a plane and I'll take care of getting you unemployed. Just don't confront anyone, don't take any chances, act dumb."

"That won't be hard." Tom snickered. Then he saw that Mitch was troubled. "You're really serious, aren't you?"

"Aren't you?"

He had a point.

Tom finally asked, "What kind of an excuse are you gonna give her to get me away if I find out I'm an unwitting dope pusher?"

Mitch answered, "I'll just tell her we're getting married, and I want you to come live with me."

"I almost wish that were true."

TWENTY-ONE

Tom and Kevin took a morning flight to Chicago and were met at the airport by a well-groomed woman named Marion and two thugs she seemed to treat as slaves. She told them the showing of the collection—seven trunks filled with coats—would be held at her mansion in Glencoe, and that's where they would be staying. If they wished to get around Chicago and enjoy themselves, a car would be at their disposal.

They were driven to Glencoe in a limousine with the woman smoking up a storm, but never saying a word. They turned into the estate and passed through huge iron gates; the place was surrounded by a red brick wall and the grounds seemed endless. Filled with huge chunks of ice, Lake Michigan lined one end of the property, and the land was covered with snow. Giant old oak trees surrounded the magnificent house, which had several Cadillacs and Continentals parked in front of it. Another thug came out and acted as the doorman, while yet another served as butler.

They were led to their "quarters", a big room with a view of the lakefront, the covered swimming pool, and the garages. They watched the truck drive up. The trunks were unloaded and brought into the house to a room directly beneath theirs.

They dined alone in a private sitting room. Roast chicken and vegetables on a little table with white linen napkins and finger bowls. Marion joined them after dinner for a glass of sherry, and Tom tried to pick her brain. "Are you a personal friend of Madame Oluspenskaya?"

"Oh, in a way. We met in Europe some time ago. Is there anything you boys need to make you more comfortable?"

"No, thanks, we're fine. Good chicken. Are you running the showing?"

She shook her head. "I am a coordinator, a go-between."

Tom shot Kevin a look that said: *She's running heroin, the old bitch.*

"If you'd like to go into the city tomorrow, I could make some suggestions. . ."

"No, thanks," Tom said. "I lived here once. I know the place pretty well. Will you need us at all during the week?"

"Most likely not, but you must be available on short notice. I think the Countess told you we may ship the designs back at a moment's notice. Don't stray too far."

We'll hang around right under your nose, if it's okay with you. "We're at your service," Tom said pleasantly.

"I just want to see the Art Institute," Kevin said. It was true, he did; he remembered trips to Chicago when he was a child, getting lost amidst the treasures of the marvelous museum. But he was also saying it to throw off any suspicions she may have had. "I'm really here on a sightseeing trip. I usually don't do this work."

The woman stood. "Now, is there anything you'd like for the night?"

Tom said, "I figure we'll watch a little TV."

She cracked a smile. "Fine." It disappeared. She seemed in a hurry, preoccupied. "Breakfast will be between—"

A thug entered, playing butler, and announced the arrival of someone he addressed as, simply, "The Man"

She waved him away. "Breakfast between eight and nine, right here. The maid will take your order. A good night to you then," and she hurried out to greet "The Man".

Once back in their room, Tom said, "When they get all the heroin unloaded, they'll probably send us home."

"You don't know it's heroin so stop saying that," Kevin insisted.

"Well, whatever it is."

"It could be birdseed. We don't know anything yet." Kevin looked out the window. "Maybe they're planning on doing it the other way as well, maybe they refill the trunks and send something back."

Tom walked up and stood next to him, his arm on the boy's shoulder. "Look at that goon out there. You can tell he's got a gun in his jacket. It's freezing out there. Those fucking rags aren't worth that kind of protection."

"You think they're guarding us?"

"Naw. I really think she just figures we're two kids who don't give a rat's ass."

"What are we going to do?" Kevin asked, poking Tom under the arm. "Play Scrabble?"

"Stop!" He was laughing. "That *tickled*. . ."

Kevin tickled him to the bed and they rolled over and over, and finally Tom pinned him down. There was a moment when their eyes met and it happened, that feeling, that sudden shock of something between them, and they both wondered if this time, finally, they'd go beyond it—

But no, they stopped. Tom dropped Kevin's arm as he felt something in his loins. "Promise no tickling?"

"What's in it for me if I don't?"

"I feed you to Marion and her 007 henchmen."

"One was pretty hunky," Kevin giggled.

"Shit." Tom got up and started putting on his winter jacket, scarf, gloves.

"Where are you going?"

"We, Kev, *we*. We're going for a walk."

"Nobody 'goes for a walk' in this weather."

"Come on, we gotta see what's going on around here. It's a perfect way to do it, like we're just going out to play in the snow. I want to peek in that room downstairs and see what gives."

Kevin shivered, both at the thought of the cold and the sleuthing. He dressed for warmth. "I'm ready."

Tom opened the door. "Come on, let's go make snow angels."

They went down the hall and descended the steps. The door to the first floor hall was closed and they didn't dare open it, because they heard voices from behind. They went outside instead, and walked around the front of the house, away from the goon who was still standing guard in the back.

They looked in all the windows. They saw lovely wood-paneled rooms, the mahogany reflecting the shimmer of crystal chandeliers. Overstuffed sofas filled corners of rooms, roaring fireplaces, huge paintings of ancient looking faces, and an ancient man sitting in a rocker, smoking a pipe. "Nothing much I'd call a clue," Kevin said sarcastically.

"Watch that man," Tom said, staring through the glass pane at the old gent gently rocking. "The pipe is actually a laser beam capable of slicing our heads off in a flash."

"You are so full of shit. . ." Kevin brought his knee up and hit Tom in the ass. They laughed and tripped over one another, and Kevin caught Tom just as he was about to fall into an evergreen. It was ridiculous, and they realized it. They rounded the back of the house and saw that the goon was gone. Tom pointed toward a bright light on the snow. It was coming from the window directly beneath their room. They went toward it.

They crouched down and sneaked up. They really didn't expect to see anything interesting, but it was fun to think this was finally the big clue they'd been searching for. Tom pulled a branch down and stuck his head up right under the corner of the window. The curtains were parted enough just to see—and suddenly he was speechless, suddenly he was trembling. He was astonished and fearful. His hand tugged at Kevin's jacket and soon both heads were looking in. Kevin was equally surprised.

The room was filled with fluorescent light. In the center was a long aluminum table which looked as though it belonged in an operating room. Instruments were on the end of it, as well as a small scale and weights and several test tubes. The three trunks were in a corner; one was open and all the coats had been removed and were hanging on a clothes rack on the other side of the door. On the table a long roll of white was encased in plastic, a big sausage of white powder. Sitting there, on a metal stool, flanked by one of the thugs and a well-dressed man with a diamond on his finger, was Marion. She was dressed all in white, her hair tied back with a white kerchief, and she was carefully slitting the bag and removing some of the contents.

"She looks like a fucking nurse," Tom whispered.

"That guy with the rock on his finger has to be 'The Man'."

"Kev, I think that's snow."

"What?"

"Snow. Cocaine."

"Jesus. Tom, I'm scared."

Tom stared in amazement, wonder. "I don't believe it. I never expected to just drop in on it like this."

"Tom, let's get out of here. Do what Mitch said. Let's get to the airport, call him, and get on a plane."

"Yeah, my stomach's suddenly aching."

Kevin moved back, carefully stepping over the bushes, and Tom put his foot on what he thought was a rock. When his full weight was on it, it snapped, loudly, and he realized he was on the bottom rung of a trellis. "Kev!" he shouted, and then it toppled against the window, breaking the huge pane into hundreds of pieces. Houston rang in his head, breaking windows haunting him again. A piece of glass hit Tom in the face and blood ran down under his left eye, but he didn't notice. Floodlights were going on all around, even in the trees at the back of the property. Dogs were barking. Hell was breaking loose.

"*Run!*" Tom yelled, forgetting how difficult it was for Kevin to do that. But he tried. They started around the house, toward the front gate, and Tom smashed right into the burly goon who already had his gun drawn. The impact knocked the pistol to the snow. The man fell, Tom on top of him. Kevin thought fast and kicked the goon's head down into the white, and they took off in the opposite direction.

Tom rounded the trees, zigzagging through them toward the dark at the back of the property. "Come on, Kevin, come on!"

Kevin tried to keep up. He dragged his right leg along painfully, sweating. He called to Tom in an already hoarse voice, "No, no, the water—we're trapped!"

Tom thought quickly. "Over the wall!" He turned for the high brick wall. "Over the fucking wall!" He could feel his feet freezing and burning at once, the blood on his face turning to ice as he ran, ran hard, fearing for his life. It wasn't fun anymore, it wasn't a game. This was the real thing, and he was crying and didn't even know it.

Tom knelt and yelled, "Use my leg, Kev, jump over with my leg!" Kevin ran toward him, centered his left foot directly on Tom's thigh, and flung himself up to the top of the brick dividing line. He flipped over and fell into mud and snow on the other side, into darkness and safety.

Then Tom landed next to him with a thump.

And bullets blew the top of the bricks into little red fragments.

"They're *shooting* at us!" Kevin screamed, not believing it. "Tom, Tom, where . . . what. . ."

Tom pulled him to his feet. "Run, Kev, oh please, you have to run!"

And again he tried. He followed Tom through the dark yard, around an empty swimming pool half-filled with snow, through a gate, through yet another yard. Another shot whizzed by them, but it didn't register; everything was going by as if they were on a speeding train, and their ears were immune to any sounds other than the pumping of their hearts.

They ducked into a long passageway between the garages.

Kevin was about ten yards behind Tom. When he came up and slid down next to him, he was in agony. "I can't run anymore . . . my leg, my leg. . ."

The sound of the dogs came closer. "We've got to get to a street, to a busy street where they can't . . . we've got to, if I have to carry you. . ." He pulled Kevin up and dragged him down the passageway. There were lights ahead, at the end a street, a thoroughfare. . .

Suddenly, there was an explosion of gunfire. A garbage can jumped into the air. Tom squealed in pain, twisted around, crashed to his feet. "Tom!" Kevin cried, reaching for him.

But Tom got up. They had to keep moving. Blood gushed from Tom's sleeve. He held it with his free hand, pressing snow to it, the snow that stuck to his hand when he fell. "Come on, Kev . . . just a little . . . come on. . ."

"Fuckers!" Kevin screamed back at the unseen figures chasing them. "Dirty fuckers!" He thought he couldn't stand the ache any longer, couldn't stand seeing the blood soak Tom's clothes. He was going mad. This was not happening. It was too silly. It was something you see in a movie or on television. He thought he couldn't take another step, couldn't breathe another breath—

Suddenly he was at the street. Tom was already across the big wide thoroughfare, waving, jumping up and down. Lights were everywhere. "Kevin, come on, come on!" he heard Tom shout. And he gave it one more try, just as he felt he was going to pass out, one more run, one last effort to get to Tom, and then it would all be over, it would be all right.

It happened so fast and silently it was as though it were choreographed. The car seemed to come out of no-where. Kevin was caught in the headlights. He only saw a blur of twinkling light on top of him. He had no idea what was happening.

But Tom saw it. He saw it and it flashed in his head, and he knew he would see the horror again and again and again. He hollered at the driver to stop, *please* stop, and he saw the car skid even though he didn't hear the brakes, and then the impact, a dull thud, as Kevin flew into the air and came down again, doubled in a heap in the cinders and dirty snow at the side of the road.

The truck Tom had been flagging when Kevin dashed into the street had stopped already. And a car behind that. The car which hit Kevin went out of control and smashed into a closed gas station, shearing off two of the pumps, and there was an explosion and suddenly the whole area was illuminated by fire.

Tom ran to Kevin, and held him. He promised him it would be all right. He was aware of people standing around him. "Please," he said, cold and numb, "he needs help, he needs—"

"Come on," a voice said, "we'll get him to a hospital."

They dragged Kevin to the car and put him on the back seat. Tom got inside and moaned, "Go, please, go," and then felt the car jerk as it started to move.

Kevin opened his eyes and said, "My stomach . . . it hurts like I ate too much." Tom pulled open Kevin's coat and his own stomach tightened and he held back retching as he saw the ripped flesh. How had the impact done this when his coat wasn't even ripped? Blood was pouring from Kevin's chest and abdomen, and Tom let out a weak moan, pressing his hands there, feeling numb and incomplete, praying all the time it would stop, hoping he could keep the blood in him, keep him alive.

Kevin looked up and his eyes seemed to flicker. He was alert. Tom thought he never looked so beautiful; his face was untouched, perfect, the eyes bright as ever, almost happy. "What happened?" he whispered. Tom shook his head, biting his lip, begging God what was going to happen would not happen. Keven moaned and there was a small gurgle in his throat. Blood came from the corner of his mouth. His eyes seemed to grow wide and he tried to speak again, but all Tom could make out was, ". . .so cold . . . love you."

And then he died.

Tom would not admit it—even though he held his lifeless form in his arms for nearly fifteen minutes, even though the back seat was swimming with all the blood Kevin had had in his young body, even though the lids over his bright eyes no longer closed.

Only when the frail old nurse came to him in the emergency room, the nurse who looked like Kevin's grandmother, only when she held his hand and told him he must accept it, his friend had passed away, only then would he accept it. And only then did he close his eyes and feel the agony and the loss. Only then did he allow his heart to break. He put his head in his hands and sobbed. "I killed him. It was my fault."

She took his head and held him, tried to comfort him,

but he began screaming. He tore the bandage off his arm and blood gushed again. He held the woman by the shoulders and shook her and cried, "He's dead! He's dead and I did it!" A doctor and orderly came in and forced him down and gave him an injection.

Two days passed in a blur. So much happened, it seemed hard to recall it in his mind, as if he were floating in space, a puppet with no control over who was pulling his strings. The police questioned him, the narcs questioned him, the FBI talked to him. The information he provided enabled them to put a dent in one of the largest cocaine rings in the country. He sifted through thousands of mug shots. He looked at a line-up and identified two of the thugs he'd seen at the mansion. He managed a smile when the police told him the cocaine had been recovered in a truck en route back to the Countess, still neatly stashed inside the fur coats. He returned with the FBI—and a slew of TV, newspaper and magazine reporters—to the house in Glencoe and identified it. And then was blasted with questions under the glare of lights. Finally, everyone left him alone.

It was then that he cried for the first time. Alone, in the hotel room they'd provided for him, he curled up sideways on the bed and cried his heart out. He'd told them everything without concern for himself. Every detail, every painful truth about the outrageous benefactress who employed him, the delightful, zany Zena, the woman who'd murdered his best friend. Maybe she would seek revenge on him one day and maybe the effort was futile in the long run, for someone was bound to take her place and continue trafficking drugs as much as ever. But at least . . . at least he could help get the people who had killed an innocent young man. Kevin. Kevin was dead. *Dead.* He wanted to think it was simply unbelievable, but the word would not register in his head. It was true. And the ache in his heart was so strong he felt he could not bear it.

At one a.m., he found himself dialing the phone.
Mitch was going to hear it soon enough on the radio or
television. He had to get himself together and warn him,
prepare him. He also needed some good legal advice—
what was he to do once he left the guarded hotel room?
"Mitch," he said, knowing he woke him up, "go into the
den. Hang up in there and pick up in the den. I've got to
talk to you. Don't ask—just do it, Mitch." He waited
while the line was silent. Then Mitch picked up. And
Tom felt a sense of relief flooding his veins. "Oh, God,
Mitch, I need you so badly. . ."

"Tom, what's happened? Where are you? I've never
heard you sound like this."

"Kevin's dead. Christ, Mitch, Kevin's dead and I
didn't listen to you—"

"Dead? What the—? Tom, are you drunk? You're not
making sense—"

"*You think it makes sense to me?*" Tom screamed.

"Stop it! Tell me what's happened."

Tom told him the whole story. He was shaking, angry,
sad, ashamed. And he suddenly thought of Rachel, what
she would say, what she would tell him, and he *knew*
that once and for all the whole truth had to come out.
"Mitch, I wasn't always guarding her trunks. That's
only been going on for a short time. I was a . . . I was a
hustler for her before that. I've been a male prostitute
for years."

There was only silence at the other end of the line.

"Mitch, say something."

"I don't believe you."

"She runs a call boy service and you're the only one in
all of L.A. who doesn't know it. I couldn't tell you because I was sure you'd leave me."

"I don't believe it." But he did. It was in his voice. He
knew it was the truth.

"Help me, Mitch. I need to know what to do. I can get
on a plane and—"

"Tom, you didn't tell them about that part of it, did you? About the prostitution?"

"I told them everything. I'm never going to lie again to anyone in my life. It'll help put her away for the rest of her life. They already knew. They told me she's also behind a child pornography thing I never even heard about. I hope she rots in hell."

Mitch's voice was now brittle and distant. "Tom, do you realize what you've done? To us? Jeremy's gonna—Paula's gonna see you—everyone who's ever seen us together is gonna read about it and—" He stopped, his own anguish cutting him off, choking him. And then he shouted, "Goddamn you! God *damn* you!"

"I . . . I'm sorry."

"How could you do this to us? It's the end, don't you realize that? There's nothing left, nothing. You ruined it all. I could have helped you if only you'd let me know, if only. . ." He coughed and sucked in his breath and he moaned, ". . .fucking liar," and then Tom heard Paula in the background, asking what was wrong, what had happened, and the line went dead.

In a trance, Tom dialed Sandy and said, "I can't tell you what happened—if I have to say it all again, I'll crack, but you have to do me a favor. . ."

"Tomcat, what's wrong?"

"I'm in Chicago and you have to go up to my house, right now, this very minute, and get Blizzard. And take anything you can carry out, my clothes and records, books, anything you can get. You might see cops up at the big house, but ignore them unless they hassle you. Get Blizzard and take care of him till I get back. Please, Sandy, do it."

"Yes, right away. Can't you tell me what happened?"

"It'll be in the papers. Sandy, thank you, I can't tell you how much it means to me. Don't worry, I'm all right. I'll be there soon."

He hung up and collapsed.

* * *

He spent two days in seclusion in the hotel. His stubble grew and his hair was matted in dull knots from sleeping with a pillow over his head, and his eyes were puffy and bloodshot. But he had to pull himself together to make the plane, and he did, moving as if in a trance, going through the motions as if living an illusion.

He went back to California, but not to Los Angeles. The funeral was held in San Diego, a small, simple service with only Kevin's parents, grandparents, and close relatives and friends. Tom sat in the back of the chapel during the service. He heard the minister talking about Kevin having been an honor student, a good son, his suffering as a child, never complaining. Tom wanted the man to talk about his unselfishness, his love, his inner beauty which overcame a limp and pain, his dreams.

When the cemetery prayers were concluded, Tom saw Kevin's mother's eyes lock into his. She came to him. "Tom, I just want you to know we're glad you're all right." She gently put her fingers on the sling holding his arm. "Kevin always said you were his best friend. You did so much for him that no one else had been able to do . . . you. . ." She could not continue.

Her husband took over. "We're all sorry you were hurt. And we hope you'll still consider our home yours, and come out and see us often. It's gonna be lonely now."

How absurd it was, Tom thought. He should be comforting *them!* Tom looked at Kevin's father. His face was ashen, his eyes dead with grief. "I'm so sorry," he whispered, and then walked to the casket and looked down.

"He's going to be next to his grandfather," a voice said, and Tom looked up to find Kevin's granny standing next to him. "And he won't feel another day of pain, ever." She tried to smile, tossed a rose to the casket, and was helped away by an usher.

Then Tom looked up and out over the bleak, sun-drenched land, and wondered how it could have turned out like this, how God could be so cruel?

There was no answer. He turned and walked back to the car he'd rented and drove to the airport. Seven hours later, he was in New York.

TWENTY-TWO

Rachel had read it all and talked to him by phone, but to hear the whole story from his lips was agony for her. And Tom did talk now, after a hot bath and dinner, after a nap. He talked until he hurt. It was so senseless, two kids playing games and suddenly finding themselves in the midst of the kind of thing you only read about. It was so overwhelmingly sad.

When he finished the story, ending with Kevin's grandmother at the grave site, Rachel just stared at him. He knew what she was thinking, and he avoided her eyes as long as he could. But he finally gave in, as if there were no resistance left inside him any longer. "When did you realize he was in love with me?" he asked. There. It had finally been vocalized.

"That day at the airport. It wasn't difficult, Tom. You just had to see the way he looked at you, heard how he spoke of you. It was enough. He wanted so much for you, so much of what he'd denied himself for so long: happiness. He was devoted to you. And he loved you deeply."

Tom put his head down and nodded.

She waited, but nothing more came. Finally she said, "Tom, can't you even now admit it?"

"Yes! Okay, I loved him!" He faced her and let it out.

"I *did,* damn it, and I *wanted* him! But I fought like mad because I couldn't face it, it would have complicated things too much and it was already so good on its own. I thought if we slept together . . . it would . . . it would get all messy, with Mitch, you know, and I figured we could keep our friendship without having to take risks." He looked at her for some kind of approval, but got nothing. "I thought it was the right thing!"

"I know, I know." She held him. "Tommy, the only thing you can do for him now is everything he wanted you to do when he was with you. Grow up and take the world by its ears and shake it, make your music and make a mark. If this teaches you that one thing—to stop being selfish, to take the other person's feelings into consideration for—"

"I don't need to hear this, not now." His head felt like a steel drum and guilt was choking him; he thought he'd collapse if told one more time that he'd done it all wrong. She was saying things he could not stand to hear.

"You *must* listen, you *must* hear, or Kevin died in vain. You knew how much he wanted you, how he adored you, and yet you didn't let that matter to you. *You* called the shots. The relationship was what *you* decided."

"Please," he begged, trying to cover his ears.

She pulled his hands down. "Stop acting like a child."

"I can't take anymore! When's it gonna let up?"

"Oh, Tommy, little cat, I'm not trying to dump on you all at once." She pulled him to her breasts. "Don't blame yourself for Kevin, it would have happened another way, another time. You don't have control over that. But do tell yourself perhaps it was meant to teach others a lesson, in your case how to be a man, how to love without holding back, how to be honest."

He put his head to the pillow and closed his eyes. "Annie used to say something: *Flowers grow best in horse manure.* All I see is shit. Kevin's gone. Mitch is gone. Chloe's locked up. Even Zena—" He stopped himself and groaned. "How could she have done that to me?" He pulled himself up from thinking about her, before the rage infected him. "I don't even have a place to live anymore."

"So do what Annie said, look at the flowers. You've got your cat. You've got Sandy. You've got me. You may have lost a piano, but you've still got your fingers. And one thing you never really considered. Yourself."

He smiled slightly.

"And you're not sure about Mitchell. You hit him pretty hard all at once, how can you fault his reaction? Can you imagine the hurt and revulsion you caused him? But if what you told me is true, if he really was preparing to leave his wife before this happened, then he may very well find this is the time to do it, because it's all out now, no matter how much it may have shamed him or how much it cost him."

He took her hand and said no more.

Tom stayed at Sandy's apartment for a few days. He spent a great deal of time with the police and FBI and others in dark suits who questioned him. One night a guy grabbed him when he stepped from his car—Sandy had been smart enough to take a cab to his house—to load up his car with his clothes and drive it to her place —and held him by the throat. Tom recognized him as one of Zena's former hustlers. "Man, you're fuckin' lucky she didn't keep names in books, or you'd be dead like the other creep!" the guy spit at him. "You remember, they come after me, you're gonna get your fuckin' neck busted." And he stomped off into the night.

But that was the only incident.

Tom tried to put his life together. He had some money saved and there was a contract to score a TV film, but he had no piano, no place of his own. So he hit the apartment trail, depressed each night as he returned, for nothing matched the cottage up in the trees.

When he finally gave up trying to recreate what had been before, when he faced the fact that this was another beginning, he found a place. It was a small apartment in Hollywood. The building was somewhat secluded, and it had a hill behind it filled with grass and trees where Blizzard could romp as he'd been used to doing. He was starting to claw Sandy's furniture to death; he wanted the outdoors again.

So they moved in. He gave the cat three days to learn this was home, see where the food would be each morning, get comfortable—trying out the various windowsills —with the same old sun. Then he let him out and Blizzard carefully sniffed the hillside and let the other cats in the neighborhood know he was in residence, here to stay; he got a few scratches and a furless ear in that territorial announcement, but soon he was coming and going as if he owned the place.

Tom rented a spinet from the Hollywood Piano Rental Company. Sandy had gotten most of his personal things out of his house; what he needed for the kitchen he bought. He had everything. Everything but Mitchell.

He made several attempts to reach him. His secretary first promised he would return his calls; she herself had sounded surprised to hear Tom calling, as if he had some nerve. Then she started to say, "I'm sorry, Mr. Birney is in conference." Mr. Birney? Since when didn't she call him Mitch in front of Tom?

Finally, Tom reminded her Mitch had been "in conference" a total of eight days, and she changed her story to "I'm sorry, but Mr. Birney has gone on an extended vacation. I don't know when he's due back."

Feeling desperate one afternoon, Tom drove to Century City and confronted the girl. Mitch wasn't there. He had left, not on vacation, but on an extended leave of absence. At that moment his name was being removed from his door.

As he left, the secretary said to him, "Why don't you leave him alone." And he just looked at her. Dumb cunt would never understand.

Tom drove to Westwood. He simply had to see him, no matter what it cost. He knew he would be at home, hiding there, trying to run from this as he'd run from everything in his life. What had he said about wanting to confront things? About being cautious? This was one time Tom was going to force him into saying the hell with caution—he simply had to see him and hear from his own mouth what the future for them was going to be.

He parked the car across the street from the little house. Nothing had changed, it was just like the day he'd driven up there with Kevin and felt so humiliated. There were people out, some kids playing together in a yard down the way, and everything seemed normal and untouched. But the shades were drawn in the Birney house. Tom panicked—had they gone away already?

He jumped out of the MG and crossed the street. He stopped for a moment and started up the front walk. All of a sudden he heard, "Uncle Tom, Uncle Tom!" Tom had not noticed, but Jeremy was one of the kids playing a few houses away. Jeremy ran to him and Tom lifted him high into the air. "I thought you were never coming back and I saw you on the television but mommy said—"

"Don't you touch my children! Put him down!" Paula was standing in the doorway, her face flushed, her fist clenched.

Tom was startled. He put Jeremy down.

"In the house, Jeremy Allen, right this minute."

"But mom. . ."

"You *heard* me," she screamed, "in the house this *instant!*"

Jeremy ran inside and she shut the door on him. "What do you want?" she asked Tom.

"Is Mitchell home?"

"No."

"I don't believe you."

"He isn't here. Leave us alone. Haven't you done enough harm?"

"But I must see him. I can't live with it this way, I need to talk to—"

"*You* can't live with it?" She took a step toward him and looked at him as no one had ever done in his lifetime. "You miserable little bastard, do you know how you've embarrassed us, held us up to—to *ridicule!* I can't show my face. My husband lost his job. Our friends have turned on us. My children, how do you think this has affected them? God, have you once considered how you've made us suffer? And you have the . . . the gall to come here and face me and tell me *you* can't live with it." She closed her eyes for a moment and tilted her face up as her hands tightened on her skirt. "I wish to God *you* were the one who was killed!"

Tom told himself he should run.

But he stopped himself. He faced her head on. "I'm truly sorry about what happened, but there was no other way. You must understand something underneath all this, something vitally important—we *loved* each other. It wasn't dirty and sleazy and wrong. We loved each other and it was right and good and I can understand you must be hurt and shocked, but we—"

"*Hurt and shocked?*" she screamed. Neighbors were beginning to gather around the yard, watching silently. "Hurt and shocked? Me? *Me?* Oh, you don't know anything, you don't know anything at all, do you?"

Tom didn't understand what she was saying. "I just want to *see* him—"

"You're so stupid," she said, walking toward him, a grin on her face suddenly. "Look at you standing there, the righteous lover, telling me you really *loved* each other. How goddamned stupid can you be?" She took a breath and then spit it at him: "*You actually thought you were the first one, the first of his boyfriends?"*

Tom's shoulders sagged. He felt as though he were sinking into the earth. She's lying. She's got to be lying.

She laughed in his face. "Hah! You weren't even the *best* of them. Now get out of here and leave us alone."

He didn't move. He just stood there, numb, shaking, the ache in his soul so strong he didn't even know where he was.

"Go! Go away! Leave us alone!" She screeched at him but still he did not move. Tears flooded her cheeks and she whirled around, looking for something, anything— she grabbed a flower pot and threw it at him. She missed. It crashed on the cement behind him and the crowd watching began to move back, talking, agitated now. "Go *away,* damn you! *Go away from here!"* She picked up another pot and flung it at him and he saw it coming and tried to protect himself, but it hit him in the side of the head and he fell to his knees, stunned, and then realized what was happening. The bullets were flying again and he had to run. He crossed the street and got into his car. She was screaming still, following him, a flower pot in both hands. One struck the lid of the trunk and broke into several pieces. *"Faggot!"* she screamed. *"You dirty filthy faggot!"*

Tom started the engine and turned his head just as he saw the other clay pot coming at him. It fell into the front seat, and dirt and geranium leaves filled the interior. As he turned, he saw the faces from the window of the house, under the shade, the two children watching their mother, watching him. He sucked in his breath and stepped on the gas.

Just as the car started to move, she looked for something more to throw—there was nothing—and in her desperation she tried to kick the car, but fell to the street, crying, screaming, sobbing, holding her head in her hands as she knelt there on the pavement.

In the rearview mirror, Tom saw the crowd dispersing, moving away from the sideshow, embarrassed. But one lady remained, and bent down to help Paula to her feet.

He drove and drove and found himself at the beach. He sat on the deserted lifeguard stand where he and Mitchell had held each other to keep warm. There was no one to keep him warm now, and he sat alone and lonely, listening to the sound of the surf, remembering all the soft loving words Mitch had ever whispered to him. Everything sounded so empty now, so hollow, as distant as the lights of a ship he could see way out on the water.

All the times before, the water seemed to take fire from the moon, it had filled his soul with a secret yet cold excitement. But tonight the moon was dull, and whatever fire had burned so strongly before was now extinguished.

Two weeks passed and Tom brooded. Richard Douglas called several times, told Tom he understood what he had gone through, but it had nothing to do with his job and talent, and the best thing in the world to do was to work. He needed the music, he still wanted Tom, and he offered a few weeks' extension. He encouraged him and assured him he believed.

But Tom couldn't work. He kept thinking of Mitch. Why had he been denied a good-bye? Why had he not been able to speak to him? No matter what she said, didn't he deserve that? He still failed to believe it totally and completely. He needed to hear it from Mitchell's lips. He wanted to talk to him more than he wanted to live, but he never dared dial the phone.

Each time his own phone rang, his heart raced with the possibility it could be Mitch, but it never was. It was Douglas or the police or Rachel or someone else, never Mitch. Then one night, very late, the phone rang and his heart beat faster. Who would call so late? He picked it up and it was Sandy and she was crying. "Tomcat, it's over. Chloe . . . they just called."

"What?"

"Tomcat, she died, tonight. Tomcat, can we go to her?"

"Oh God. Oh dear God." He closed his eyes and lay back and felt the numbness again.

"Tomcat, I wanna take her home to mama and daddy."

"I'm coming, Sandy. I'm coming."

What Tom didn't know was Chloe had tried to commit suicide at the institution the day after Kevin's death. She had drunk a half gallon of bleach which had been left in a restroom by a janitor at night; she had come close to death that evening from internal bleeding, but hung on by a thread. Sandy was informed a day later and was told nothing could be done, that the doctors had worked hard and long and it seemed there was no hope for her. She decided to keep the news from Tom; he'd had enough grief.

"Tom, her body just couldn't take it. She'd been all messed up inside with the pills and liquor," she said as they drove up the coast.

He shook his head. "You know, we knew it was going to happen some day. But not now. And I thought . . . I thought when it did, I just wouldn't care anymore. But . . . but I. . ." He could hardly speak. He was crying. "Oh, God, when is it all going to stop?"

"I don't know, Tomcat. I don't know."

When they stopped for gas, they got out to stretch their legs, sharing a Coke and bag of peanuts. "Tom, what I don't understand is why you put up with her for so long? I'm her sister, I know why I did. But why you? Did you really love her so much?"

He shook his head and closed his eyes.

"You feel guilty?"

"A little." He sat on the hood of the car and faced

her. "Sandy, I never really knew the answer to that until now. It suddenly, well, I don't know, it's like it rose up from deep inside me someplace. Remember when Chloe and I would visit you on Sundays back in Chicago, when we'd come for dinner? Well, every time we left, your mama would give me a hug and whisper to me, 'You take care of my Chloe, ya?' And I'd promise I would. I always promised her I would. She worried about her all the time." Tom took a deep breath. Sandy put the Coke bottle down and held his hands. "Sandy, your mom called me two weeks before the two of you left, two weeks before she died."

"What?" Sandy's eyes widened. "I didn't know that. She never told me."

"She didn't call to ask me why I hadn't seen her the whole time she was living here in California. I think she knew it was because I couldn't be around Chloe. She even tried to hide the hurt she felt at my never even calling. But she said she was worried, she said she was going to die soon." Sandy's fingers stiffened against his flesh. "She said, 'Vladimir's gone and I'm gonna go too,' and I just didn't think anything of it, I thought she was just feeling melancholy. I said something like, 'Oh, come on.' But she said, 'Tom, I want to ask only one favor. When I go, you take care of my Chloe. She's got nobody to take care of her. You promise me, ya?' " Tom took a deep breath and whispered, "And I promised her."

"Oh, God," Sandy said. Tom slipped off the hood and put his arms around her. "Oh, Tomcat. . ."

"Sandy, it wasn't even conscious. I mean, all this time I myself have been wondering why I put up with all the shit, the suicide calls, the abuse. Now I know. And you know what?" He pulled back to look into her eyes again. "Your mother had no right to ask that of anyone, and I should never have accepted the responsibility. I should have come to my senses long ago."

"Tomcat," Sandy said, "it's all over now. Mama had her promise from you for as long as it was needed. You don't have the responsibility anymore. It's over."

Tom nodded. "Well."

"Well."

"I guess we better get going."

"I guess."

They got back into the car, and drove the rest of the way in silence.

They were able to see her for a few minutes. She had lost a great deal of weight and looked almost pretty again. A peaceful smile creased her face, as if she were finally spared the demons. Sandy was reinforced by the smile; she knew Chloe was never going to suffer again. But it disarmed Tom; he remembered that same look only one time before, when they'd lived together in Chicago. He turned away, because he could not face her or the responsibility of the past, even in death.

And so they went to Illinois again in the snow, and the family gathered for the burial of the third member of the Kosenkowski family in less than two years. There seemed to be a sense of doom in everyone's words that frightened Sandy and made her want to get out of there. But the girl bravely went through the paces.

Tom was shell-shocked.

He had brought Cinch out from New York. She didn't want to come at first, but said she was glad she did when she saw Tom and Sandy. After the service, she could not bear to go back to the house; Sandy didn't want to either. "They're all going to be looking at me, wondering when *I'm* going to go." So the three of them went to a bar and said to hell with the family. They drank to Chloe, the spirit of Chloe and, as Cinch said she was sure Chloe would want, they got rip-snorting drunk and celebrated.

Tom stayed in Chicago two days to help Sandy with

lawyers and accountants and morticians and all the other vultures who descended. Only when he was leaving did Sandy show him the letter. It had been handed to her the night they went up to Camarillo. A nurse told her she'd found it in Chloe's pocket, and thought Sandy would want it, and know what to do with it. It was addressed to Tomcat:

My beautiful Tomcat, when the spirit has left, the body serves no function. I'm tired of dragging it around. I tried so hard to hate you because you fucked me out of my life. I failed because despite what you did, I loved you. You didn't do it to be mean, I know that, you did it because you were scared. But I was too, more than you even, and I gave you my life. I put it in your hands. It was a mistake, it was wrong.

I had been taught the thing in life to aim for was a man to take care of you. Despite my genius and flair and outrageous gifts, I looked for something that mundane, and I offered my everything on a plate to you. I never had the strength to take it back. I kept thinking you would still take care of me. I went crazy waiting—I am crazy waiting still. The madness is gone with the spirit now and I feel dreadfully sane (what a bummer, man!), and there is nothing left but an emptiness I cannot bear any longer.

I don't blame you. I just know it was all wrong, it was not meant to end this way. It should have been so much better for us both. I loved you too much, Tomcat, and that was my mistake. I gave up my *self*.

We will meet in another life and we'll do it right then. We'll marry and give the world wonderful things. There is nothing in the world left to laugh about now, so why stick around and be bored? I

shall always be a part of you. . .
I love you, Tomcat,

Chloe

It was written in the familiar scrawl on the yellow legal
paper he remembered so well. He'd once written her a
farewell letter; now it was her turn. He folded it and sat
there looking down at the grey brightness of the clouds,
and told her spirit that he was sorry.

When he got back to Los Angeles, he did not loosen
his hold on the dream. He sat for three days, morosely
waiting for Mitchell to call. Richard Douglas reached
him and Tom said he was progressing. But he didn't
touch the keyboard. He was paralyzed. He reread letters
Mitch had written him, lovesick, romantic letters. He
wallowed. Facing facts would have been too hard. The
worst part was he knew what he was doing, sitting on his
ass like a goddamn rock, and he loathed himself for it.

But then it happened. The phone rang exactly at ten
one morning. "Hello?"

"Tom? Are you awake?"

He gulped. His body seemed weightless suddenly. It
was *him!* Mitch was on the phone.

"Tom? Hello?"

"Ye . . . yes. It's me." He could barely find words. His
heart was pounding. He'd finally called. Everything was
going to be all right.

"I want to see you. Meet for coffee?"

"Sure. When?"

"Right now. How about Theodore's on Santa
Monica? It's between us."

"Yeah, sure." Tom felt there was so much more he
should be saying, but he was blank. Just hearing
Mitchell's voice again made him feel so much better.

"In fifteen minutes, then? All right?"

"I'll be there."

Mitch seemed to be waiting for something from him as well. There was a pause and then he said, "Well, see you soon."

"It's good . . . good to hear your voice again." There was no reply. "I'm leaving right now. 'Bye." Tom ran out of the house, grabbing just his jacket, and drove all the way to the coffee shop with his heart in his throat, a big smile creasing his face.

Tom waited out front for Mitch. He tried to act calm when the BMW drove up, but anyone could see his anticipation, his hunger for a touch, a hug, a kiss, any sign of affection from the person he still told himself he loved more than anyone on earth. But he played it by the rules and just said hello, letting Mitch pat him on the shoulder gently; then they went inside.

They slid into a booth in a far corner. "You look awful," Mitch said to him.

"You too."

"Yeah, well, life hasn't been too good lately."

They ordered coffee.

"Tom, this is going to be hard for me. I wasn't going to do it, but I couldn't leave without seeing you—"

"*Leave?*"

"I've done a lot of thinking in the days since it happened. I was so involved with what came down on our heads, with having to try to explain it and apologize for it and try to hide it, try to make people like parents comprehend, try to—" He stopped himself. "What I started to say is I lost sight of the fact that Kevin died. It hit me just recently. How senseless. I'm sorry."

"Chloe is dead, too."

Mitch's eyes were blank for a moment. "They both died loving you," he said quietly.

Tom didn't know what to say. The waitress brought coffee and he sipped it and felt it burn his tongue. "I think the problem was I was never able to love anyone more than I loved myself, no one but you."

Mitchell slowly shook his head. "No, don't kid yourself. You didn't. Anyway, it doesn't matter anymore. I came to tell you Paula and I and the kids are moving to Connecticut. My dad pulled some strings and a rural judgeship is mine. It's a whole new way of life, in a town where they don't read newspapers. I think maybe we can start again, try one more time."

Tom felt his eyes welling up. "I hoped it would be different. I thought we—"

"You gave me no choice! Can't you see that, can't you see what you *did?* It was too late. The damage had been done. I really loved you and I never had any suspicion that you weren't telling me the truth about everything. But to find out the hard way. . ."

"I never lied about loving you."

Mitch looked away. "It doesn't matter. What I came to ask, to beg you for, is that you never try to see me again, ever. What's done is done, and it's completed, finished. Seeing you today proves it, it puts a finish to it. I don't want you showing up one day to confront Paula, I don't want you to come walking down the road five years from now, I don't want to see you again, ever."

Tears fell down Tom's cheeks. He held the empty mug in both hands, twisting it around and around.

Mitch brought his hand up and touched Tom's arm lightly. "I just want to leave you knowing I really cared, Tom, I really did. I loved you as I've loved no other person in my life and—"

Tom yanked his arm back and shouted, *"Bullshit!"*

Everyone in the restaurant looked at him.

Mitch said, "Keep your voice down."

"I don't care what anyone thinks. Don't give me all that crap, you don't need to do that—what are you trying to do, ease your conscience? You using that *caution* you always talked about?" Tom jumped up and ran out the door.

Mitch followed and grabbed Tom just outside the door, forcing him to face him. "I didn't want this, I didn't want a scene. But you've turned it into one. Just let me tell you you'll never know what was really there, what I was really willing to do for you, you'll never know. You'll never know because you can't begin to understand what the truth about anything is." And he turned and walked away, toward his BMW.

Tom shouted, "You know what's going to happen? You're gonna find some kid in the supermarket up there in Connecticut, some other blond with a nice ass a month or two from now, and you know what, it's gonna be the same fucking thing all over again!"

Mitch jerked to a stop and twisted around to face him. "Yeah," he shouted, seething, "you're right, you're absolutely right! *Only next time I'll pick a guy who isn't a goddamn pathological liar!*" He got into the car, slammed the door, and drove away.

Tom started the MG, put it in reverse instead of first, and rammed into the steel post behind him. The taillight broke into several pieces. He beat on the steering wheel with his fist, shouted *"Fuck you!"* to a woman who was trying to say something to him, and sped out of the parking lot and down the curb and into traffic, narrowly missing colliding with a truck.

He drove straight to the airport through blinding tears.

TWENTY-THREE

She had never seen him looking so unhappy, so cried-out and weak, so terrible. He just looked at her as she opened the door, his big blue eyes pools of anguish. "Oh, Tommy."

"Can we go to Rockefeller Center?" he asked, standing there in the hallway. "Please. Just for a walk."

Rachel got her coat and boots, and found him a big thick knit muffler for his nose and chin, and a sweater to go under his thin khaki jacket. She could see he had come without planning, not even bringing an overnight bag. He'd gotten on a plane and come directly to her apartment.

New York was covered with snow and everyone was shivering in one of the worst winter storms in years. West End Avenue looked like a ski run, and Tom and Rachel felt the icy air sting their cheeks and crawl up their noses. The sky was dark and the temperature down near zero as the white stuff crunched underfoot. It was very much like the day they first met, and Tom needed to return to the very spot.

It was nearly one in the morning, too late for skating; Rockefeller Center was almost deserted at that hour. The city was strangely mute, for the snow consumed the sounds of the few cabs plowing through the drifts with chains and tire studs. Tom was glad it was so wintery, quiet, peaceful, it was what he needed.

He didn't say anything until they were standing looking down at the ice rink. His breath formed a round cloud of white in the air in front of his face. "I let them all down," he said clearly. "Chloe died loving me, and so did Kevin, and Mitch said he really did. I trashed him that he didn't, but I thought I was going crazy, I couldn't take anymore. If I hurt them all so much, why did they love me still?" He wasn't looking for an answer, and she wasn't about to give him one. It was his turn to talk.

He pulled the scarf up around his ears. "Let's walk a little or we'll freeze to death. And I've had enough of death to last me a. . ." His voice trailed off. They joined arms and began to trudge through the heavy snow. "This is the way I always think of New York, not in summer, it's horrible then. I love winter. Remember when we met?"

"It's locked in me for the rest of time."

"I came up and asked if you wanted to skate because I didn't have a partner and didn't want to go it alone."

"And I hadn't been on skates in fifteen years."

"Still, you tried."

"Are you kidding? For you I'd have walked a tightrope from that building to that one." She pointed. It was a very long way.

"First thing I noticed was your eyes."

"Yours too. Like small shooting stars. That's how they look right now."

"Honestly?"

She looked at his eyes. "But troubled and hurt. Stars do remain stars, but they lose their glow sometimes."

"Yes, I know. God, do I know. I couldn't stop myself —I cried a river on the plane—and I was sitting next to a nun, of all things, and she thought I was cracking up. She kept trying to be helpful and said, 'Do you want to talk about it, my son?' She asked if I were in pain and I said yeah and she asked where and I just shook my head and she wanted to get the stewardess but I assured her an aspirin wouldn't cure it. Then she asked if it was trouble with my wife or sweetheart and that's when I really broke."

"Tommy, what happened? You still haven't told me."

"He called me this morning. He wanted to meet for coffee. I was sure this was it, I had been right, I had believed blindly and I had been right, and you were finally wrong and so was his wife and so was everyone." He took a deep breath as they crossed Sixth Avenue. "But it was to say good-bye, tell me he was giving in to all the pressure and going off to live the straight life in Connecticut."

"Connecticut?"

"It's anonymous. His father got him a job. They're going to live in a big farmhouse and be The Waltons."

"Tommy, you're trashing again."

"I don't mean to. Jesus, it's hard to accept because he's not going to be happy and he *knows* it and yet he's *doing* it!"

"Was it a scene?"

"Yes. I went nuts. Fucking nuts. I couldn't help it. I dented the shit out of the car and drove like a madman —got a speeding ticket on the freeway but it didn't even phase me—and went right to TWA and put a ticket on Master Charge—"

"You have a Master Charge?"

"Mitch helped me get it months ago." He winced, as even that recollection pained him. "He let the decision be made for him, I know it. He didn't make it himself, *she* made it for him, *his parents* made it for him."

"Did you ever think *you* may have made it for him?"

Faced with her penetrating eyes, he finally nodded. "Well, I can always say he gave me a cat. No one else ever did that for me."

"Let's go home," she said softly, sadly.

They started toward the steam rising from the entrance to the subway. As they descended the wet steps, the heat burned their cold faces. It was damp and they felt chilled down there in the bowels of New York. All the way home, he spoke not a word; his head bounced on her shoulder and their hands found each other's fingers and held on.

She made him cocoa.

Alone, in the kitchen, she had time to think. She knew she had to put motherly feelings aside, a lover's feelings aside; it was time to be brutally frank with herself. She'd known the time was coming, but she hadn't expected it this soon. She had to do what was best for him. But also for her. And in this case, it would be the same thing.

She leaned against the sink and rubbed her eyes. She knew what would have to be done to save both their lives. There was no denying this was the time to do it, and it pained her that there was no putting it off. She stirred the cocoa and sugar and nutmeg and vanilla and poured it into the big mug with the marshmallows. Oh, how she wanted to give in! She wanted to walk in there and go on as before, but she knew she could not.

She brought him the cocoa. He drank it with both hands, sitting cross-legged on the bed. "Tommy, you've got to accept what happened."

"I do."

"No, you really don't. You can't yet. You're pretending to be strong now for me, giving me what I want to hear. You really can't accept it until you're free from all the dependencies which are basically bad for you, and for the other person."

"Jesus, I *am!*" Zena was gone. Kevin. Chloe. Mitchell. Who the hell was left? He was emotionally free of his mother and the pall of young Texas life that he'd carried around inside him for so long. He could accept all of it.

"No, you don't understand. I want to ask you a question. Have you done anything with your music in the last few weeks, with all this happening?"

He shook his head. He hated it, the control his emotional life had over his creativity. "Every time I've sat down at the piano I do exactly that—just sit there. I can't concentrate on anything."

"When's the score due?"

"I don't know, in a few days. But who cares? I fucked it up. You won't ever be interviewing me for album notes."

"What's with the self-pity? You could do that score in a matter of hours."

He faced her, growling. "But I've lost interest, don't you see? Can't I wallow for a while, huh? Why can't I do that?"

"You had six hours in the sky to grieve with the good sister and you can cry your eyes out to me all night long if you like. But that's all the time you get. Life goes on."

"Oh, yeah? Why? Why the fuck does it have to go on? Jesus, why can't it just stop sometimes? It isn't right that it goes on! It violates. . ." Tears streamed down his face. She wanted to hold him and dry his eyes, but she didn't dare. It was the hardest thing to do—to sit there and do nothing—but she knew she would ruin everything she felt was best if she so much as touched him. "I loved him," he sobbed, "and I loved Kevin and Chloe . . . oh, God. . ."

She said nothing, turned out the light, and sat still on the edge of the bed. He curled around the pillows, on his side, and moaned, "I'm so tired . . . hold me . . . hold me. . ."

He drifted off to sleep before he could see she had no intention of holding him. It was a restless sleep, nightmarish visions having their play with him still. He awoke the next day at noon. She was in the living room. He could see she hadn't been to sleep. She was in the dress she'd had on the night before, on the sofa drinking tea. He was confused. "I . . . you weren't in bed?"

"Get dressed, Tom," she said, getting up. "I'll put up some tea for you."

"But—".

"Do it. It's cold in here, the wind is coming up the street from the river. You can hear it whistle through the panes." She had been sitting listening to the dull howl ever since the sun had risen. The dreary, grey sun. Even the tea seemed brighter, with a tart slice of lemon. It was the perfect setting for this day.

He came into the dining room in his clothes. His beard was beginning to show a little now, and his hair looked in need of washing. She wanted to draw a tub for him and pour in the Pears and watch him lather up his beautiful silky fur. She would lick him clean like a little kitten. But she stopped herself, for she had other plans for him.

"Tom, listen to me. You've always trusted me and said I'm the wisest person you've ever known. That I've always been right, even when you didn't see it at first."

"Yeah, but—"

"Please *listen* to me, don't say anything until I'm done." She sat down at the table and faced him. "I'm sure I'm right about what I have to say. Tom, you now have a chance you've never had before—a chance to really be the person you were put on this earth to be. You think it's all gone, Mitch and Kevin and Chloe, even what you had with the Countess, you think the world has turned against you and you've got nothing left. But you do. You've got *yourself!* You and your talent and your dreams and plans, and now you've got the knowledge that experience brings, painful experience, and you can only rise from that.

"We've told each other our dreams and we planned on realizing some of them together. We won't go to Paris, Tom. No more travels. We'll have to settle for memories of our trip to Santa Fe and a walk through the Cloisters."

He was getting the drift of what she was saying now. But it could not be true. It was unthinkable. Impossible. *"No,"* he moaned, his throat tightening, his stomach contracting, feeling as though someone were strangling him.

"You've got one crutch in life and I'm it, Tom. I'm it because I wanted to be and I relished that position, but now I must relinquish it. I'm very much in love with you and what kind of future is there for us? I'm forty-four and you're twenty-five and what happens the next time a sexy lawyer with dark hair comes up to you at the Christmas tree lot? I can't go on wondering when or even if you'll show up, waiting for the few chances or whims or business or whatever it is that brings us together. I don't want any longer to be the buffer for unequal relationships with your friends and lovers. It would just put me in the same position, being in a relationship that isn't equal. There's no future in it for me."

He sat with his mouth open, looking stunned.

"I've been there, Tommy, all the time, and I've loved every moment of it. My arms were made to hold you, our lovemaking was perfect, we talked deep and we talked silly, and we did wonderful things together. But every time you leave I hurt a little. I don't want any longer to be the person you choose to hug and hold and love only when you have a rough time in life. I don't want you coming to me only when you have a problem. Oh, how I needed you the time Barry was missing, and how desperately I hoped you'd come, on your own, even when I told you not to. Yes, I was hurt that you didn't. You didn't understand my needs, just as you didn't understand Kevin's or Chloe's."

He sat facing her and his head pounded. He thought he could take no more. He was shaking.

"Tom, you've got to believe me that this is harder for

me than it is for you. You'll fill the void because you're younger and more resilient and you'll bounce back and come to realize you don't need a mother's arms anymore. What counts is that you've now got the chance to be a man for the first time in your life—Mitchell finally gave you that opportunity. I can't and won't take that away from you."

"Let's go to bed," he said feebly, clutching for anything to stop him from drowning. "Let's make love. Stop talking. I want to make love to you."

She shook her head. "It would be too easy. And I'm not Mitchell, I couldn't take it. It was too rough last time and I'm afraid my body wouldn't survive what would happen now."

He looked as if he didn't comprehend a word she spoke.

She took his hand and held it. "Tom, admit something to yourself—the one real love affair you've had in your life was a homosexual one. And the strong but unfulfilled love for Kevin, that was male also. *You are a homosexual.* You must admit it for what it is—no woman will ever satisfy you the way Mitchell satisfied you. There's nothing wrong with that. Go with that and embrace it and find joy in it. Don't fight it. Don't want to make love to me because you lost your male lover. . ."

"I don't believe I'm hearing this," he moaned. But he was hearing. And understanding every word.

And then she finally said it: *"I must ask you to leave."* It reverberated in his head. He heard Mitch's voice: *I don't want to see you again, ever.* "Those are the hardest words I've ever had to speak. Harder than telling my husband I wanted a divorce. I'm taking the gamble that you're going to be all right, never better, in fact."

"I'm going to kill myself."

"Oh, stop talking like Chloe. You won't kill yourself. You're not strong enough. You're too ambitious. You love yourself too much. But I'll take the gamble, and if

I lose, I promise on my mother and on my son, I'll be in the graveyard every day, on my knees, *mea culpa*, because I'd never be able to live with myself again for a moment. But you'll land on your feet. Cats always do."

"Stop with the cat talk already!" he cried angrily. He jumped up and went to the living room window and looked out at the grey winter sky through the grille.

Her voice was suddenly sharp and pointed. "I've heard that crappy tone from you too many times. Stop moaning. So the world dumped on you. Take the responsibility, you brought it down on yourself, you know. It seems to me you've had it pretty easy until now. When have you suffered? Were you ever able to comprehend the kind of suffering Kevin went through? Or the emotional hell Chloe experienced? The difficulty Mitchell must have had just living from day to day, self-condemned to a life he despised? And you feel sorry for *yourself?*"

"Oh, this is supposed to mean nothing, just because everyone I know had it rough? What about you? Don't *you* have something to cry about? Didn't *you* suffer more than me somewhere along the line?"

She turned her head. "Yes," she said softly, "somewhere along the line I did, but you wouldn't understand, and it isn't important that you do. I'm not important here. You are. Trust yourself. You don't want to take the chance to sink or swim, you want a raft under you all the time. Believe in yourself and maybe you'll grow up to be president or king or something. Or—better yet —a pianist."

He looked at her with pleading eyes. "You don't mean it. Please say you don't mean it. I can't lose you. There's nothing left."

"You have *you,* Tommy." She kissed him on the forehead for the last time—his mind flashed to Mitch doing the same thing; he thought he was literally falling apart. She whispered, "It would be too easy to go on like this.

Too safe. And ultimately, I've dreaded this day for so long, but you will see it had to be, and that it was for the best. My little kitten, I'll love you forever, but you must go. You've outgrown the nest, and there's a world waiting."

Dazed, he went through the motions of putting on his coat and wrapping the muffler she'd given him to wear the night before around his neck. It was sleepwalking, moving in a nightmare; it would be over soon. Everyone in his life had been shot down, ducks in a shooting gallery, gone, but this was no carnival, no midway. She opened the door. She couldn't look at him. And after she closed it, he was sure he heard her crying against it, leaning against it, that big heavy West End Avenue door, and he prayed that it would open again.

He stood there for a long time, but it did not open, and when he finally pressed the elevator button, he knew it would never open for him again.

The cold made him shiver, for he had been sweating. He moved through the snow, crossing the Drive to Riverside Park. People looked like mummies, walking winter suits with slits for eyes in their stocking caps, head-to-toe insulation that moved. Was this New York City? No, it had to be Tahoe, the main street at Big Bear. He walked and went nowhere, trembling, crying, hoping someone would mug him and ease the pain. He prayed a ton of snow would fall from a tree and bury him forever. But the snow was all underfoot and it was even too cold for muggers to move fast.

He wasn't sure how he ended up in an apartment overlooking the river. He had blanked out after he went into the bar. All he knew was he'd been drinking as fast as they could be set up, and a boy who reminded him of Kevin was talking to him. But he heard Kevin's voice, not this boy's, and he moved away.

Then he was in the apartment with a stranger, a thin,

willowy young man he had never seen before. Who he was or what they might have said to one another, he didn't have the foggiest idea. He was in bed with him and he was fucking him as he'd never fucked anyone in his life, man or woman, with sadistic movements and a frenzy of energy he never knew he could possess. And then, suddenly—

Brrrrrup. Brrrrrup. Brrrrrup.

He cocked his head back and the memories flooded through. Annie. Glass breaking. Houston. Johnny Mathis. The feeling he had to get away, away from the overpowering revulsion, the sensation of—

Brrrrrup. Brrrrrup. Brrrrrup.

He turned his head and saw the tone arm in the center of the record near the bed. He pulled out of the boy and hit the record with his hand so hard he knocked it right off the base of the turntable. The boy cringed in a corner, cowering, thinking his trick had gone mad.

Then the sound was gone and madness was curtailed; the temporary insanity lifted, and it as as though it cleared his head. He looked around the strange room, at the naked boy, out the window at New Jersey, and he wondered what he was doing there. Oh, he knew why. Yes, he did. And he knew he had to get out of there because in a moment he wasn't going to be able to breathe, he was going to be sick.

He started putting his clothes back on and the boy said, "Whadaya, nuts?"

Tom said nothing. His head was pounding.

"Somethin' I said?" the boy asked, pissed. His voice was growing in anger, high-pitched, pointed. "What'sa matter, Muscles?" He was on his knees on the bed now. "You always do this, give this kinda show? Pound a guy's ass like you're hammerin' nails and then take a flyer, huh? Ya broke my goddamn record player. What the fuck's your problem?"

Tom ignored him. How could he hope to even begin

to explain? How could he tell him he didn't remember anything, that he was running away from himself, that. . .? *I have to go home.* That's it, that's all. *I must go home.*

The boy put his hands on his hips. "Boy oh boy, this is one fuckin' performance! Great show, like goin' to the movies and seein' only the first reel or somethin'! What are you, Miss Preview? Miss Sneak Preview? You *bastard!* You came here to fuck me! I dragged you all the way from the fuckin' bar and you tease me with your dick and then walk out on me? You got some nerve, you asshole!"

Tom felt sorry for him, but he couldn't give a damn about this person. The queen would get over the rejection. He had something more important to do now.

The boy chased him down the hall, naked, down the stairs, screaming all the time. "Okay, go, you cunt! Get the fuck outta here, I didn't think you were such hot shit anyhow, ya know? You're nothin' much with your big dick and a suntan you got in a bottle from Bloomies! Don't try and come back, you shit! You hear me? You hear me, you *shit?* You *turd!* You *cunt! Cunnnnnnnnnt!*"

Tom ran out into the street and fell to his knees in the snow. Everthing came up as he retched, all the beer and bile, the hurt and frustration. He washed his mouth with snow and got up and felt dizzy, but he stood his ground until he spied a cab and waved it down. He collapsed into the back seat and moaned one word. "Kennedy."

TWENTY-FOUR

He turned on the light over the piano and sat down. Blizzard settled in near his feet. It wasn't a Yahama grand, but it *was* a piano. The tea kettle would stay hot over the low flame, and he'd sharpened several pencils and had a stack of tapes ready.

He had come home, fed the cat, showered, washing off the vomit, the boy, the snow and sweat, the plane ride, the past. As the water prickled his scalp he admitted to himself that she had been right about one thing. He still had his fingers. And he'd show her. He'd write a goddamned score that would *show her!* Revenge burned in him until he sat on the bed drying his hair.

Then he relented, gave in, didn't try to fight it anymore—what was the point? The reason he'd come home had nothing to do with revenge or spite. Damn! It was so hard to admit, especially when the world had fallen in on his head, when his heart was broken, when he wanted to go on running and crying, but she had been right. She had been wise, she had spoken the truth. It was time for a test, kitten or tomcat, winner or loser, man or boy. And he remembered the words of Mrs. Jensen as clearly as if the old lady were in the room herself: "*. . .you could really do it someday . . . I want a promise from you that you'll keep practicing and really become someone. . .*"

The light in his window stayed on all night long as he pictured the film in his mind, the mountains, pine trees, lovers sitting beside a babbling brook, and he wrote music that spoke of wind and sunshine and fresh green pines and harsh storms; he even wrote of water drawing fire from the moon. He thought of Mitch in his winter jacket, his arms around him on the lifeguard stand, of Chloe lying under a piano, of Kevin standing shyly at the side of the pool, trying to hide his bad leg, his eyes so bright and shining. He thought of Zena masquerading as the Grand Duchess Anastasia, and of Rachel cuddled up to him in her big bed, watching him over the rim of her reading glasses far down on her nose as he drank cocoa. He recalled all the love from so many, in such different ways, which gave him strength, purpose, and his fingers moved as his spirits soared. The people who had loved him were gone, but they remained in his heart. Maybe what he was doing was saying, in the best way he knew how, that he was sorry, that he'd learned, and that maybe, just maybe after all, he really did know how to love. She was right. He had himself, a cat and a piano, and it was enough; they had not loved him in vain.

Music, beautiful music, a painful but joyful noise, filled the air. When the sun rose, it stopped. He got up from the bench and opened the windows. Blizzard yawned and woke from his dreams, stretched his paws out like little starfish in front of him, and shook off the night as Tom rustled his fur.

While Blizzard consumed his morning tuna, Tom had one last glass of tea, the two of them breakfasting there silently. There was nothing to be said; Blizzard understood everything, and he seemed to smile. He licked his chops, washed behind the ears, and leaped to the window, up and out into the sunshine, off to stalk the impossible butterfly or elusive lizard, out on yet another adventure.

Tom went into the bedroom. He took off his robe and

slipped in under the covers. For the first time in many weeks, he slept soundly and peacefully.

About an hour later, Blizzard came back in and curled in a warm ball at his feet.

EPILOGUE

Dear Sandy,

By now you should be back in the frozen Midwest, so here's a friendly voice to greet you. You've got to write and tell me all about Greece—working for TWA does have its advantages, right? I know, I know, I should have married you just to get the passes.

Wanted to bring you up-to-date. I hate not seeing you for such long stretches of time. Sorry for the delay in answering your last letter, but I had a deadline on the score for my first feature film. Yes, it finally happened! (And Jane Fonda is the star, how about that?) I can't tell you how pleased I am with it. It is the best music I've ever written. You know what? Success is such a quiet thing. It's not so much seeing your name up there on the credits, it's the day you see a rough cut with some of the music added and you *feel* it is right, you feel it *working*. So different from what I used to think "making it" was all about.

Best of all, I received a note from Rachel—yes, Rachel, after four years—telling me she thinks the score is smashing and she's writing the album jacket notes herself. I guess God had a scheme behind the madness after all. Sandy, I can't tell you how good it was to hear from her after so long, and I pray someday soon we'll be able to see one another in person, for I believe we're very different people now from who we were then. At least I am. To tell the truth, I wouldn't want her to have changed at all.

Patrick sends his best. His shop is taking off, and he finds it more fulfilling each day. Not only is everyone in Westlake Village into gourmet cooking, but they're demanding the finest utensils, and he's making money at that, but the real satisfaction comes from the cooking classes he's giving. Three nights a week now. We're moving soon. That's the biggest news of all. We bought a house—brand new, authentic English country manor house—that sits atop a mountain and overlooks the world. Let's hope it never rains again in Southern California, or we'll be at the bottom of the hill somewhere; but I guess that risk is part of living in Lotus Land. The new place will be closer to Pat's shop, and much more conducive to my work. I'm finding Los Angeles too distracting as I grow "older". Blizzard will have a new castle in which to roam.

Speaking of cats, Kevin's parents' cat had a litter, and they gave me a beautiful kitten the last time I went to visit them. She's all white with one blue eye and one green eye and the sweetest lap-cat disposition you'd ever imagine. I'm calling her Christmas. You'll fall in love when you visit.

And do plan to visit soon. We both miss you. You know, Sandy, life gets better each day. There was a time you well remember when I sincerely wondered if I'd survive the hell coming down. I know now that I never would have made it to today had my life not fallen apart back then. And I guess that's what it's all about. I'm feeling . . . I don't know how to put it—mature? No. Patrick says the word is "peaceful", and I think he's right. I feel very much at peace and in touch with my life. I feel in control finally, as if I have the reins in my own hands now. And Pat has been so supportive of that.

I remember what you said when I first told you I felt I was falling in love with him, how you wondered how someone like me, someone *crazy* like me, could feel that way about a person so quiet and uninterested in show business and all that jazz that my life's been about. But he possesses all the qualities which I don't have, and I draw from them, the tranquility, the honesty, so many simple pleasures. And my talent and mad artistic ways have enthused and inspired him. He has the beauty of Mitch, the undemanding love of Kevin, and a great deal of the wisdom of Rachel. And so much more in his own right. I ask you, am I not blessed? What I'm trying to say is he makes me happy. And I him.

Write soon. I ¶t3&#M./+h ———Christmas just jumped up on the keys. Love you.

A thousand meows,
Tom

There are a lot more where this one came from!

ORDER your FREE catalog of ACE paperbacks here. We have hundreds of inexpensive books where this one came from priced from 75¢ to $2.50. Now you can read all the books you have always wanted to at tremendous savings. Order your *free* catalog of ACE paperbacks now.

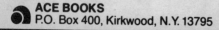

ACE BOOKS
P.O. Box 400, Kirkwood, N.Y. 13795